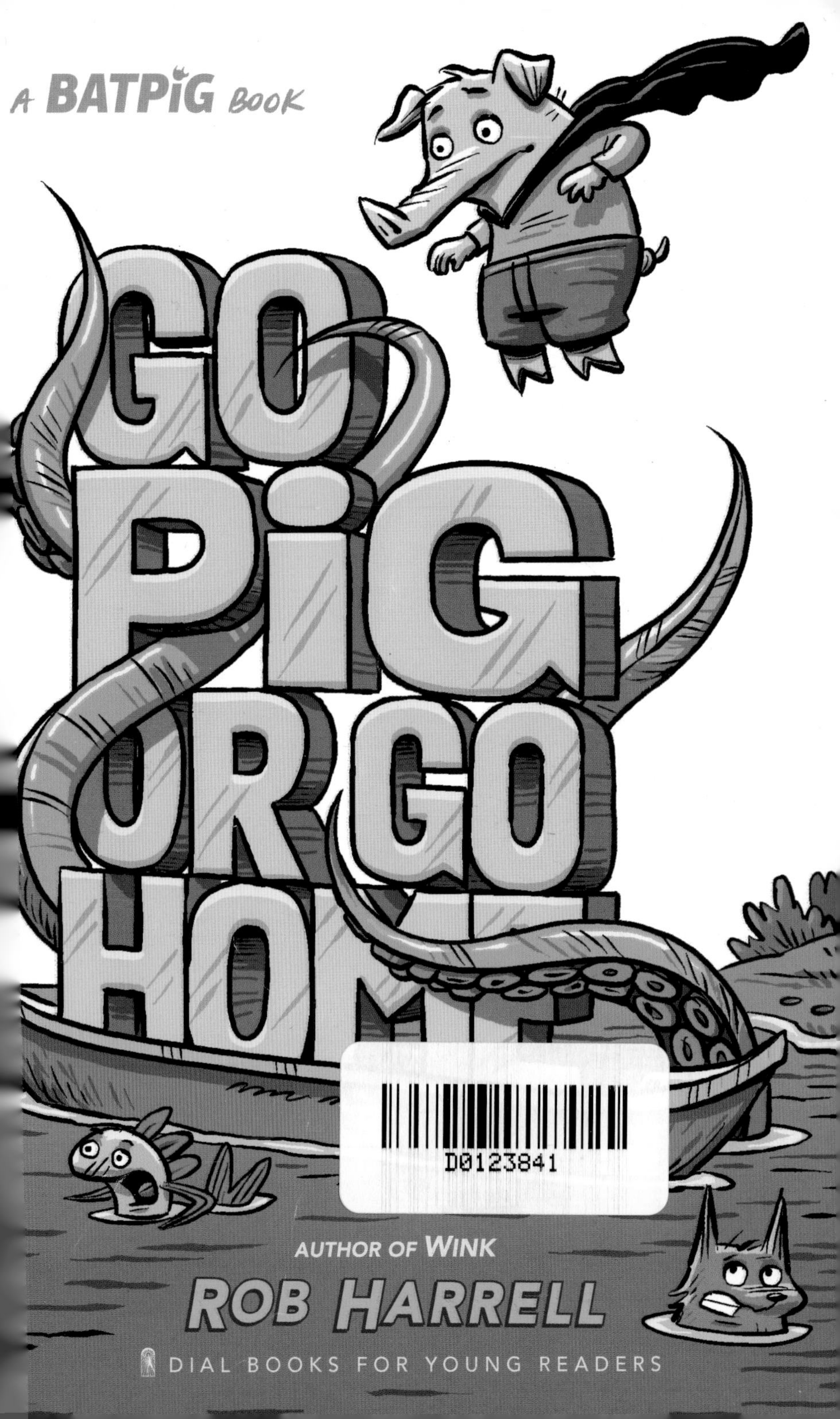

A BATPIG BOOK
GO PIG OR GO HOME
AUTHOR OF WINK
ROB HARRELL
DIAL BOOKS FOR YOUNG READERS

Dedicated to Lee Salem,
for opening the door

DIAL BOOKS FOR YOUNG READERS

An imprint of Penguin Random House LLC, New York

First published in the United States of America by Dial Books for Young Readers,
an imprint of Penguin Random House LLC, 2023

Copyright © 2023 by Rob Harrell

Visit us online at penguinrandomhouse.com.

Library of Congress Cataloging-in-Publication Data is available

Manufactured in China

ISBN 9780593531945 • 10 9 8 7 6 5 4 3 2 1

TOPL

Design by Jason Henry

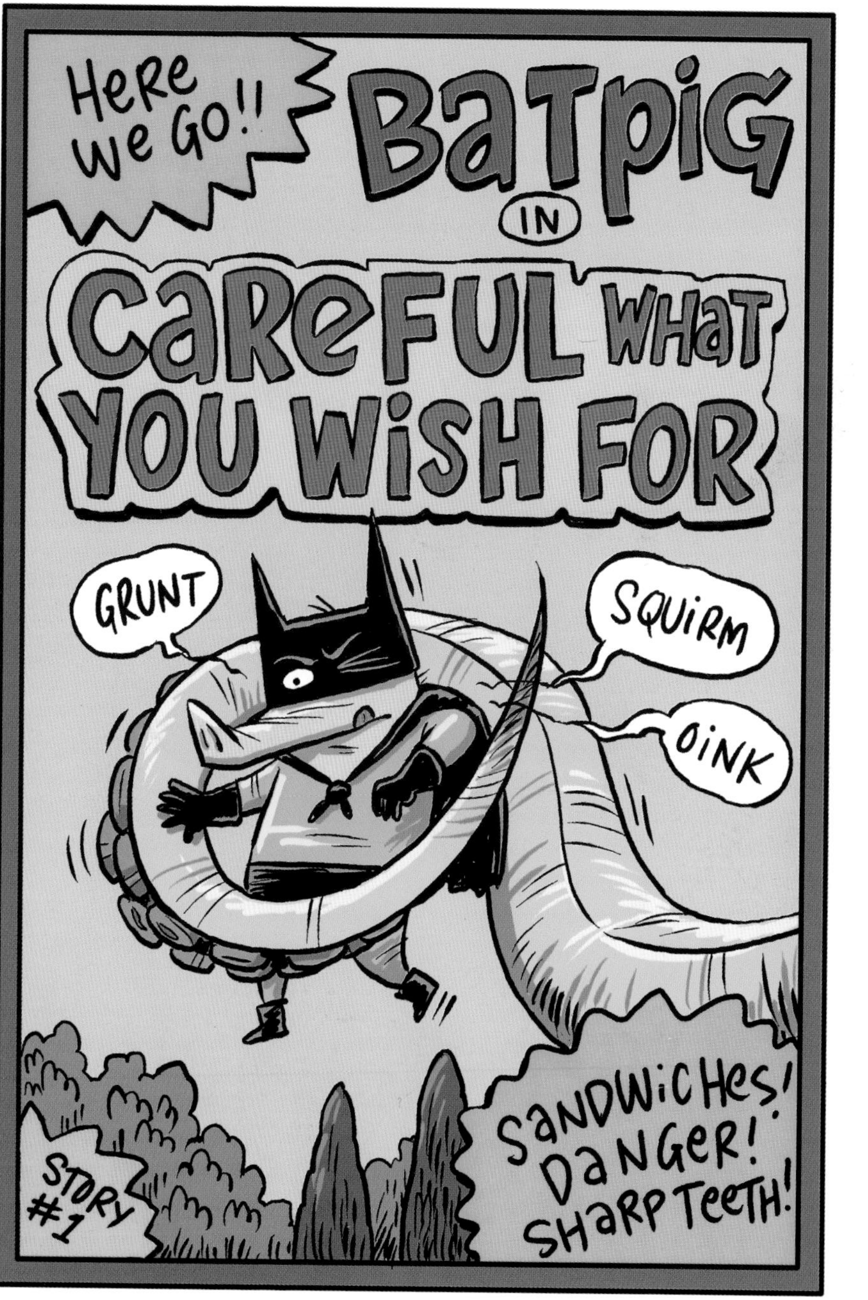
Here we Go!!
BATPIG
IN
CAREFUL WHAT YOU WISH FOR
GRUNT
SQUIRM
OINK
STORY #1
SANDWICHES!
DANGER!
SHARP TEETH!

CHAPTER ONE

"BETWEEN TWO SLICES"

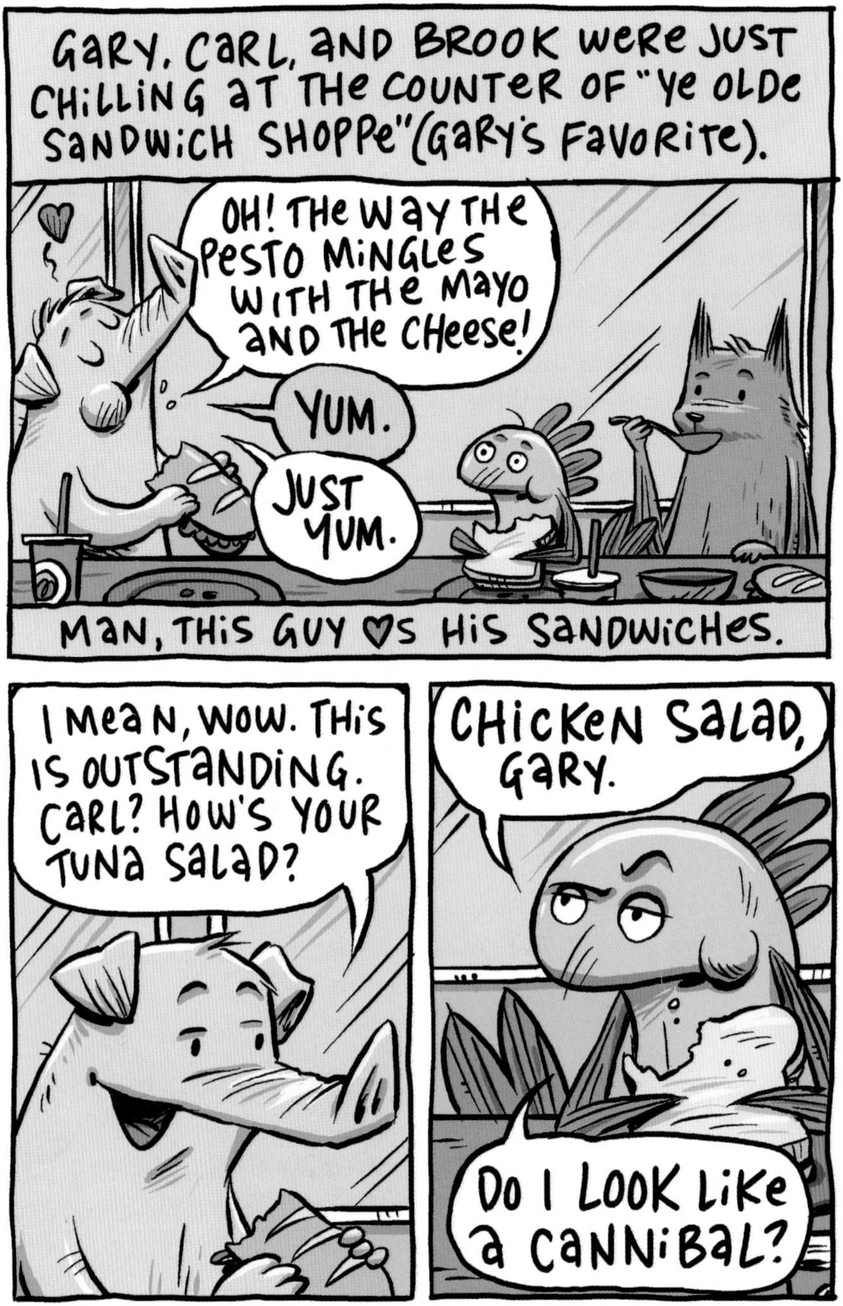
GARY, CARL, AND BROOK WERE JUST CHILLING AT THE COUNTER OF "YE OLDE SANDWICH SHOPPE" (GARY'S FAVORITE).
OH! THE WAY THE PESTO MINGLES WITH THE MAYO AND THE CHEESE!
YUM.
JUST YUM.
MAN, THIS GUY ♥S HIS SANDWICHES.
I MEAN, WOW. THIS IS OUTSTANDING. CARL? HOW'S YOUR TUNA SALAD?
CHICKEN SALAD, GARY.
DO I LOOK LIKE A CANNIBAL?

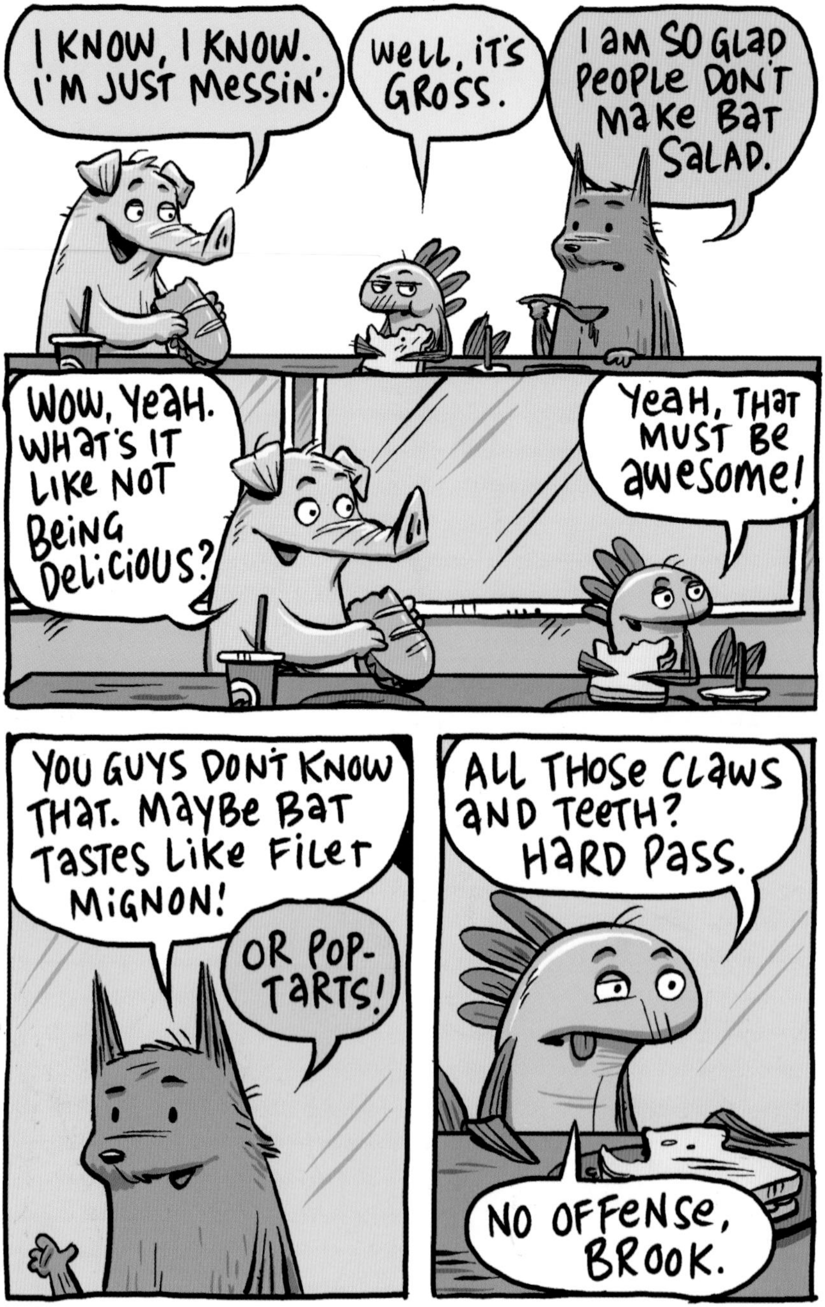
I KNOW, I KNOW. I'M JUST MESSIN'.
WELL, IT'S GROSS.
I AM SO GLAD PEOPLE DON'T MAKE BAT SALAD.
WOW, YEAH. WHAT'S IT LIKE NOT BEING DELICIOUS?
YEAH, THAT MUST BE AWESOME!
YOU GUYS DON'T KNOW THAT. MAYBE BAT TASTES LIKE FILET MIGNON!
OR POP-TARTS!
ALL THOSE CLAWS AND TEETH? HARD PASS.
NO OFFENSE, BROOK.

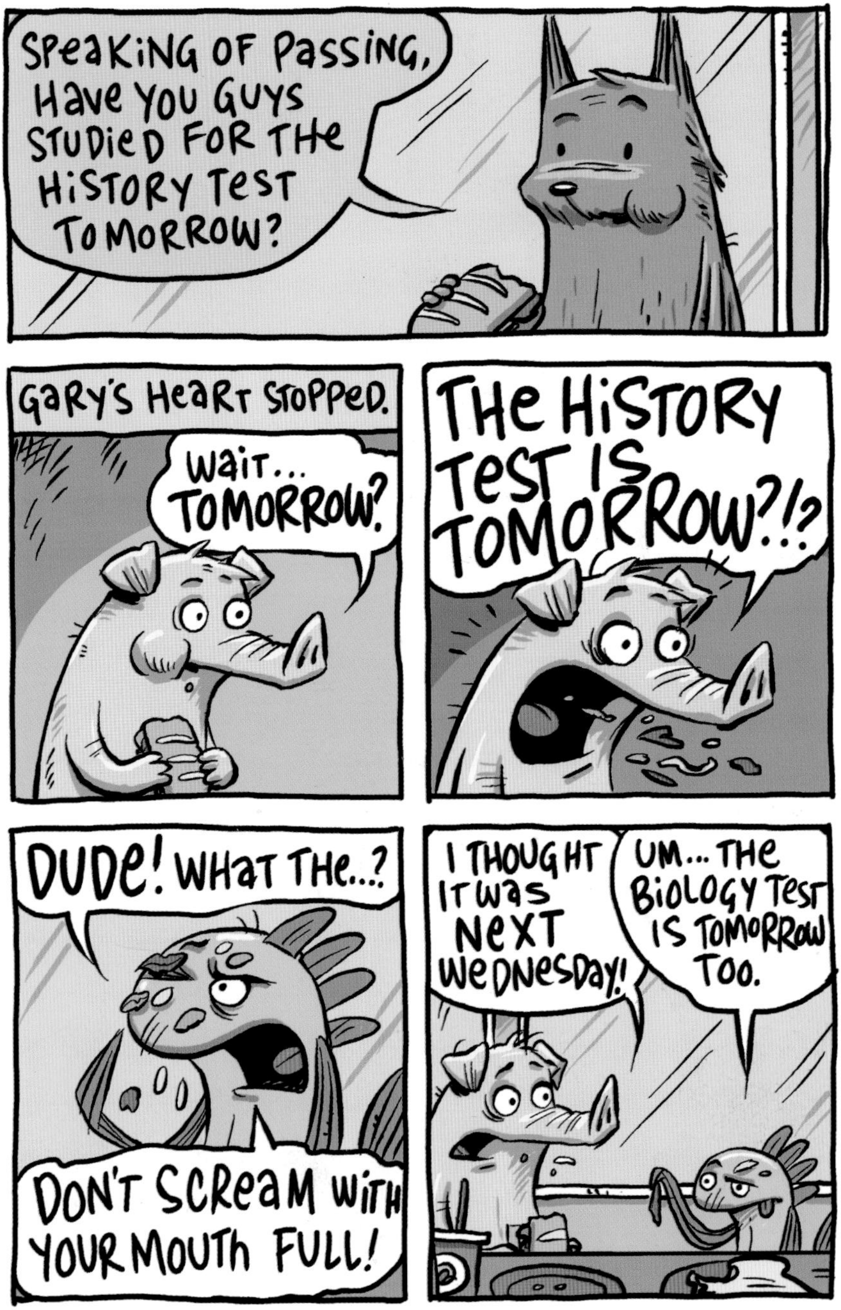
SPEAKING OF PASSING, HAVE YOU GUYS STUDIED FOR THE HISTORY TEST TOMORROW?
GARY'S HEART STOPPED.
WAIT... TOMORROW?
THE HISTORY TEST IS TOMORROW?!?
DUDE! WHAT THE...?
DON'T SCREAM WITH YOUR MOUTH FULL!
I THOUGHT IT WAS NEXT WEDNESDAY!
UM... THE BIOLOGY TEST IS TOMORROW TOO.

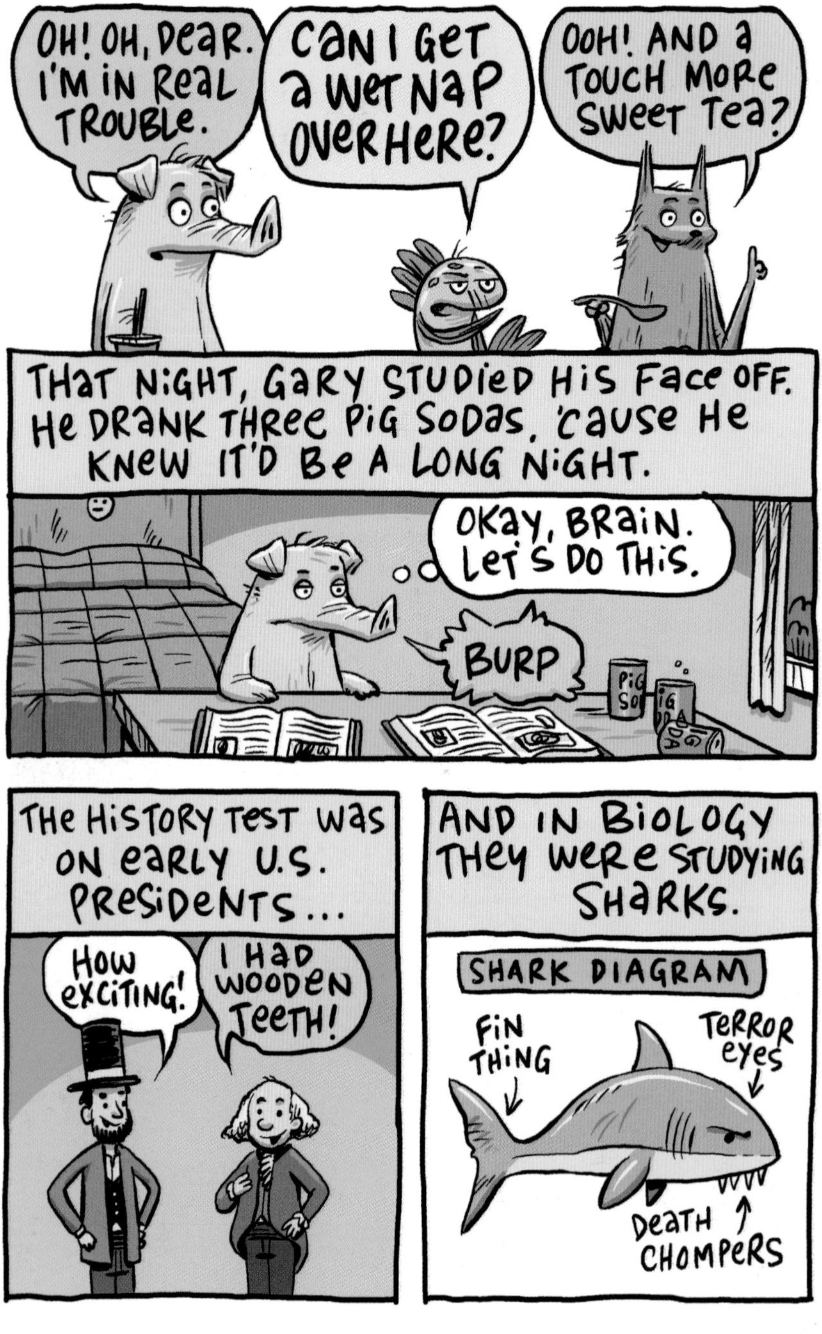
OH! OH, DEAR. I'M IN REAL TROUBLE.
CAN I GET A WET NAP OVER HERE?
OOH! AND A TOUCH MORE SWEET TEA?
THAT NIGHT, GARY STUDIED HIS FACE OFF. HE DRANK THREE PIG SODAS, 'CAUSE HE KNEW IT'D BE A LONG NIGHT.
OKAY, BRAIN. LET'S DO THIS.
BURP
THE HISTORY TEST WAS ON EARLY U.S. PRESIDENTS...
HOW EXCITING!
I HAD WOODEN TEETH!
AND IN BIOLOGY THEY WERE STUDYING SHARKS.
SHARK DIAGRAM
FIN THING
TERROR EYES
DEATH CHOMPERS

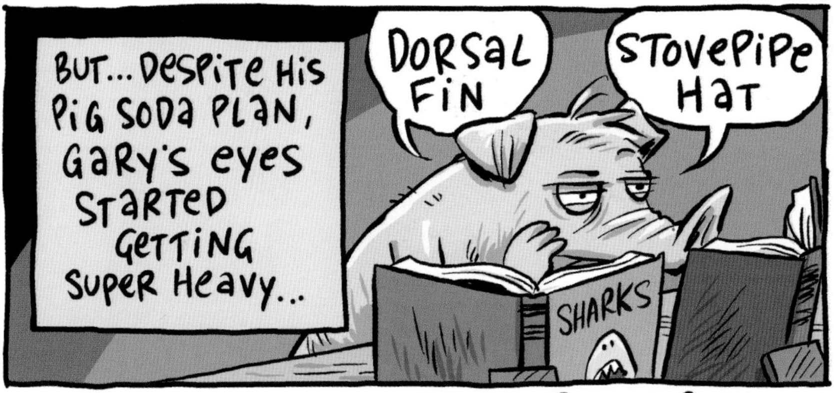
BUT... DESPITE HIS BIG SODA PLAN, GARY'S EYES STARTED GETTING SUPER HEAVY...
DORSAL FIN
STOVEPIPE HAT
SHARKS

HE DECIDED TO GO OUT TO FIGHT SOME CRIME TO WAKE HIMSELF. REALLY BATPIG IT UP, YOU KNOW?

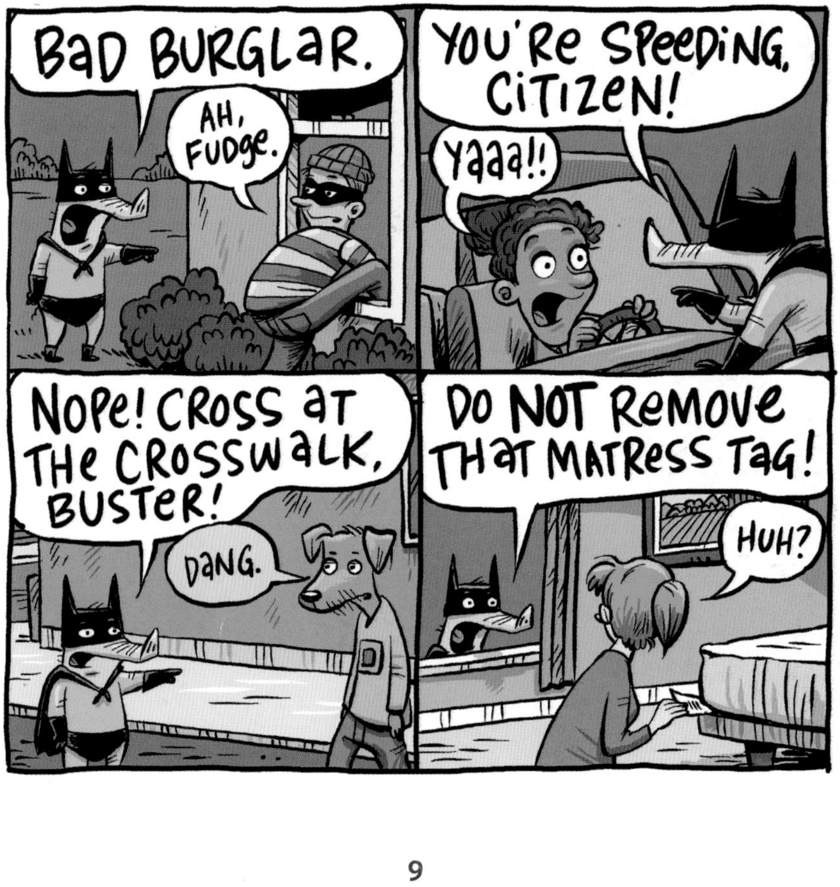
BAD BURGLAR.
AH, FUDGE.
YOU'RE SPEEDING, CITIZEN!
YAAA!!
NOPE! CROSS AT THE CROSSWALK, BUSTER!
DANG.
DO NOT REMOVE THAT MATRESS TAG!
HUH?

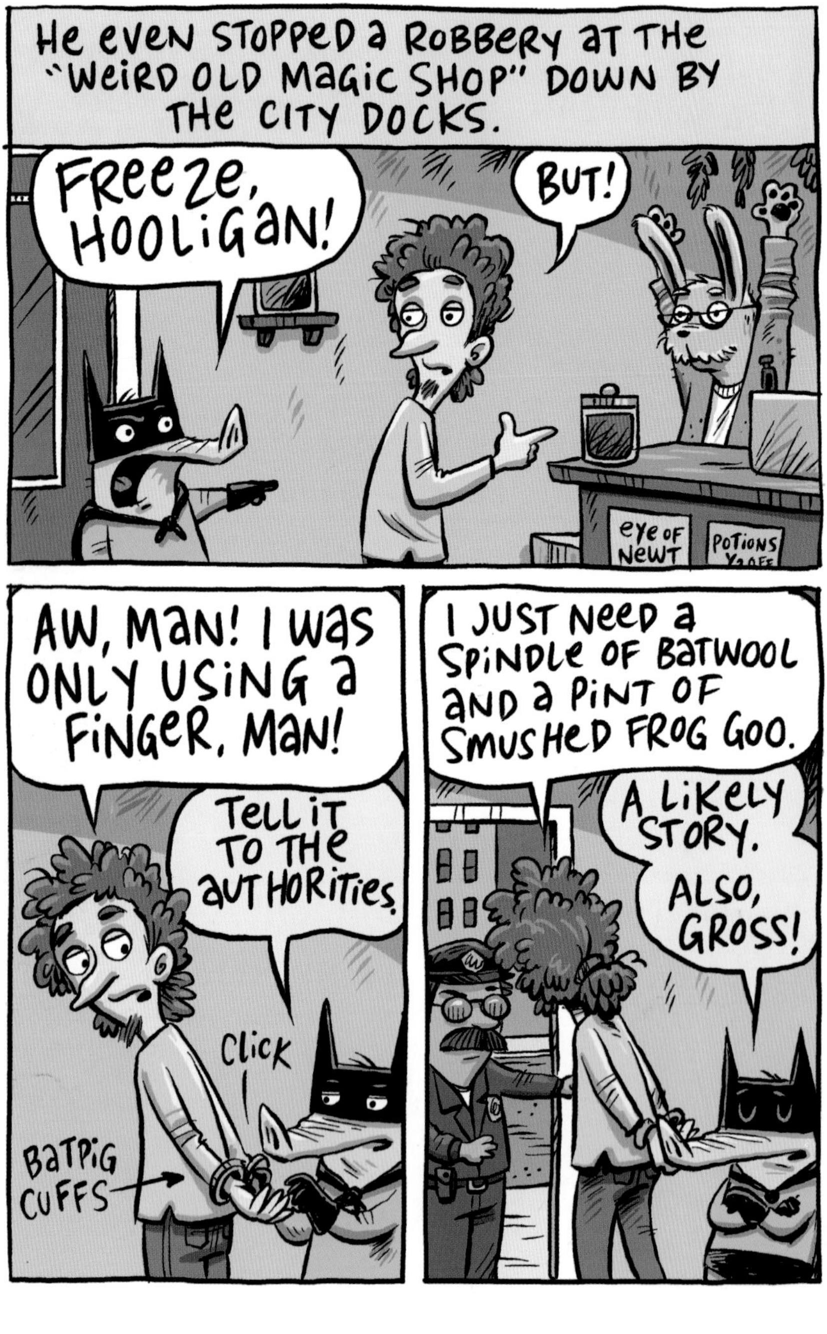
He even STOPPED a ROBBERY aT THE "WEIRD OLD MAGIC SHOP" DOWN BY THE CITY DOCKS.
FReeze, HOOLIGAN!
BUT!
eye OF NeWT
POTIONS
AW, MAN! I WAS ONLY USING A FINGER, MAN!
TELL IT TO THE AUTHORITIES.
CLICK
BATPIG CUFFS
I JUST NEED A SPINDLE OF BATWOOL AND A PINT OF SMUSHED FROG GOO.
A LIKELY STORY.
ALSO, GROSS!

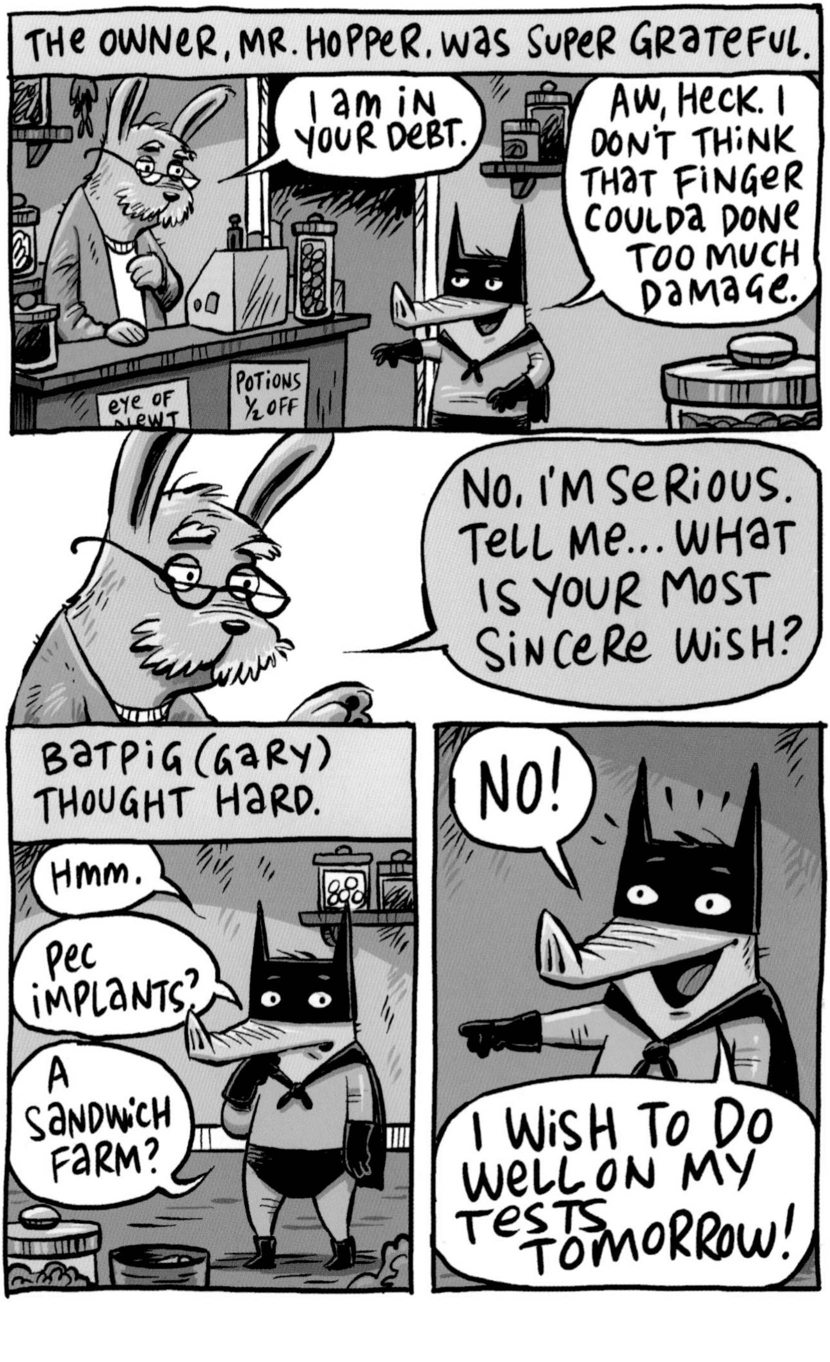
THE OWNER, MR. HOPPER, WAS SUPER GRATEFUL.
I AM IN YOUR DEBT.
AW, HECK. I DON'T THINK THAT FINGER COULDA DONE TOO MUCH DAMAGE.
POTIONS ½ OFF
NO, I'M SERIOUS. TELL ME... WHAT IS YOUR MOST SINCERE WISH?
BATPIG (GARY) THOUGHT HARD.
HMM.
PEC IMPLANTS?
A SANDWICH FARM?
NO!
I WISH TO DO WELL ON MY TESTS TOMORROW!

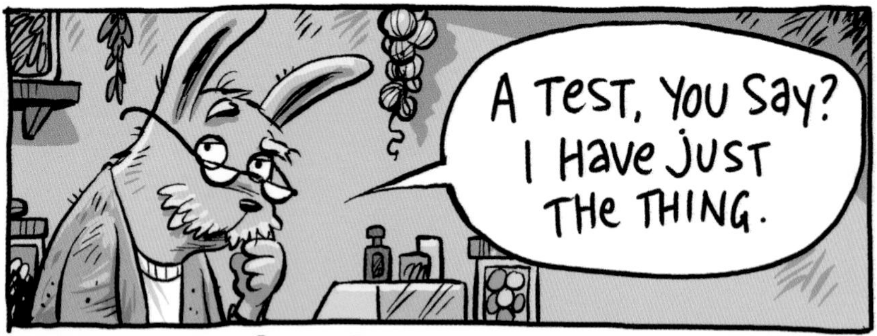
A TEST, YOU SAY? I HAVE JUST THE THING.

THE OLD RABBIT HOBBLED TO THE BACK ROOM FOR A BIT, AND CAME BACK HOLDING A SMALL POUCH.

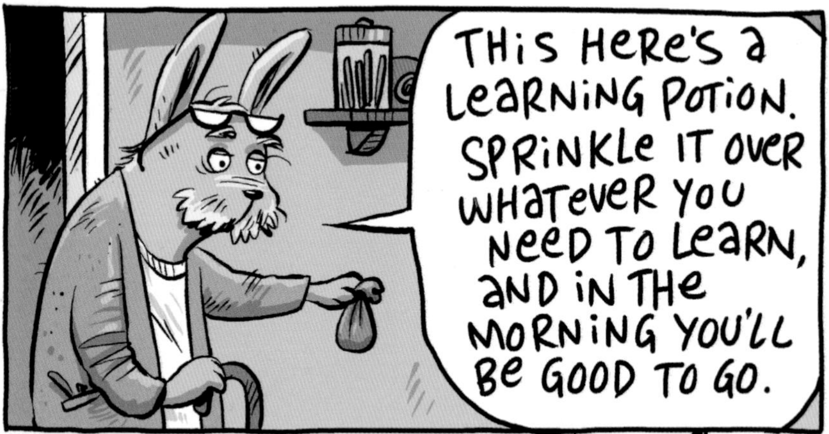
THIS HERE'S A LEARNING POTION. SPRINKLE IT OVER WHATEVER YOU NEED TO LEARN, AND IN THE MORNING YOU'LL BE GOOD TO GO.

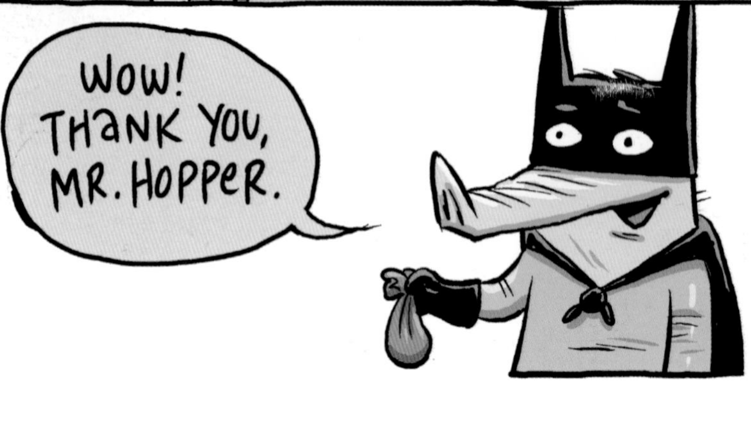
WOW! THANK YOU, MR. HOPPER.

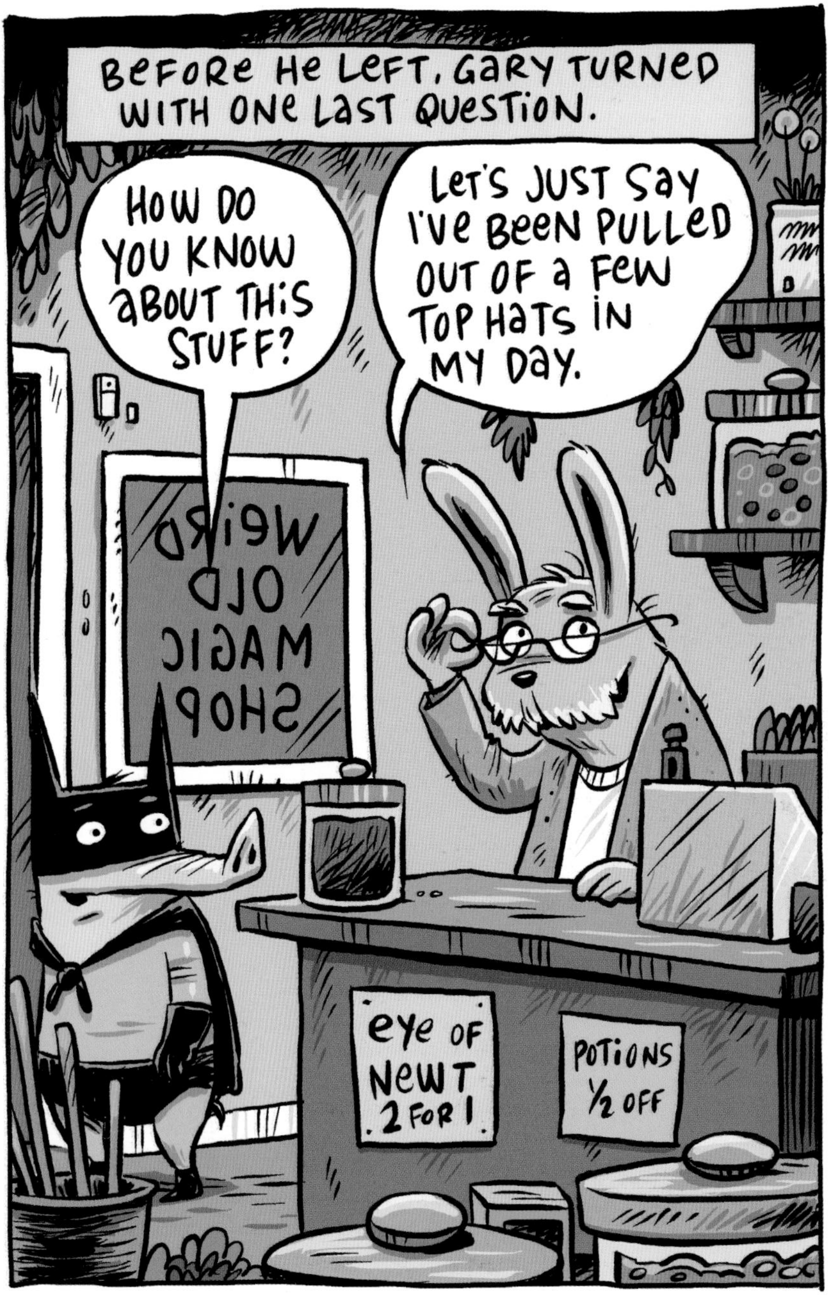
BEFORE HE LEFT, GARY TURNED WITH ONE LAST QUESTION.
HOW DO YOU KNOW ABOUT THIS STUFF?
LET'S JUST SAY I'VE BEEN PULLED OUT OF A FEW TOP HATS IN MY DAY.
WEIRD OLD MAGIC SHOP
EYE OF NEWT 2 FOR 1
POTIONS 1/2 OFF

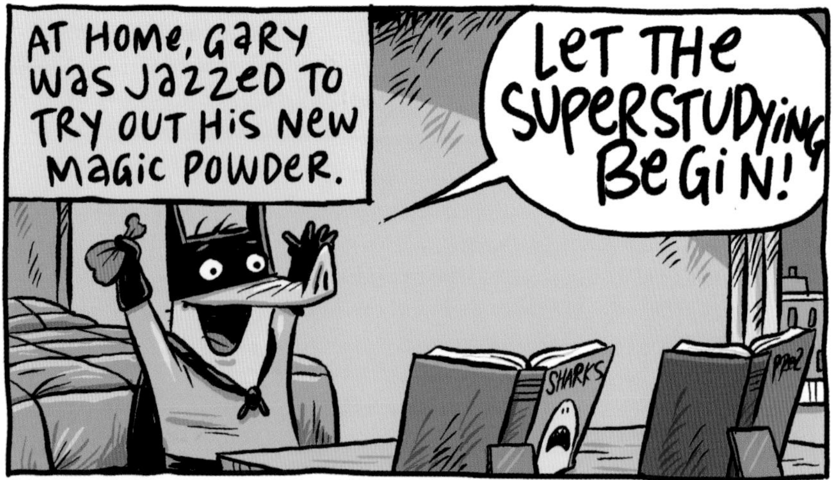
AT HOME, GARY WAS JAZZED TO TRY OUT HIS NEW MAGIC POWDER.
LET THE SUPERSTUDYING BEGIN!
SHARKS
PREZ

AFTER SOME THINKING ABOUT HOW TO WORD IT, GARY GAVE IT A SHOT.

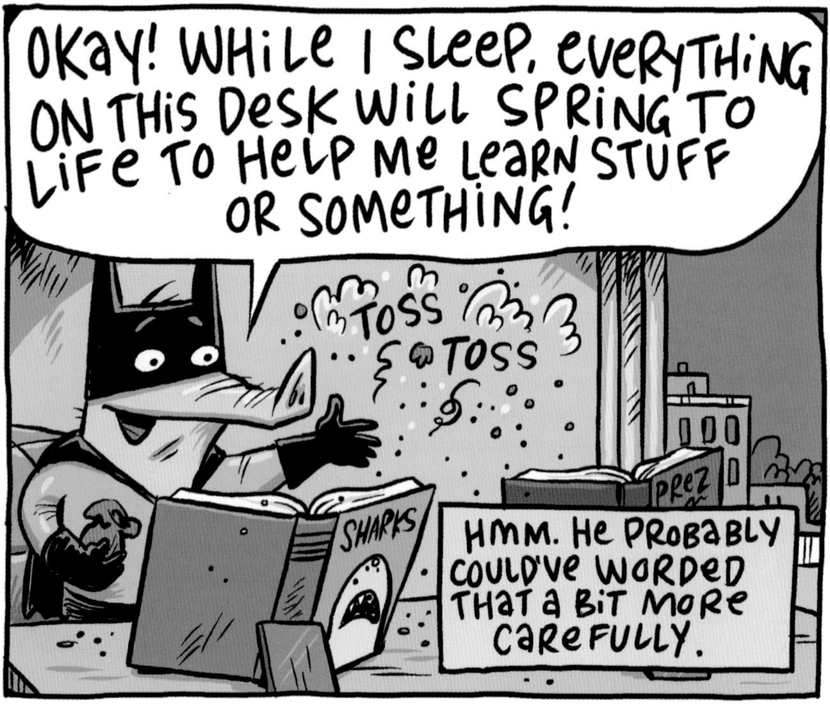
OKAY! WHILE I SLEEP, EVERYTHING ON THIS DESK WILL SPRING TO LIFE TO HELP ME LEARN STUFF OR SOMETHING!
TOSS
TOSS
PREZ
SHARKS
HMM. HE PROBABLY COULD'VE WORDED THAT A BIT MORE CAREFULLY.

CHAPTER TWO

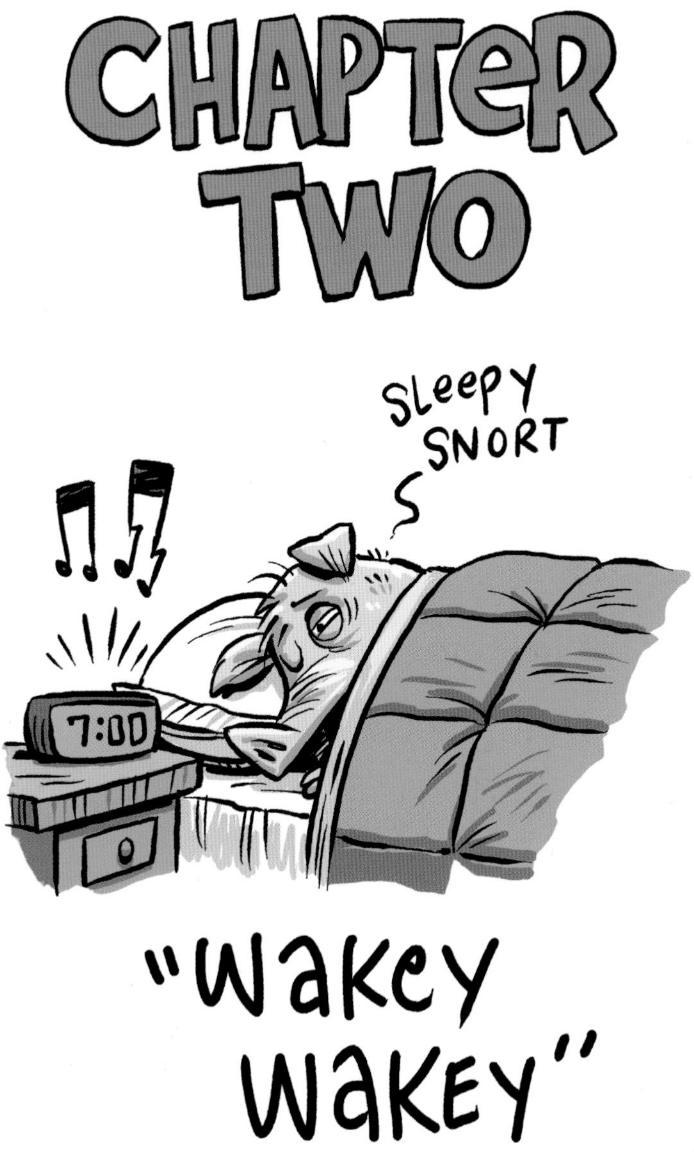
SLEEPY SNORT
7:00

"WAKEY WAKEY"

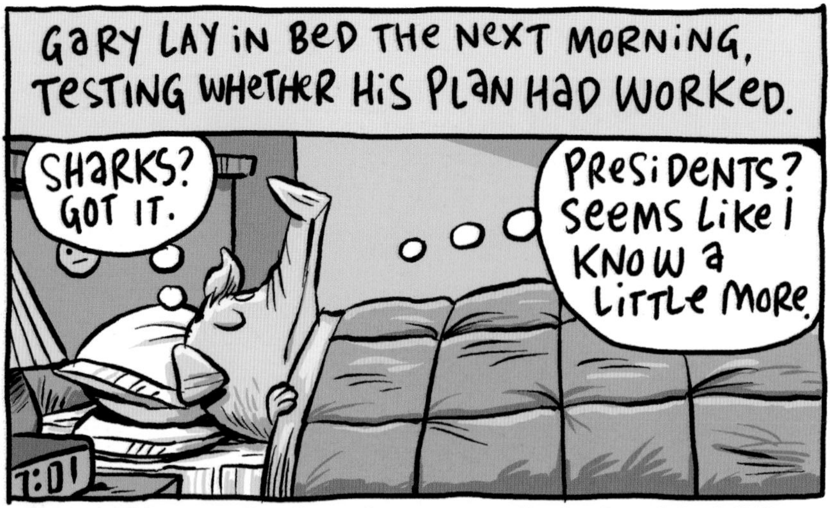
GARY LAY IN BED THE NEXT MORNING, TESTING WHETHER HIS PLAN HAD WORKED.
SHARKS? GOT IT.
PRESIDENTS? SEEMS LIKE I KNOW A LITTLE MORE.
7:01

ALL SEEMED GOOD, UNTIL HE OPENED HIS EYES AND SAT UP.

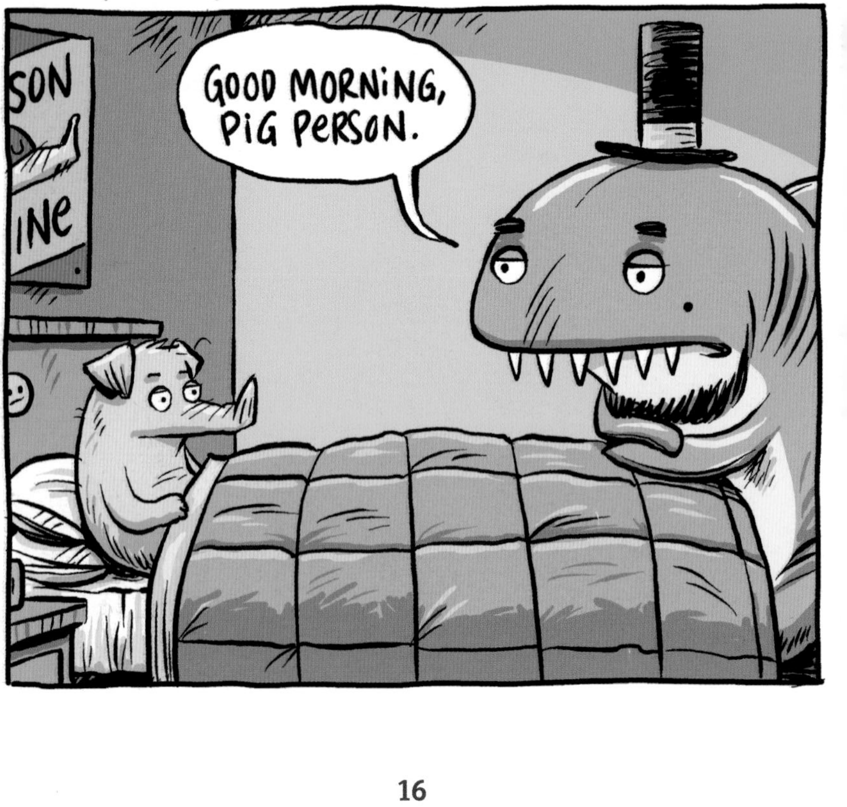
GOOD MORNING, PIG PERSON.

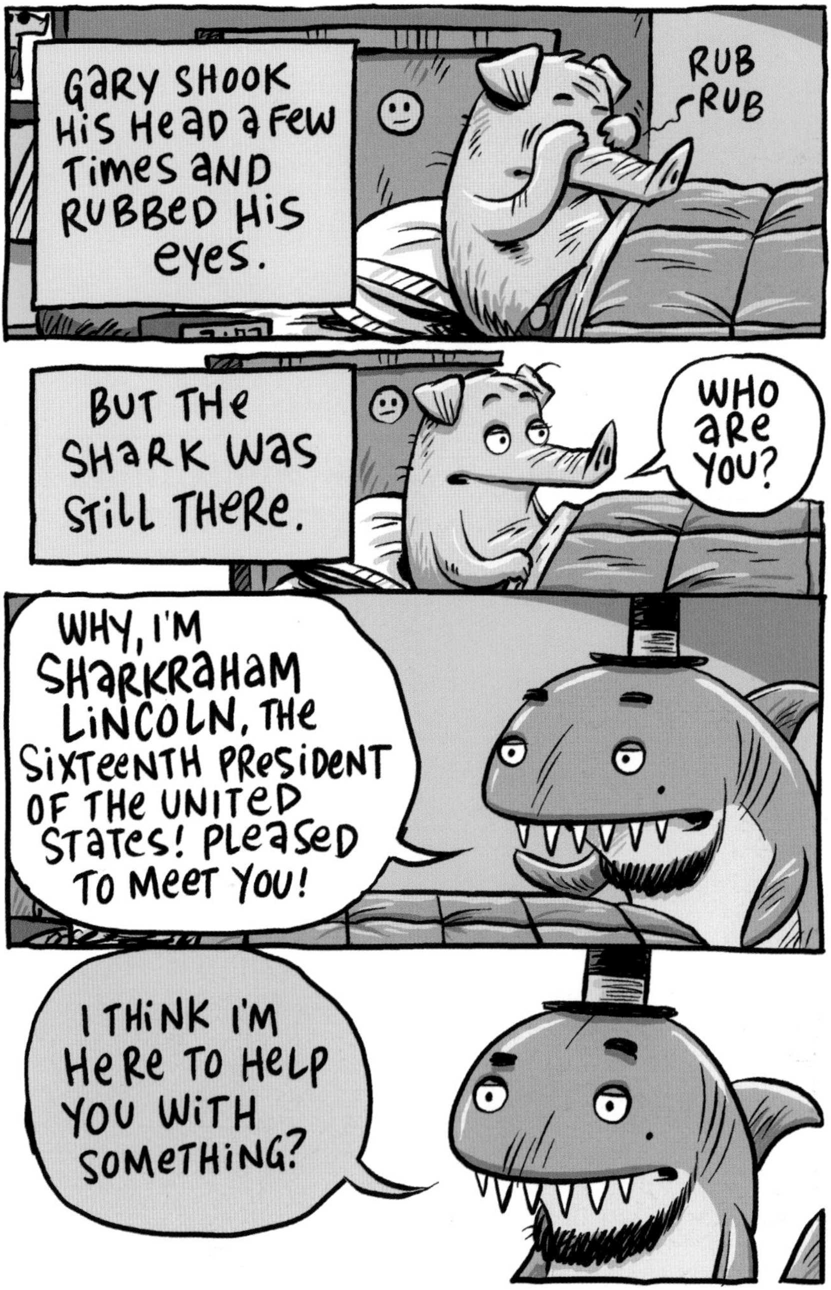
GARY SHOOK HIS HEAD A FEW TIMES AND RUBBED HIS EYES.
RUB RUB
BUT THE SHARK WAS STILL THERE.
WHO ARE YOU?
WHY, I'M SHARKRAHAM LINCOLN, THE SIXTEENTH PRESIDENT OF THE UNITED STATES! PLEASED TO MEET YOU!
I THINK I'M HERE TO HELP YOU WITH SOMETHING?

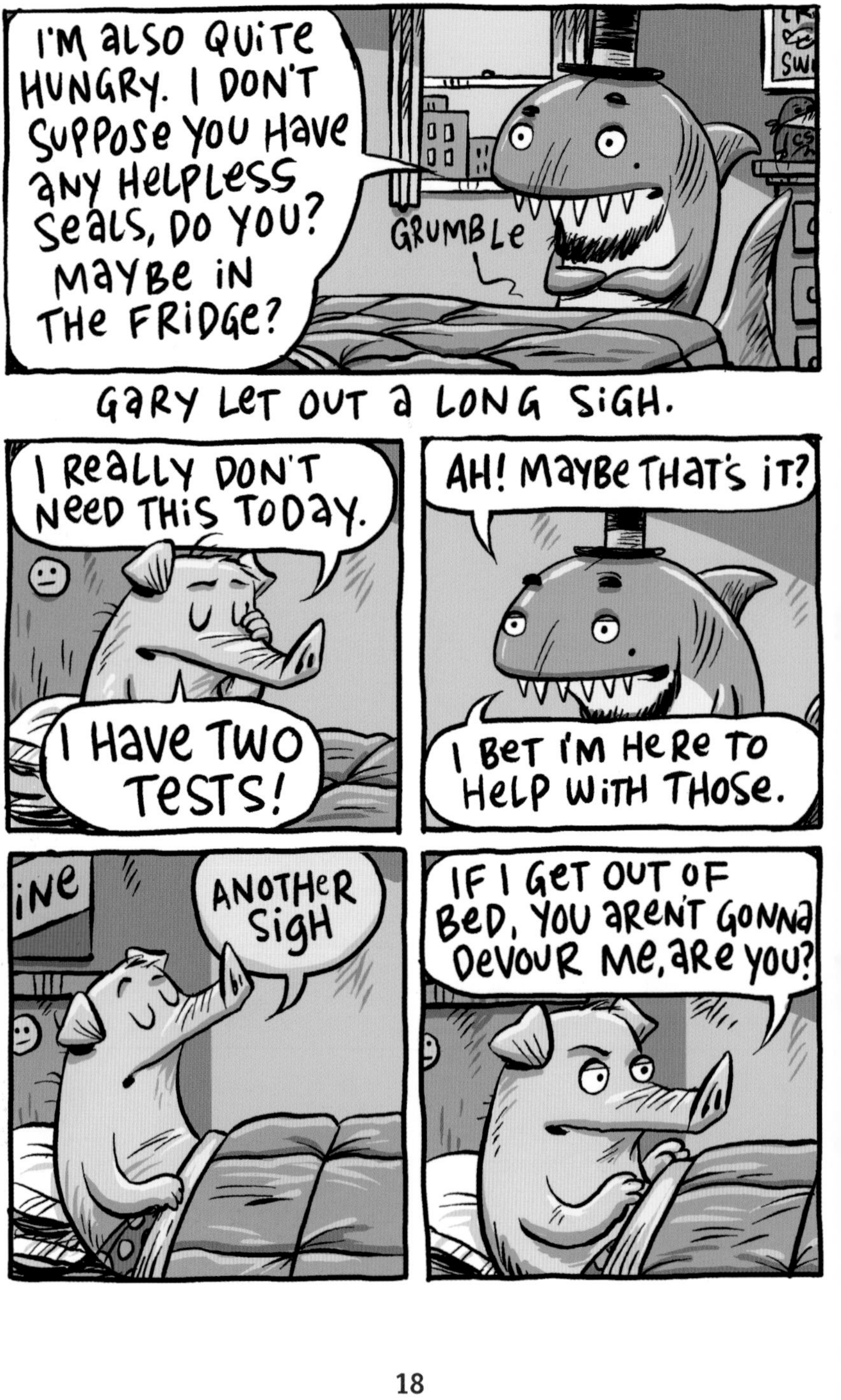
I'M ALSO QUITE HUNGRY. I DON'T SUPPOSE YOU HAVE ANY HELPLESS SEALS, DO YOU? MAYBE IN THE FRIDGE?
GRUMBLE
GARY LET OUT A LONG SIGH.
I REALLY DON'T NEED THIS TODAY.
I HAVE TWO TESTS!
AH! MAYBE THAT'S IT?
I BET I'M HERE TO HELP WITH THOSE.
ANOTHER SIGH
IF I GET OUT OF BED, YOU AREN'T GONNA DEVOUR ME, ARE YOU?

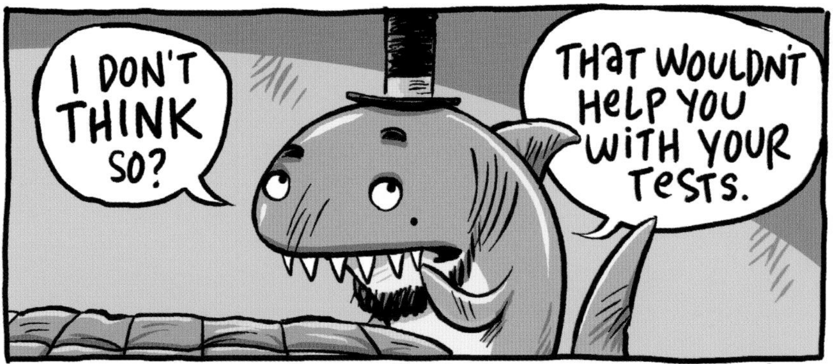
I DON'T THINK SO?
THAT WOULDN'T HELP YOU WITH YOUR TESTS.

GARY GOT READY FOR SCHOOL WHILE HE THOUGHT ABOUT HOW TO GET RID OF HIS POLITE BUT UNWELCOME GUEST.

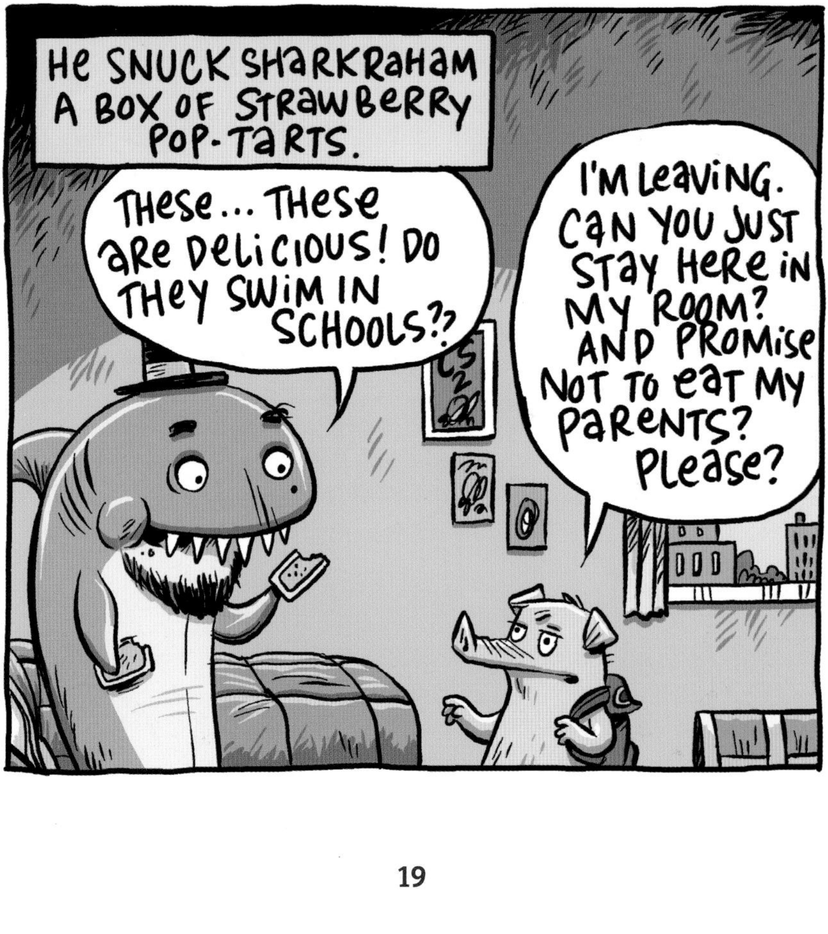
HE SNUCK SHARKRAHAM A BOX OF STRAWBERRY POP-TARTS.
THESE... THESE ARE DELICIOUS! DO THEY SWIM IN SCHOOLS??
I'M LEAVING. CAN YOU JUST STAY HERE IN MY ROOM? AND PROMISE NOT TO EAT MY PARENTS? PLEASE?

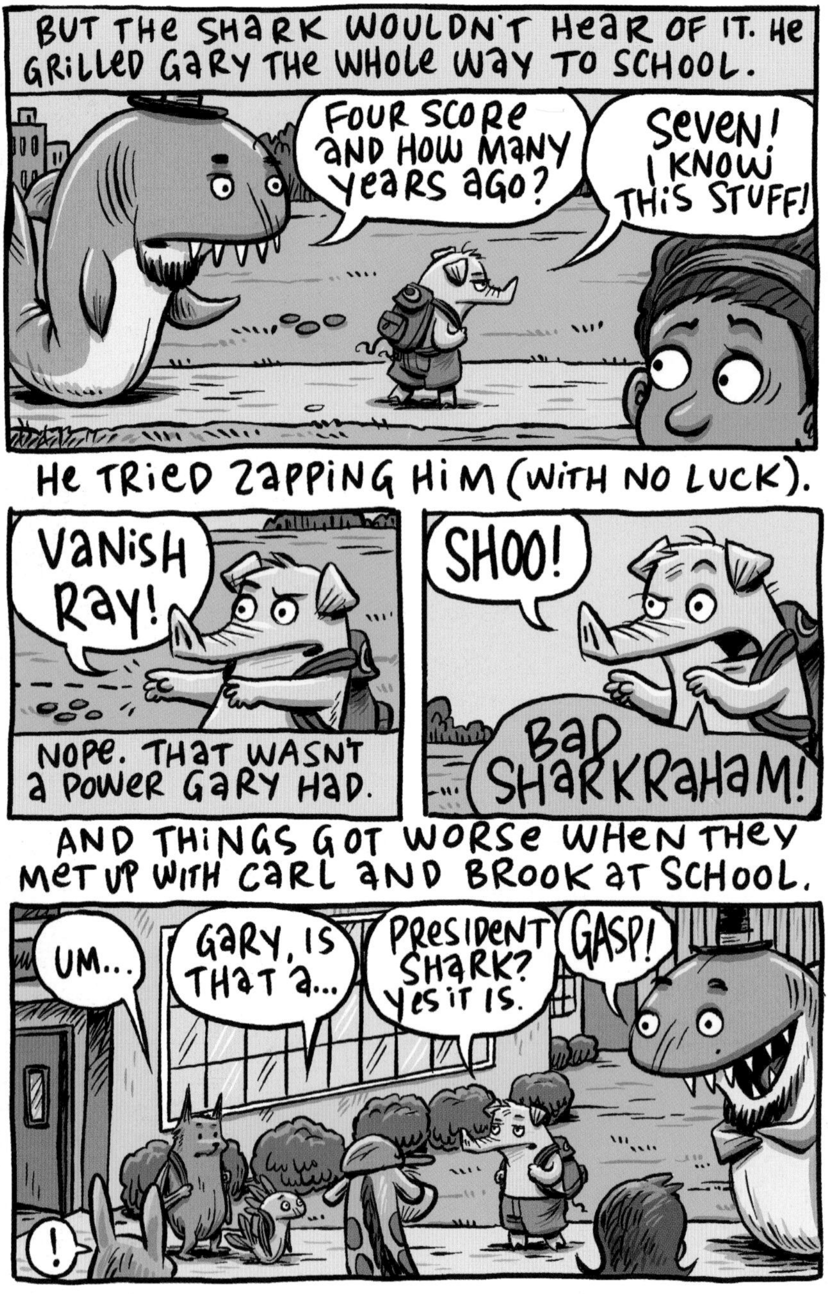
BUT THE SHARK WOULDN'T HEAR OF IT. HE GRILLED GARY THE WHOLE WAY TO SCHOOL.
FOUR SCORE AND HOW MANY YEARS AGO?
SEVEN! I KNOW THIS STUFF!
HE TRIED ZAPPING HIM (WITH NO LUCK).
VANISH RAY!
NOPE. THAT WASN'T A POWER GARY HAD.
SHOO!
BAD SHARKRAHAM!
AND THINGS GOT WORSE WHEN THEY MET UP WITH CARL AND BROOK AT SCHOOL.
UM...
GARY, IS THAT A...
PRESIDENT SHARK? YES IT IS.
GASP!
!

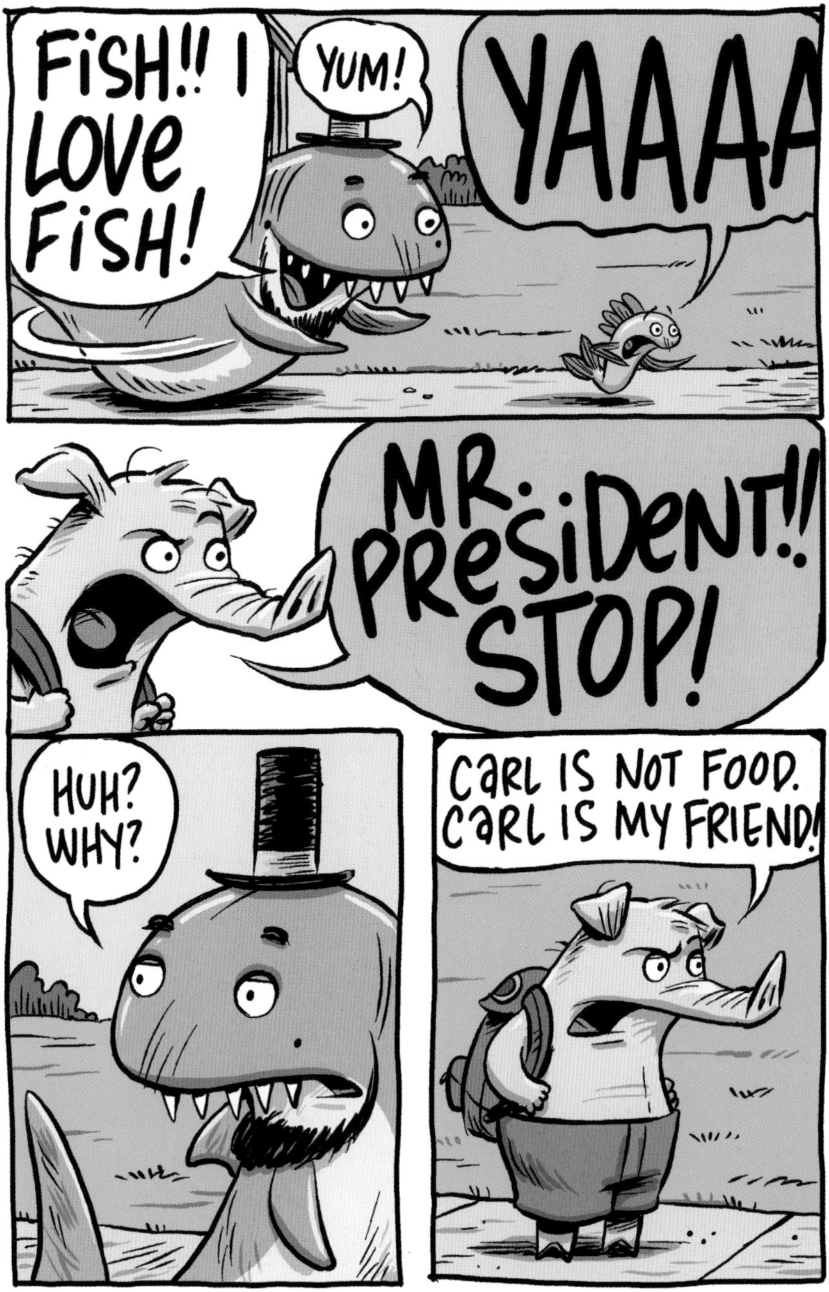
FISH!! I LOVE FISH!
YUM!
YAAAA
MR. PRESIDENT!! STOP!
HUH? WHY?
CARL IS NOT FOOD. CARL IS MY FRIEND!

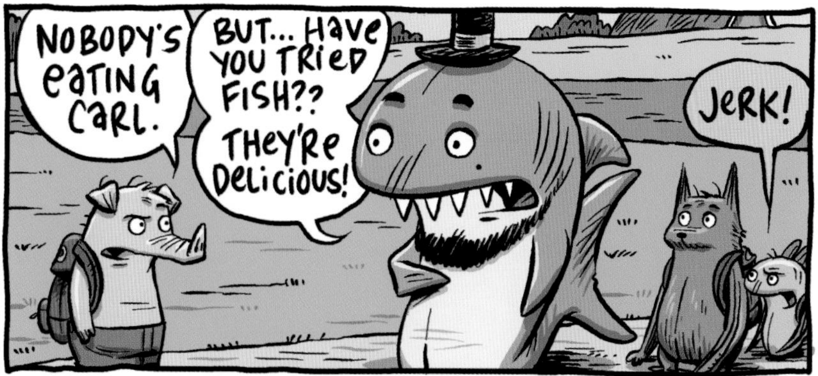
NOBODY'S eating CARL.
BUT... Have YOU TRIED FISH?? THEY'RE DELICIOUS!
JERK!

GARY STASHED SHARKRAHAM IN THE JANITOR'S CLOSET. (ONLY GIVING MR. GUFFIN ONE NEAR HEART ATTACK DURING SECOND PERIOD.)

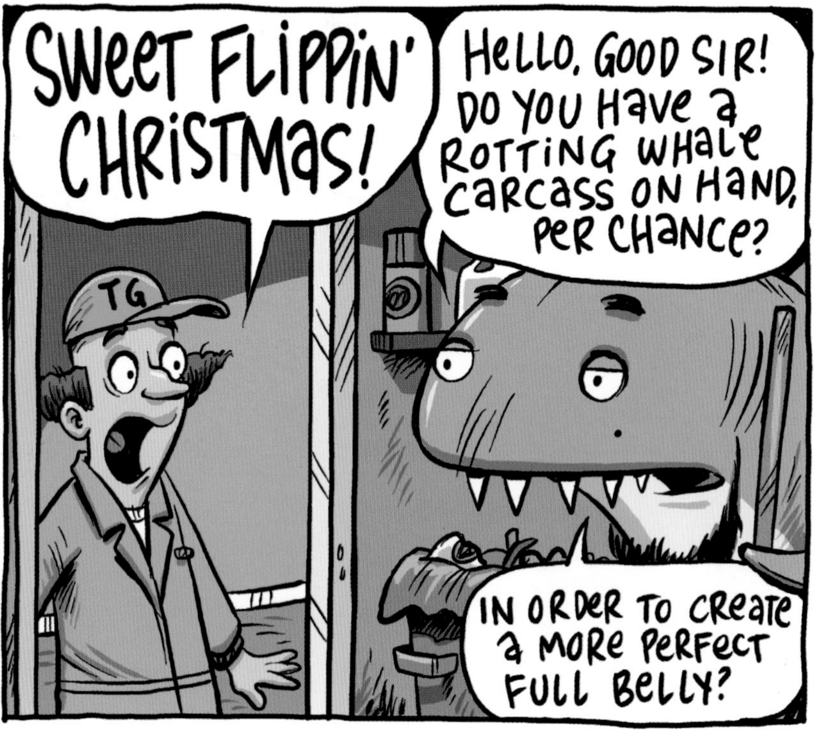
SWEET FLIPPIN' CHRISTMAS!
HELLO, GOOD SIR! DO YOU HAVE A ROTTING WHALE CARCASS ON HAND, PER CHANCE?
IN ORDER TO CREATE A MORE PERFECT FULL BELLY?
TG

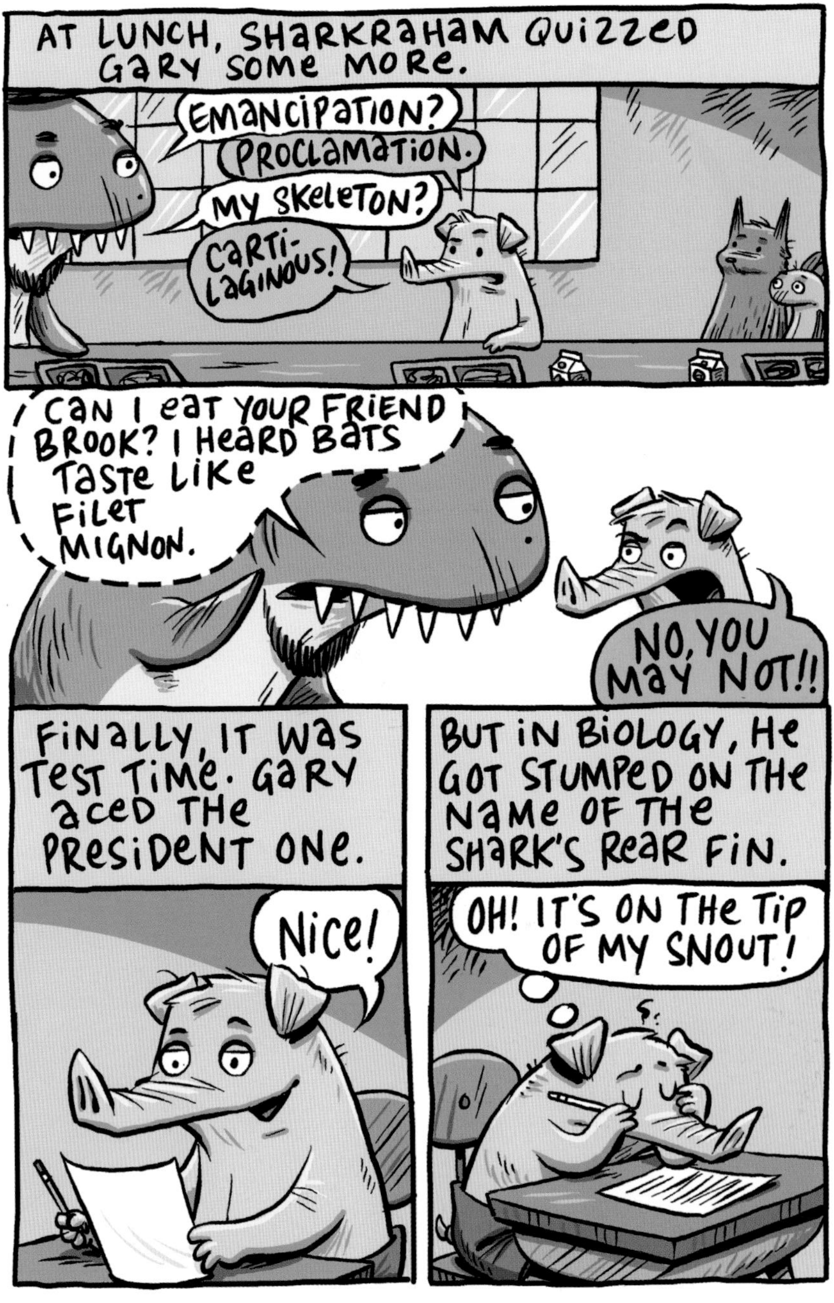
AT LUNCH, SHARKRAHAM QUIZZED GARY SOME MORE.
EMANCIPATION?
PROCLAMATION.
MY SKELETON?
CARTI-LAGINOUS!
CAN I EAT YOUR FRIEND BROOK? I HEARD BATS TASTE LIKE FILET MIGNON.
NO, YOU MAY NOT!!
FINALLY, IT WAS TEST TIME. GARY ACED THE PRESIDENT ONE.
NICE!
BUT IN BIOLOGY, HE GOT STUMPED ON THE NAME OF THE SHARK'S REAR FIN.
OH! IT'S ON THE TIP OF MY SNOUT!

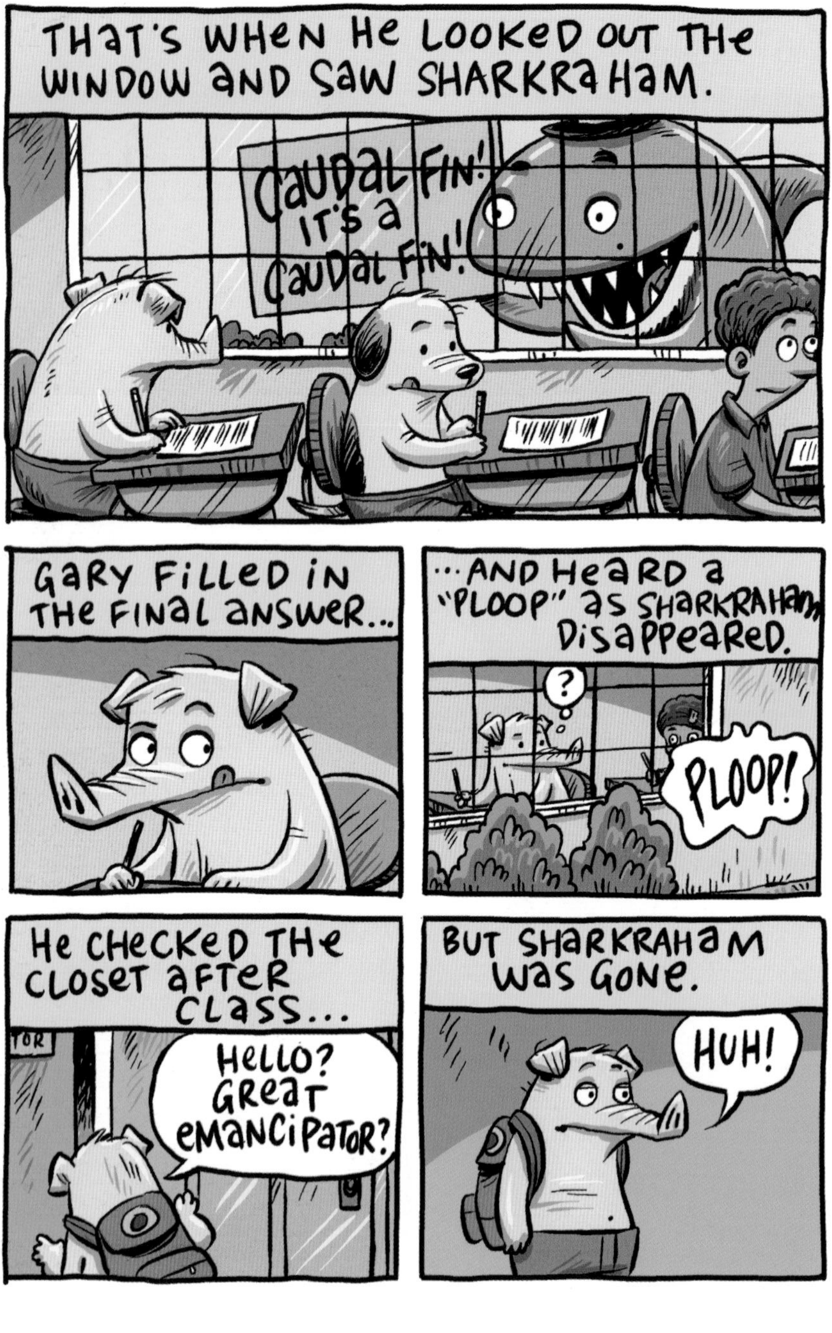
THAT'S WHEN HE LOOKED OUT THE WINDOW AND SAW SHARKRAHAM.
CAUDAL FIN! IT'S A CAUDAL FIN!
GARY FILLED IN THE FINAL ANSWER...
...AND HEARD A "PLOOP" AS SHARKRAHAM DISAPPEARED.
PLOOP!
HE CHECKED THE CLOSET AFTER CLASS...
HELLO? GREAT EMANCIPATOR?
BUT SHARKRAHAM WAS GONE.
HUH!

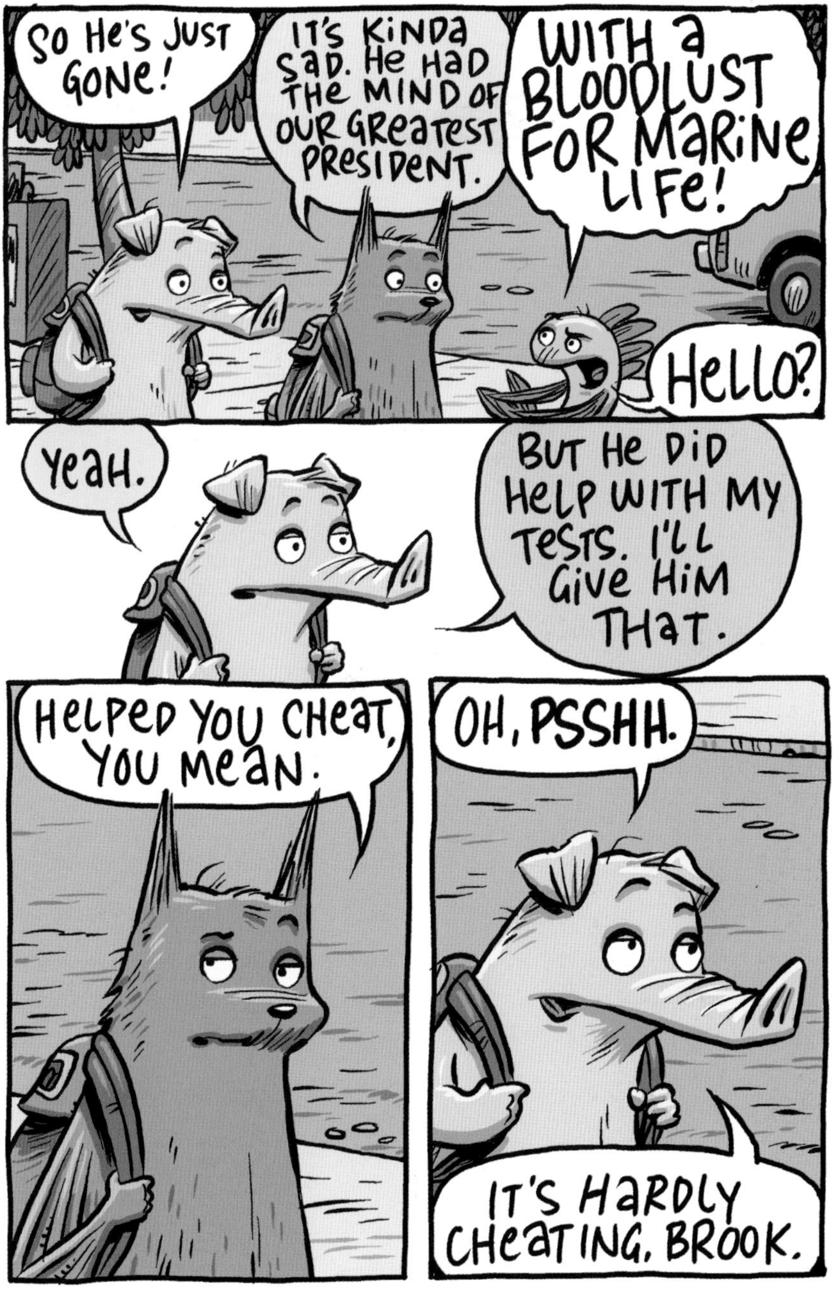
SO HE'S JUST GONE!
IT'S KINDA SAD. HE HAD THE MIND OF OUR GREATEST PRESIDENT.
WITH A BLOODLUST FOR MARINE LIFE!
HELLO?
YEAH.
BUT HE DID HELP WITH MY TESTS. I'LL GIVE HIM THAT.
HELPED YOU CHEAT, YOU MEAN.
OH, PSSHH.
IT'S HARDLY CHEATING, BROOK.

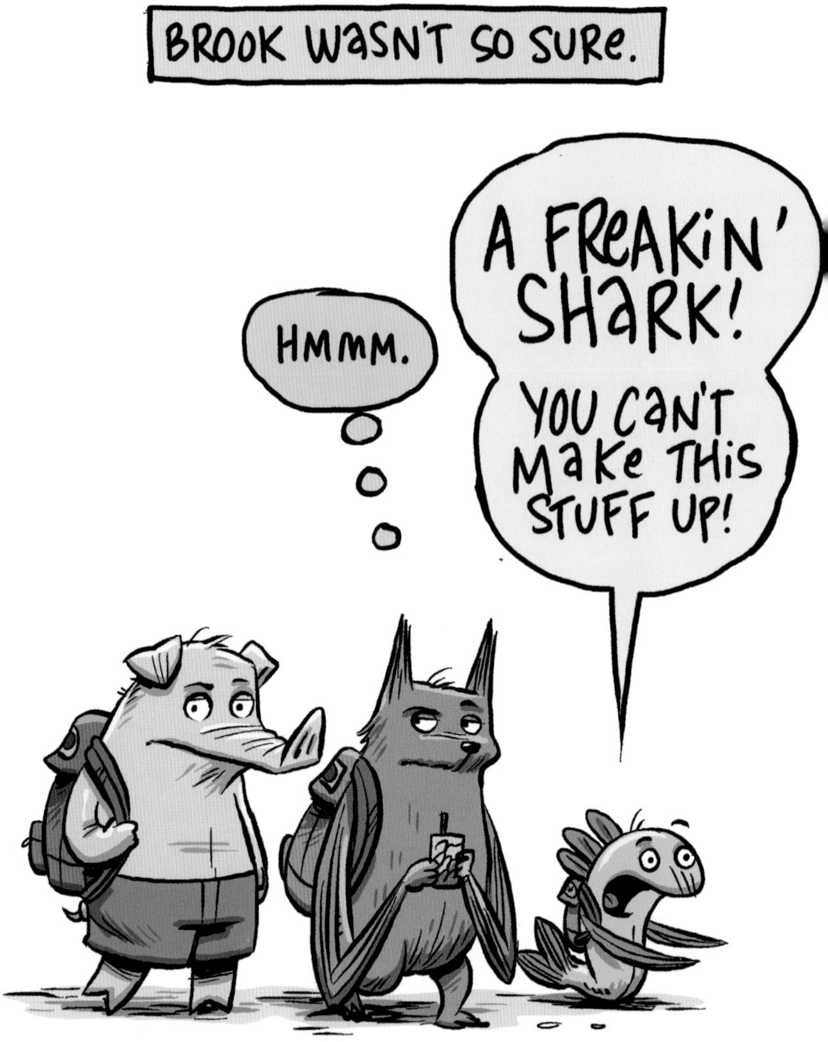
BROOK WASN'T SO SURE.
HMMM.
A FREAKIN' SHARK!
YOU CAN'T MAKE THIS STUFF UP!

CHAPTER THREE

"TROUBLE a-BREWIN'"

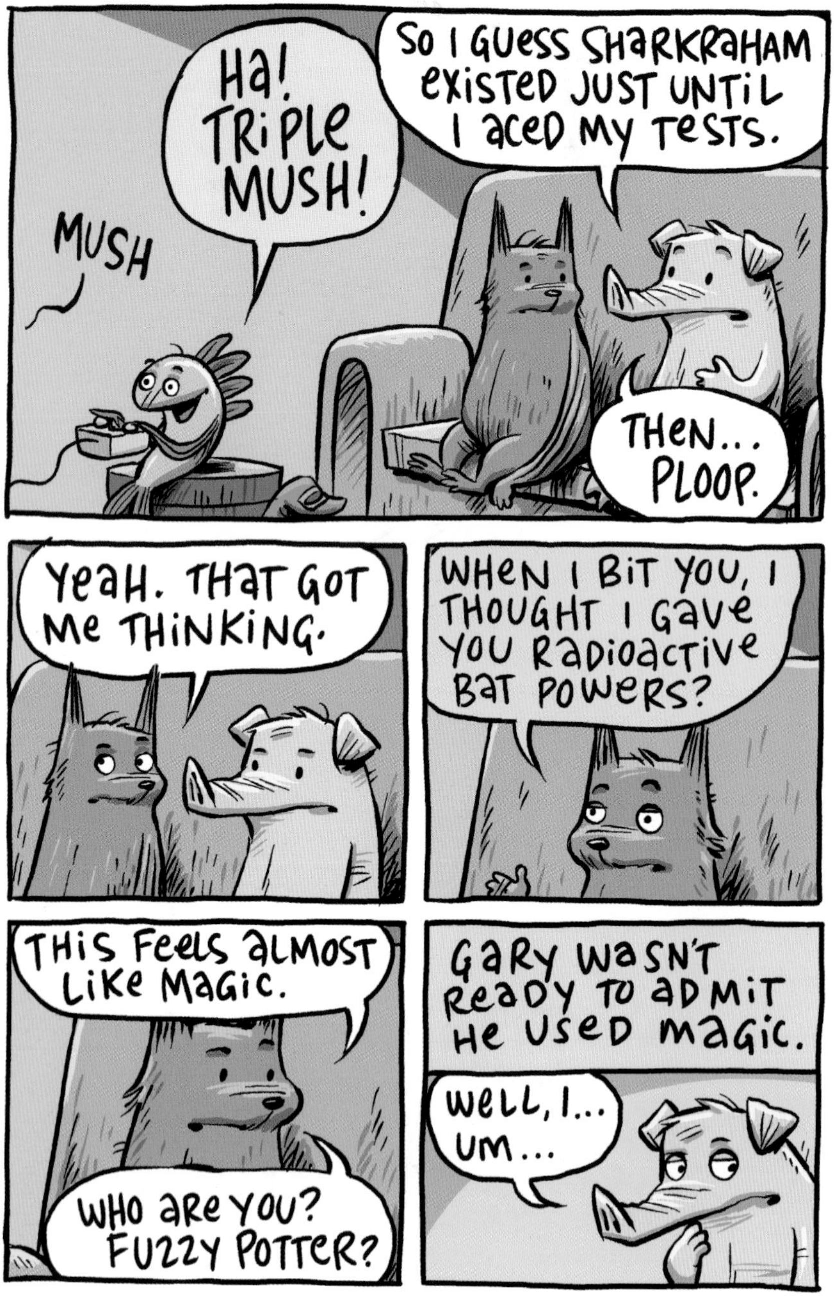
MUSH
Ha! Triple MUSH!
So I guess Sharkraham existed just until I aced my tests.
Then... PLOOP.
Yeah. That got me thinking.
When I bit you, I thought I gave you radioactive bat powers?
This feels almost like magic.
Who are you? Fuzzy Potter?
Gary wasn't ready to admit he used magic.
Well, I... um...

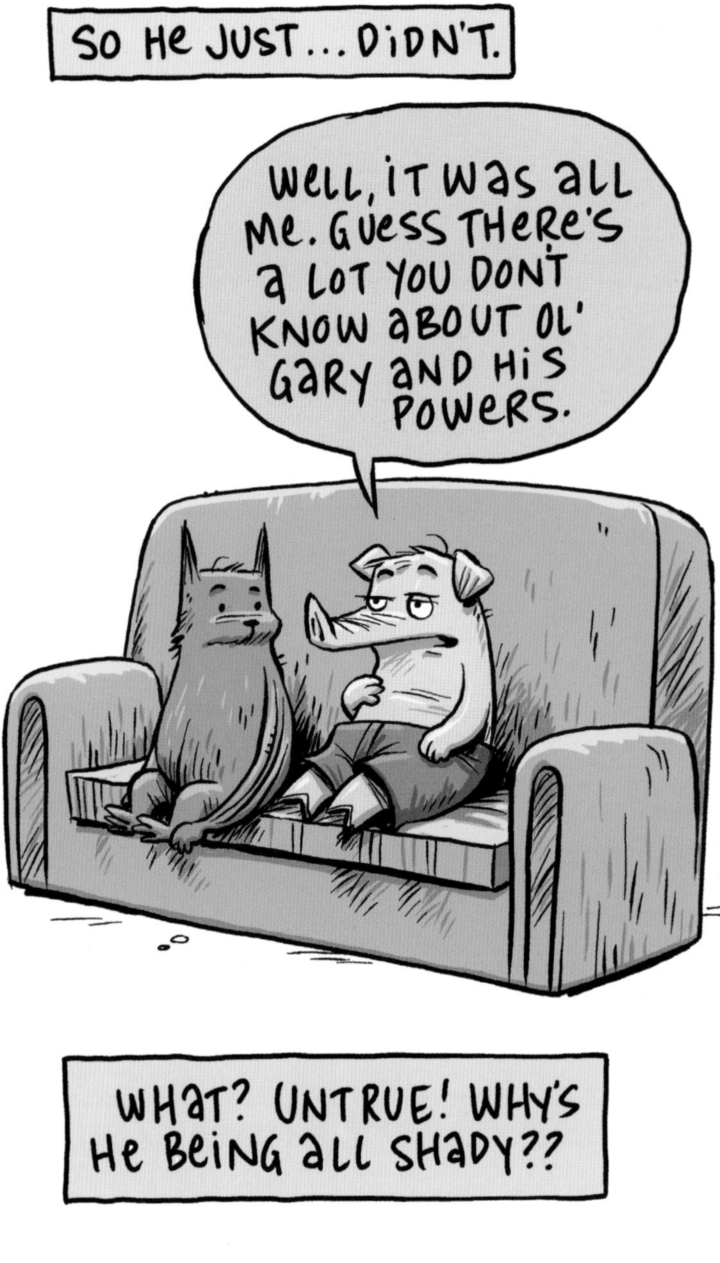
SO HE JUST... DIDN'T.
WELL, IT WAS ALL ME. GUESS THERE'S A LOT YOU DON'T KNOW ABOUT OL' GARY AND HIS POWERS.
WHAT? UNTRUE! WHY'S HE BEING ALL SHADY??

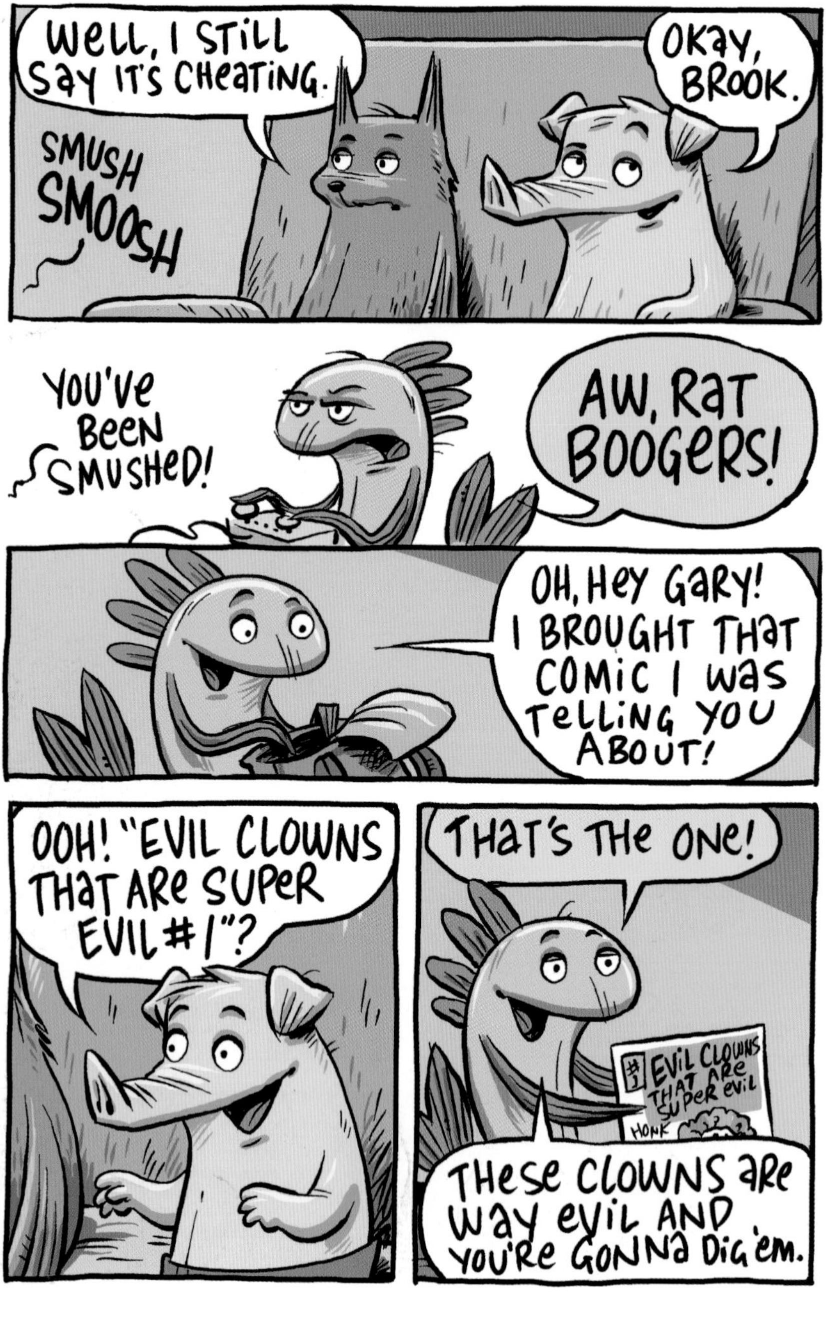
WELL, I STILL SAY IT'S CHEATING.
SMUSH SMOOSH
OKAY, BROOK.
YOU'VE BEEN SMUSHED!
AW, RAT BOOGERS!
OH, HEY GARY! I BROUGHT THAT COMIC I WAS TELLING YOU ABOUT!
OOH! "EVIL CLOWNS THAT ARE SUPER EVIL #1"?
THAT'S THE ONE!
#1 EVIL CLOWNS THAT ARE SUPER EVIL
HONK
THESE CLOWNS ARE WAY EVIL AND YOU'RE GONNA DIG 'EM.

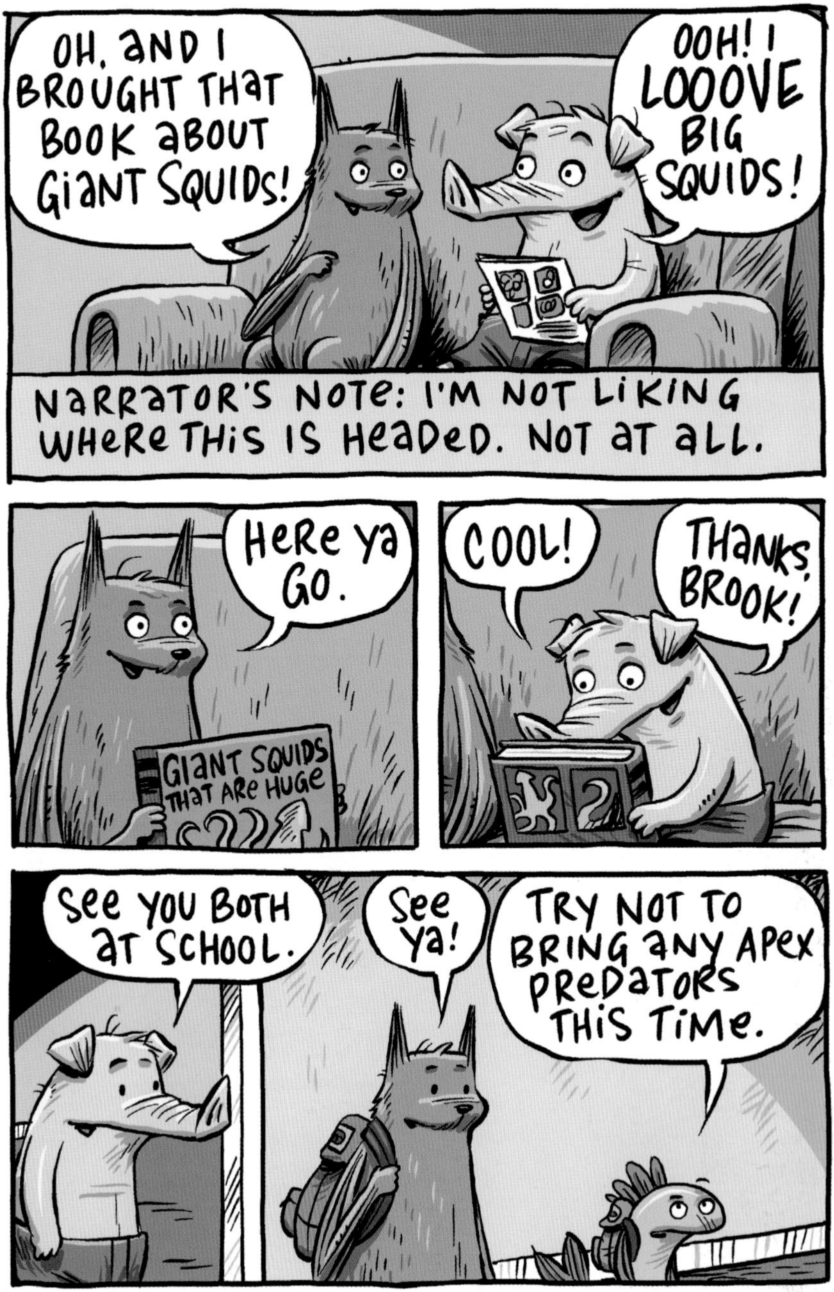
OH, AND I BROUGHT THAT BOOK ABOUT GIANT SQUIDS!
OOH! I LOOOVE BIG SQUIDS!
NARRATOR'S NOTE: I'M NOT LIKING WHERE THIS IS HEADED. NOT AT ALL.
HERE YA GO.
GIANT SQUIDS THAT ARE HUGE
COOL!
THANKS, BROOK!
SEE YOU BOTH AT SCHOOL.
SEE YA!
TRY NOT TO BRING ANY APEX PREDATORS THIS TIME.

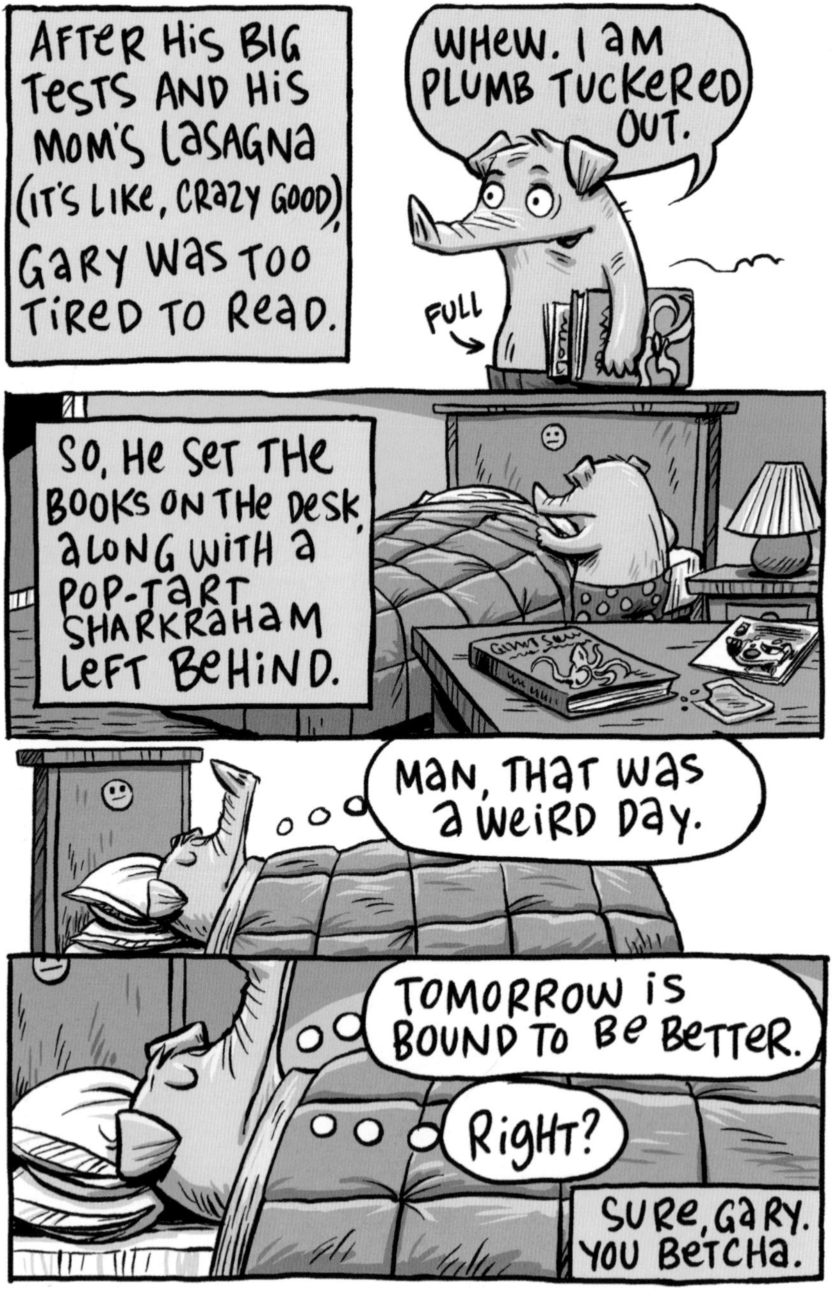
AFTER HIS BIG TESTS AND HIS MOM'S LASAGNA (IT'S LIKE, CRAZY GOOD), GARY WAS TOO TIRED TO READ.
WHEW. I AM PLUMB TUCKERED OUT.
FULL
SO, HE SET THE BOOKS ON THE DESK, ALONG WITH A POP-TART SHARKRAHAM LEFT BEHIND.
MAN, THAT WAS A WEIRD DAY.
TOMORROW IS BOUND TO BE BETTER.
RIGHT?
SURE, GARY. YOU BETCHA.

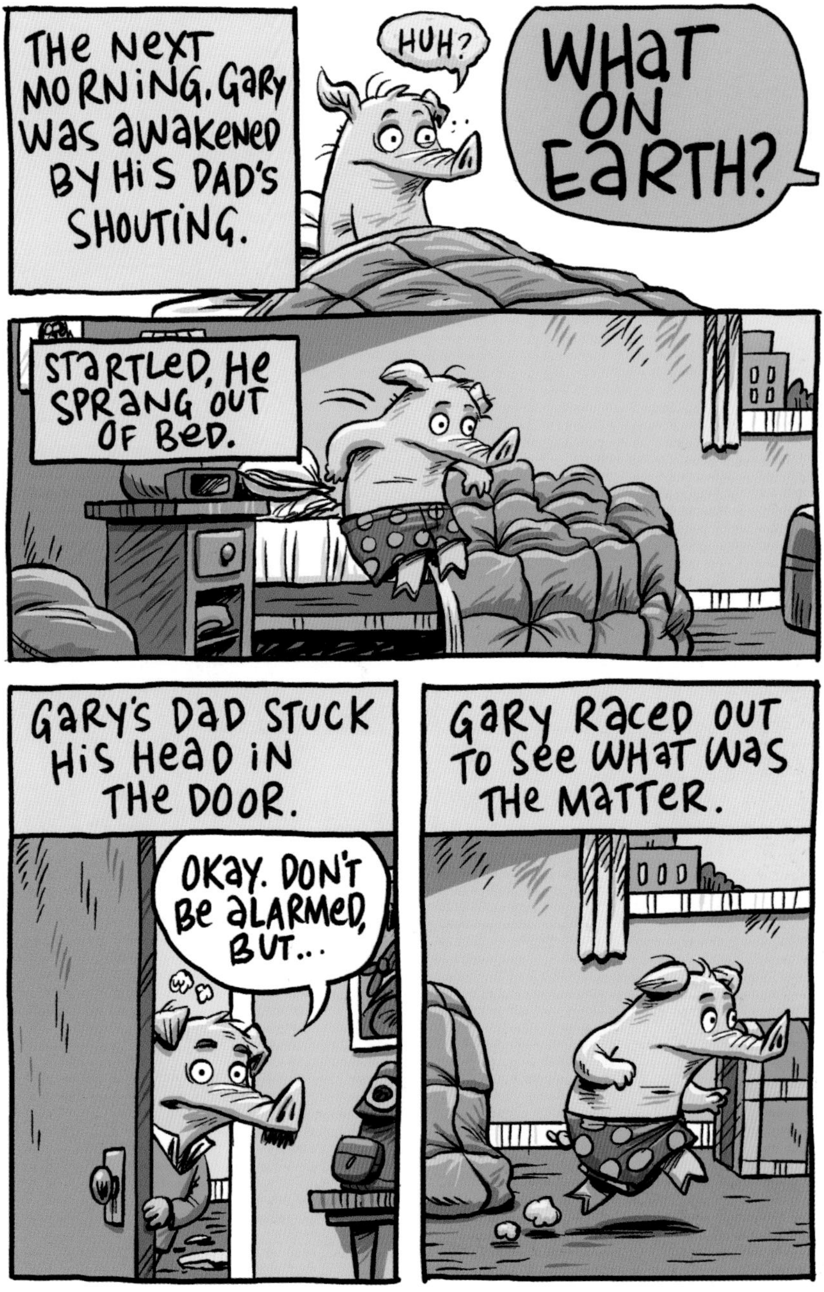
THE NEXT MORNING, GARY WAS AWAKENED BY HIS DAD'S SHOUTING.
HUH?
WHAT ON EARTH?
STARTLED, HE SPRANG OUT OF BED.
GARY'S DAD STUCK HIS HEAD IN THE DOOR.
OKAY. DON'T BE ALARMED, BUT...
GARY RACED OUT TO SEE WHAT WAS THE MATTER.

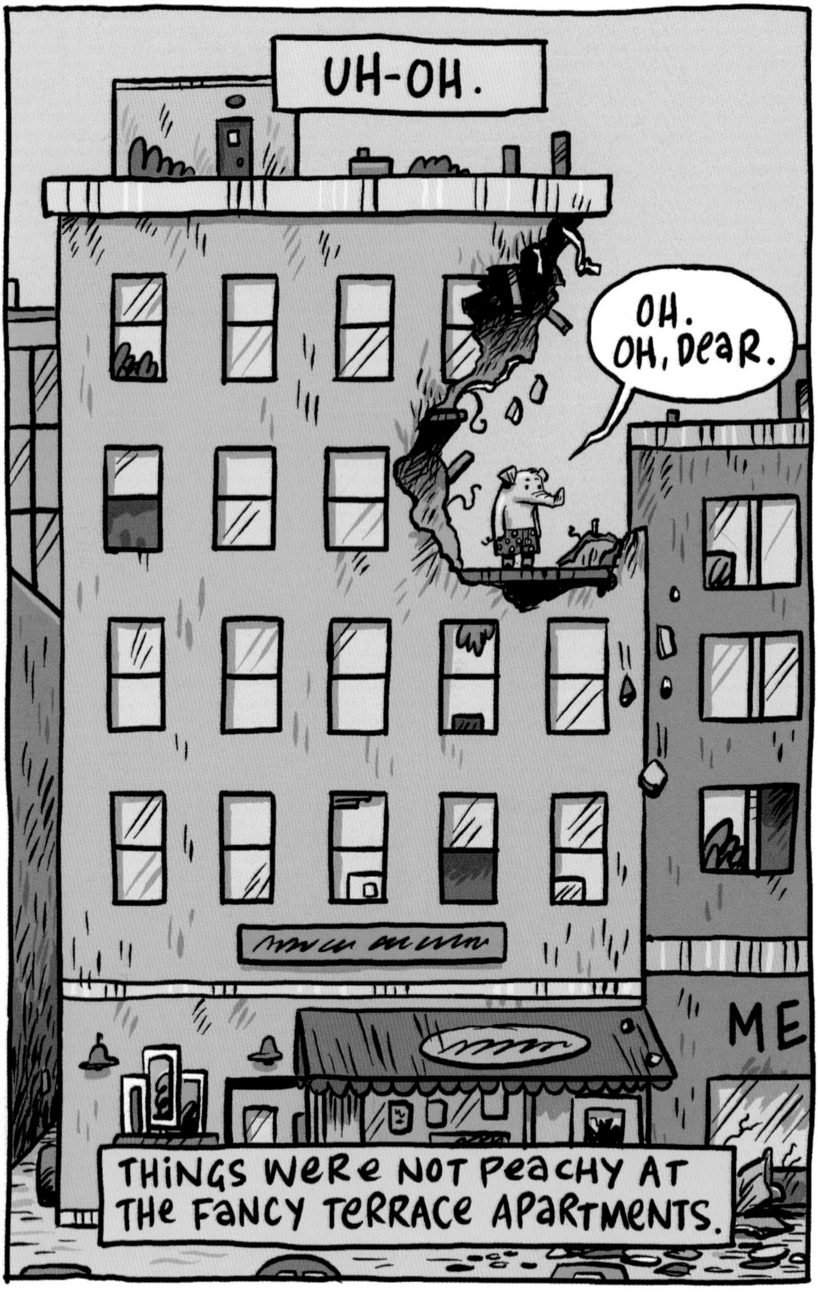
UH-OH.
OH. OH, DeaR.
ME
THINGS WeRe NOT PeacHY AT THe FANCY TeRRACe APaRTMeNTS.

CHAPTER FOUR

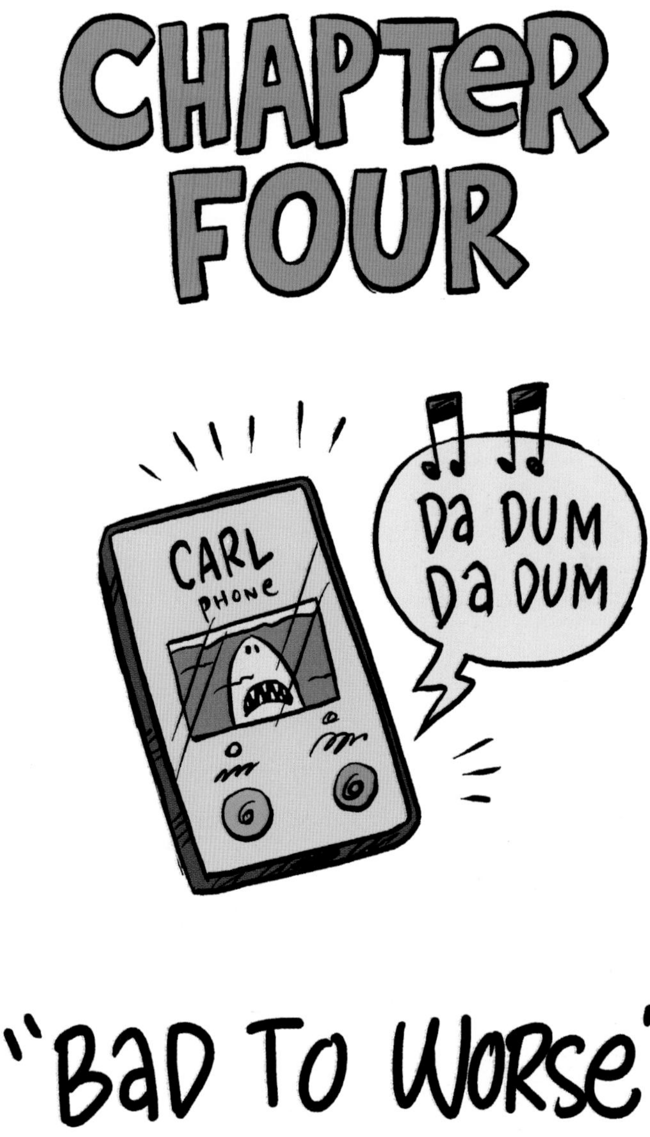
CARL PHONE
DA DUM DA DUM

"BAD TO WORSE"

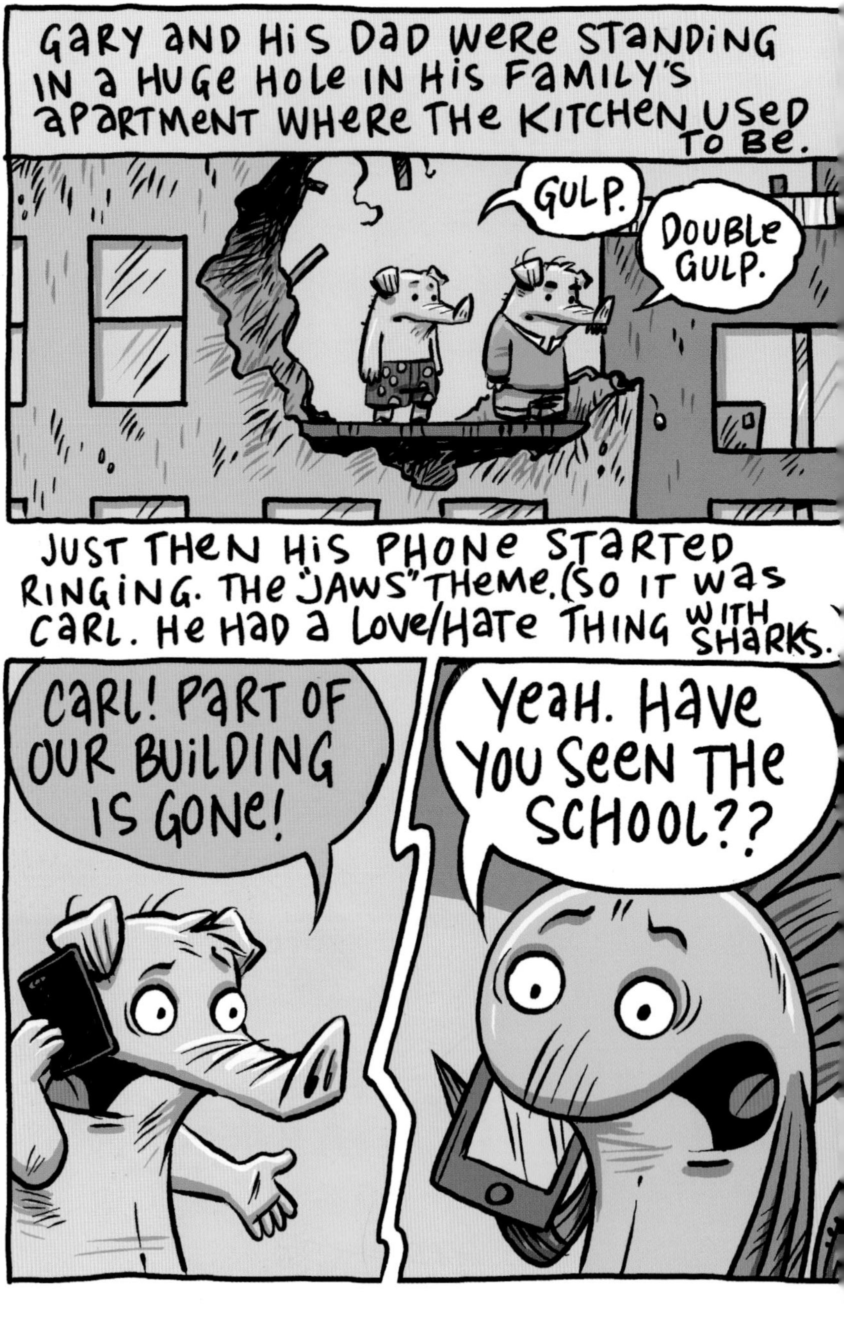
GARY AND HIS DAD WERE STANDING IN A HUGE HOLE IN HIS FAMILY'S APARTMENT WHERE THE KITCHEN USED TO BE.
GULP.
DOUBLE GULP.
JUST THEN HIS PHONE STARTED RINGING. THE "JAWS" THEME. (SO IT WAS CARL. HE HAD A LOVE/HATE THING WITH SHARKS.)
CARL! PART OF OUR BUILDING IS GONE!
YEAH. HAVE YOU SEEN THE SCHOOL??

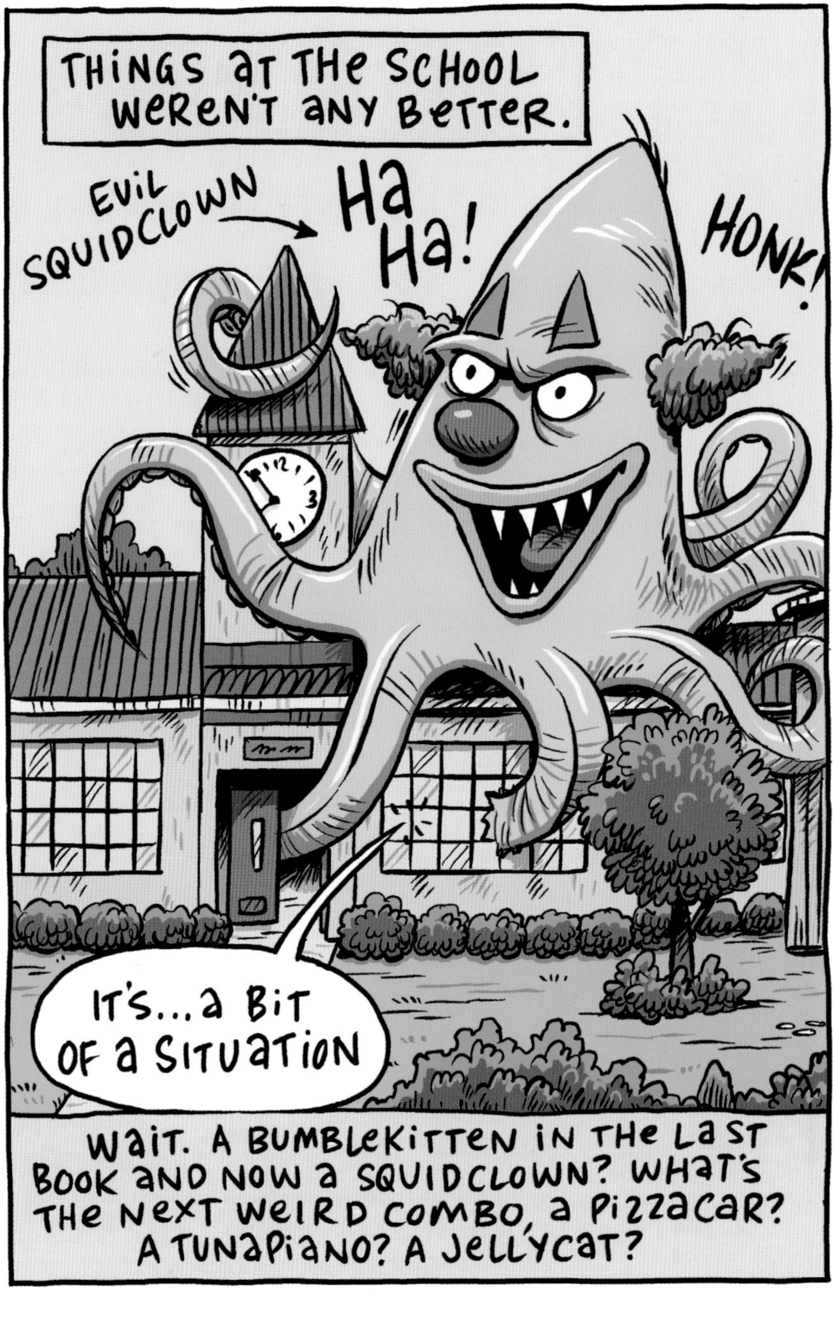
THINGS AT THE SCHOOL WEREN'T ANY BETTER.
EVIL SQUIDCLOWN
HA HA!
HONK!
IT'S... A BIT OF A SITUATION
WAIT. A BUMBLEKITTEN IN THE LAST BOOK AND NOW A SQUIDCLOWN? WHAT'S THE NEXT WEIRD COMBO, A PIZZACAR? A TUNAPIANO? A JELLYCAT?

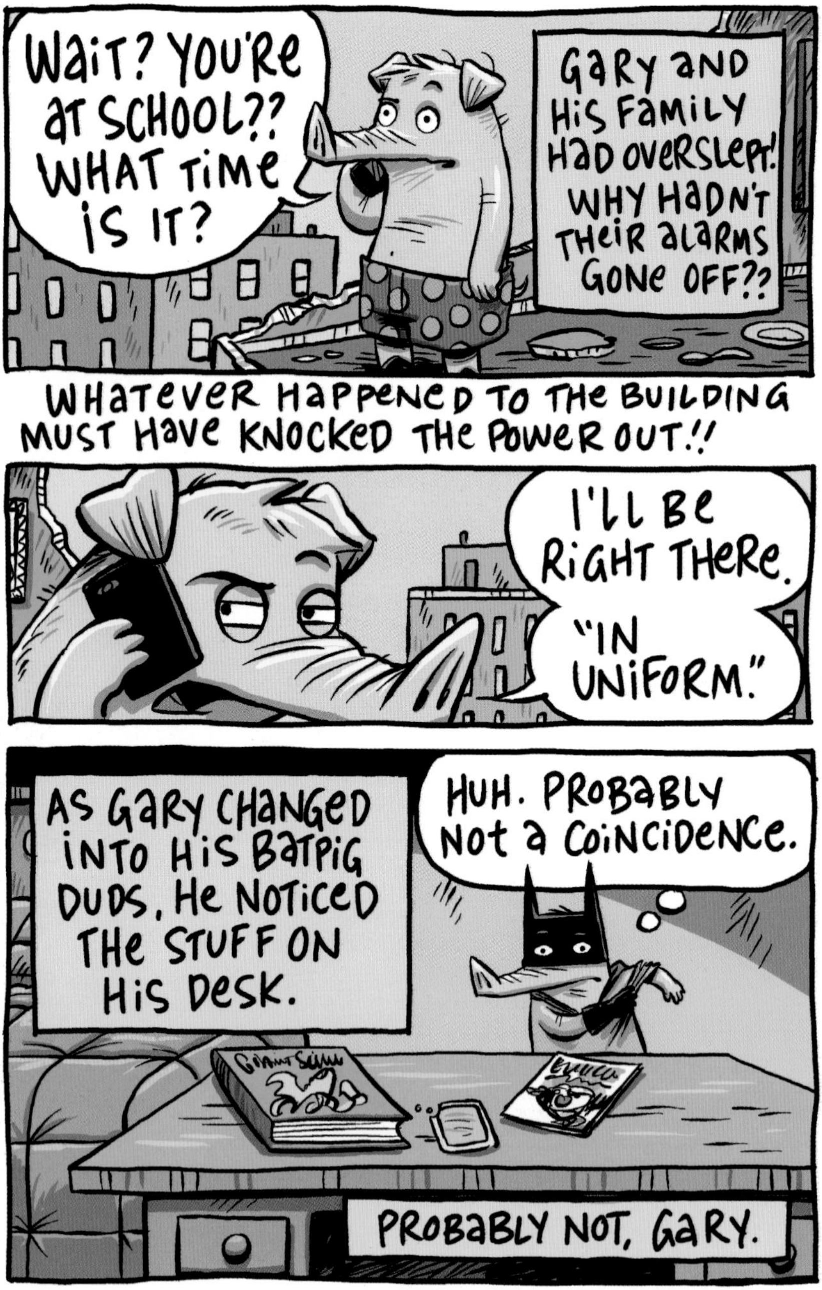
WAIT? YOU'RE AT SCHOOL?? WHAT TIME IS IT?
GARY AND HIS FAMILY HAD OVERSLEPT! WHY HADN'T THEIR ALARMS GONE OFF??
WHATEVER HAPPENED TO THE BUILDING MUST HAVE KNOCKED THE POWER OUT!!
I'LL BE RIGHT THERE.
"IN UNIFORM."
AS GARY CHANGED INTO HIS BATPIG DUDS, HE NOTICED THE STUFF ON HIS DESK.
HUH. PROBABLY NOT A COINCIDENCE.
PROBABLY NOT, GARY.

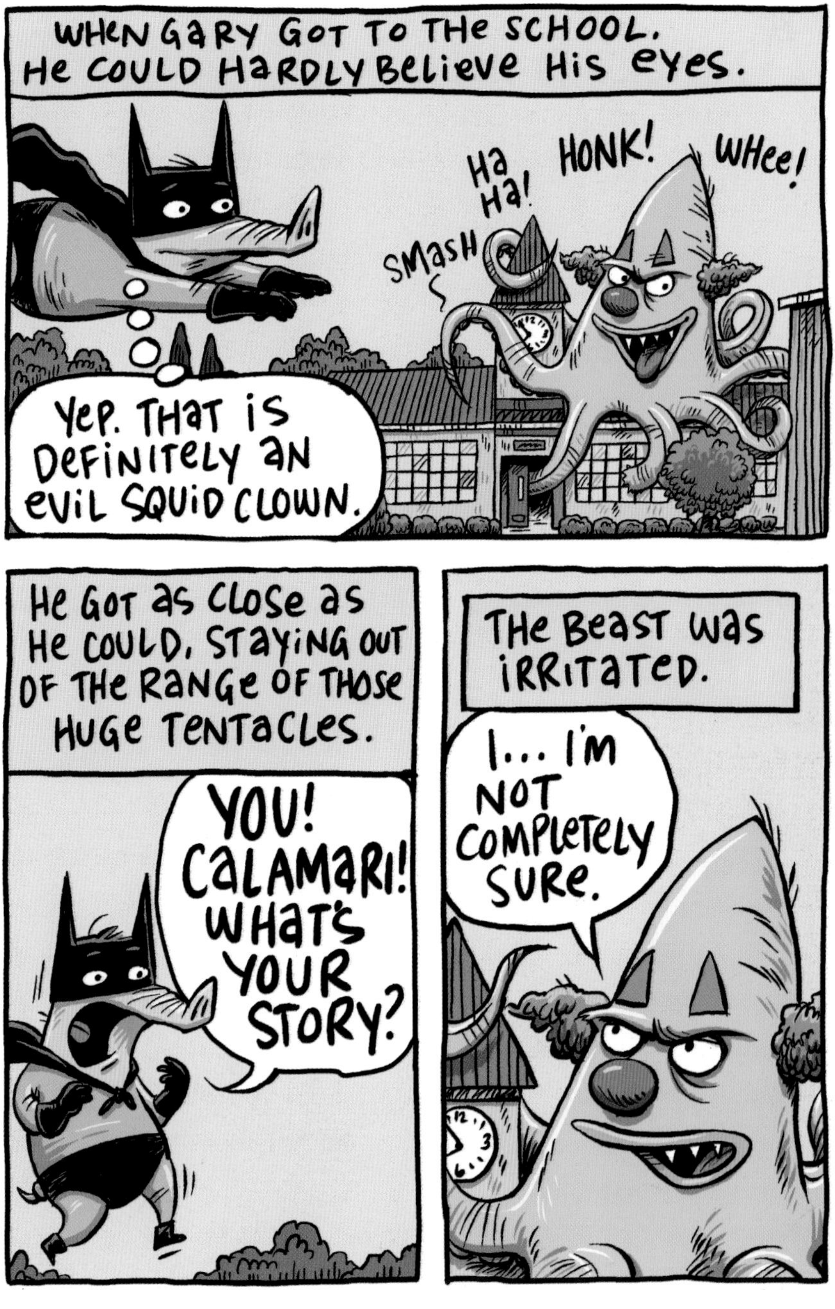
WHEN GARY GOT TO THE SCHOOL, HE COULD HARDLY BELIEVE HIS EYES.
HA HA!
HONK!
WHEE!
SMASH
YEP. THAT IS DEFINITELY AN EVIL SQUID CLOWN.
HE GOT AS CLOSE AS HE COULD, STAYING OUT OF THE RANGE OF THOSE HUGE TENTACLES.
YOU! CALAMARI! WHAT'S YOUR STORY?
THE BEAST WAS IRRITATED.
I... I'M NOT COMPLETELY SURE.

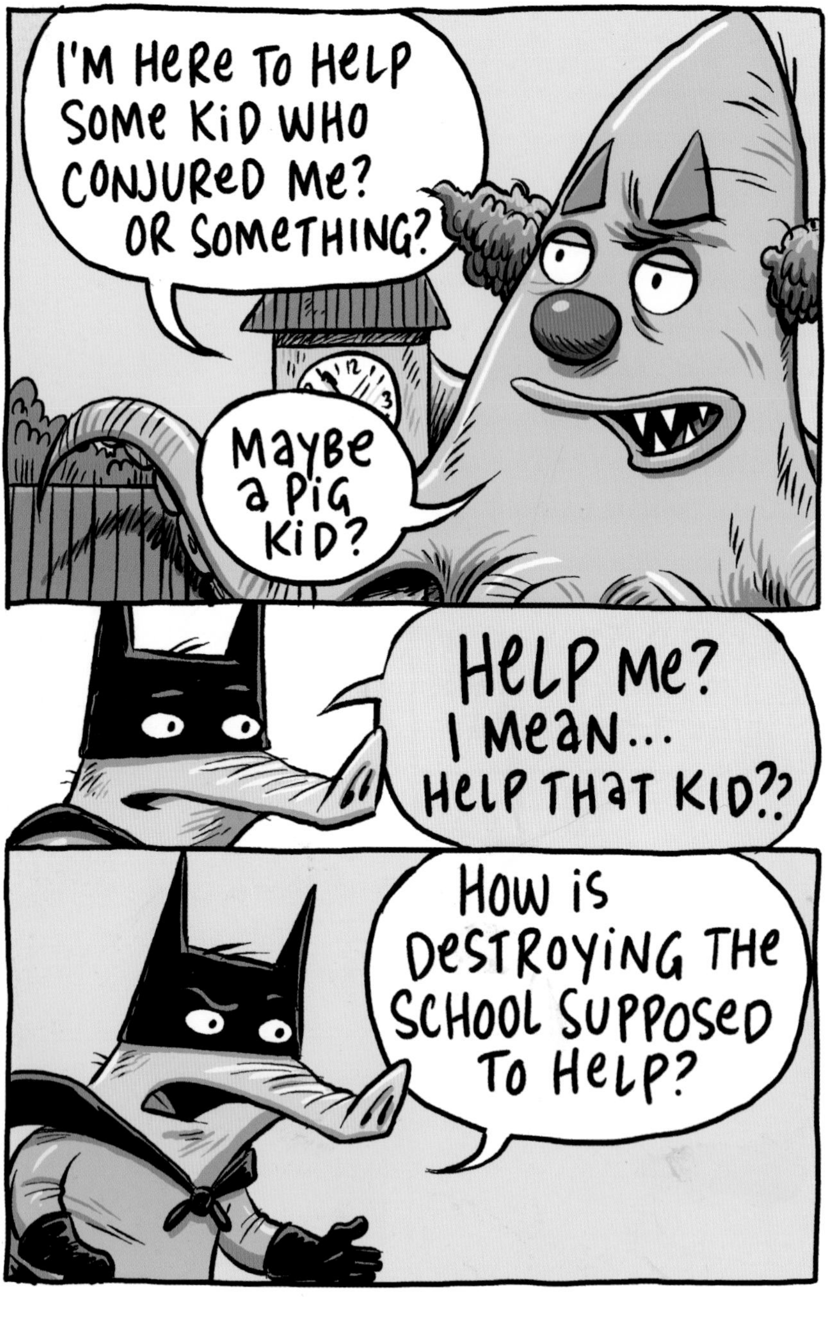
I'M HERE TO HELP SOME KID WHO CONJURED ME? OR SOMETHING?
MAYBE A PIG KID?
HELP ME? I MEAN... HELP THAT KID??
HOW IS DESTROYING THE SCHOOL SUPPOSED TO HELP?

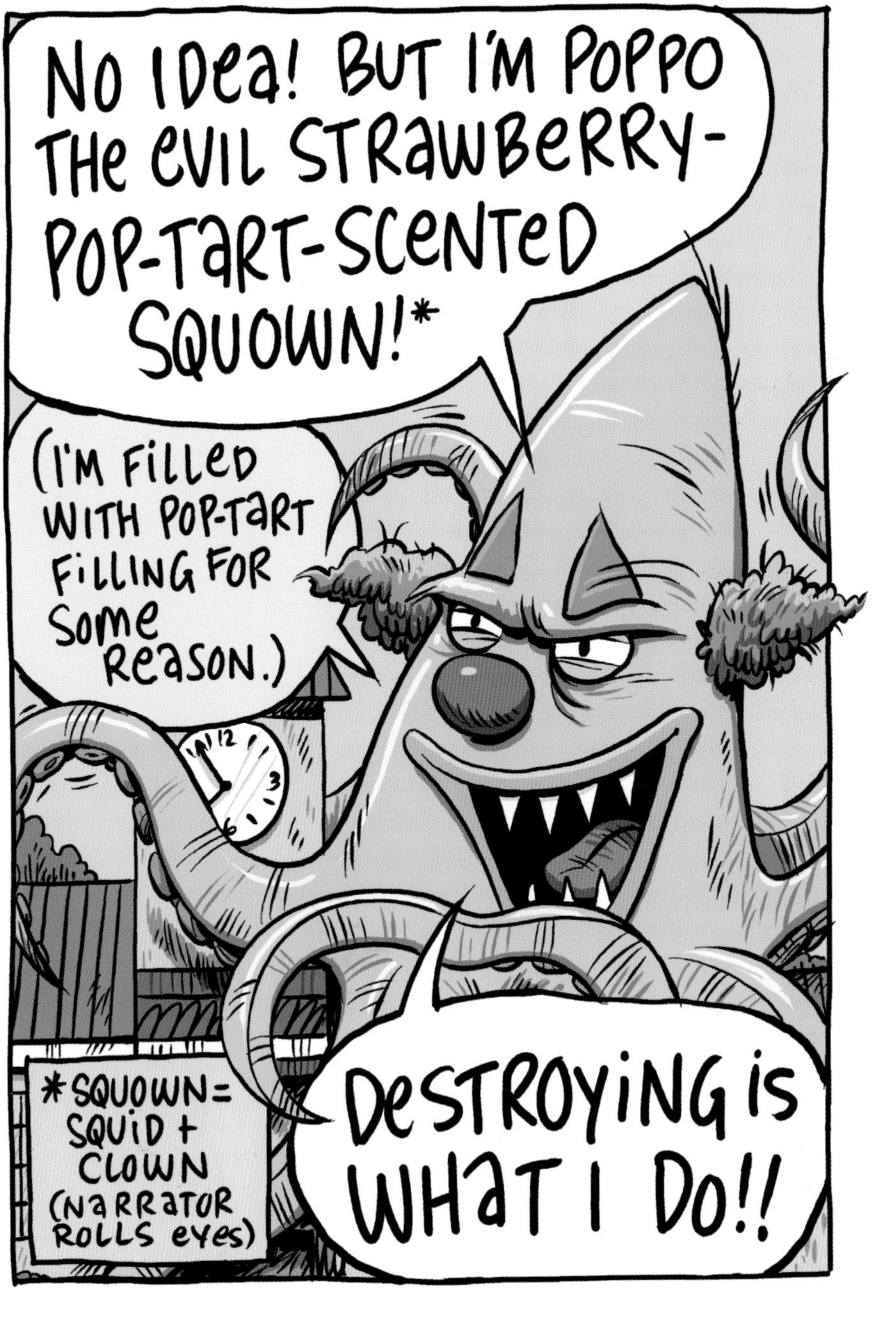

NO IDEA! BUT I'M POPPO THE EVIL STRAWBERRY-POP-TART-SCENTED SQUOWN!*
(I'M FILLED WITH POP-TART FILLING FOR SOME REASON.)
*SQUOWN= SQUID + CLOWN (NARRATOR ROLLS EYES)
DESTROYING IS WHAT I DO!!

CHAPTER FIVE

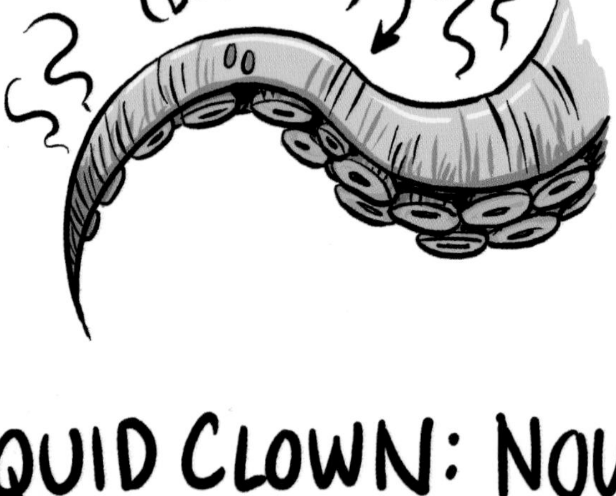
DELICIOUS BERRY AROMA (BUT EVIL)

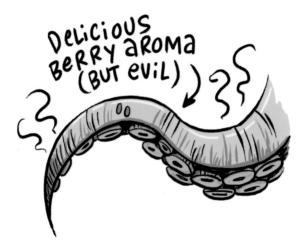

"SQUID CLOWN: NOW WITH REAL-ISH FRUIT FILLING!"

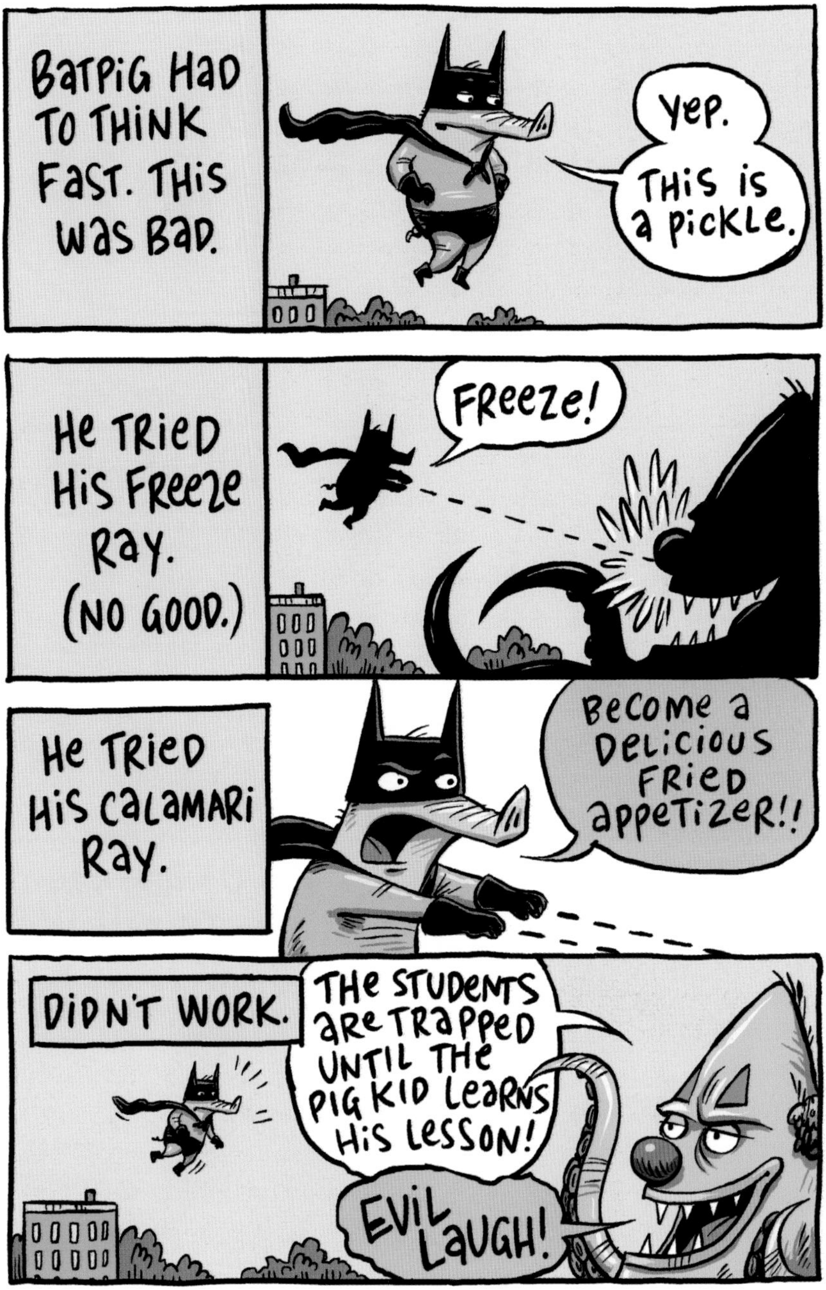

BATPIG HAD TO THINK FAST. THIS WAS BAD.
YEP.
THIS IS A PICKLE.
HE TRIED HIS FREEZE RAY. (NO GOOD.)
FREEZE!
HE TRIED HIS CALAMARI RAY.
BECOME A DELICIOUS FRIED APPETIZER!!
DIDN'T WORK.
THE STUDENTS ARE TRAPPED UNTIL THE PIG KID LEARNS HIS LESSON!
EVIL LAUGH!

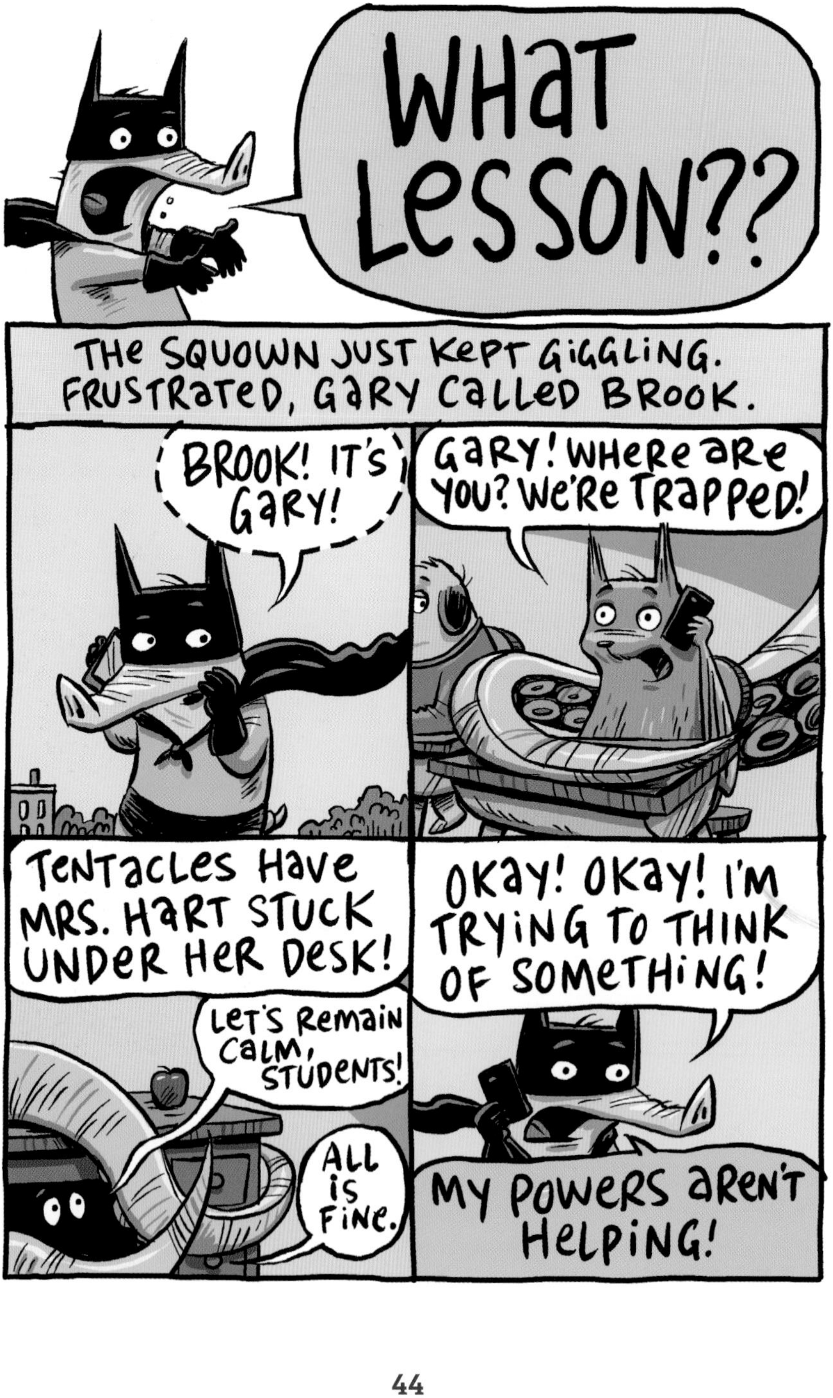
WHAT LESSON??
THE SQUOWN JUST KEPT GIGGLING. FRUSTRATED, GARY CALLED BROOK.
BROOK! IT'S GARY!
GARY! WHERE ARE YOU? WE'RE TRAPPED!
TENTACLES HAVE MRS. HART STUCK UNDER HER DESK!
LET'S REMAIN CALM, STUDENTS!
ALL IS FINE.
OKAY! OKAY! I'M TRYING TO THINK OF SOMETHING!
MY POWERS AREN'T HELPING!

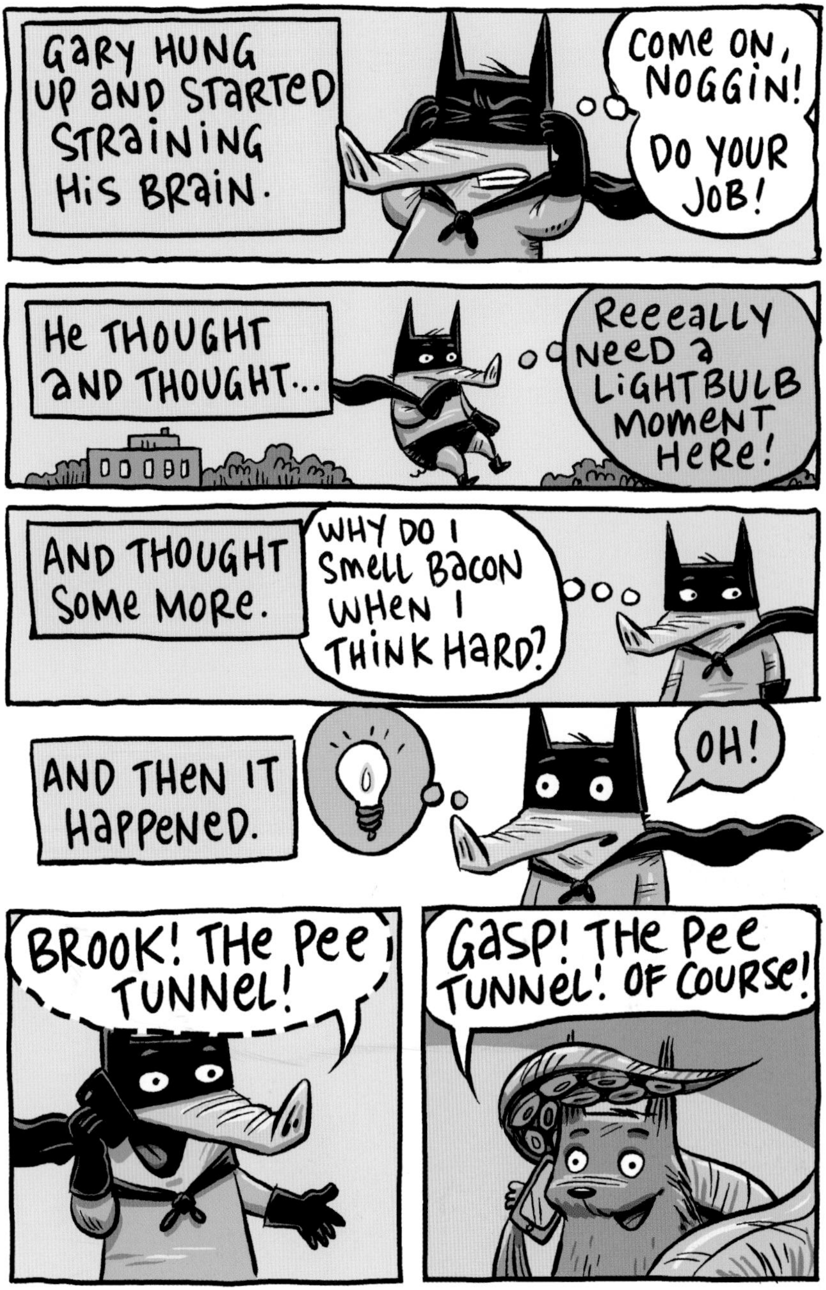
GARY HUNG UP AND STARTED STRAINING HIS BRAIN.
COME ON, NOGGIN!
DO YOUR JOB!
HE THOUGHT AND THOUGHT...
REEEALLY NEED A LIGHTBULB MOMENT HERE!
AND THOUGHT SOME MORE.
WHY DO I SMELL BACON WHEN I THINK HARD?
AND THEN IT HAPPENED.
OH!
BROOK! THE PEE TUNNEL!
GASP! THE PEE TUNNEL! OF COURSE!

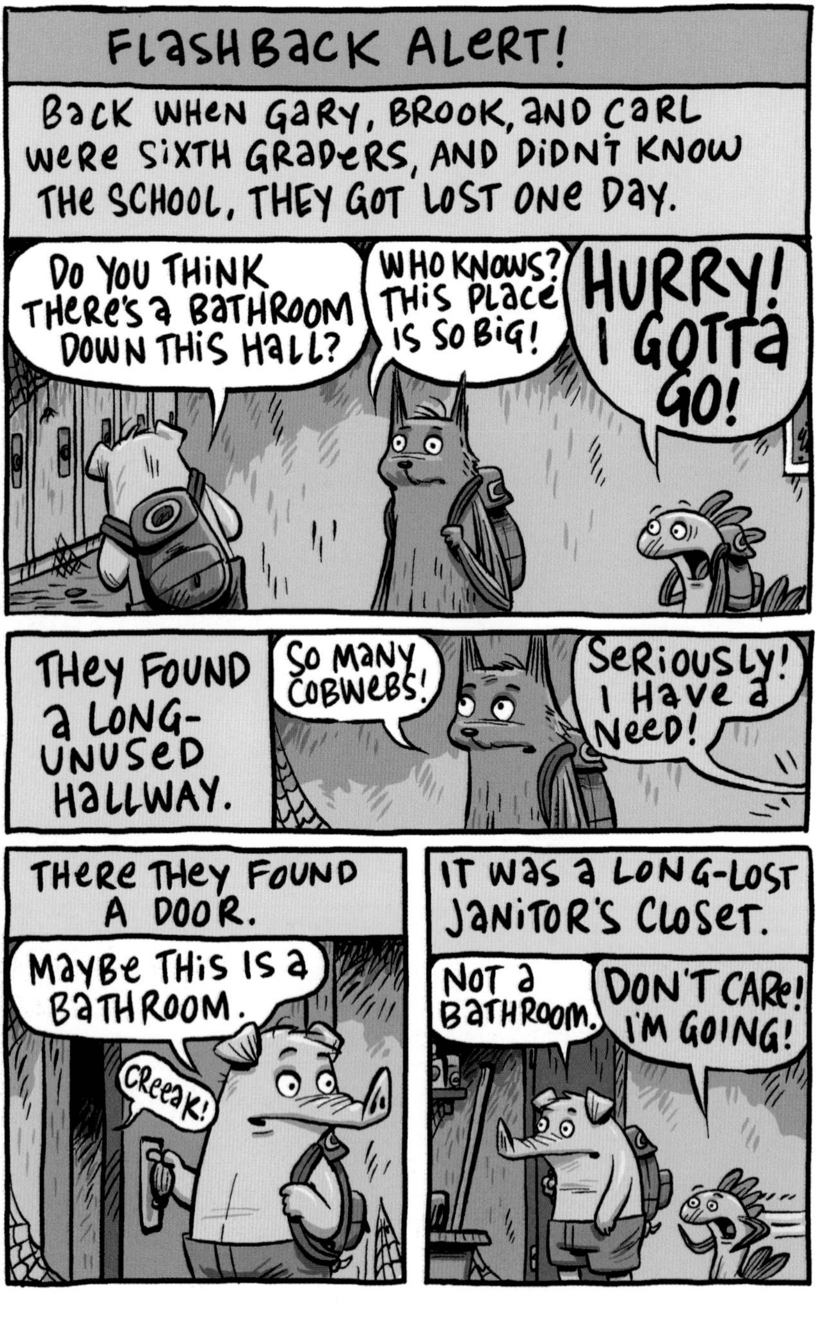
FLASHBACK ALERT!
BACK WHEN GARY, BROOK, AND CARL WERE SIXTH GRADERS, AND DIDN'T KNOW THE SCHOOL, THEY GOT LOST ONE DAY.
DO YOU THINK THERE'S A BATHROOM DOWN THIS HALL?
WHO KNOWS? THIS PLACE IS SO BIG!
HURRY! I GOTTA GO!
THEY FOUND A LONG-UNUSED HALLWAY.
SO MANY COBWEBS!
SERIOUSLY! I HAVE A NEED!
THERE THEY FOUND A DOOR.
MAYBE THIS IS A BATHROOM.
CREEAK!
IT WAS A LONG-LOST JANITOR'S CLOSET.
NOT A BATHROOM.
DON'T CARE! I'M GOING!

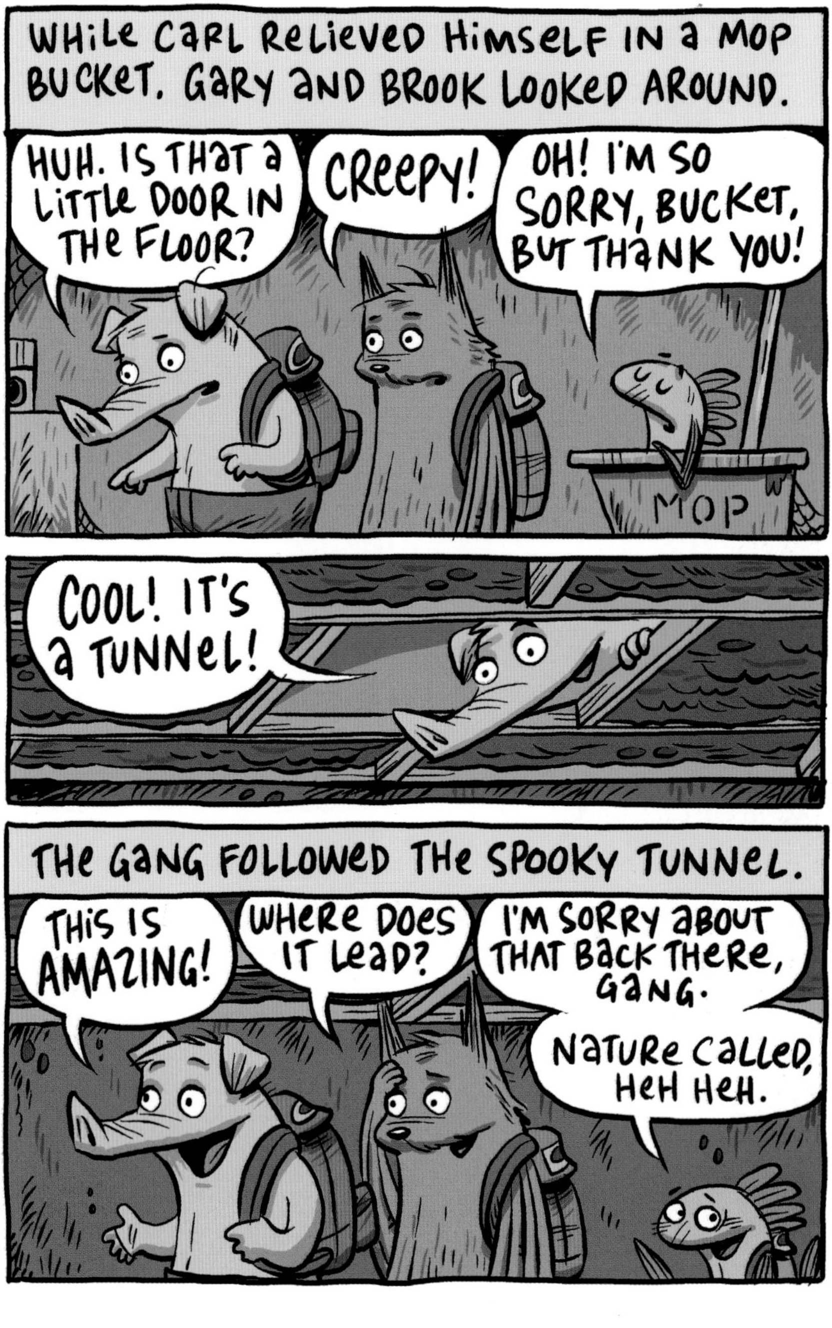
WHILE CARL RELIEVED HIMSELF IN A MOP BUCKET, GARY AND BROOK LOOKED AROUND.
HUH. IS THAT A LITTLE DOOR IN THE FLOOR?
CREEPY!
OH! I'M SO SORRY, BUCKET, BUT THANK YOU!
MOP
COOL! IT'S A TUNNEL!
THE GANG FOLLOWED THE SPOOKY TUNNEL.
THIS IS AMAZING!
WHERE DOES IT LEAD?
I'M SORRY ABOUT THAT BACK THERE, GANG.
NATURE CALLED, HEH HEH.

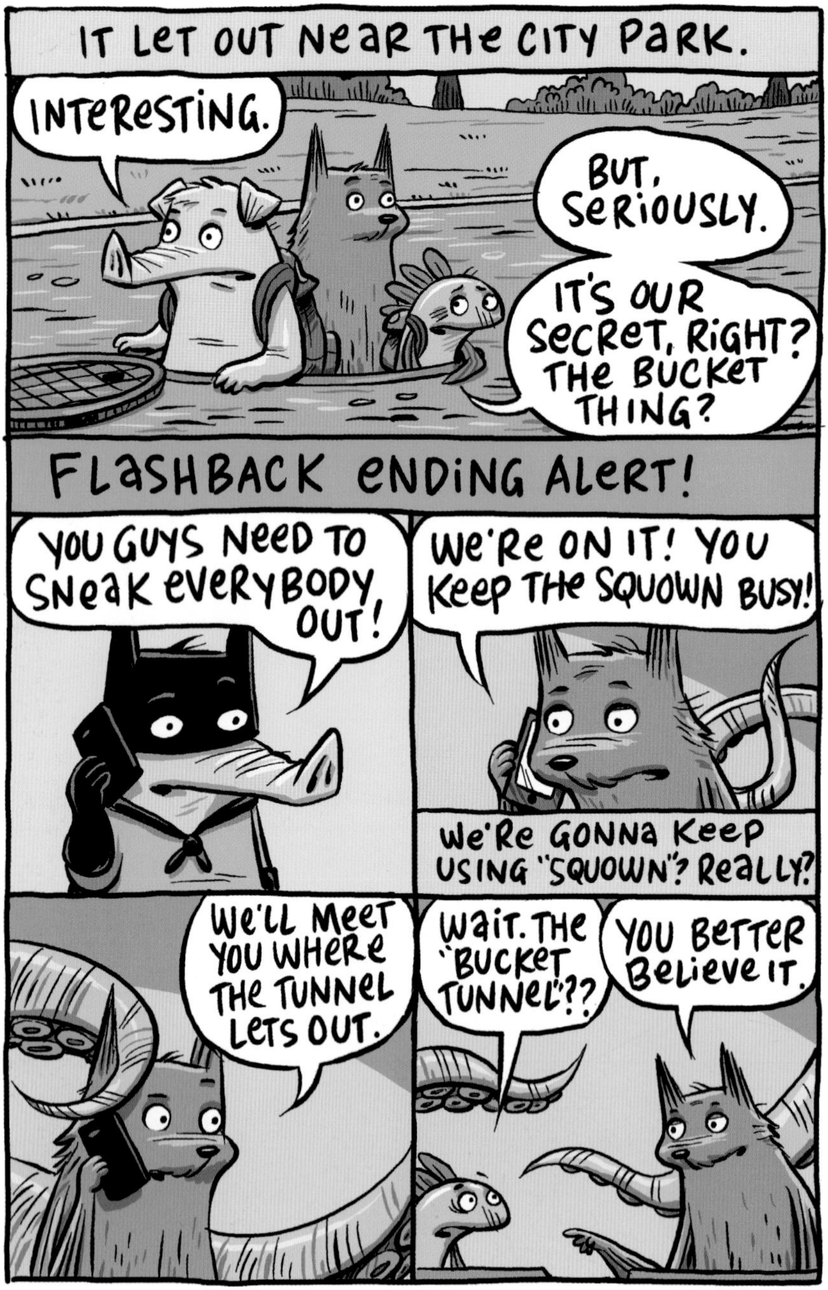
IT LET OUT NEAR THE CITY PARK.
INTERESTING.
BUT, SERIOUSLY.
IT'S OUR SECRET, RIGHT? THE BUCKET THING?
FLASHBACK ENDING ALERT!
YOU GUYS NEED TO SNEAK EVERYBODY OUT!
WE'RE ON IT! YOU KEEP THE SQUOWN BUSY!
WE'RE GONNA KEEP USING "SQUOWN"? REALLY?
WE'LL MEET YOU WHERE THE TUNNEL LETS OUT.
WAIT. THE "BUCKET TUNNEL"??
YOU BETTER BELIEVE IT.

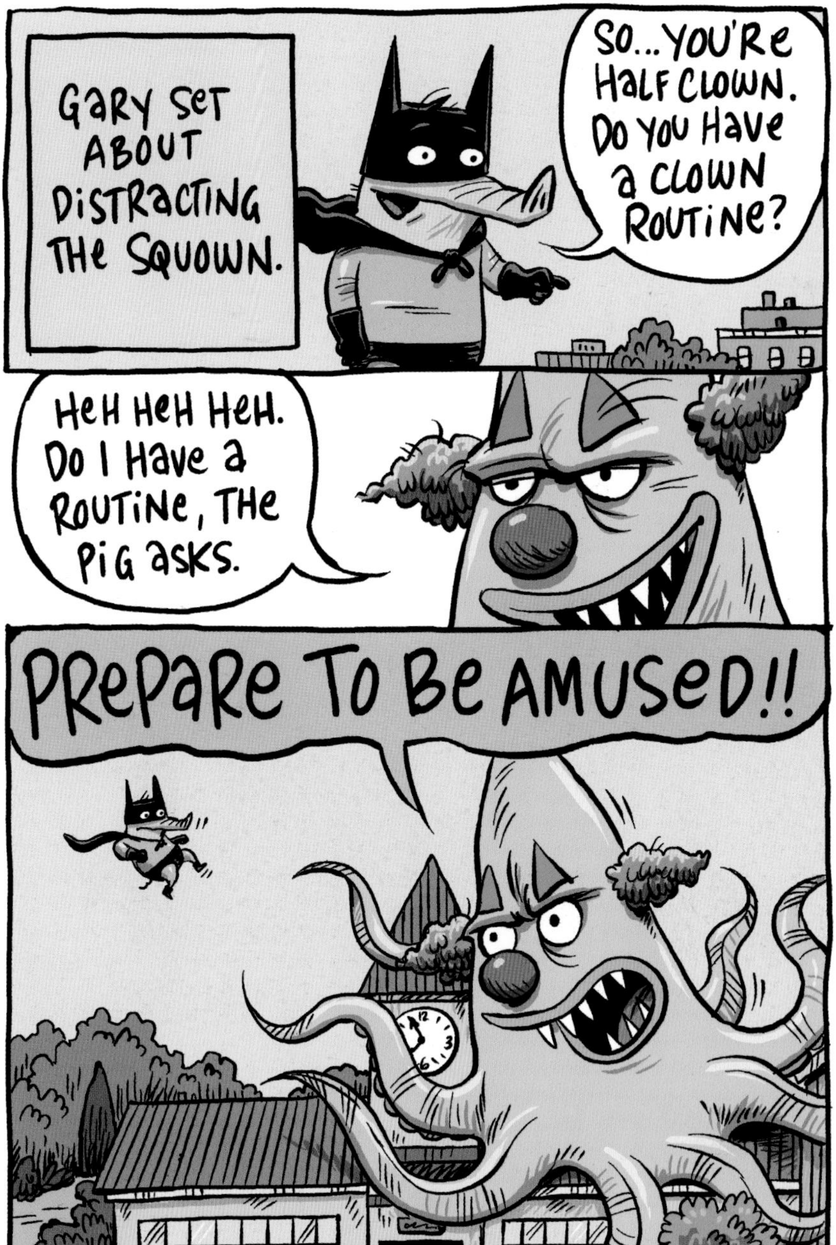
GARY SET ABOUT DISTRACTING THE SQUOWN.
SO... YOU'RE HALF CLOWN. DO YOU HAVE A CLOWN ROUTINE?
HEH HEH HEH. DO I HAVE A ROUTINE, THE PIG ASKS.
PREPARE TO BE AMUSED!!

CHAPTER SIX

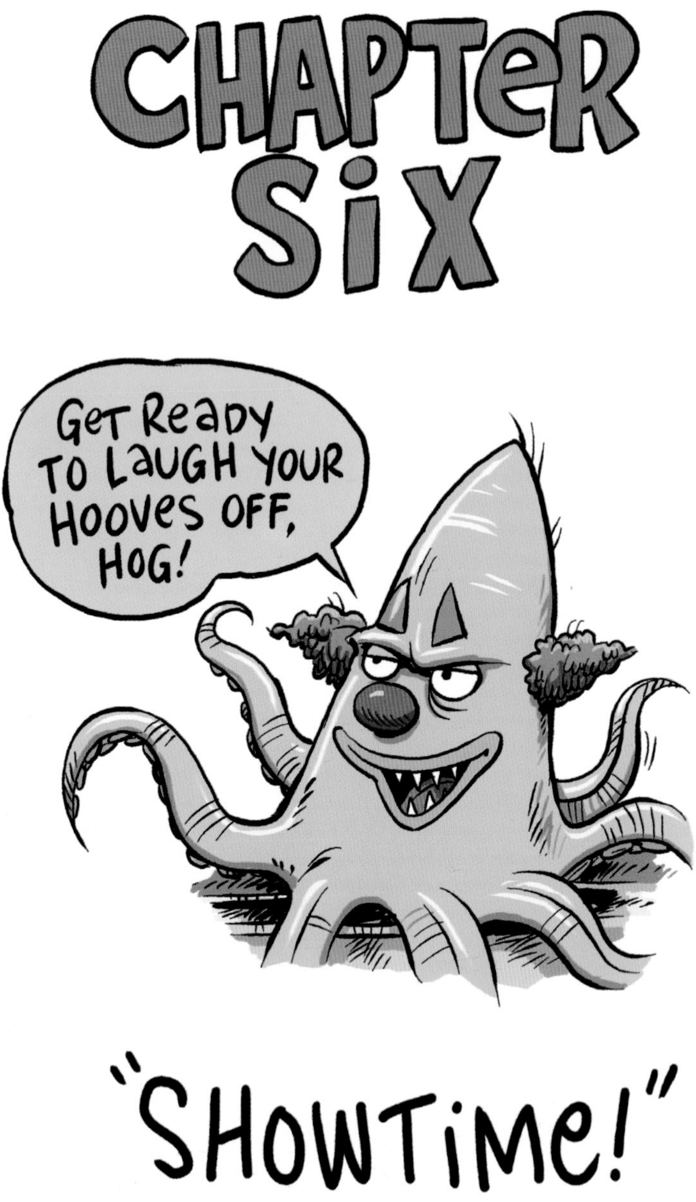
GET READY TO LAUGH YOUR HOOVES OFF, HOG!

"SHOWTIME!"

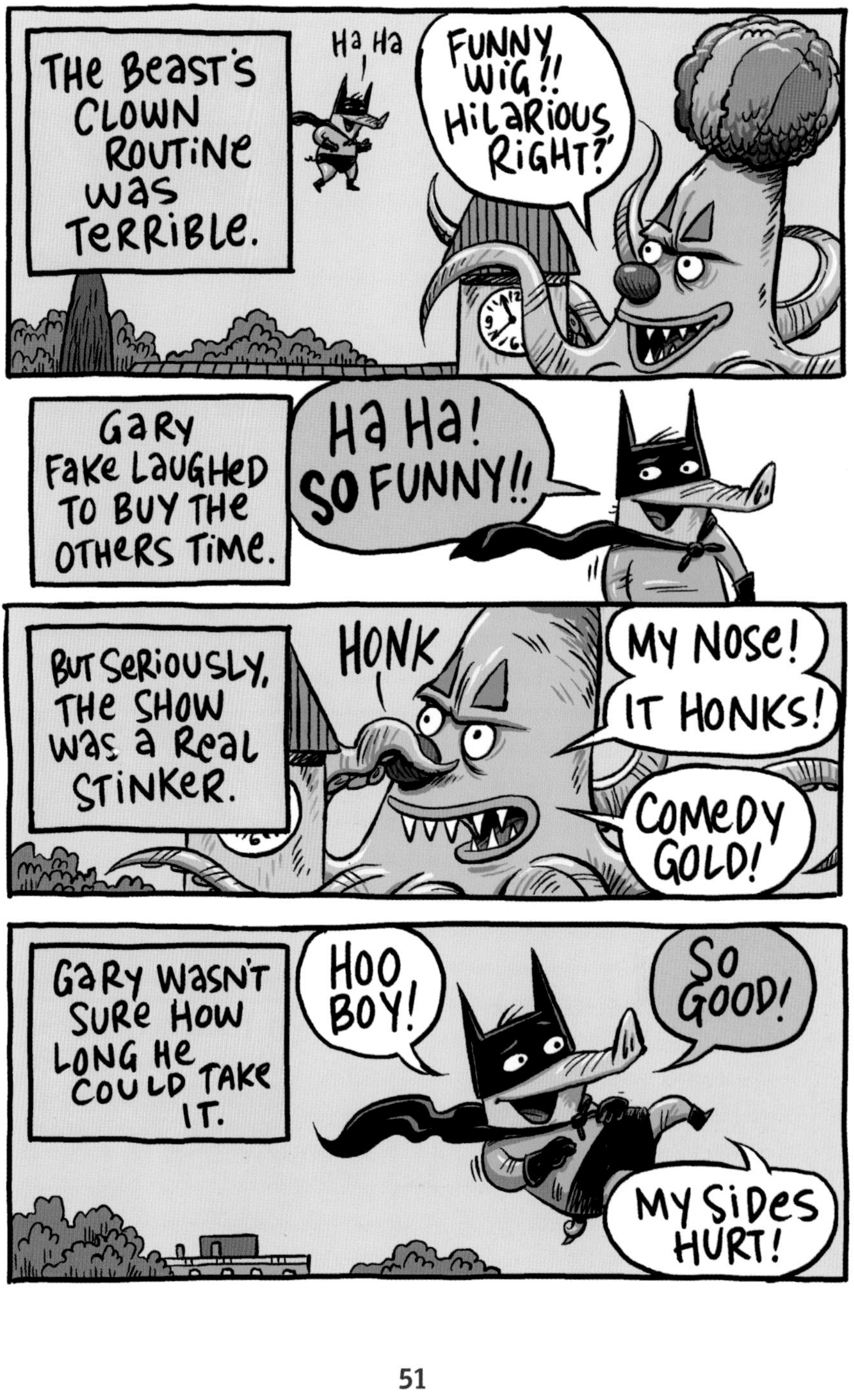

THE BEAST'S CLOWN ROUTINE WAS TERRIBLE.
HA HA
FUNNY WIG!! HILARIOUS RIGHT?
GARY FAKE LAUGHED TO BUY THE OTHERS TIME.
HA HA! SO FUNNY!!
BUT SERIOUSLY, THE SHOW WAS A REAL STINKER.
HONK
MY NOSE!
IT HONKS!
COMEDY GOLD!
GARY WASN'T SURE HOW LONG HE COULD TAKE IT.
HOO BOY!
SO GOOD!
MY SIDES HURT!

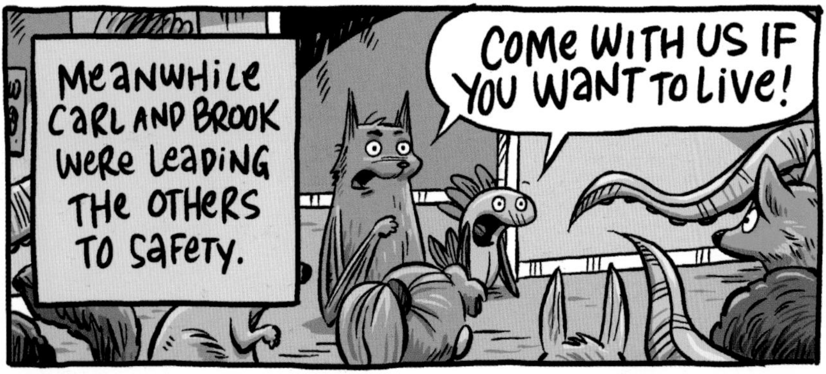
MEANWHILE CARL AND BROOK WERE LEADING THE OTHERS TO SAFETY.
COME WITH US IF YOU WANT TO LIVE!

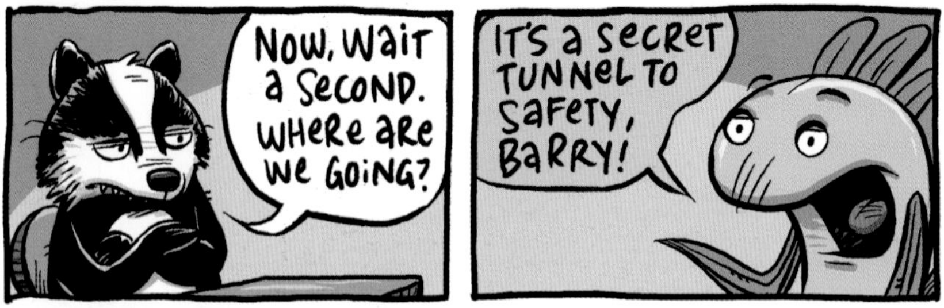
NOW, WAIT A SECOND. WHERE ARE WE GOING?
IT'S A SECRET TUNNEL TO SAFETY, BARRY!

BARRY THE BADGER WAS A BIT OF A PILL.

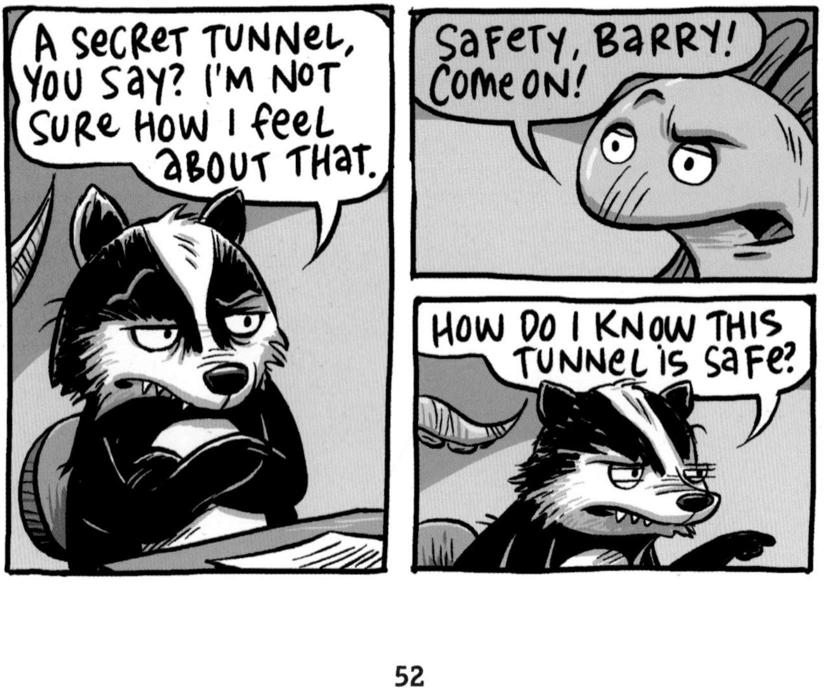
A SECRET TUNNEL, YOU SAY? I'M NOT SURE HOW I FEEL ABOUT THAT.
SAFETY, BARRY! COME ON!
HOW DO I KNOW THIS TUNNEL IS SAFE?

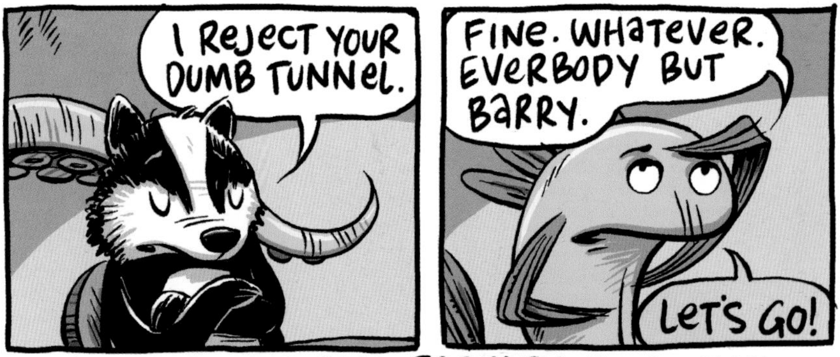
I REJECT YOUR DUMB TUNNEL.
FINE. WHATEVER. EVERBODY BUT BARRY.
LET'S GO!

THE STUDENTS AND FACULTY FOLLOWED BROOK AND CARL TO THE LONG-FORGOTTEN HALLWAY.

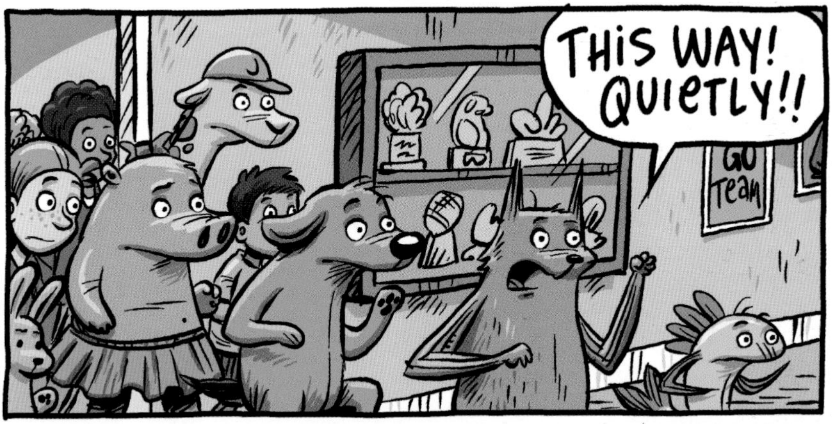
THIS WAY! QUIETLY!!
GO TEAM

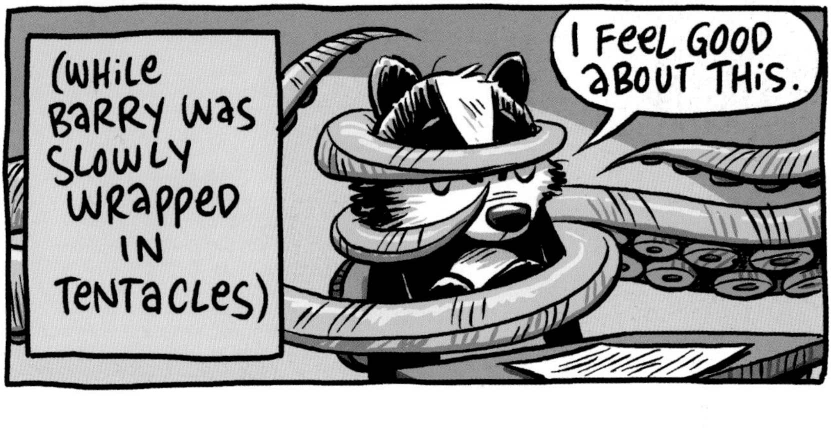
(WHILE BARRY WAS SLOWLY WRAPPED IN TENTACLES)
I FEEL GOOD ABOUT THIS.

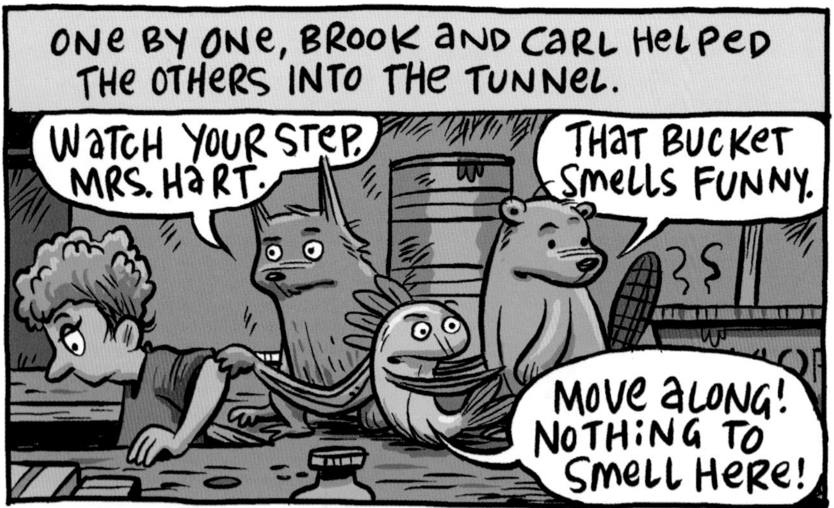
ONE BY ONE, BROOK AND CARL HELPED THE OTHERS INTO THE TUNNEL.
WATCH YOUR STEP, MRS. HART.
THAT BUCKET SMELLS FUNNY.
MOVE ALONG! NOTHING TO SMELL HERE!

THE SQUID WAS CLUELESS AS THE SCHOOL EMPTIED.

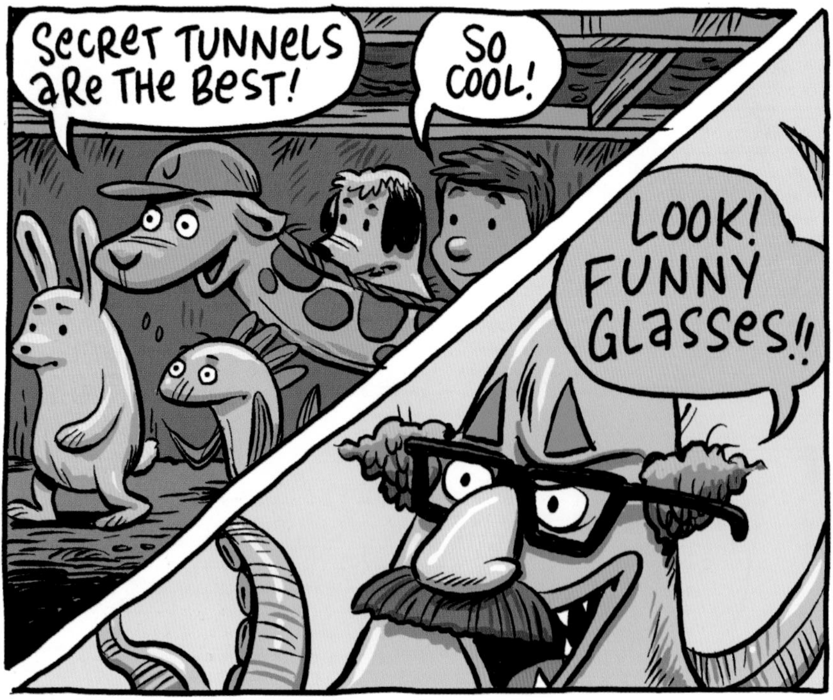
SECRET TUNNELS ARE THE BEST!
SO COOL!
LOOK! FUNNY GLASSES!!

BROOK CALLED GARY AND LET HIM KNOW WHEN EVERYONE WAS OUT OF THE BUILDING.

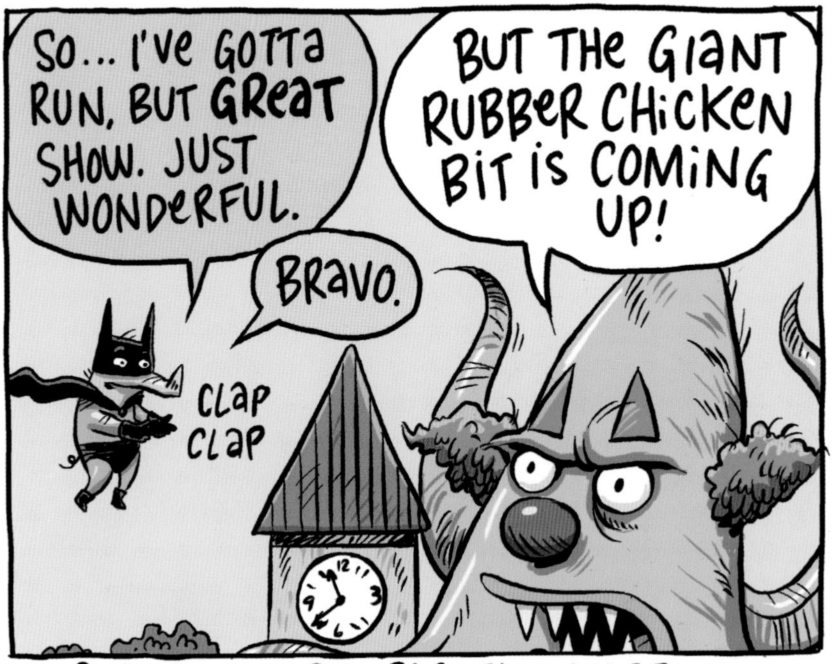
SO... I'VE GOTTA RUN, BUT GREAT SHOW. JUST WONDERFUL.
BRAVO.
BUT THE GIANT RUBBER CHICKEN BIT IS COMING UP!
CLAP CLAP

RELIEVED, BATPIG FLEW OFF.

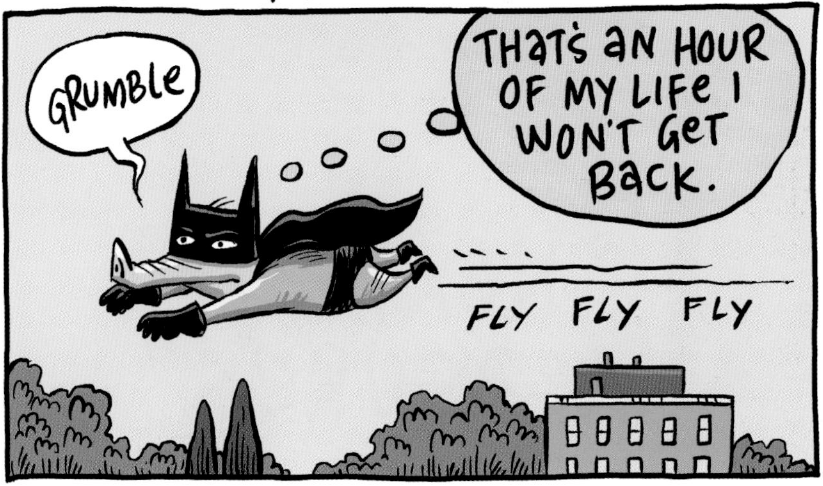
GRUMBLE
THAT'S AN HOUR OF MY LIFE I WON'T GET BACK.
FLY FLY FLY

CHAPTER SEVEN

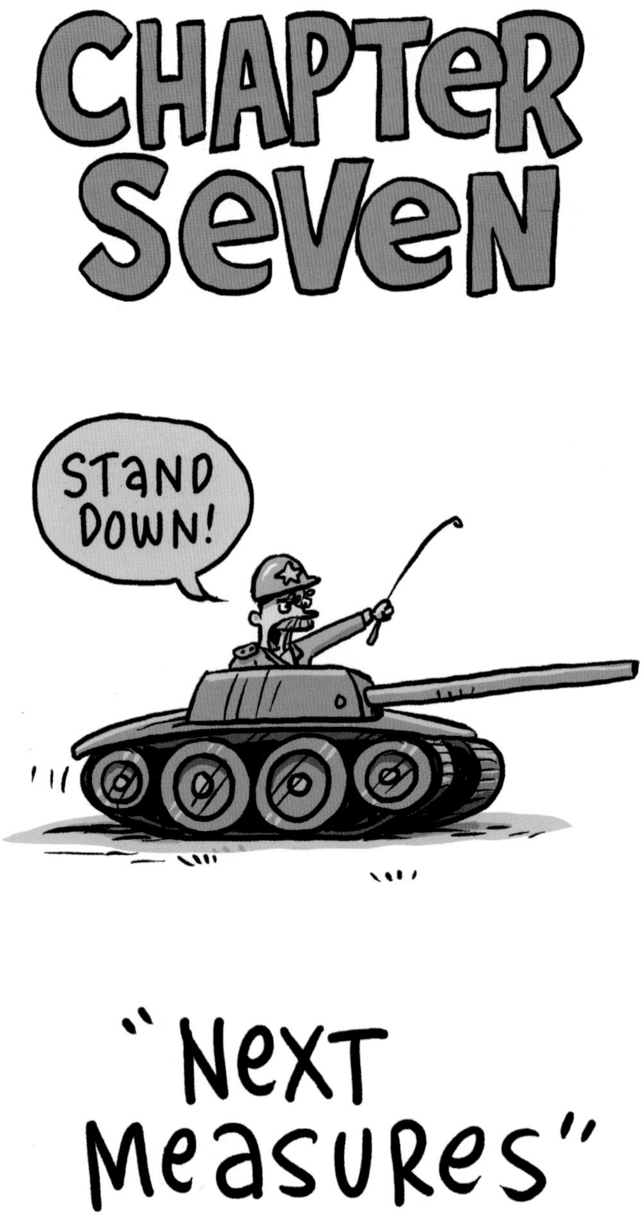
STAND DOWN!

"NEXT MEASURES"

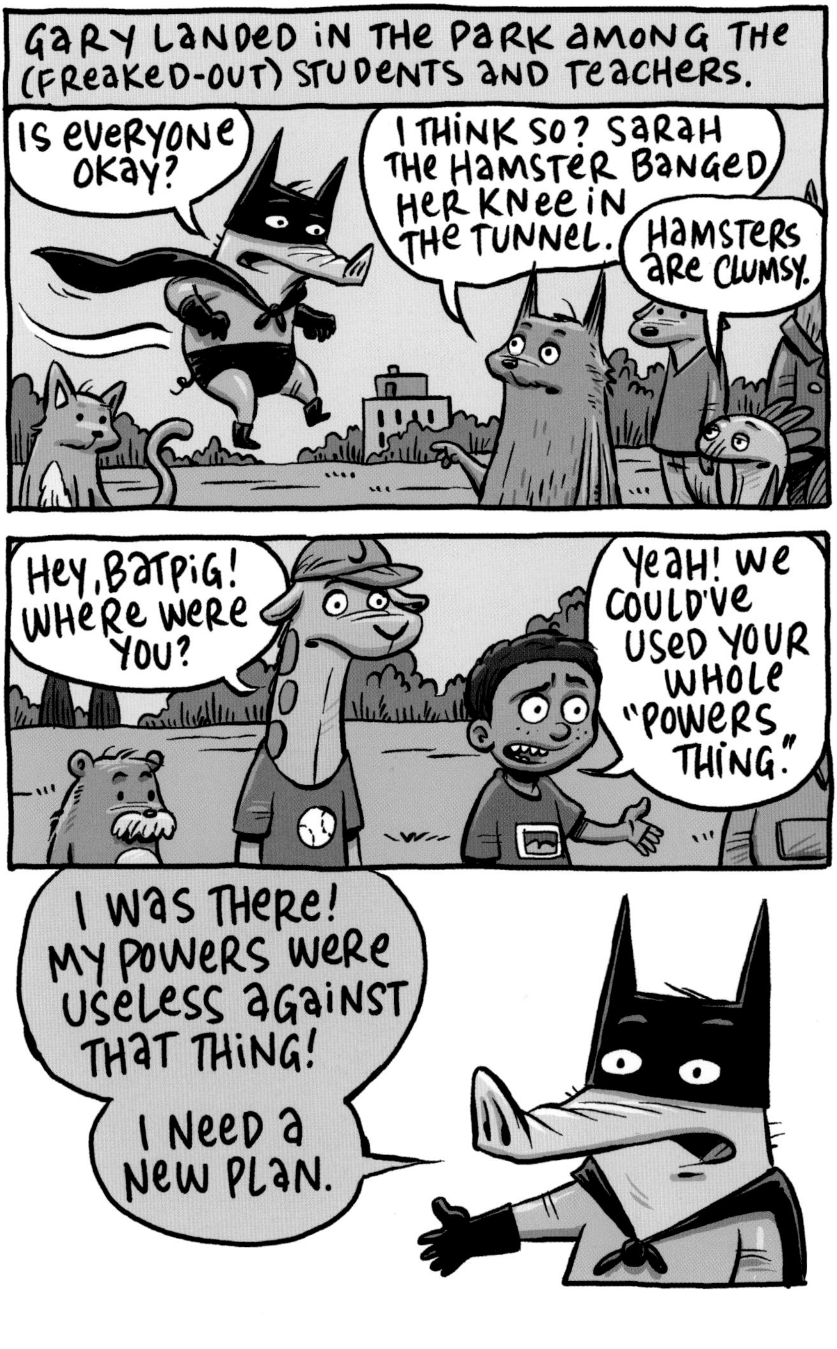
GARY LANDED IN THE PARK AMONG THE (FREAKED-OUT) STUDENTS AND TEACHERS.
IS EVERYONE OKAY?
I THINK SO? SARAH THE HAMSTER BANGED HER KNEE IN THE TUNNEL.
HAMSTERS ARE CLUMSY.
HEY, BATPIG! WHERE WERE YOU?
YEAH! WE COULD'VE USED YOUR WHOLE "POWERS THING."
I WAS THERE! MY POWERS WERE USELESS AGAINST THAT THING!
I NEED A NEW PLAN.

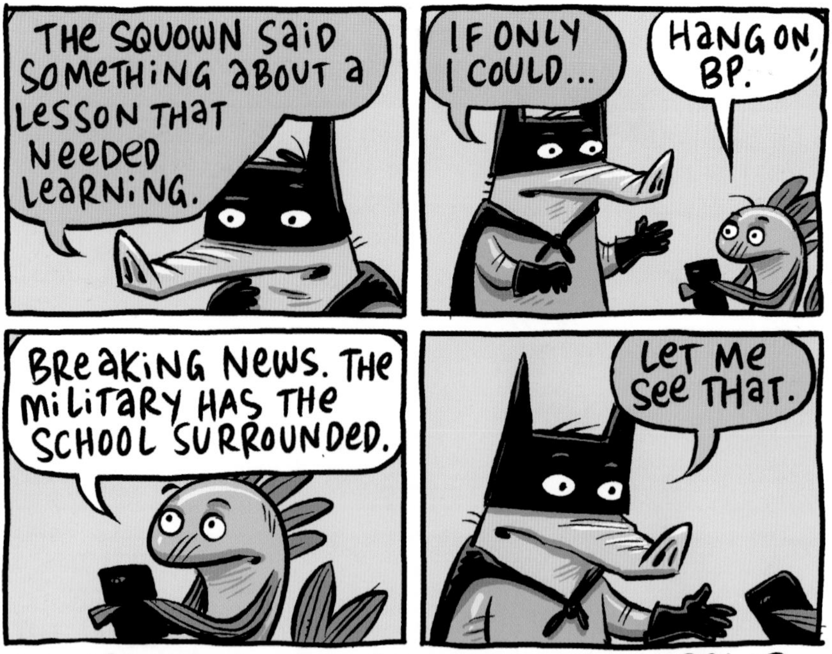
THE SQUOWN SAID SOMETHING ABOUT A LESSON THAT NEEDED LEARNING.
IF ONLY I COULD...
HANG ON, BP.
BREAKING NEWS. THE MILITARY HAS THE SCHOOL SURROUNDED.
LET ME SEE THAT.

IT WAS TRUE. THE SQUOWN WAS CIRCLED IN BY TANKS AND HELICOPTERS AND STUFF.

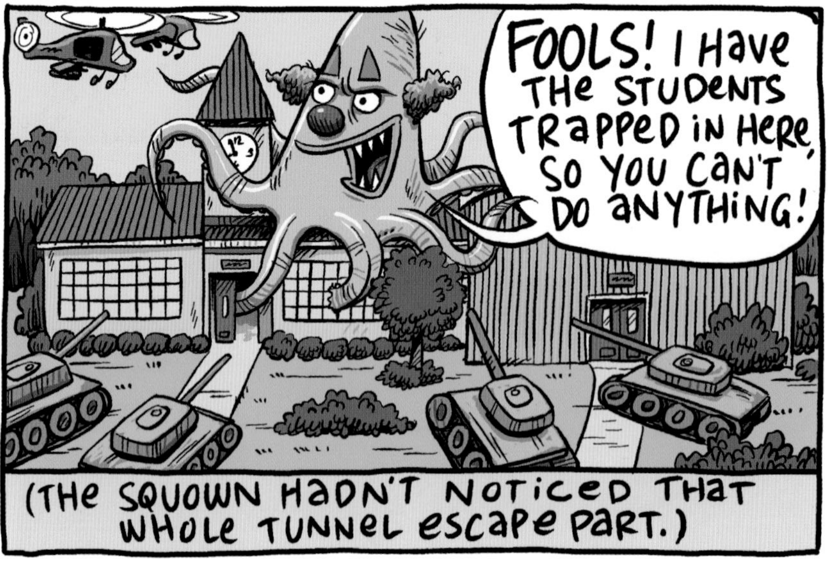
FOOLS! I HAVE THE STUDENTS TRAPPED IN HERE, SO YOU CAN'T DO ANYTHING!
(THE SQUOWN HADN'T NOTICED THAT WHOLE TUNNEL ESCAPE PART.)

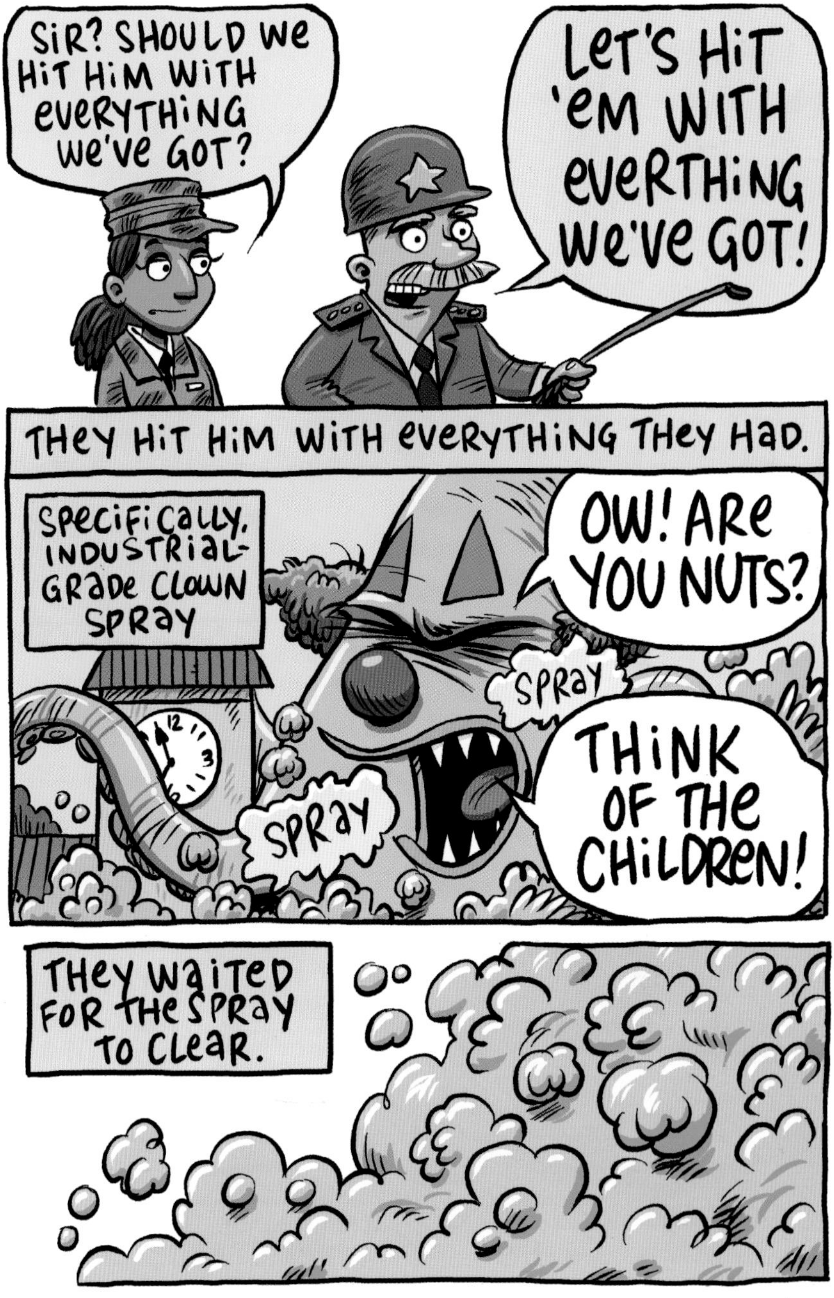
SIR? SHOULD WE HIT HIM WITH EVERYTHING WE'VE GOT?
LET'S HIT 'EM WITH EVERTHING WE'VE GOT!
THEY HIT HIM WITH EVERYTHING THEY HAD.
SPECIFICALLY, INDUSTRIAL-GRADE CLOWN SPRAY
OW! ARE YOU NUTS?
SPRAY
THINK OF THE CHILDREN!
SPRAY
THEY WAITED FOR THE SPRAY TO CLEAR.

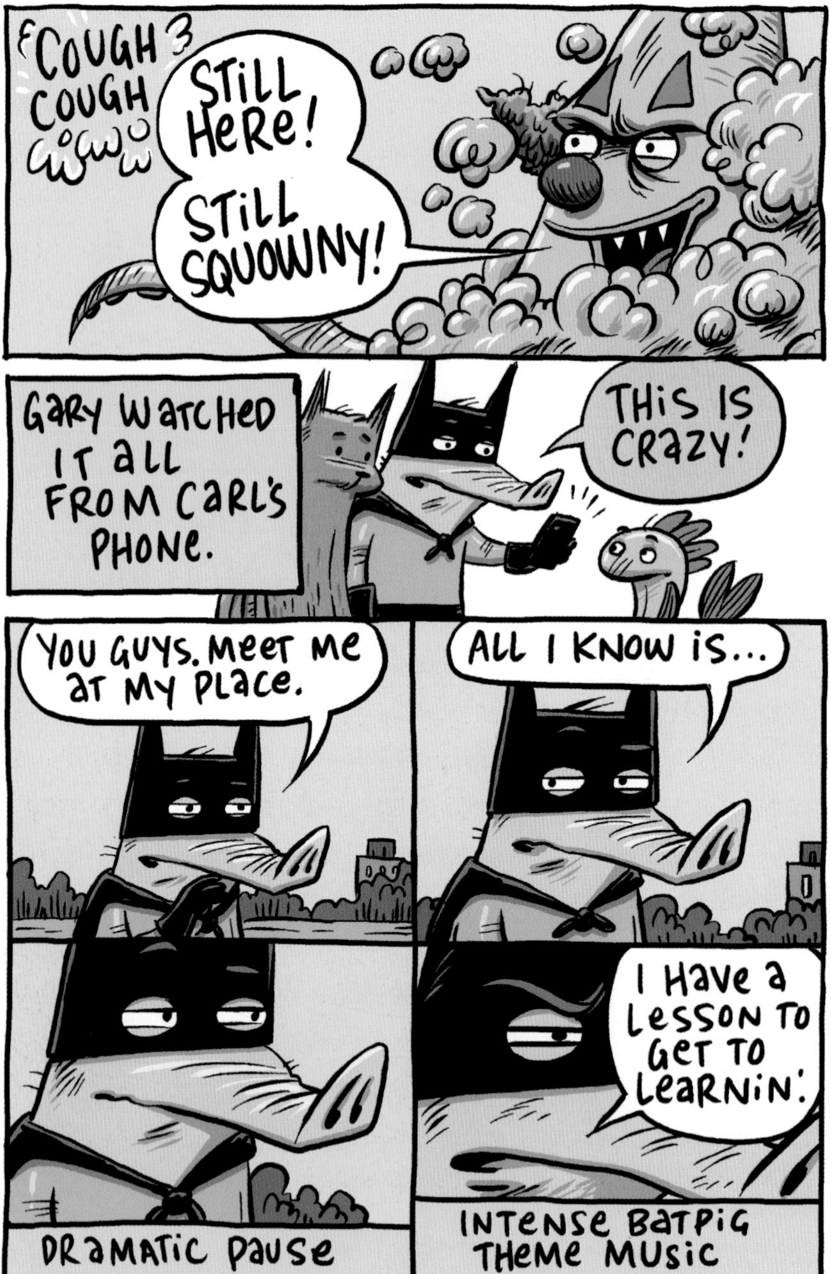
{COUGH} COUGH
STILL HERE!
STILL SQUOWNY!
GARY WATCHED IT ALL FROM CARL'S PHONE.
THIS IS CRAZY!
YOU GUYS. MEET ME AT MY PLACE.
ALL I KNOW IS...
DRAMATIC PAUSE
I HAVE A LESSON TO GET TO LEARNIN'.
INTENSE BATPIG THEME MUSIC

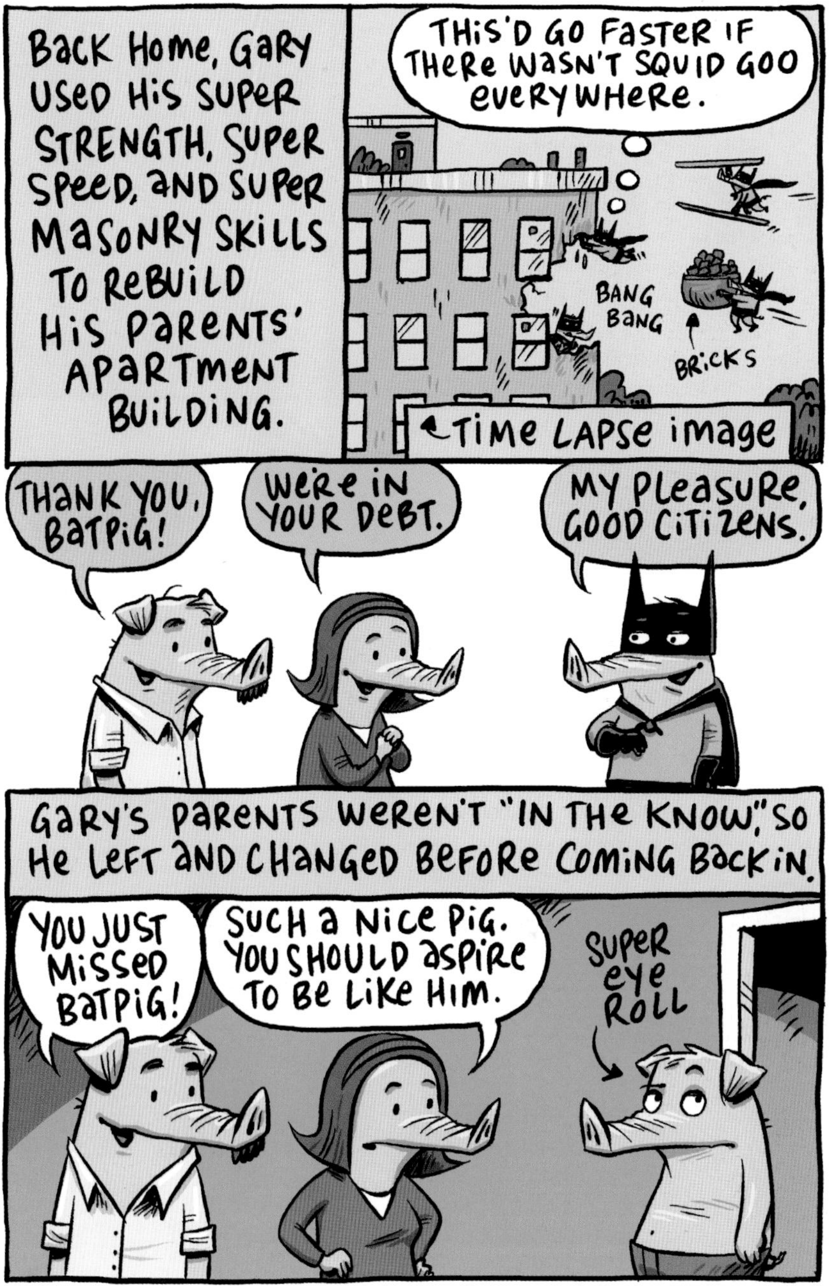
Back Home, Gary used His super strength, super speed, and super masonry skills to rebuild His parents' apartment building.
This'd go faster if there wasn't squid goo everywhere.
BANG BANG
BRICKS
Time lapse image
Thank you, BatPig!
We're in your debt.
My pleasure, good citizens.
Gary's parents weren't "in the know," so He left and changed before coming back in.
You just missed BatPig!
Such a nice pig. You should aspire to be like Him.
Super eye roll

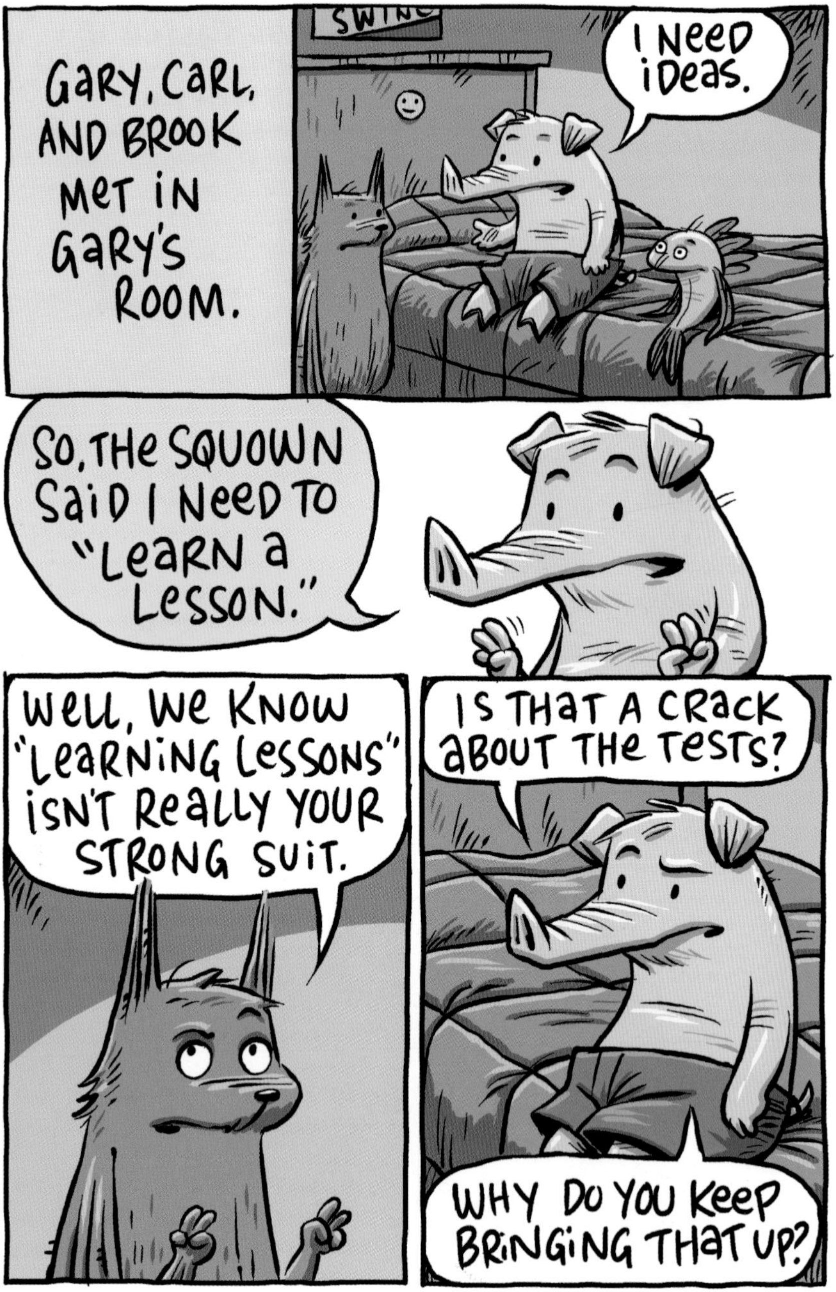
GARY, CARL, AND BROOK MET IN GARY'S ROOM.
I NEED IDEAS.
SO, THE SQUOWN SAID I NEED TO "LEARN A LESSON."
WELL, WE KNOW "LEARNING LESSONS" ISN'T REALLY YOUR STRONG SUIT.
IS THAT A CRACK ABOUT THE TESTS?
WHY DO YOU KEEP BRINGING THAT UP?

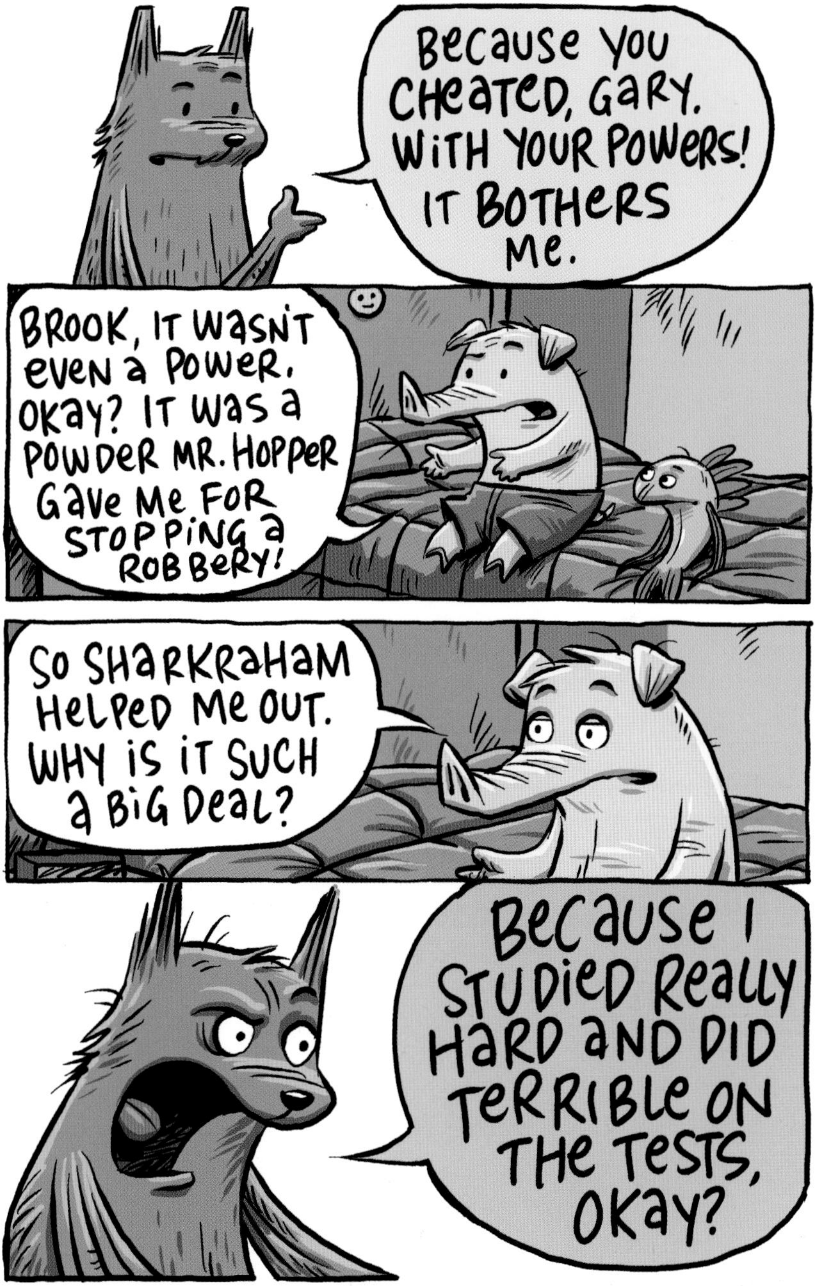
Because you cheated, Gary. With your powers! It bothers me.
Brook, it wasn't even a power, okay? It was a powder Mr. Hopper gave me for stopping a robbery!
So Sharkraham helped me out. Why is it such a big deal?
Because I studied really hard and did terrible on the tests, okay?

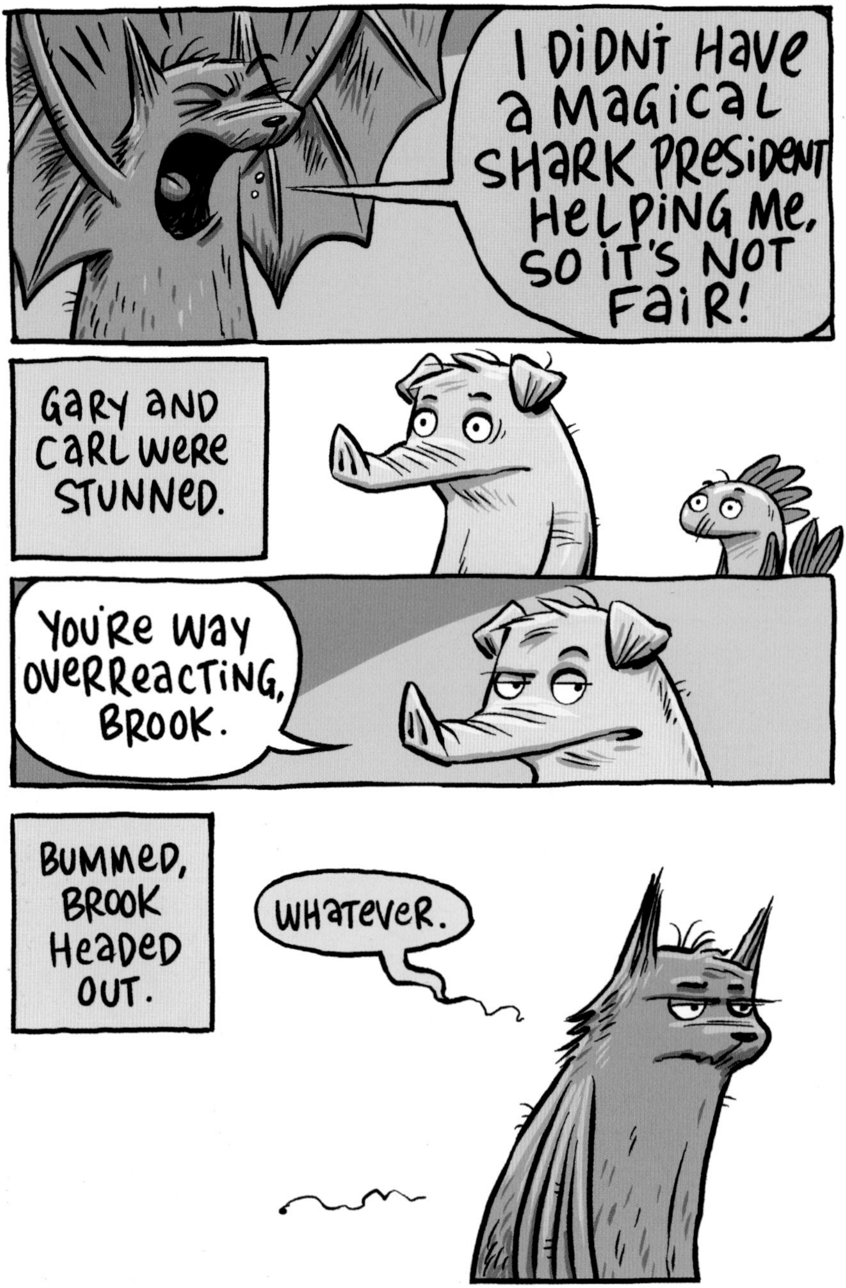
I DIDN'T HAVE A MAGICAL SHARK PRESIDENT HELPING ME, SO IT'S NOT FAIR!
GARY AND CARL WERE STUNNED.
YOU'RE WAY OVERREACTING, BROOK.
BUMMED, BROOK HEADED OUT.
WHATEVER.

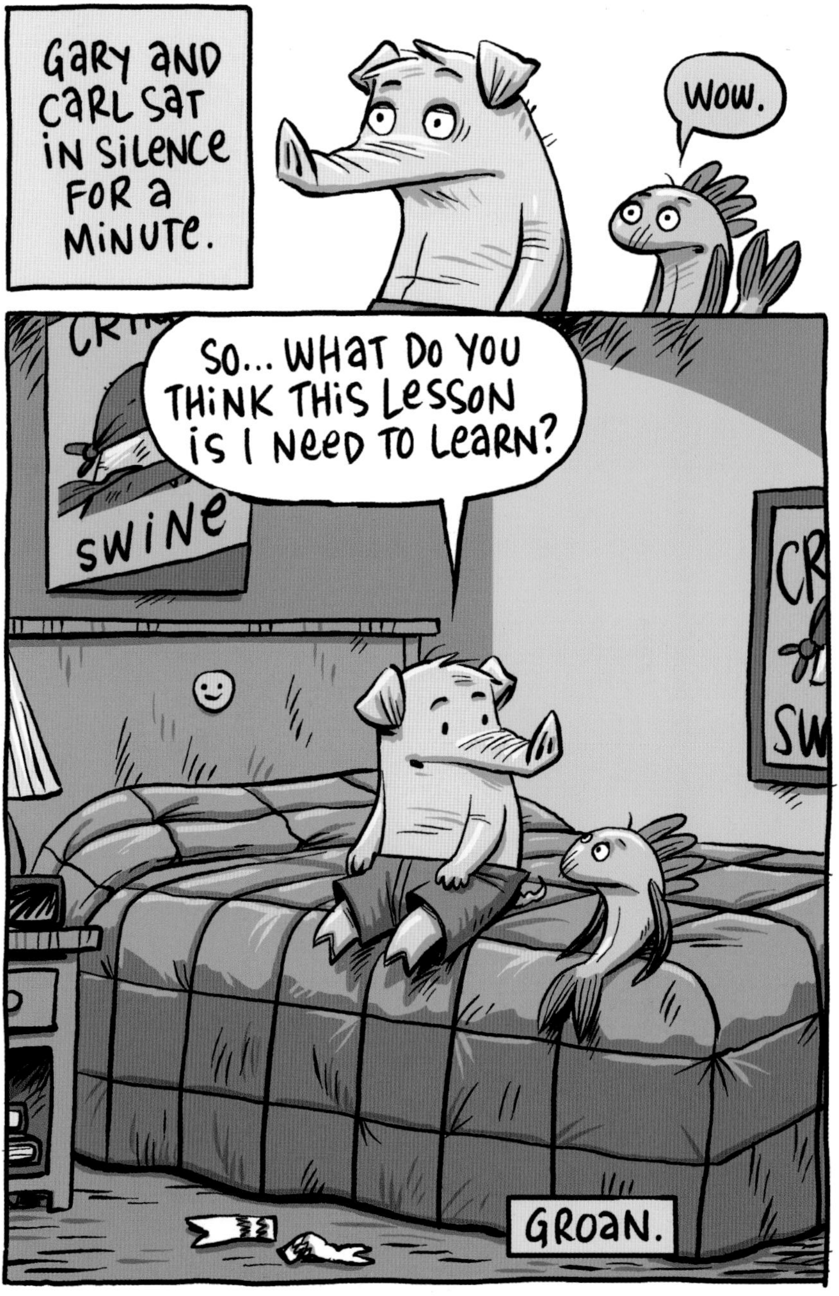

GARY AND CARL SAT IN SILENCE FOR A MINUTE.
WOW.
SO... WHAT DO YOU THINK THIS LESSON IS I NEED TO LEARN?
CR
SWINE
GROAN.

CHAPTER EIGHT

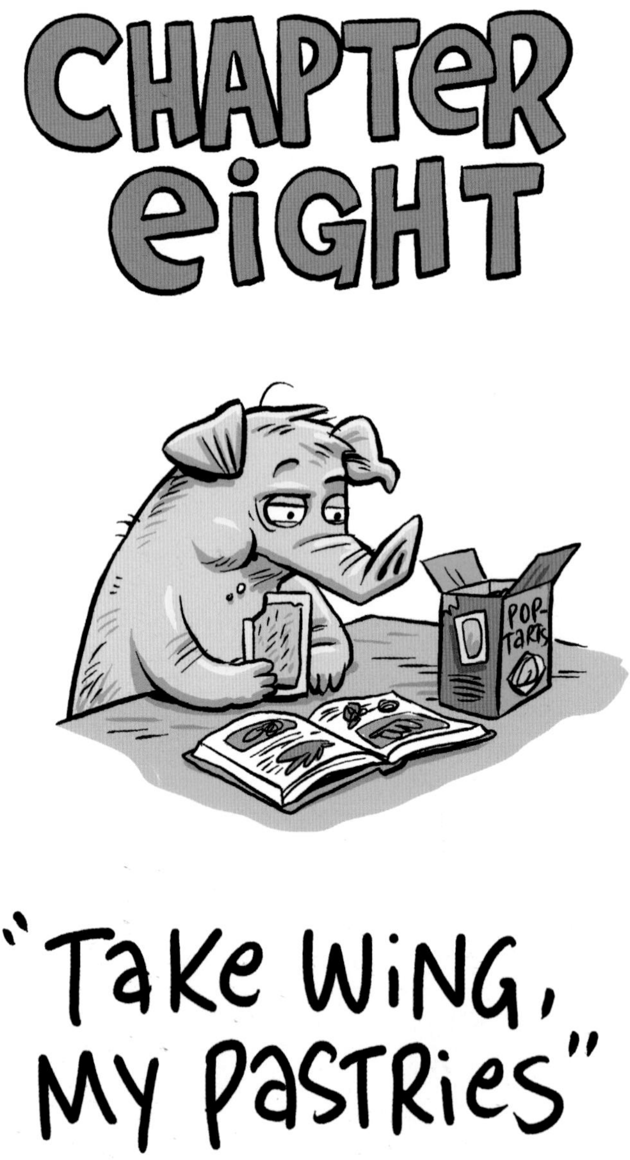
POP-TARTS

"TAKE WING, MY PASTRIES"

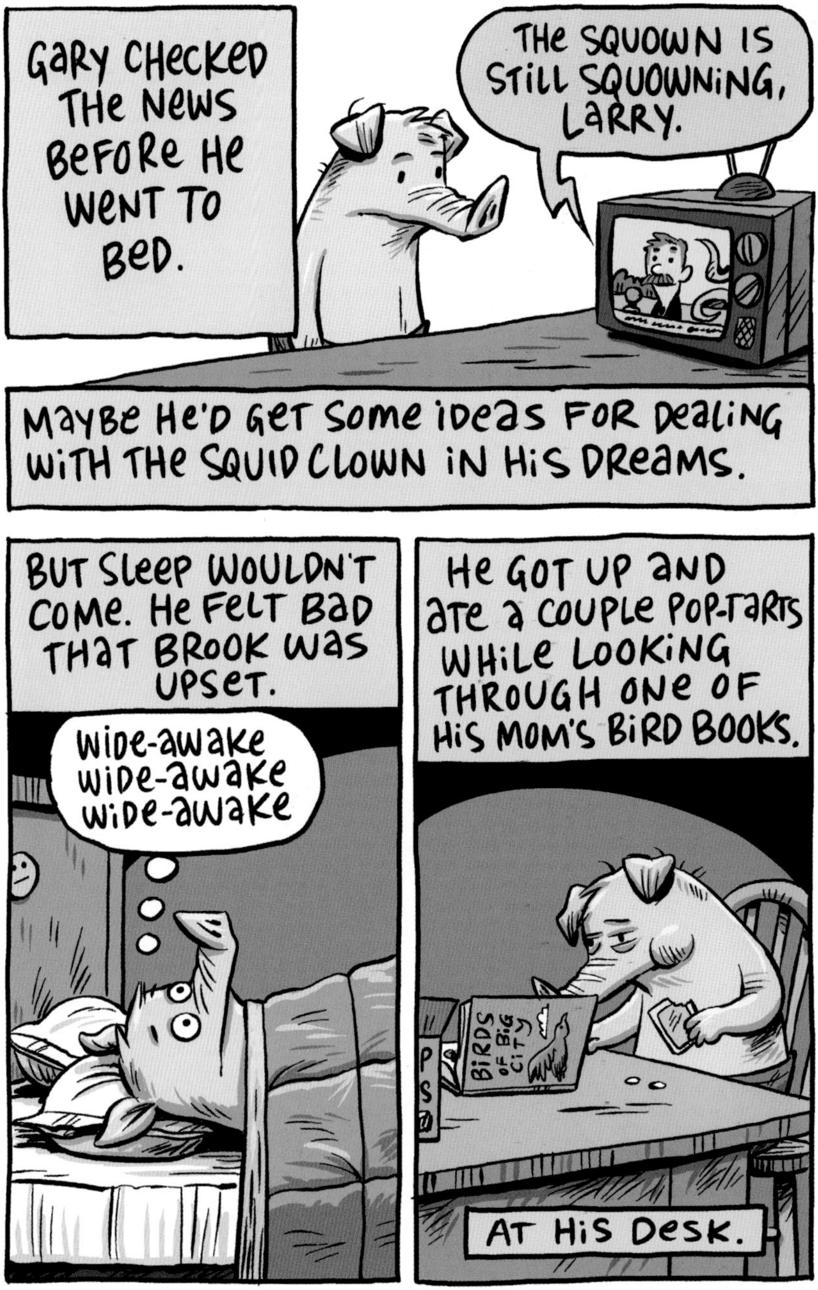
GARY CHECKED THE NEWS BEFORE HE WENT TO BED.
THE SQUOWN IS STILL SQUOWNING, LARRY.
MAYBE HE'D GET SOME IDEAS FOR DEALING WITH THE SQUID CLOWN IN HIS DREAMS.
BUT SLEEP WOULDN'T COME. HE FELT BAD THAT BROOK WAS UPSET.
WIDE-AWAKE WIDE-AWAKE WIDE-AWAKE
HE GOT UP AND ATE A COUPLE POP-TARTS WHILE LOOKING THROUGH ONE OF HIS MOM'S BIRD BOOKS.
BIRDS OF BIG CITY
AT HIS DESK.

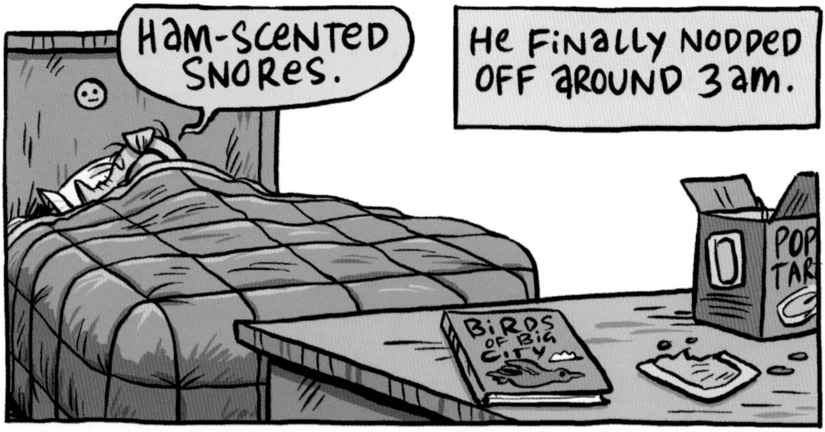
Ham-scented snores.
He finally nodded off around 3am.
BIRDS OF BIG CITY

AND WOKE TO HIS ALARM AT SEVEN.

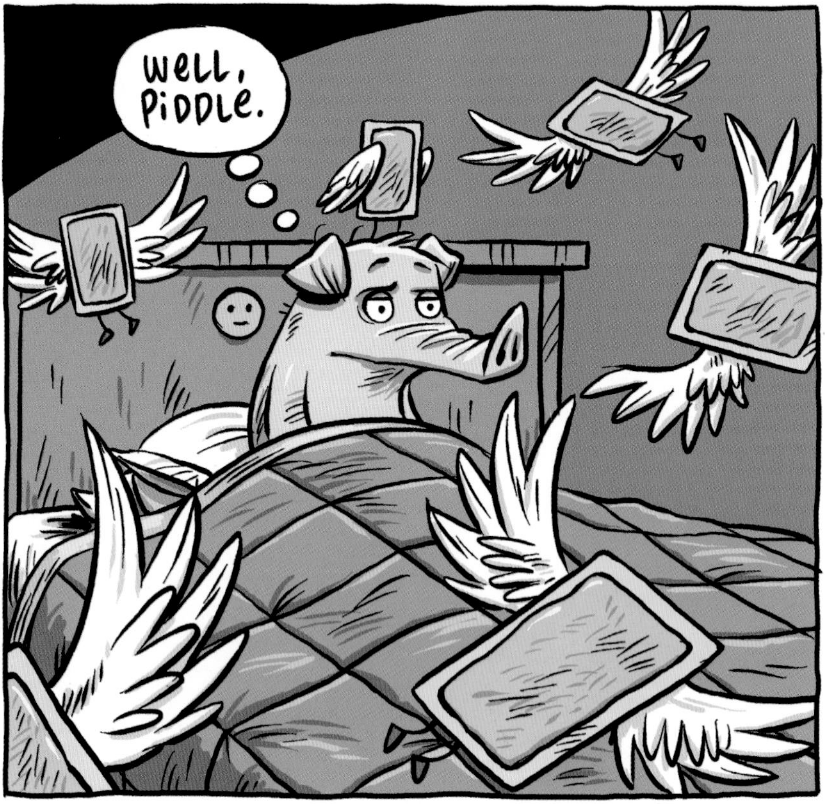
Well, piddle.

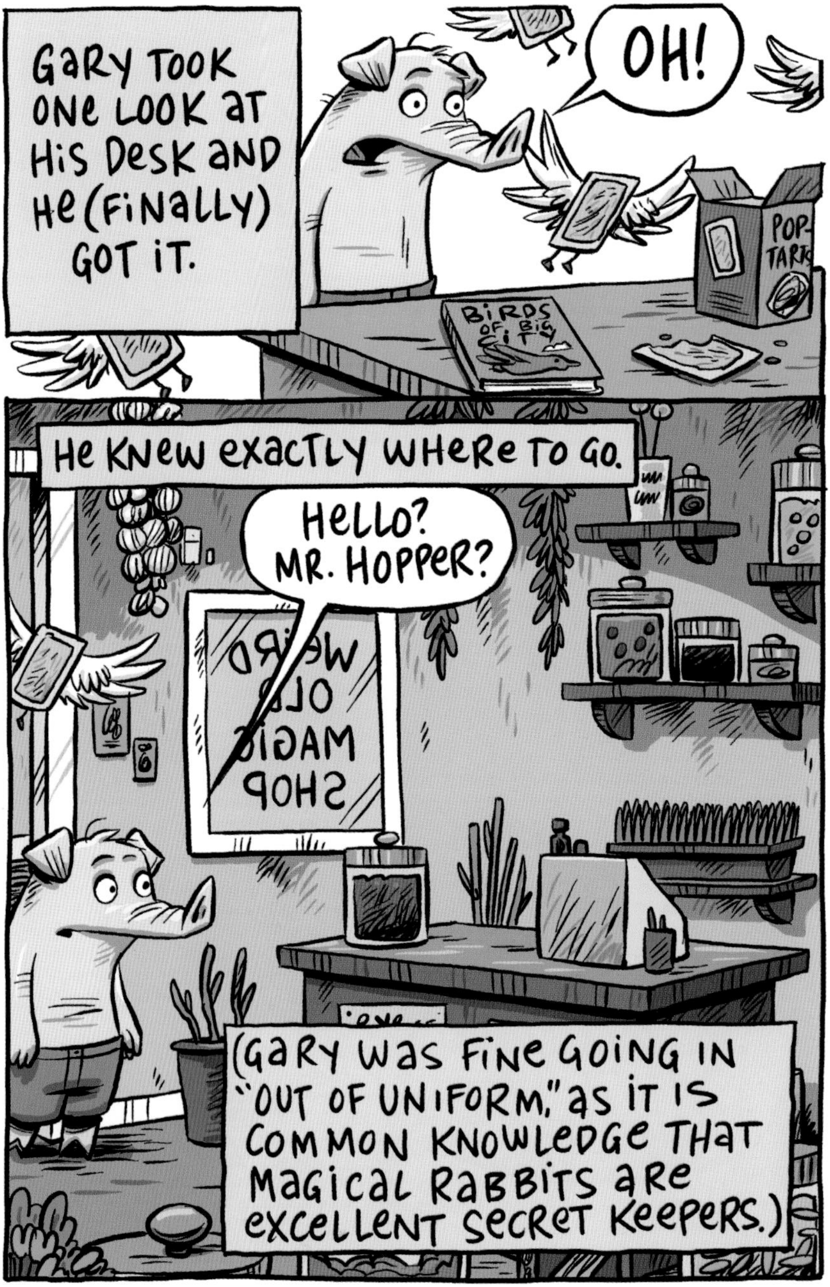
GARY TOOK ONE LOOK AT HIS DESK AND HE (FINALLY) GOT IT.
OH!
BIRDS OF BIG CITY
POP-TARTS
HE KNEW EXACTLY WHERE TO GO.
HELLO? MR. HOPPER?
WEIRD OLD MAGIC SHOP
(GARY WAS FINE GOING IN "OUT OF UNIFORM," AS IT IS COMMON KNOWLEDGE THAT MAGICAL RABBITS ARE EXCELLENT SECRET KEEPERS.)

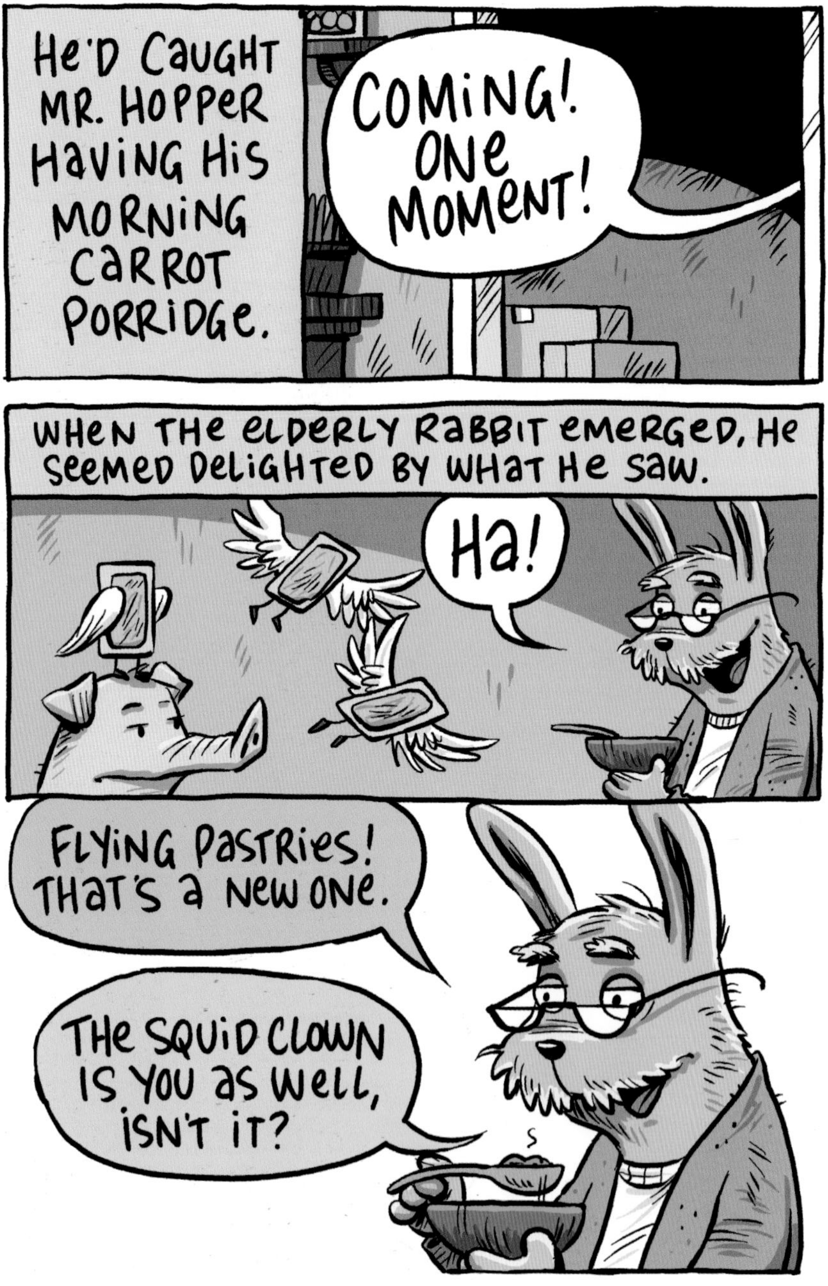
HE'D CAUGHT MR. HOPPER HAVING HIS MORNING CARROT PORRIDGE.
COMING! ONE MOMENT!
WHEN THE ELDERLY RABBIT EMERGED, HE SEEMED DELIGHTED BY WHAT HE SAW.
HA!
FLYING PASTRIES! THAT'S A NEW ONE.
THE SQUID CLOWN IS YOU AS WELL, ISN'T IT?

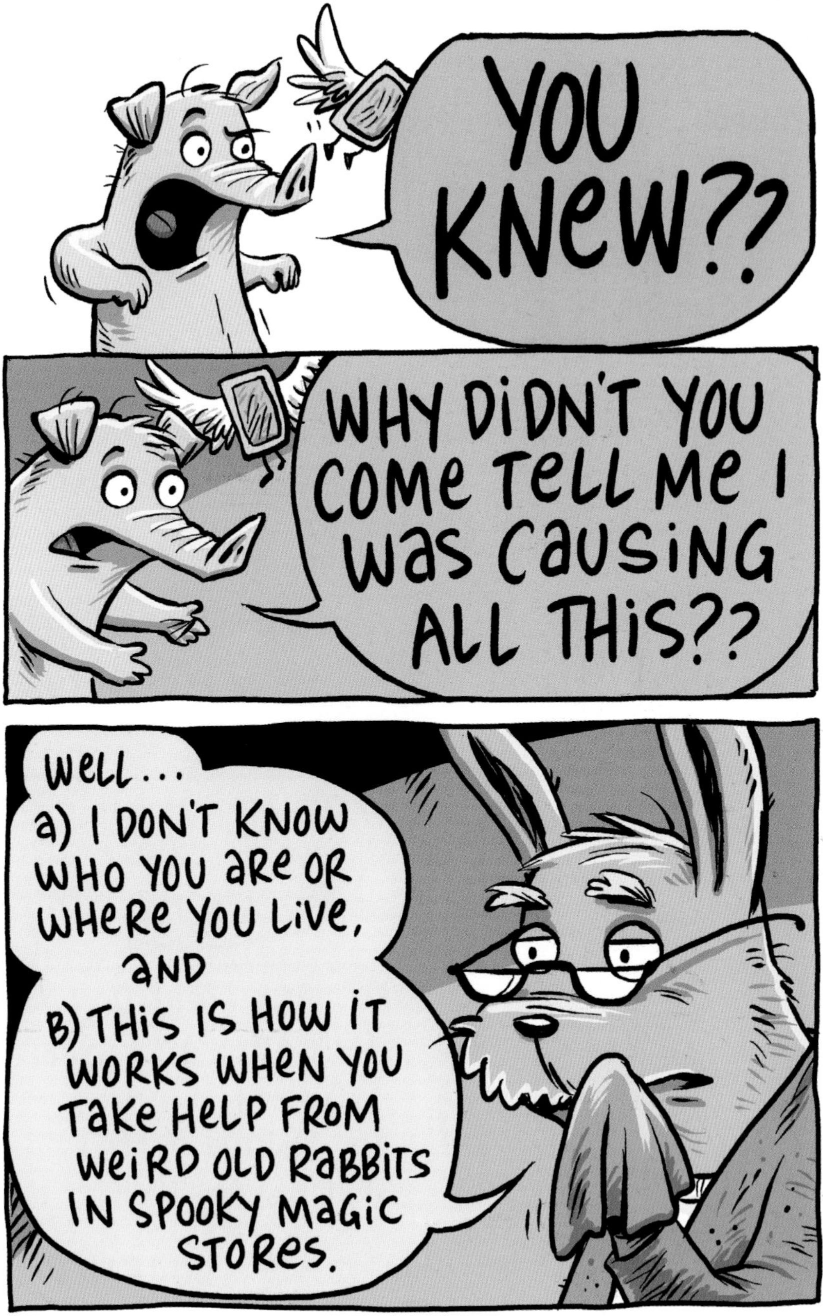
YOU KNEW??
WHY DIDN'T YOU COME TELL ME I WAS CAUSING ALL THIS??
WELL... a) I DON'T KNOW WHO YOU ARE OR WHERE YOU LIVE, AND B) THIS IS HOW IT WORKS WHEN YOU TAKE HELP FROM WEIRD OLD RABBITS IN SPOOKY MAGIC STORES.

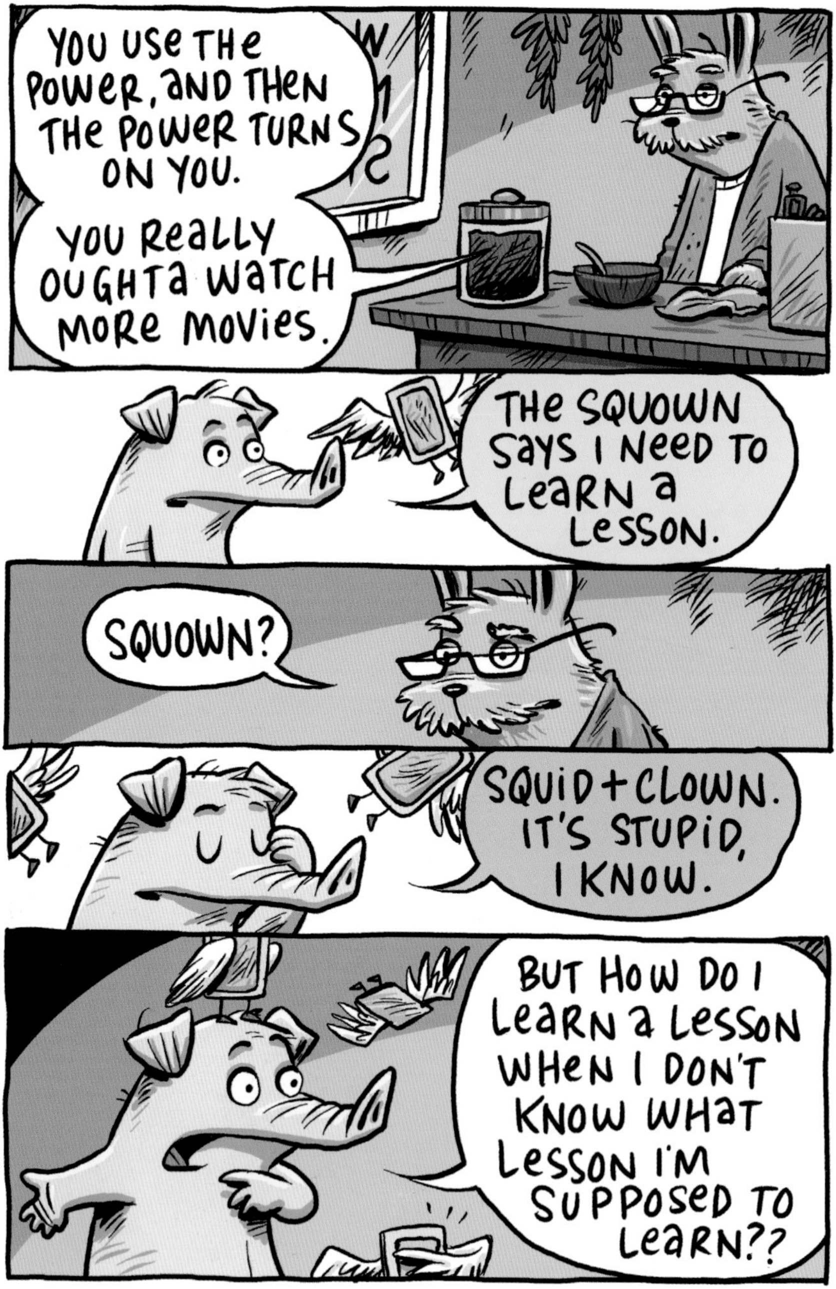
YOU USE THE POWER, AND THEN THE POWER TURNS ON YOU.
YOU REALLY OUGHTA WATCH MORE MOVIES.
THE SQUOWN SAYS I NEED TO LEARN A LESSON.
SQUOWN?
SQUID + CLOWN. IT'S STUPID, I KNOW.
BUT HOW DO I LEARN A LESSON WHEN I DON'T KNOW WHAT LESSON I'M SUPPOSED TO LEARN??

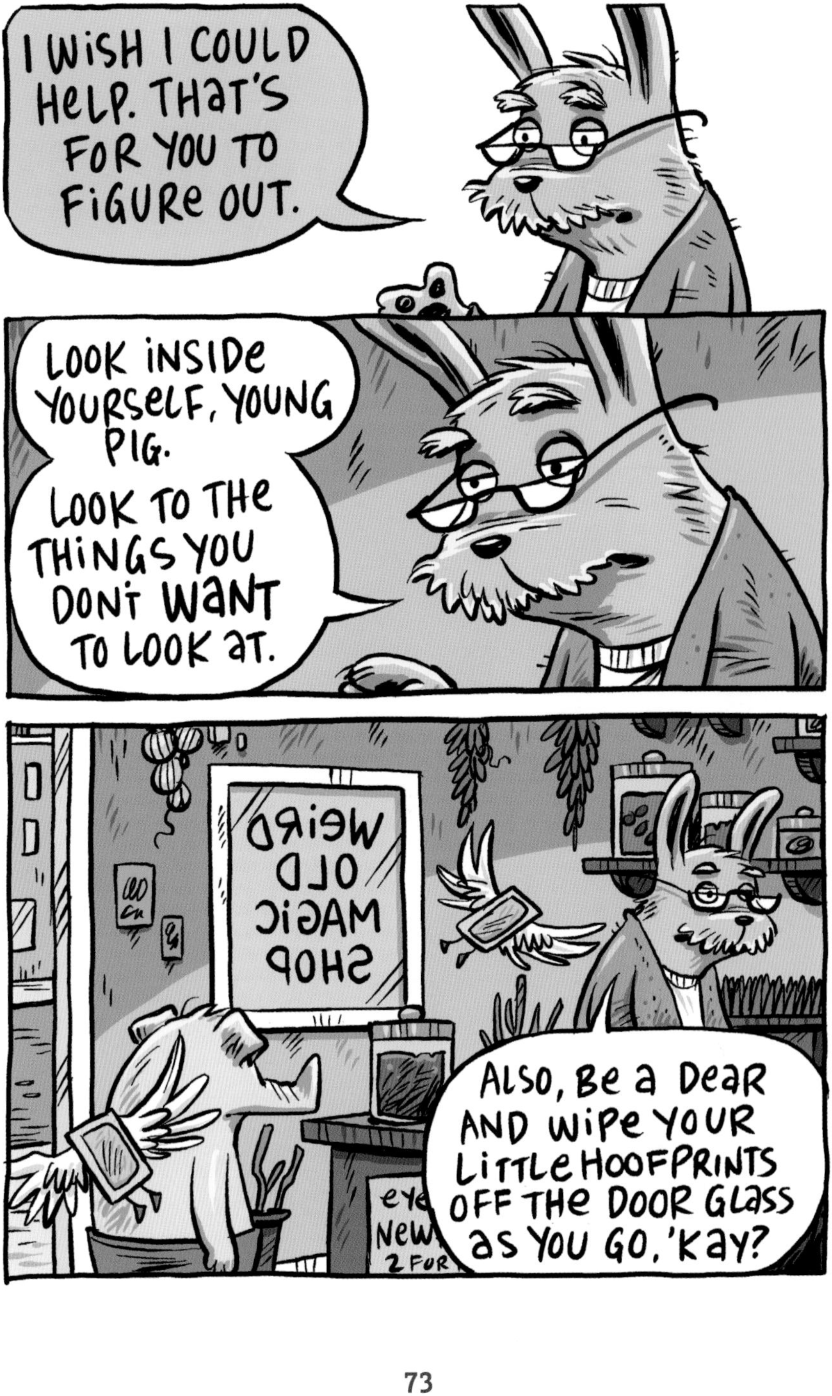
I WISH I COULD HELP. THAT'S FOR YOU TO FIGURE OUT.
LOOK INSIDE YOURSELF, YOUNG PIG.
LOOK TO THE THINGS YOU DON'T WANT TO LOOK AT.
WEIRD OLD MAGIC SHOP
ALSO, BE A DEAR AND WIPE YOUR LITTLE HOOFPRINTS OFF THE DOOR GLASS AS YOU GO, 'KAY?

CHAPTER NINE

"BACK TO BED!"

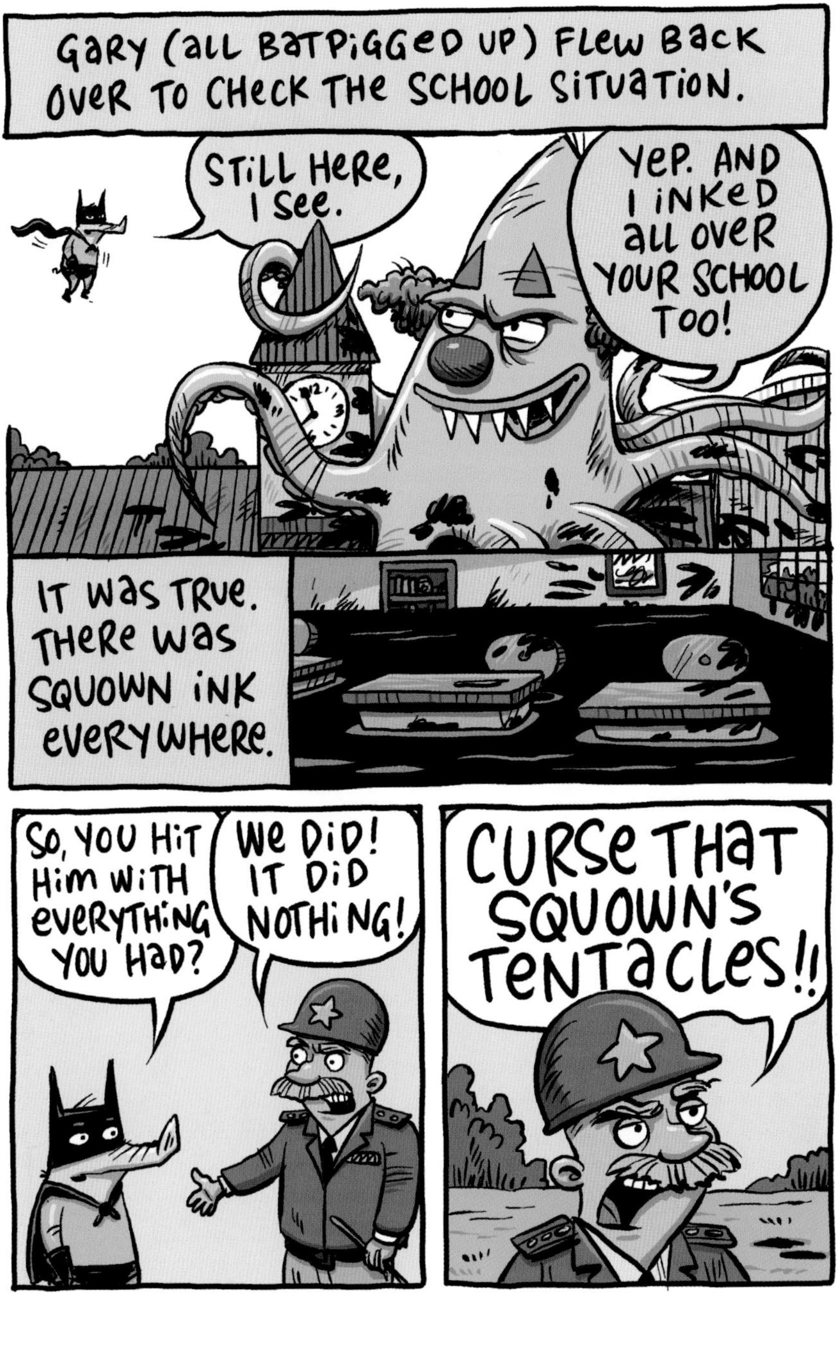
GARY (ALL BATPIGGED UP) FLEW BACK OVER TO CHECK THE SCHOOL SITUATION.
STILL HERE, I SEE.
YEP. AND I INKED ALL OVER YOUR SCHOOL TOO!
IT WAS TRUE. THERE WAS SQUOWN INK EVERYWHERE.
SO, YOU HIT HIM WITH EVERYTHING YOU HAD?
WE DID! IT DID NOTHING!
CURSE THAT SQUOWN'S TENTACLES!!

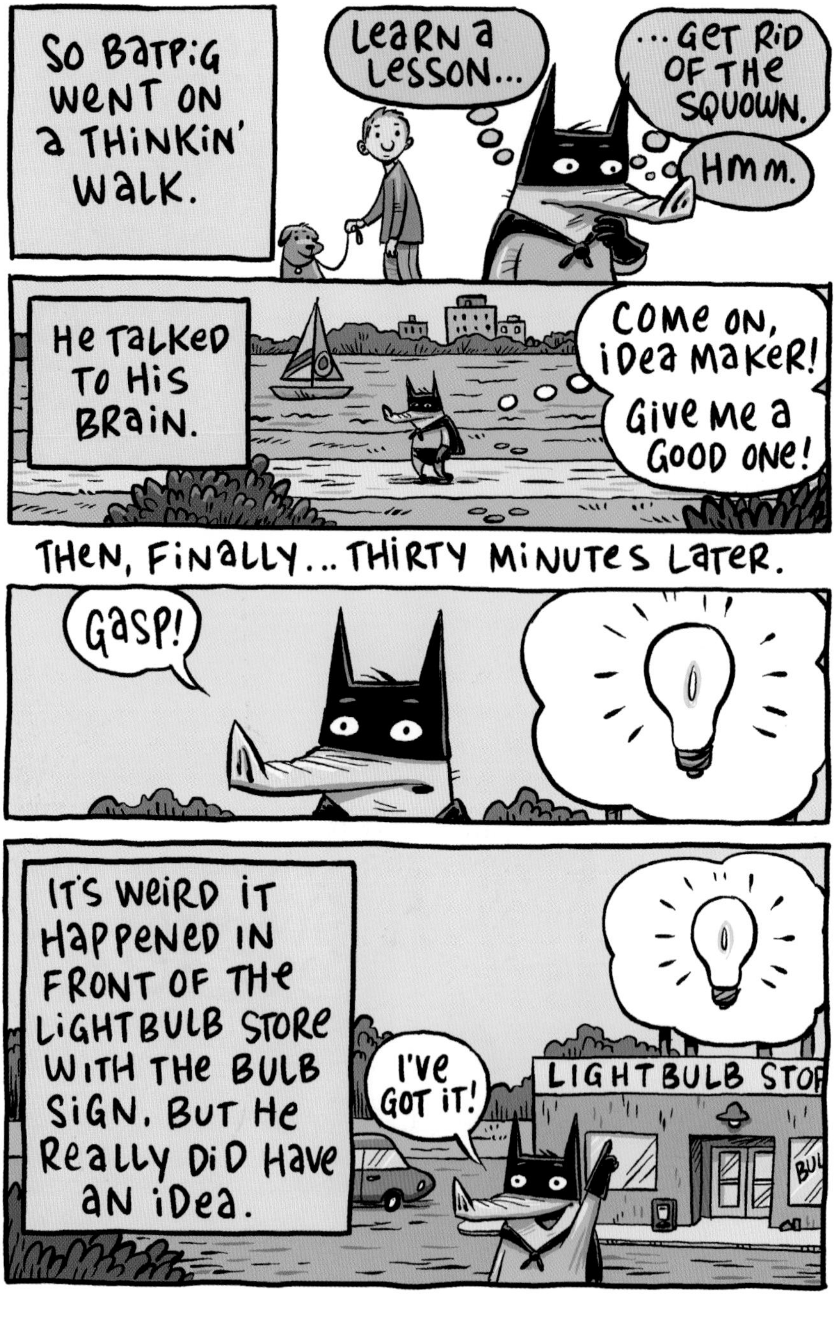
SO BATPIG WENT ON A THINKIN' WALK.
LEARN A LESSON...
...GET RID OF THE SQUOWN.
HMM.
HE TALKED TO HIS BRAIN.
COME ON, IDEA MAKER!
GIVE ME A GOOD ONE!
THEN, FINALLY... THIRTY MINUTES LATER.
GASP!
IT'S WEIRD IT HAPPENED IN FRONT OF THE LIGHTBULB STORE WITH THE BULB SIGN. BUT HE REALLY DID HAVE AN IDEA.
I'VE GOT IT!
LIGHTBULB STO

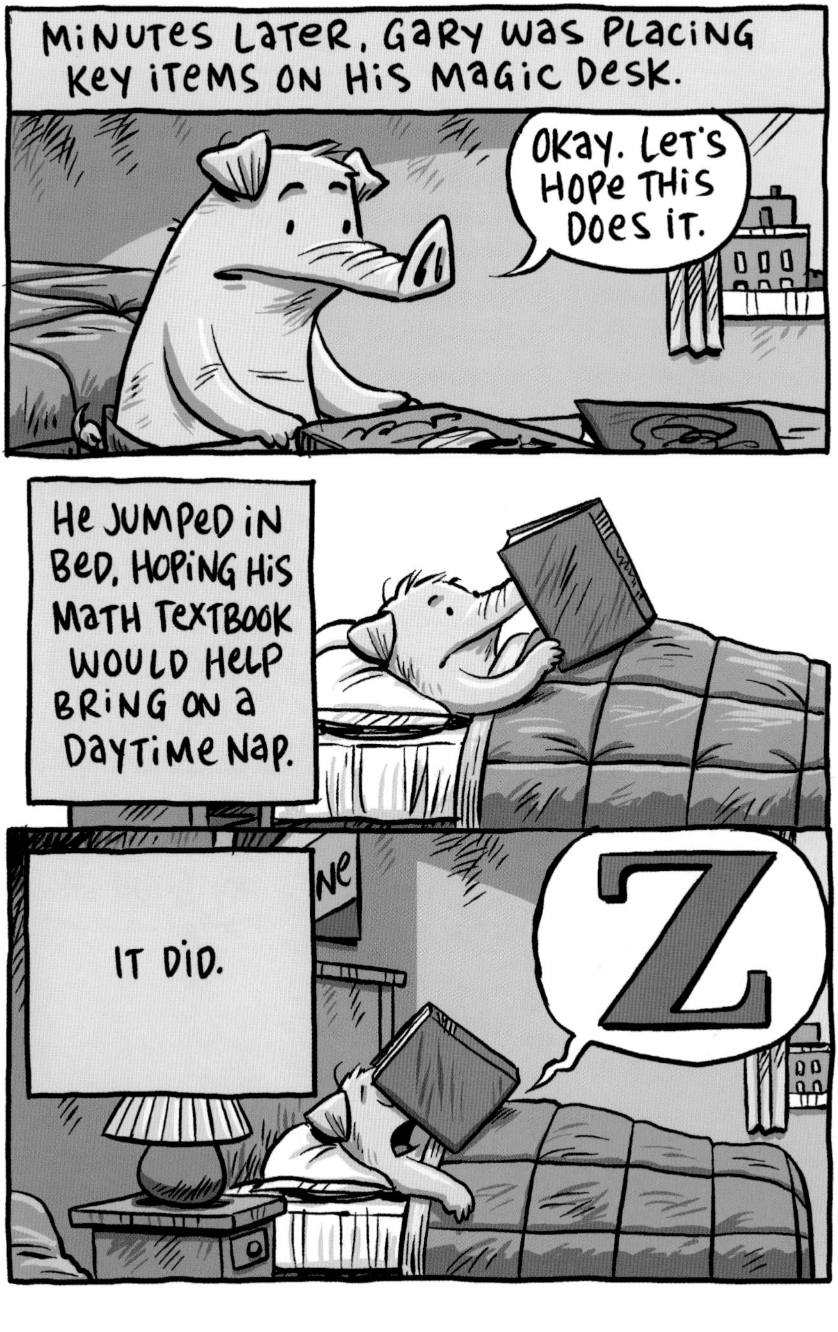
MINUTES LATER, GARY WAS PLACING KEY ITEMS ON HIS MAGIC DESK.
OKAY. LET'S HOPE THIS DOES IT.
HE JUMPED IN BED, HOPING HIS MATH TEXTBOOK WOULD HELP BRING ON A DAYTIME NAP.
IT DID.
Z

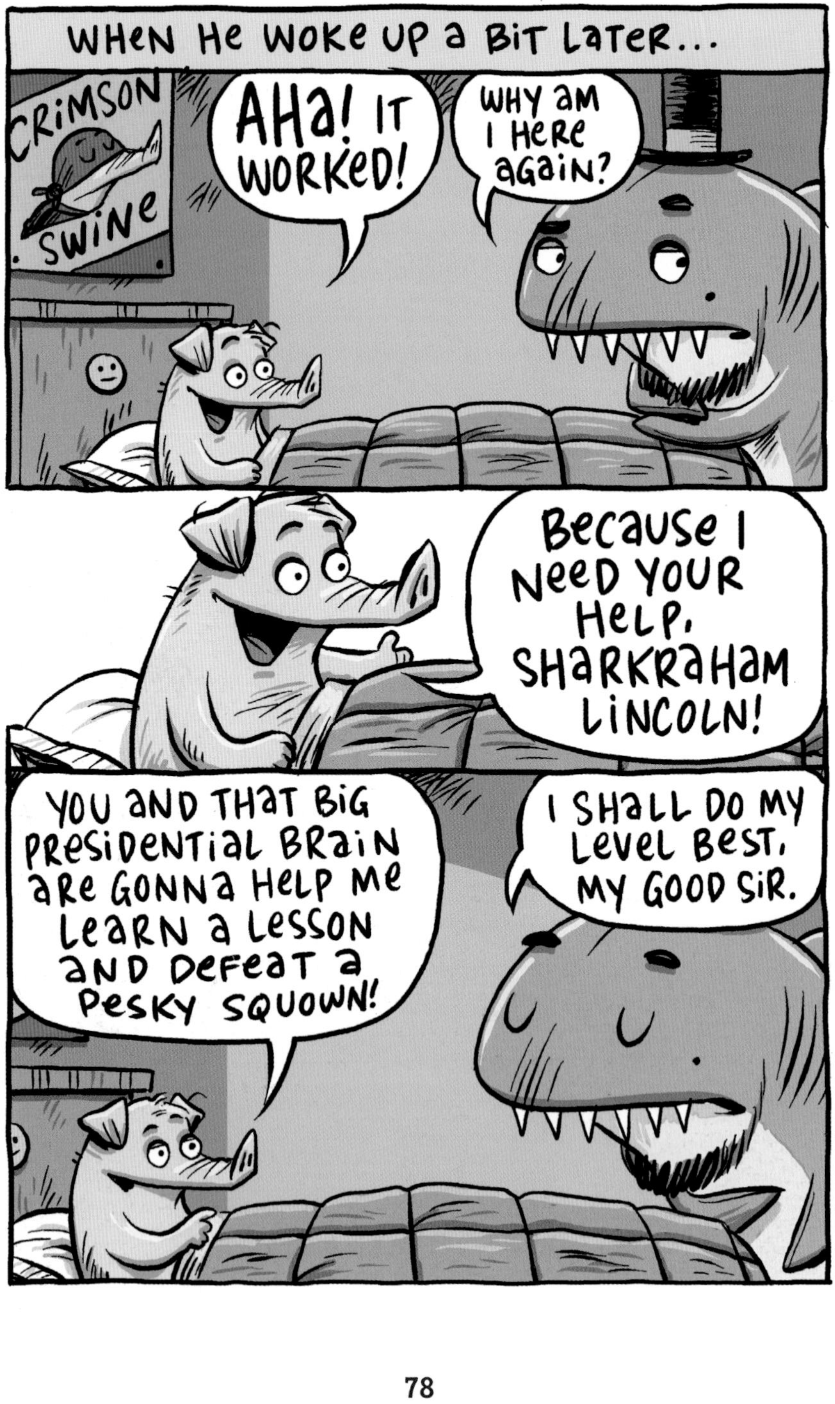
WHEN HE WOKE UP A BIT LATER...
CRIMSON SWINE
AHA! IT WORKED!
WHY AM I HERE AGAIN?
BECAUSE I NEED YOUR HELP, SHARKRAHAM LINCOLN!
YOU AND THAT BIG PRESIDENTIAL BRAIN ARE GONNA HELP ME LEARN A LESSON AND DEFEAT A PESKY SQUOWN!
I SHALL DO MY LEVEL BEST, MY GOOD SIR.

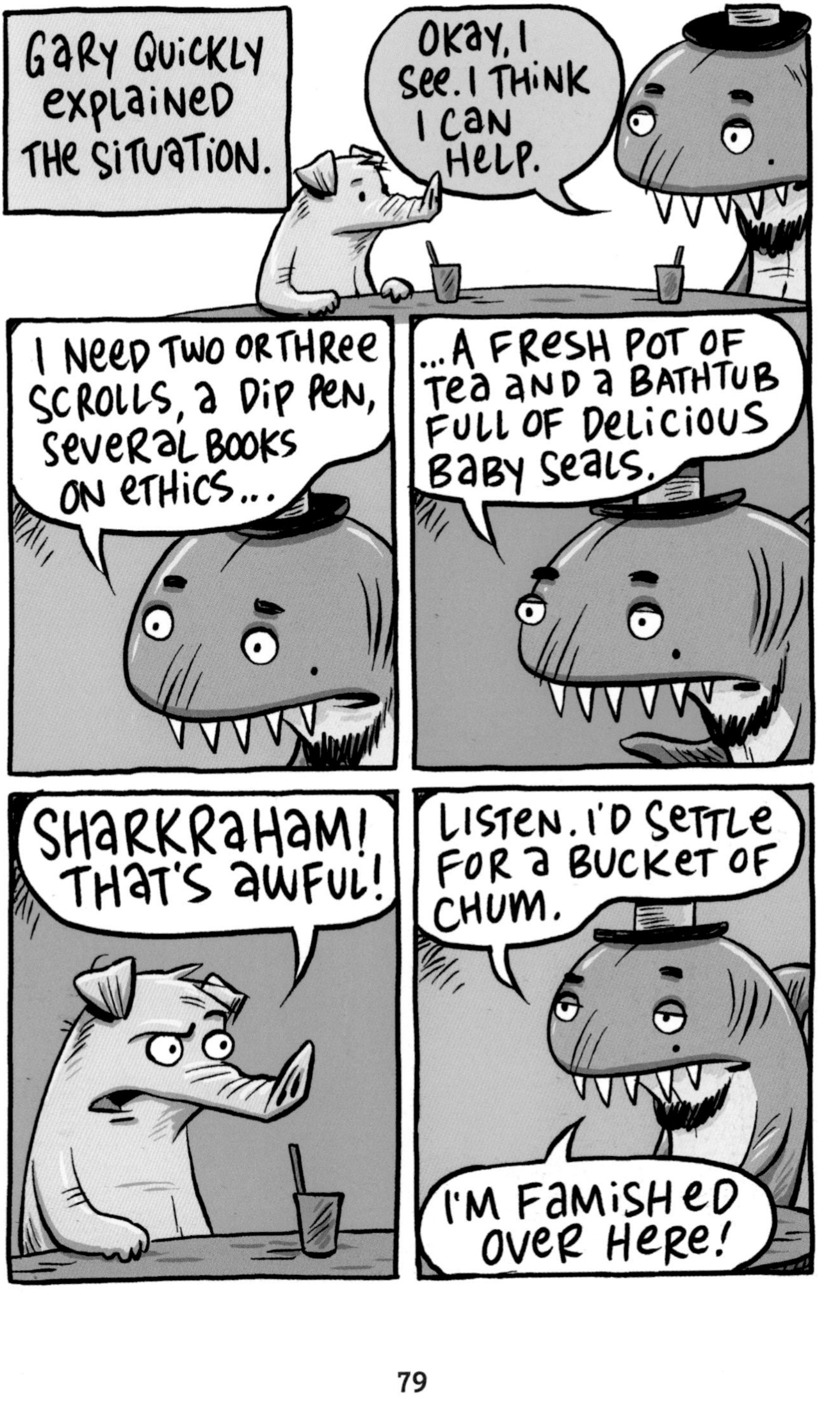
GARY QUICKLY EXPLAINED THE SITUATION.
OKAY, I SEE. I THINK I CAN HELP.
I NEED TWO OR THREE SCROLLS, A DIP PEN, SEVERAL BOOKS ON ETHICS...
...A FRESH POT OF TEA AND A BATHTUB FULL OF DELICIOUS BABY SEALS.
SHARKRAHAM! THAT'S AWFUL!
LISTEN. I'D SETTLE FOR A BUCKET OF CHUM.
I'M FAMISHED OVER HERE!

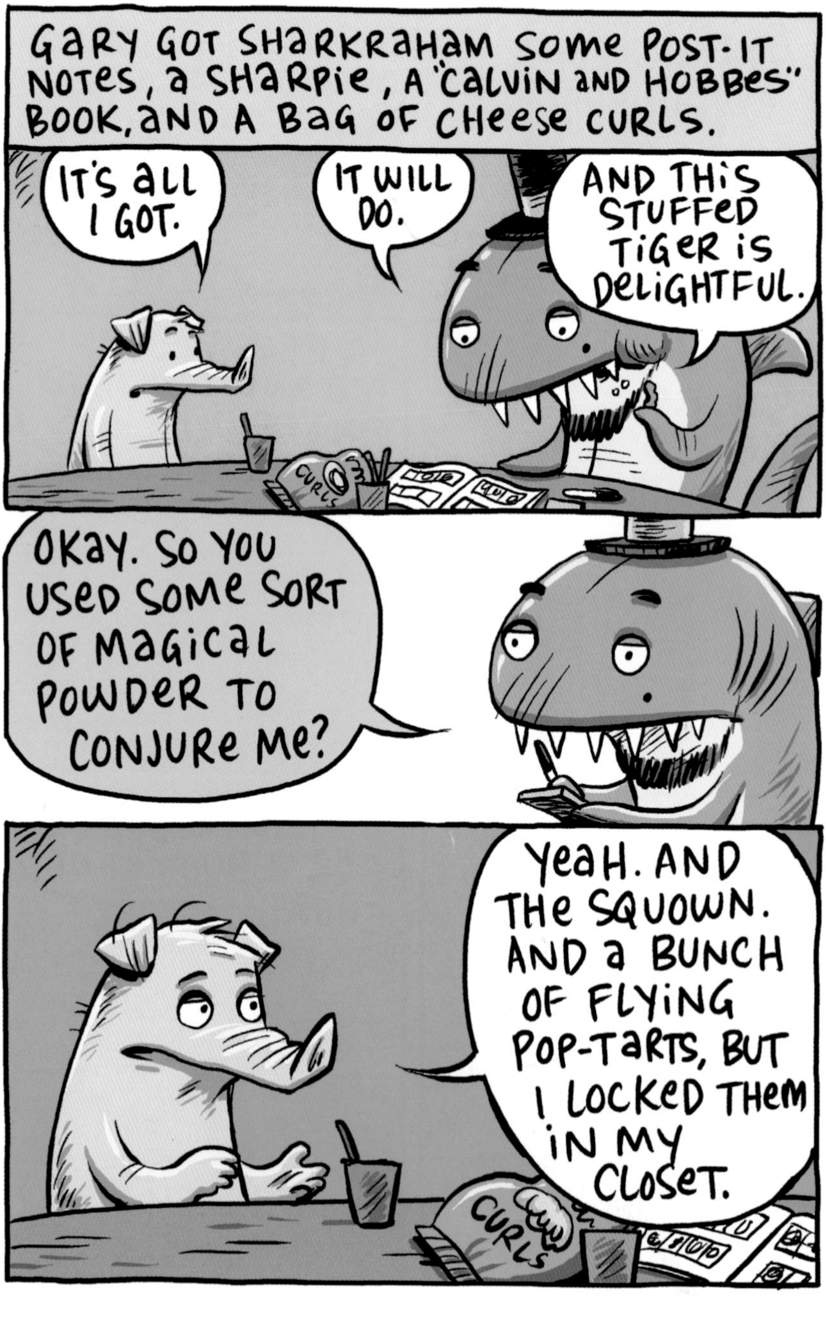
GARY GOT SHARKRAHAM SOME POST-IT NOTES, A SHARPIE, A "CALVIN AND HOBBES" BOOK, AND A BAG OF CHEESE CURLS.
IT'S ALL I GOT.
IT WILL DO.
AND THIS STUFFED TIGER IS DELIGHTFUL.
CURLS
OKAY. SO YOU USED SOME SORT OF MAGICAL POWDER TO CONJURE ME?
YEAH. AND THE SQUOWN. AND A BUNCH OF FLYING POP-TARTS, BUT I LOCKED THEM IN MY CLOSET.
CURLS

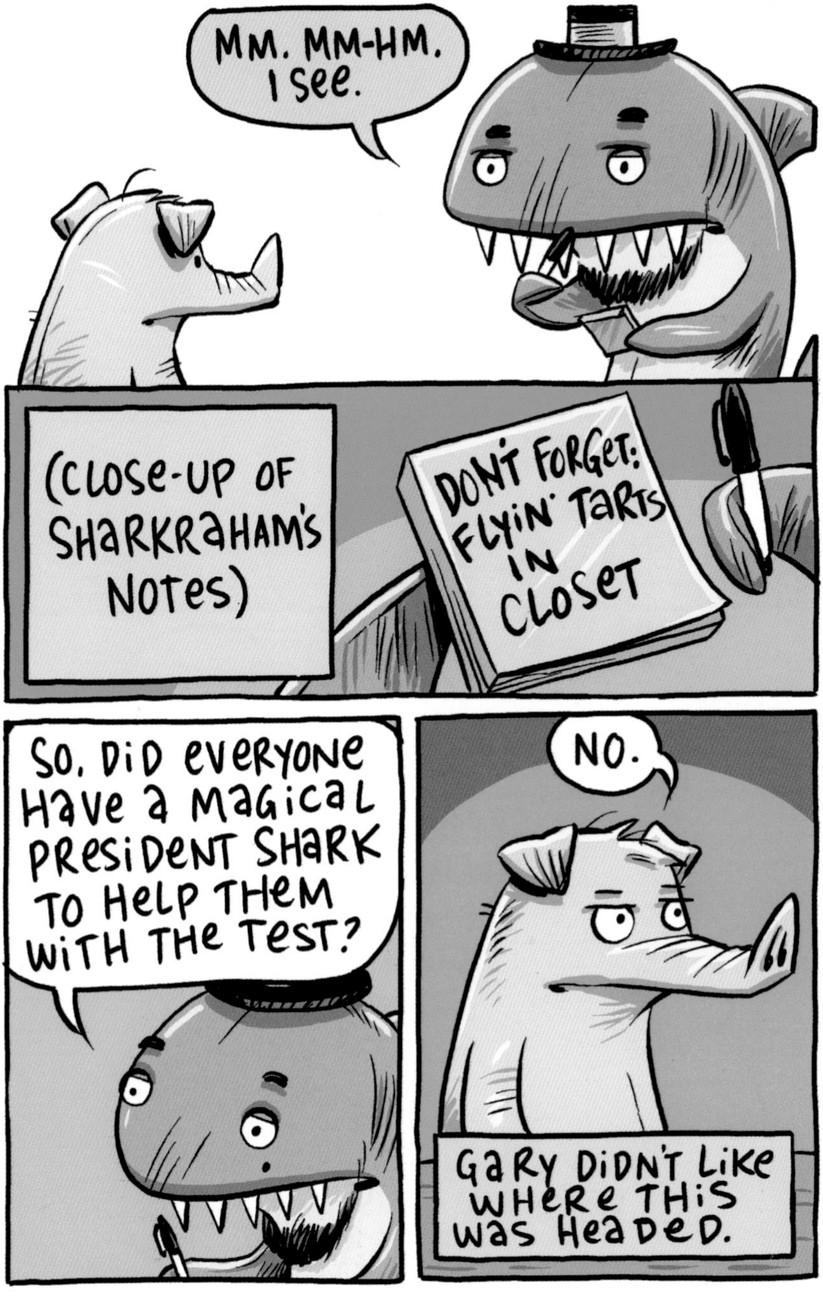
MM. MM-HM. I SEE.
(CLOSE-UP OF SHARKRAHAM'S NOTES)
DON'T FORGET: FLYIN' TARTS IN CLOSET
SO, DID EVERYONE HAVE A MAGICAL PRESIDENT SHARK TO HELP THEM WITH THE TEST?
NO.
GARY DIDN'T LIKE WHERE THIS WAS HEADED.

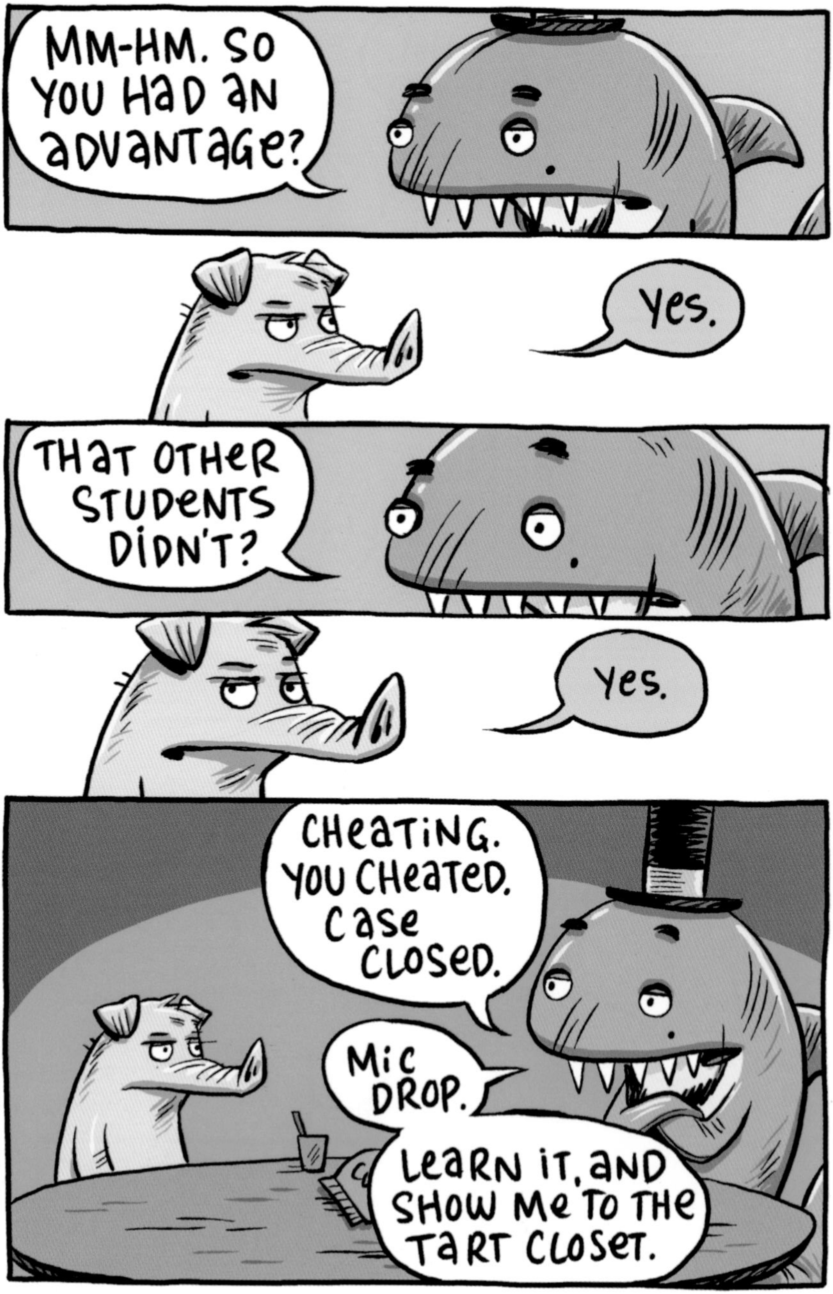
MM-HM. SO YOU HAD AN ADVANTAGE?
YES.
THAT OTHER STUDENTS DIDN'T?
YES.
CHEATING. YOU CHEATED. CASE CLOSED.
MIC DROP.
LEARN IT, AND SHOW ME TO THE TART CLOSET.

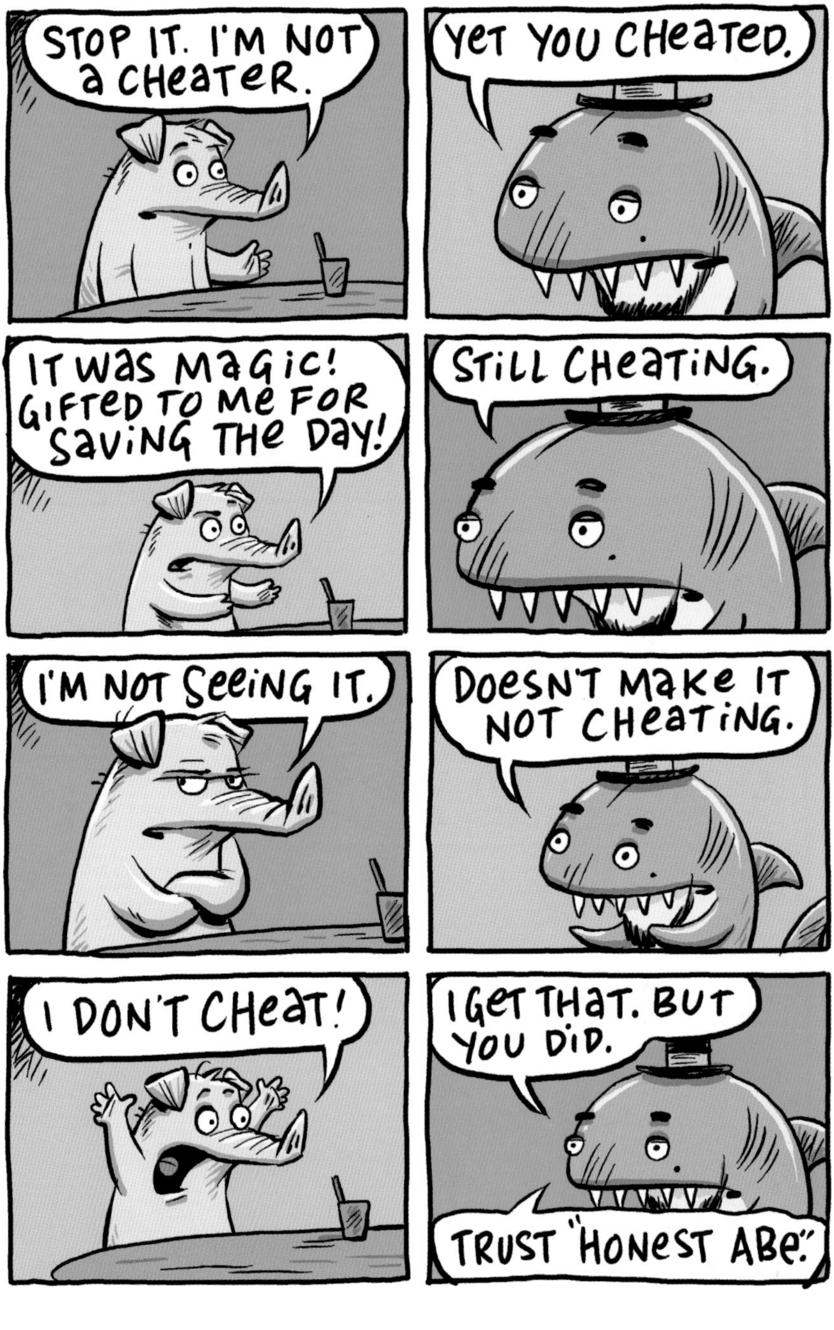
STOP IT. I'M NOT a CHEATER.
YET YOU CHEATED.
IT WAS MAGIC! GIFTED TO ME FOR SAVING THE DAY!
STILL CHEATING.
I'M NOT SEEING IT.
DOESN'T MAKE IT NOT CHEATING.
I DON'T CHEAT!
I GET THAT. BUT YOU DID.
TRUST "HONEST ABE."

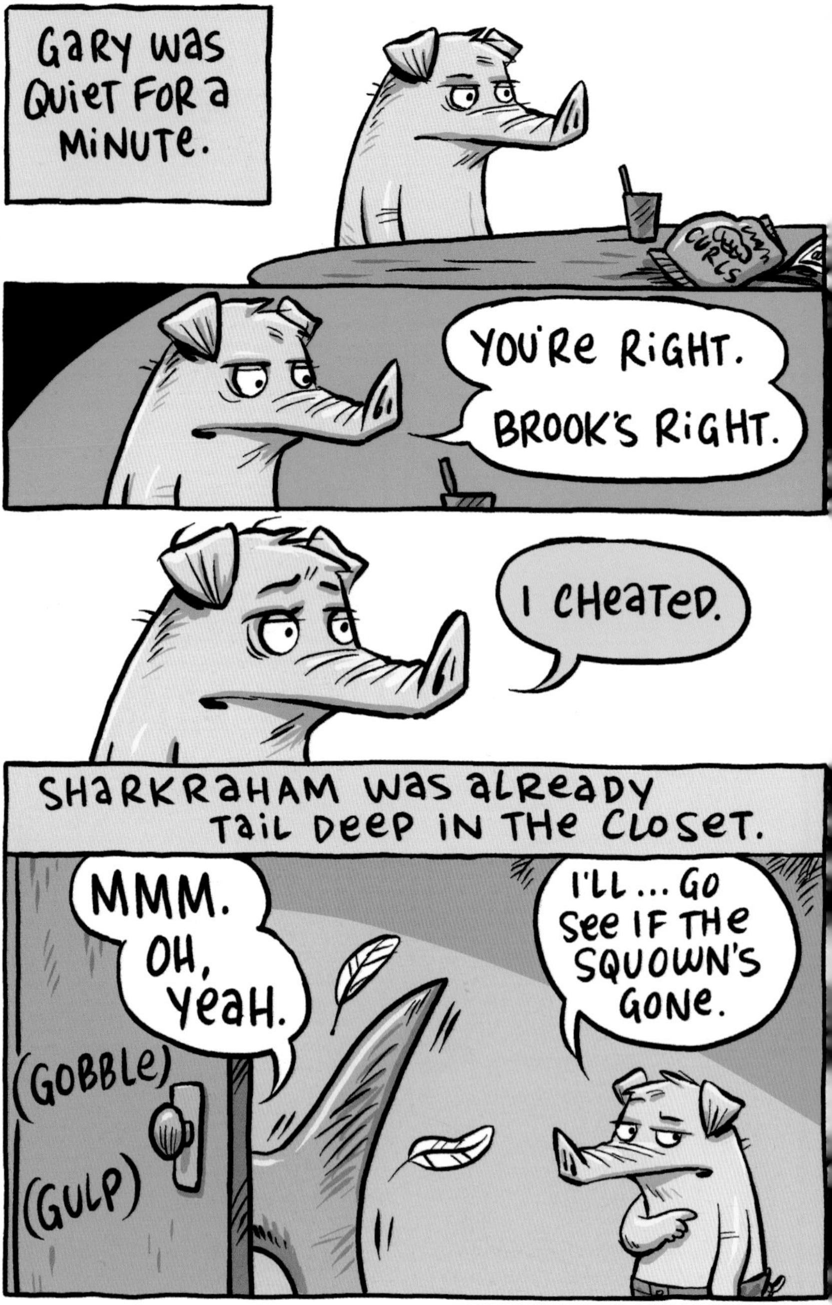

Gary was Quiet FOR a MINUTE.
YOU'Re RIGHT.
BROOK'S RIGHT.
CURLS
I CHeaTeD.
SHaRKRaHAM Was aLReaDY TaIL DeeP IN THe CLOSeT.
MMM. OH, YeaH.
(GOBBLe)
(GULP)
I'LL ... GO See IF THe SQUOWN'S GONe.

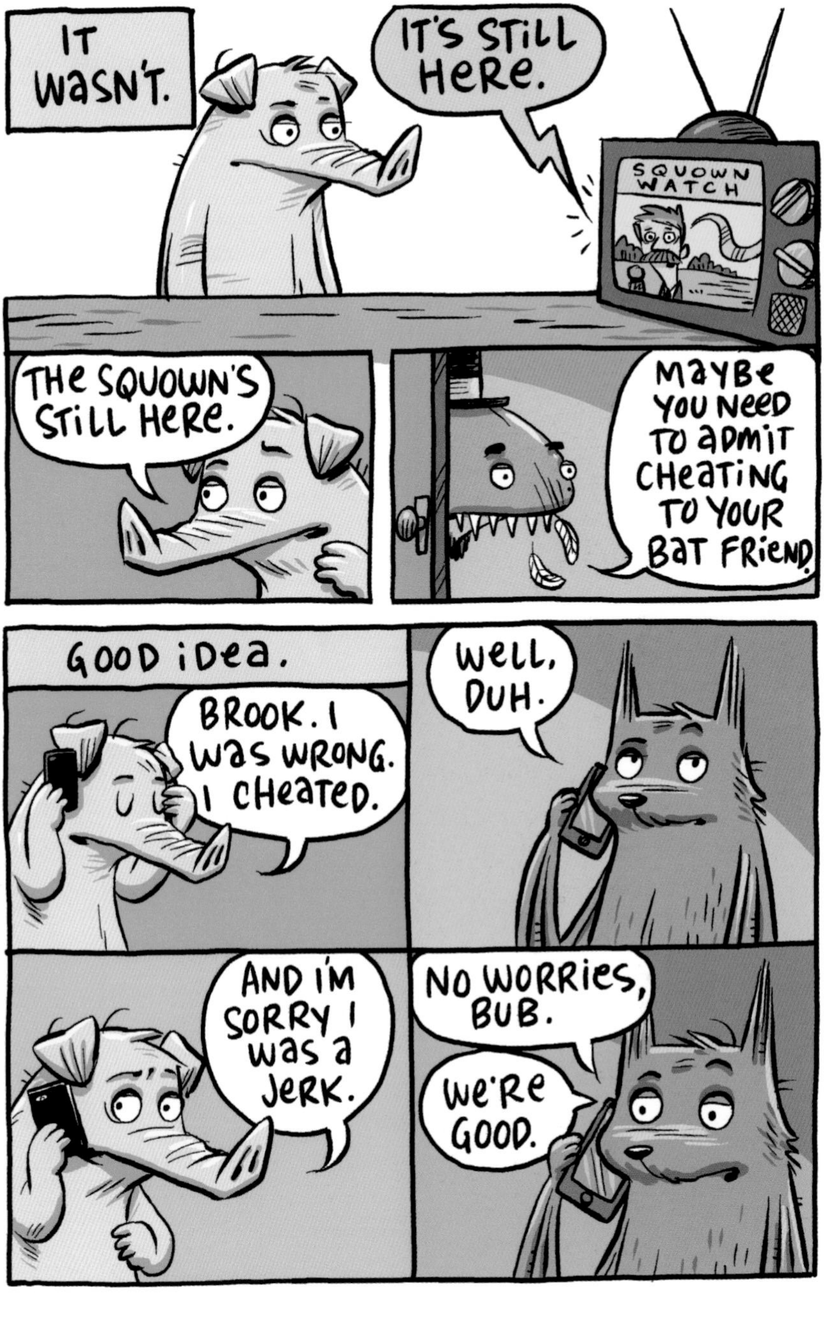
IT WASN'T.
IT'S STILL HERE.
SQUOWN WATCH
THE SQUOWN'S STILL HERE.
MAYBE YOU NEED TO ADMIT CHEATING TO YOUR BAT FRIEND.
GOOD IDEA.
BROOK. I WAS WRONG. I CHEATED.
WELL, DUH.
AND I'M SORRY I WAS A JERK.
NO WORRIES, BUB.
WE'RE GOOD.

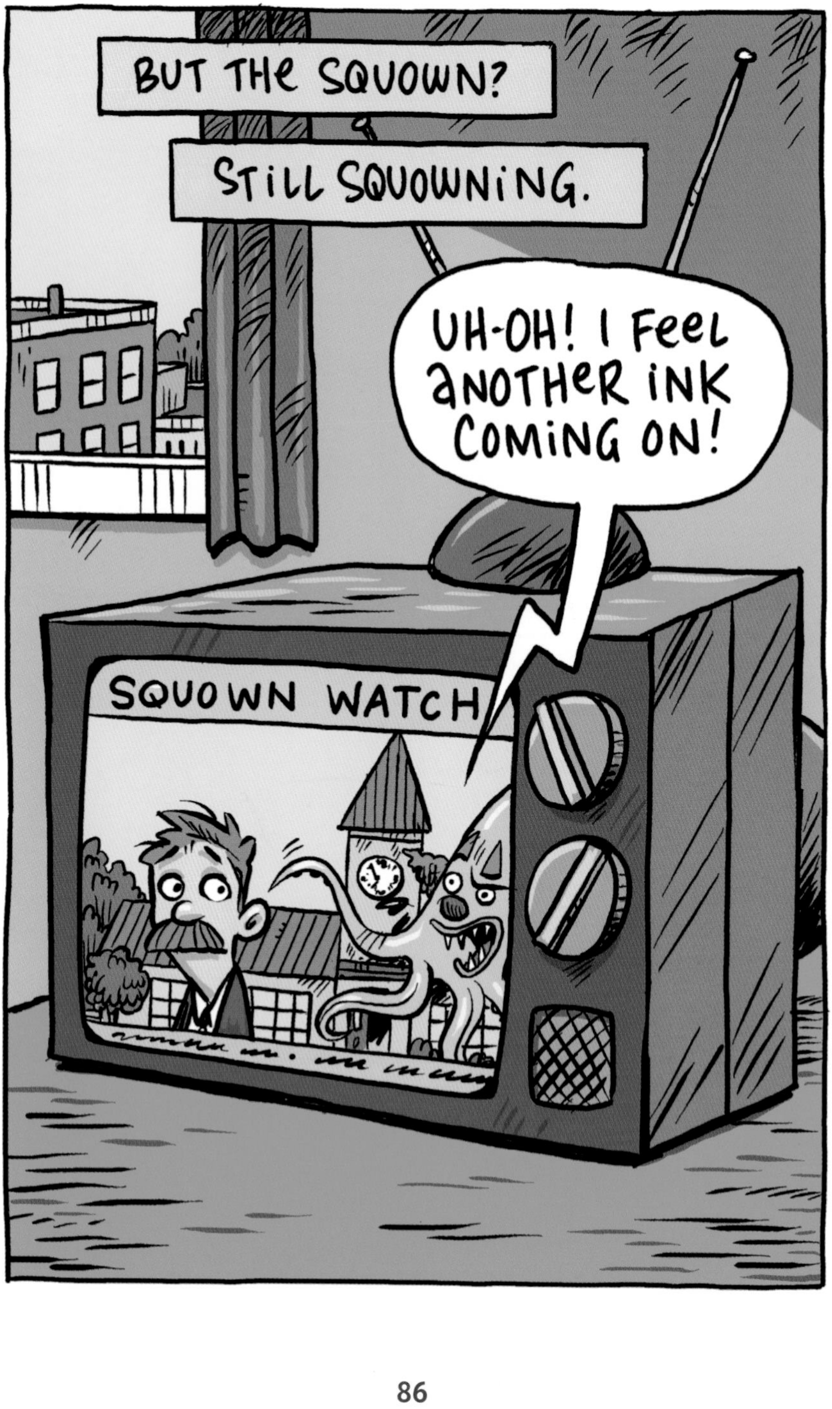

BUT THE SQUOWN?
STILL SQUOWNING.
UH-OH! I FEEL ANOTHER INK COMING ON!
SQUOWN WATCH

CHAPTER TEN

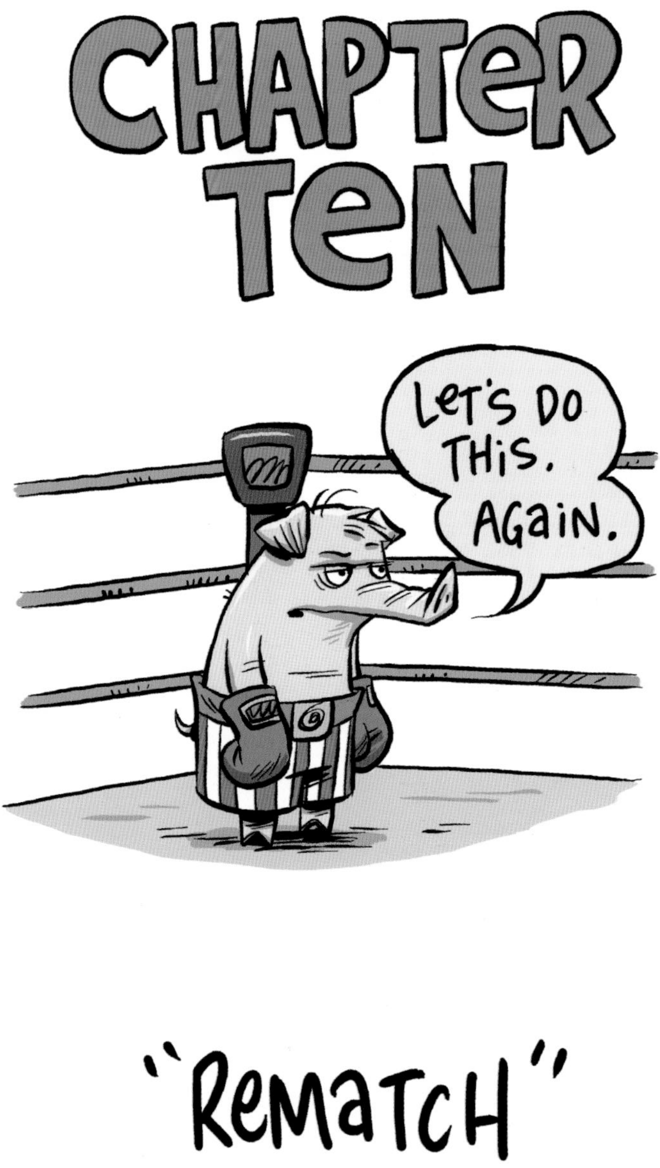
LET'S DO THIS. AGAIN.

"REMATCH"

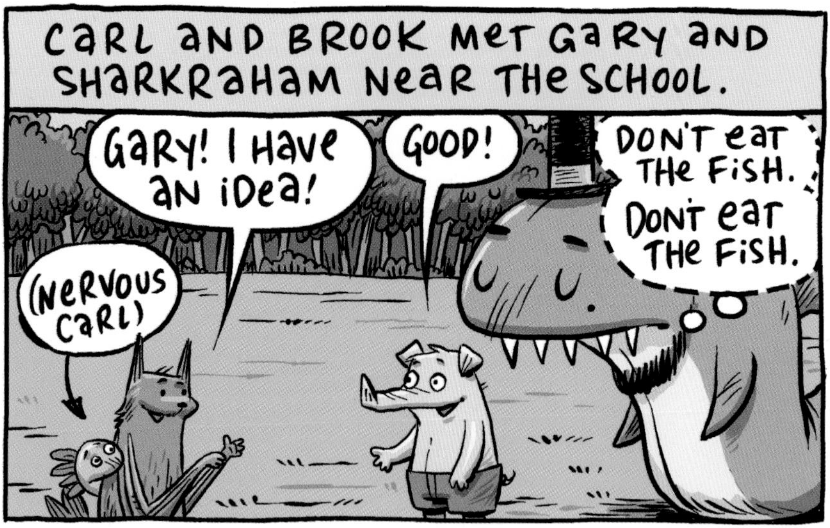
CARL AND BROOK MET GARY AND SHARKRAHAM NEAR THE SCHOOL.
GARY! I HAVE AN IDEA!
GOOD!
DON'T EAT THE FISH. DON'T EAT THE FISH.
(NERVOUS CARL)

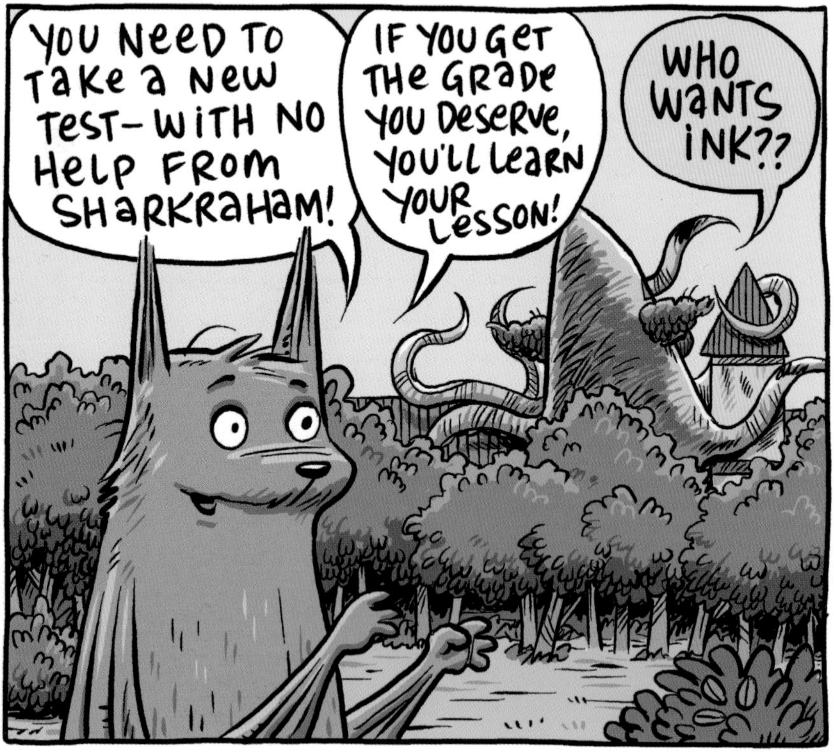
YOU NEED TO TAKE A NEW TEST—WITH NO HELP FROM SHARKRAHAM!
IF YOU GET THE GRADE YOU DESERVE, YOU'LL LEARN YOUR LESSON!
WHO WANTS INK??

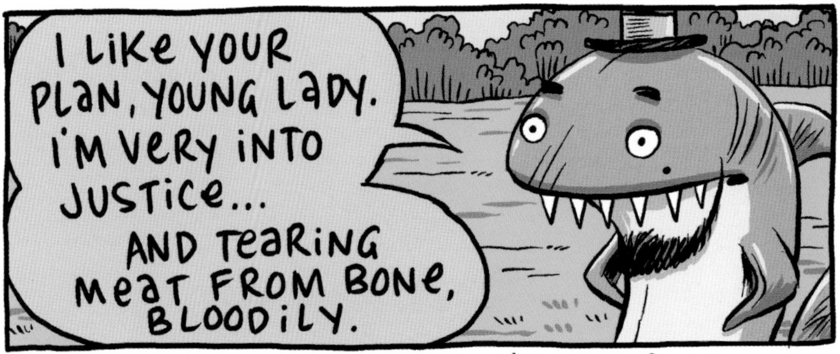
I LIKE YOUR PLAN, YOUNG LADY. I'M VERY INTO JUSTICE...
AND TEARING MEAT FROM BONE, BLOODILY.

SO IT WAS SET! MRS. HART AND MR. PONYMAN WERE CALLED. NEW TESTS AND A DESK WERE BROUGHT.

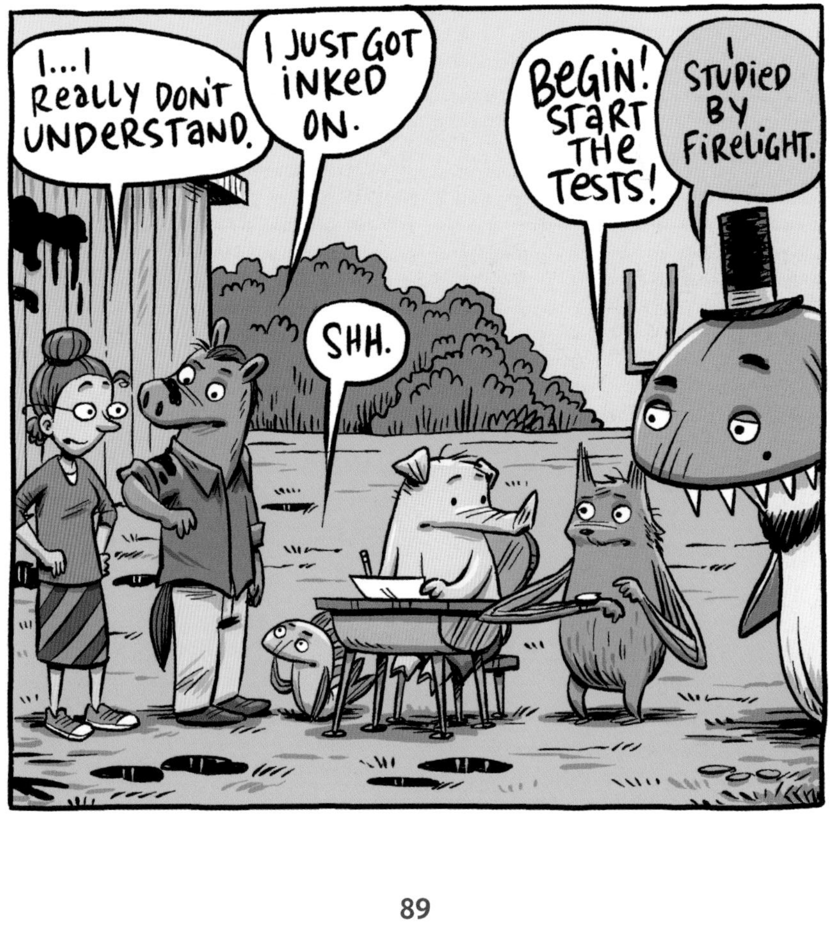
I...I REALLY DON'T UNDERSTAND.
I JUST GOT INKED ON.
BEGIN! START THE TESTS!
I STUDIED BY FIRELIGHT.
SHH.

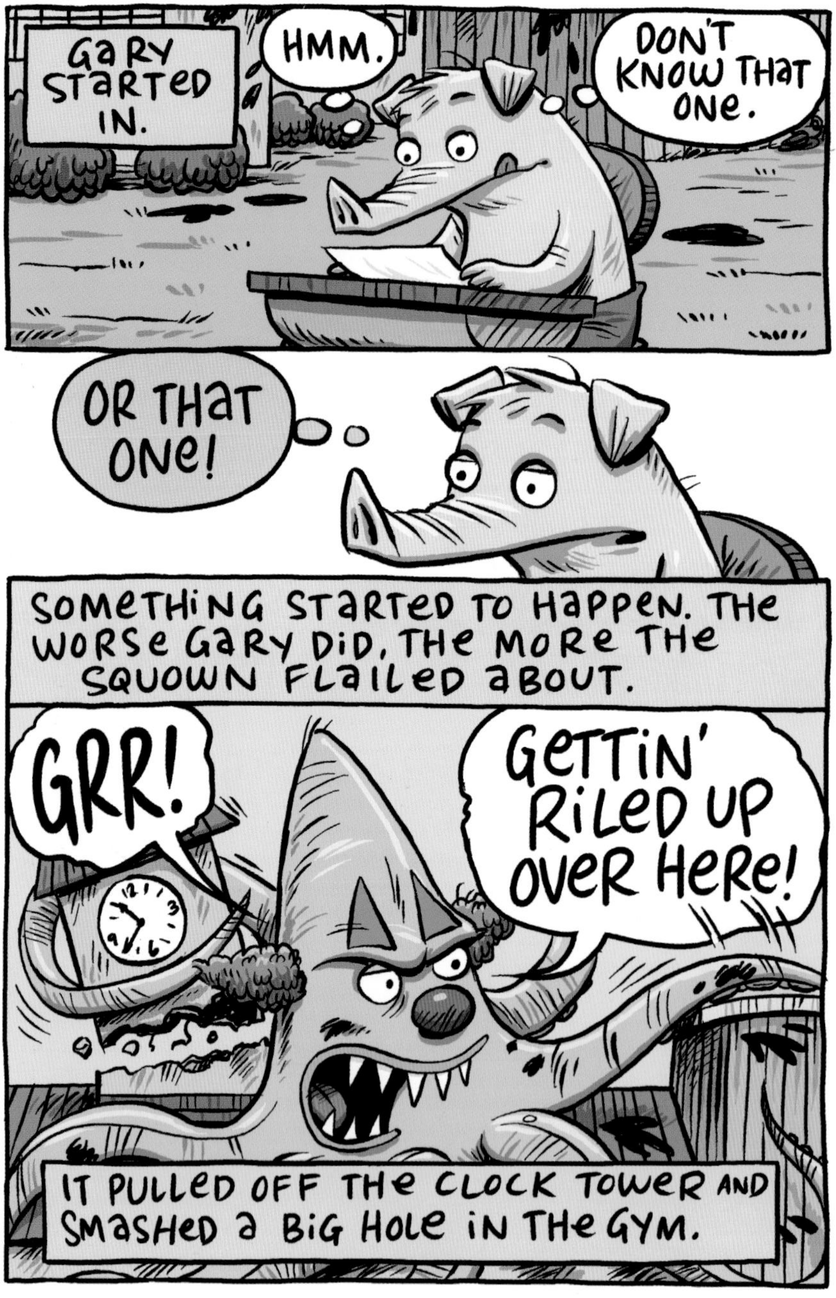
GARY STARTED IN.
HMM.
DON'T KNOW THAT ONE.
OR THAT ONE!
SOMETHING STARTED TO HAPPEN. THE WORSE GARY DID, THE MORE THE SQUOWN FLAILED ABOUT.
GRR!
GETTIN' RILED UP OVER HERE!
IT PULLED OFF THE CLOCK TOWER AND SMASHED A BIG HOLE IN THE GYM.

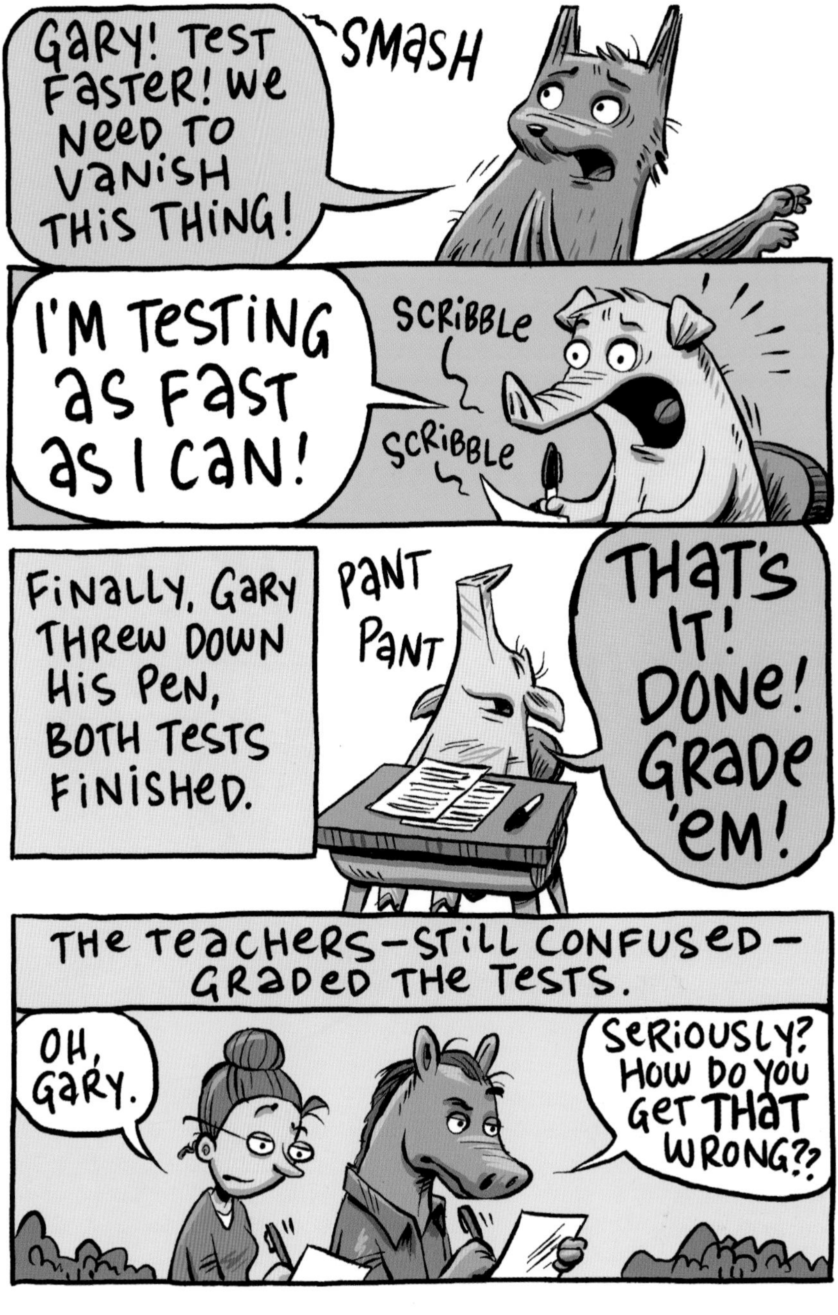
GARY! TEST FASTER! WE NEED TO VANISH THIS THING!
SMASH
I'M TESTING AS FAST AS I CAN!
SCRIBBLE
SCRIBBLE
FINALLY, GARY THREW DOWN HIS PEN, BOTH TESTS FINISHED.
PANT
PANT
THAT'S IT! DONE! GRADE 'EM!
THE TEACHERS—STILL CONFUSED—GRADED THE TESTS.
OH, GARY.
SERIOUSLY? HOW DO YOU GET THAT WRONG??

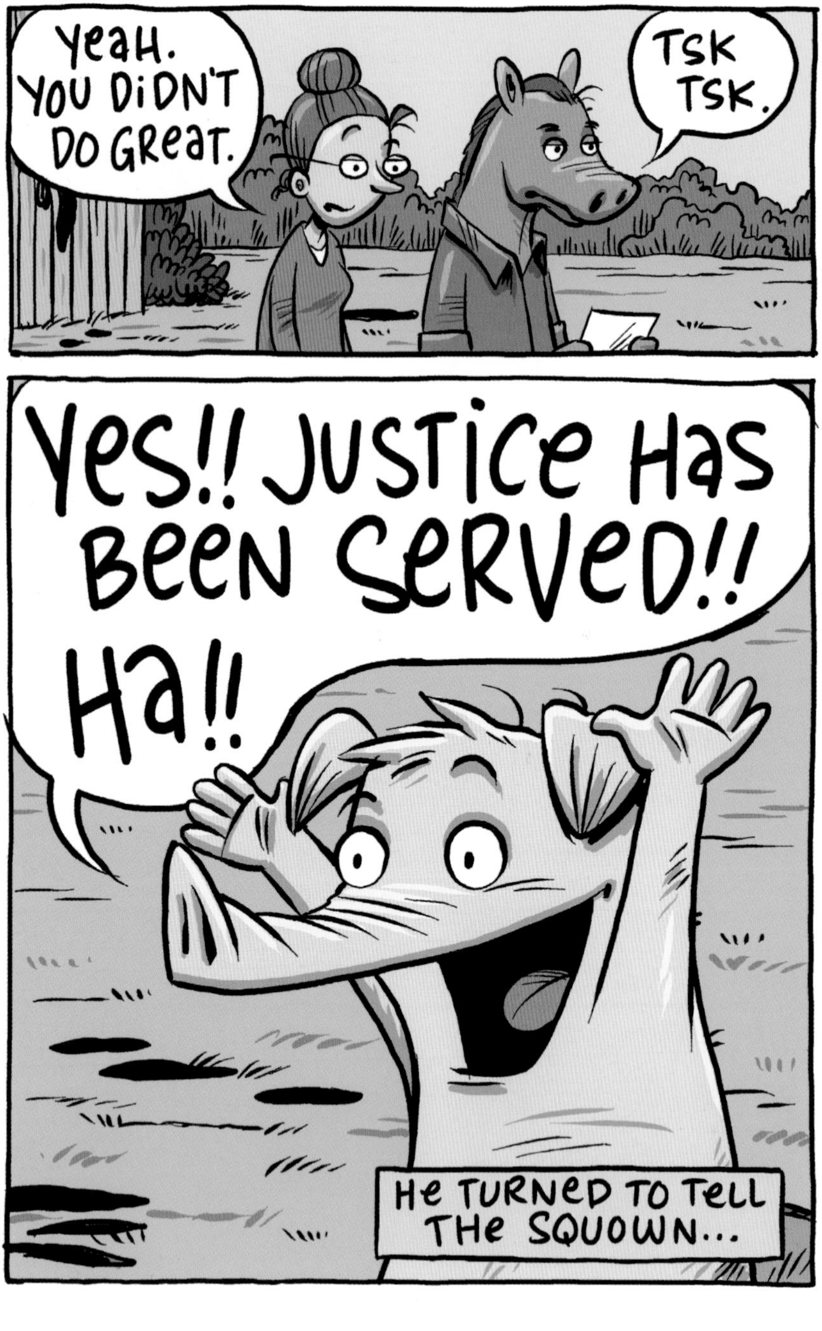
YEAH. YOU DIDN'T DO GREAT.
TSK TSK.
YES!! JUSTICE HAS BEEN SERVED!! HA!!
HE TURNED TO TELL THE SQUOWN...

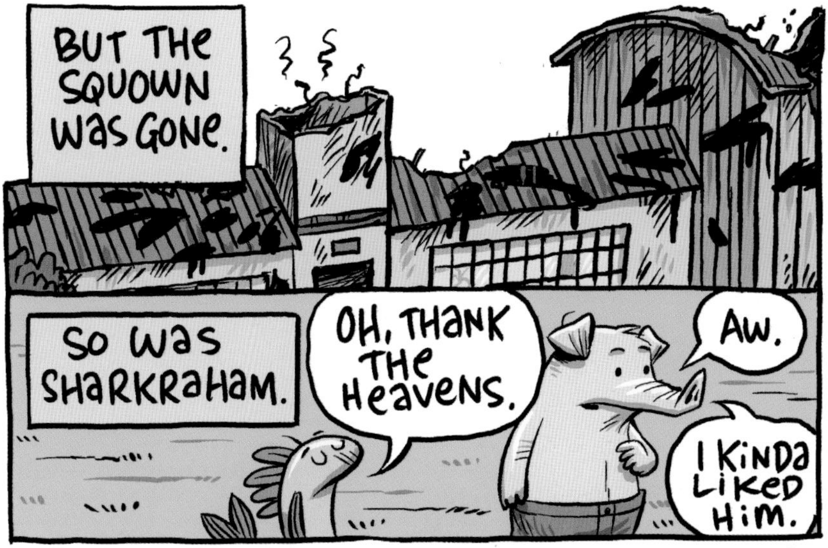
BUT THE SQUOWN WAS GONE.
SO WAS SHARKRAHAM.
OH, THANK THE HEAVENS.
AW.
I KINDA LIKED HIM.

CHEERS WENT UP! THE MONSTER SQUID CLOWN THING WAS NOWHERE TO BE SEEN.

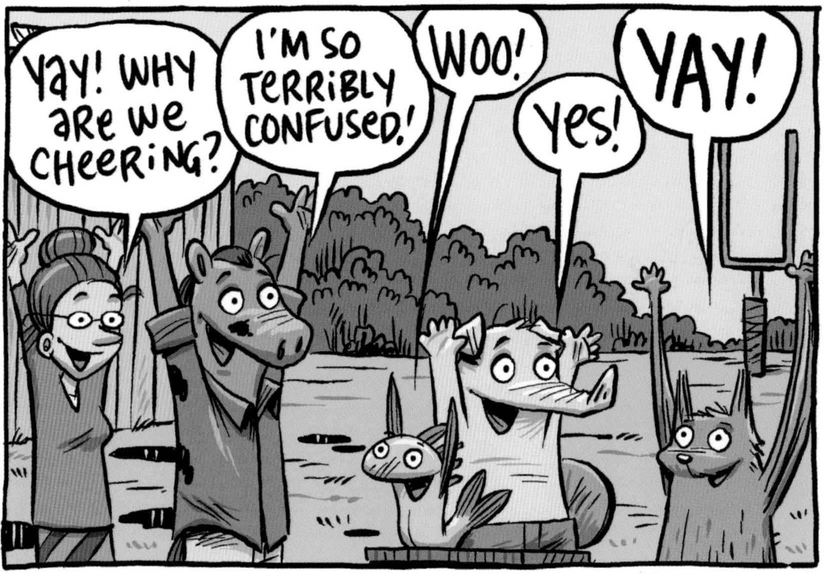
YAY! WHY ARE WE CHEERING?
I'M SO TERRIBLY CONFUSED!
WOO!
YES!
YAY!

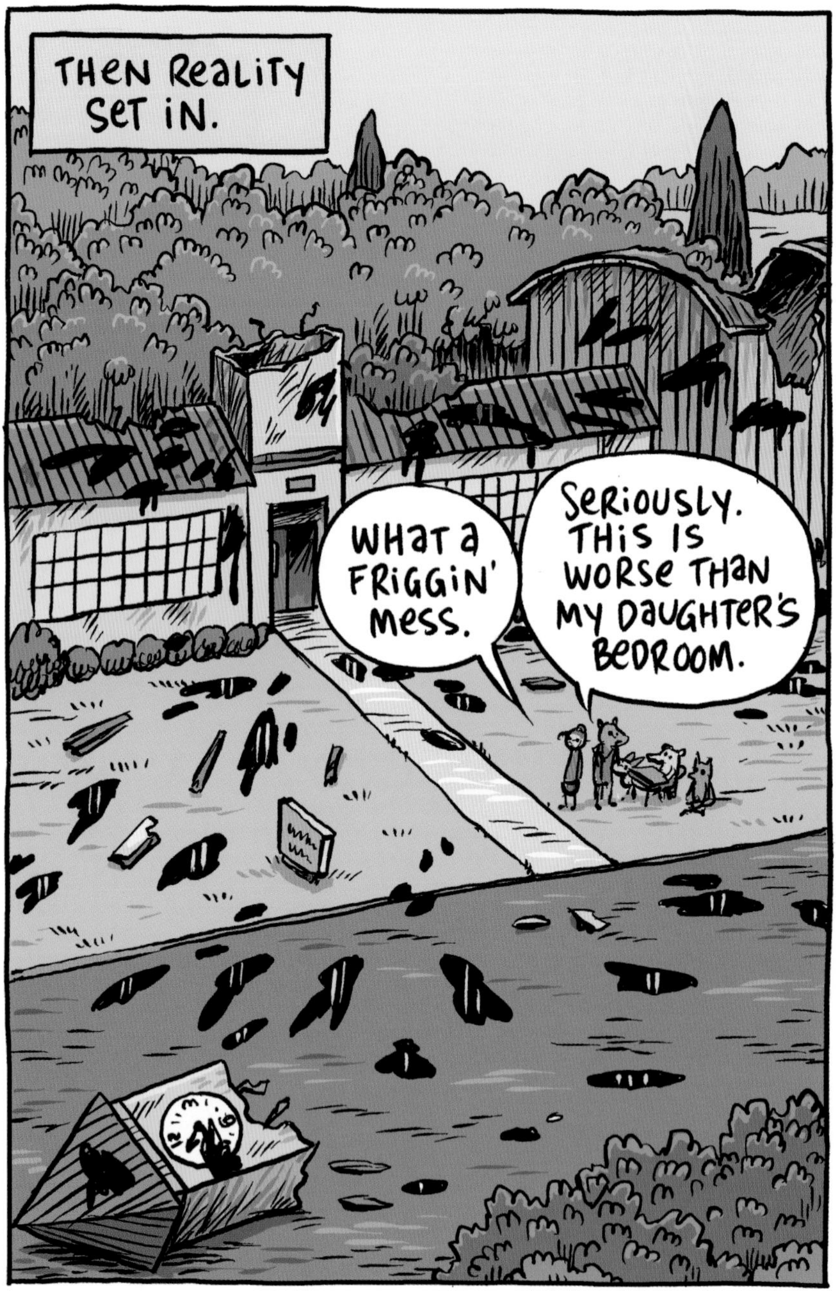
THEN REALITY SET IN.
WHAT A FRIGGIN' MESS.
SERIOUSLY. THIS IS WORSE THAN MY DAUGHTER'S BEDROOM.

CHAPTER ELEVEN

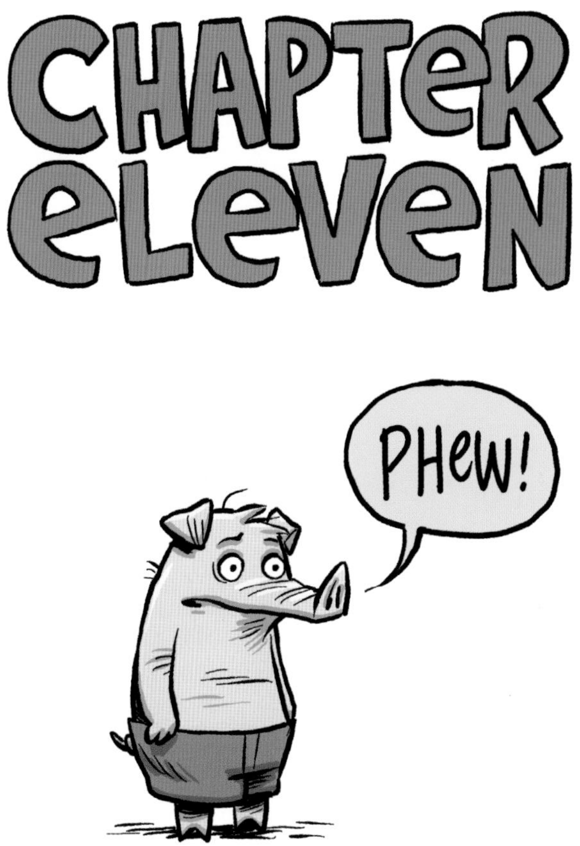
PHEW!

"LAST THINGS LAST"

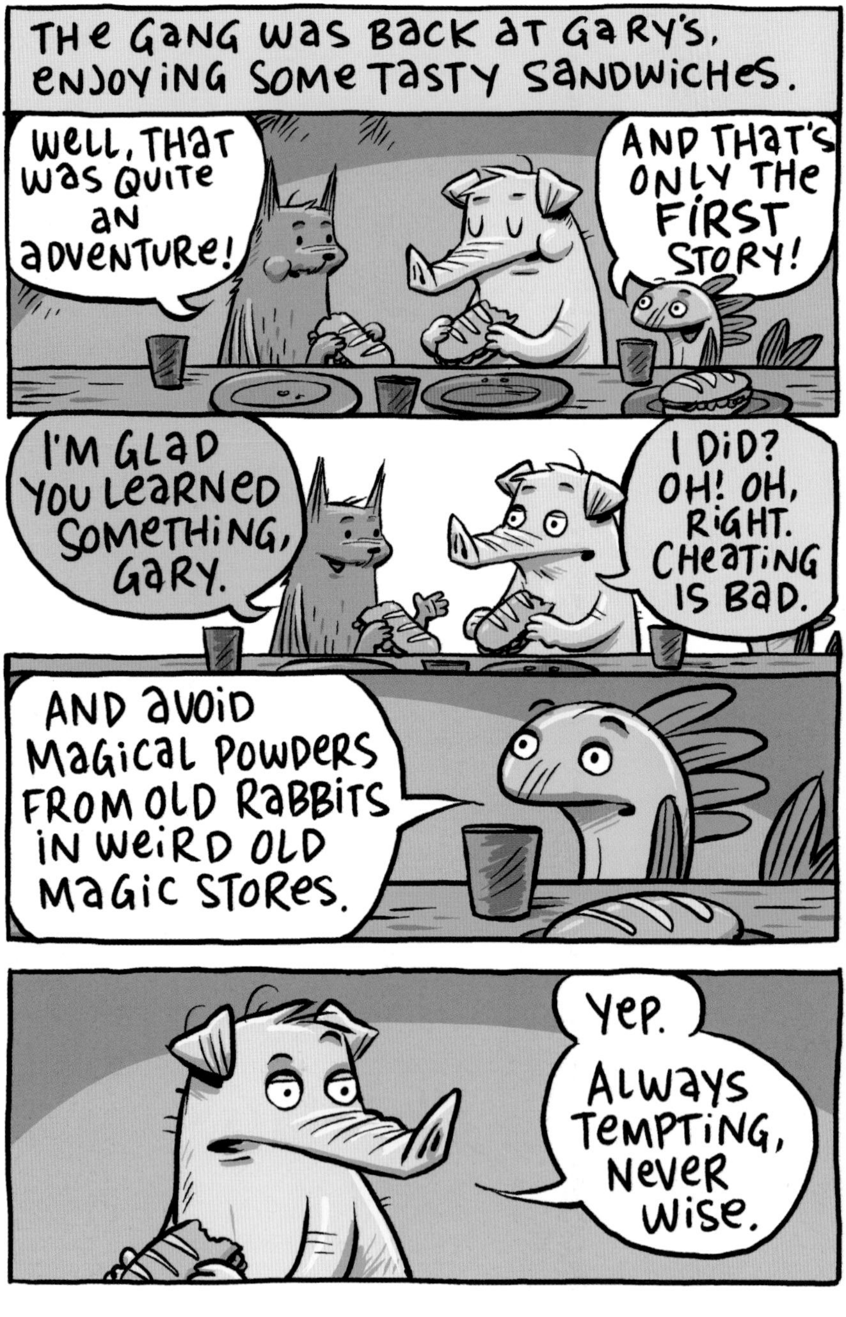
THE GANG WAS BACK AT GARY'S, ENJOYING SOME TASTY SANDWICHES.
WELL, THAT WAS QUITE AN ADVENTURE!
AND THAT'S ONLY THE FIRST STORY!
I'M GLAD YOU LEARNED SOMETHING, GARY.
I DID? OH! OH, RIGHT. CHEATING IS BAD.
AND AVOID MAGICAL POWDERS FROM OLD RABBITS IN WEIRD OLD MAGIC STORES.
YEP.
ALWAYS TEMPTING, NEVER WISE.

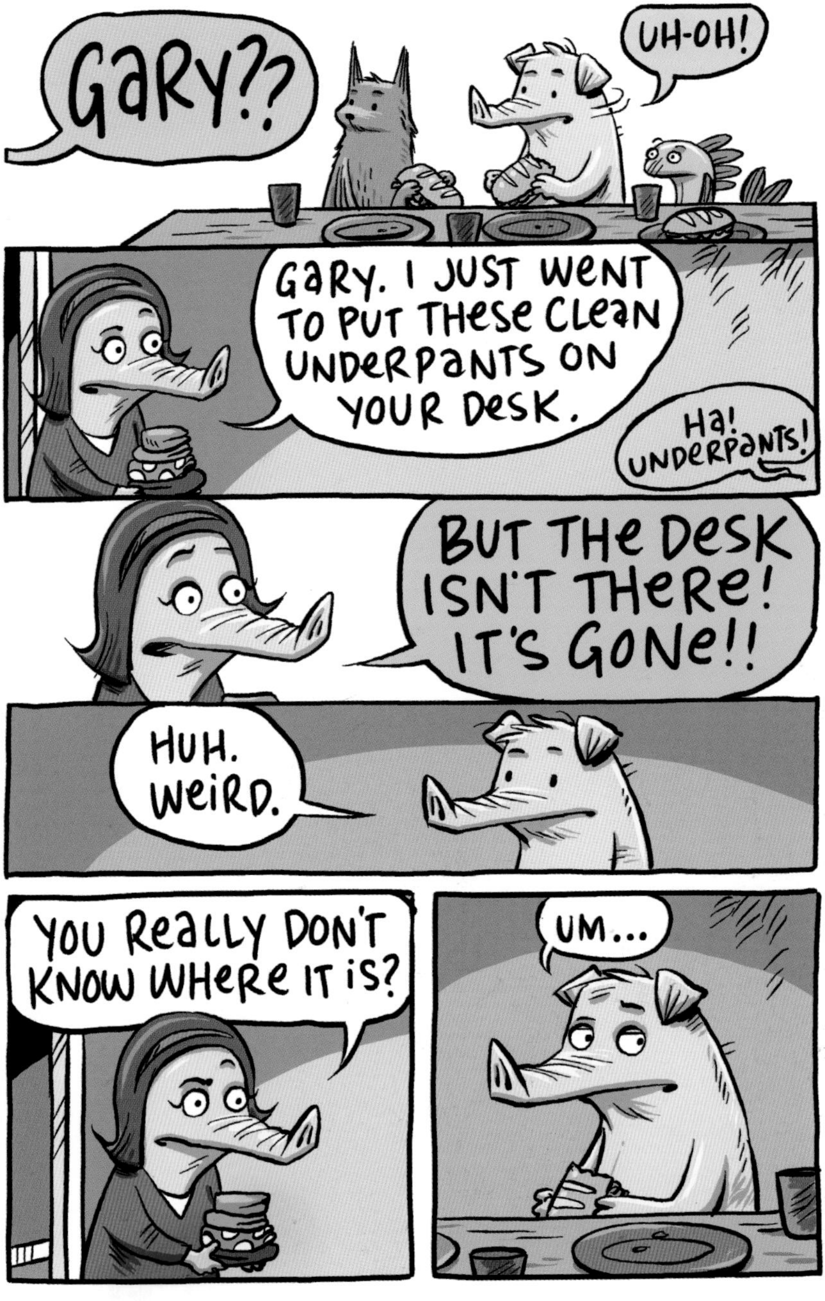
GARY??
UH-OH!
GARY. I JUST WENT TO PUT THESE CLEAN UNDERPANTS ON YOUR DESK.
HA! UNDERPANTS!
BUT THE DESK ISN'T THERE! IT'S GONE!!
HUH. WEIRD.
YOU REALLY DON'T KNOW WHERE IT IS?
UM...

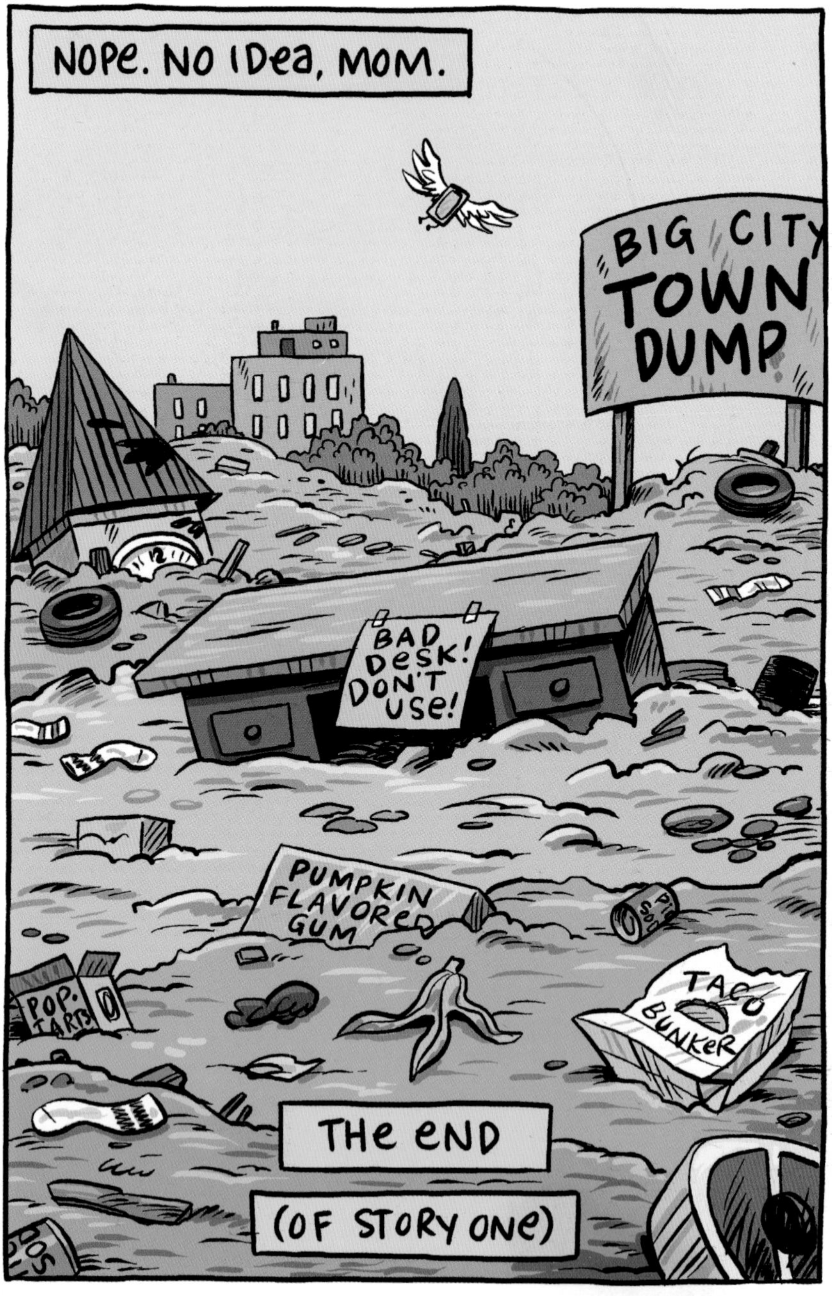
NOPE. NO IDEA, MOM.
BIG CITY TOWN DUMP
BAD DESK! DON'T USE!
PUMPKIN FLAVORED GUM
POP-TARTS
TACO BUNKER
THE END
(OF STORY ONE)

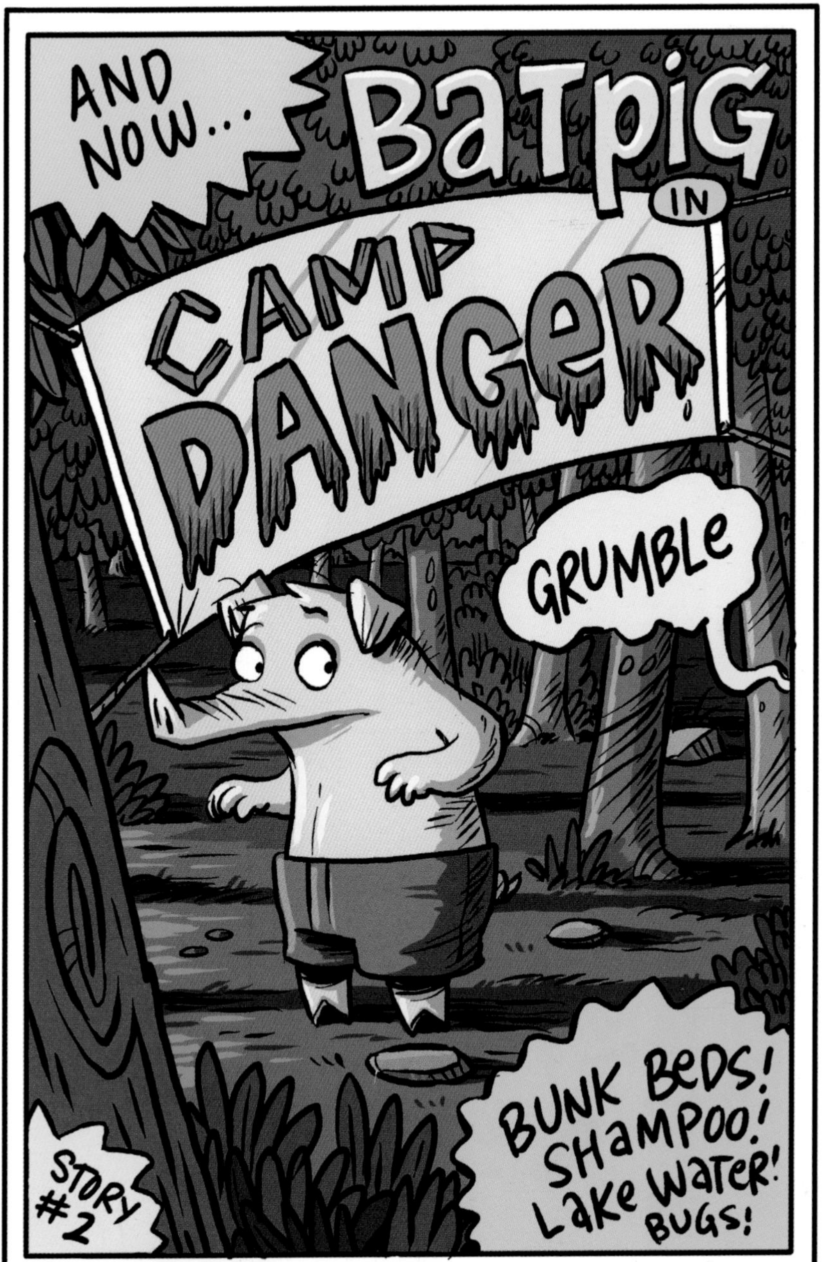
AND NOW...
BATPIG
IN
CAMP DANGER
GRUMBLE
BUNK BEDS!
SHAMPOO!
LAKE WATER!
BUGS!
STORY #2

CHAPTER ONE

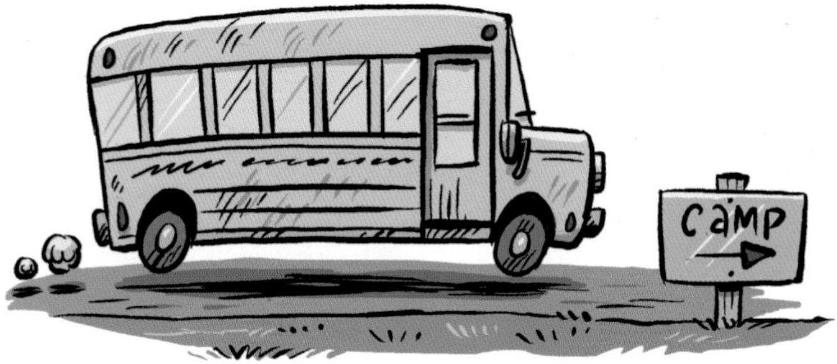
CAMP

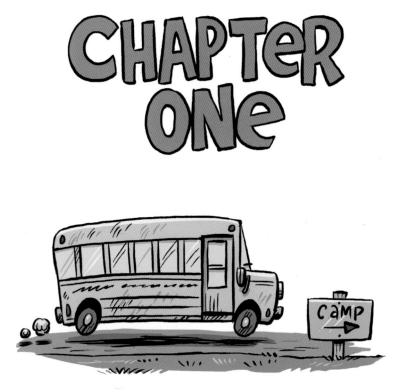

"YOU KNOW WHAT THEY SAY ABOUT THE WHEELS ON THE BUS"

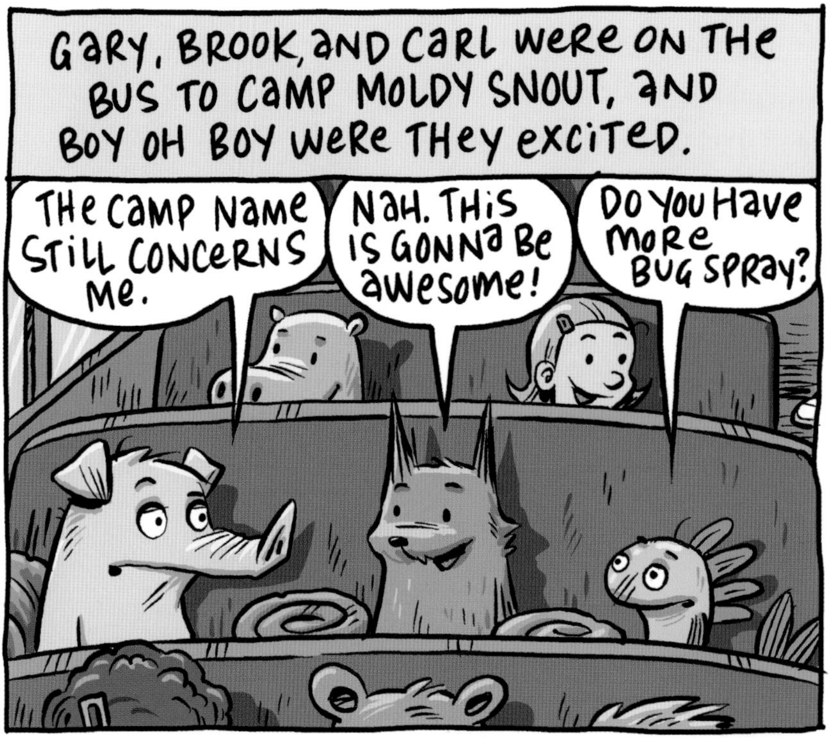
GARY, BROOK, AND CARL WERE ON THE BUS TO CAMP MOLDY SNOUT, AND BOY OH BOY WERE THEY EXCITED.
THE CAMP NAME STILL CONCERNS ME.
NAH. THIS IS GONNA BE AWESOME!
DO YOU HAVE MORE BUG SPRAY?

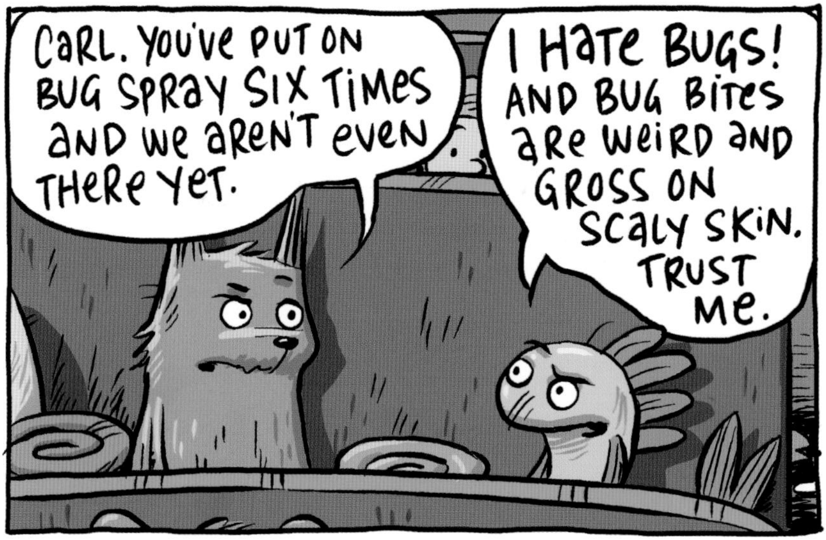
CARL. YOU'VE PUT ON BUG SPRAY SIX TIMES AND WE AREN'T EVEN THERE YET.
I HATE BUGS! AND BUG BITES ARE WEIRD AND GROSS ON SCALY SKIN. TRUST ME.

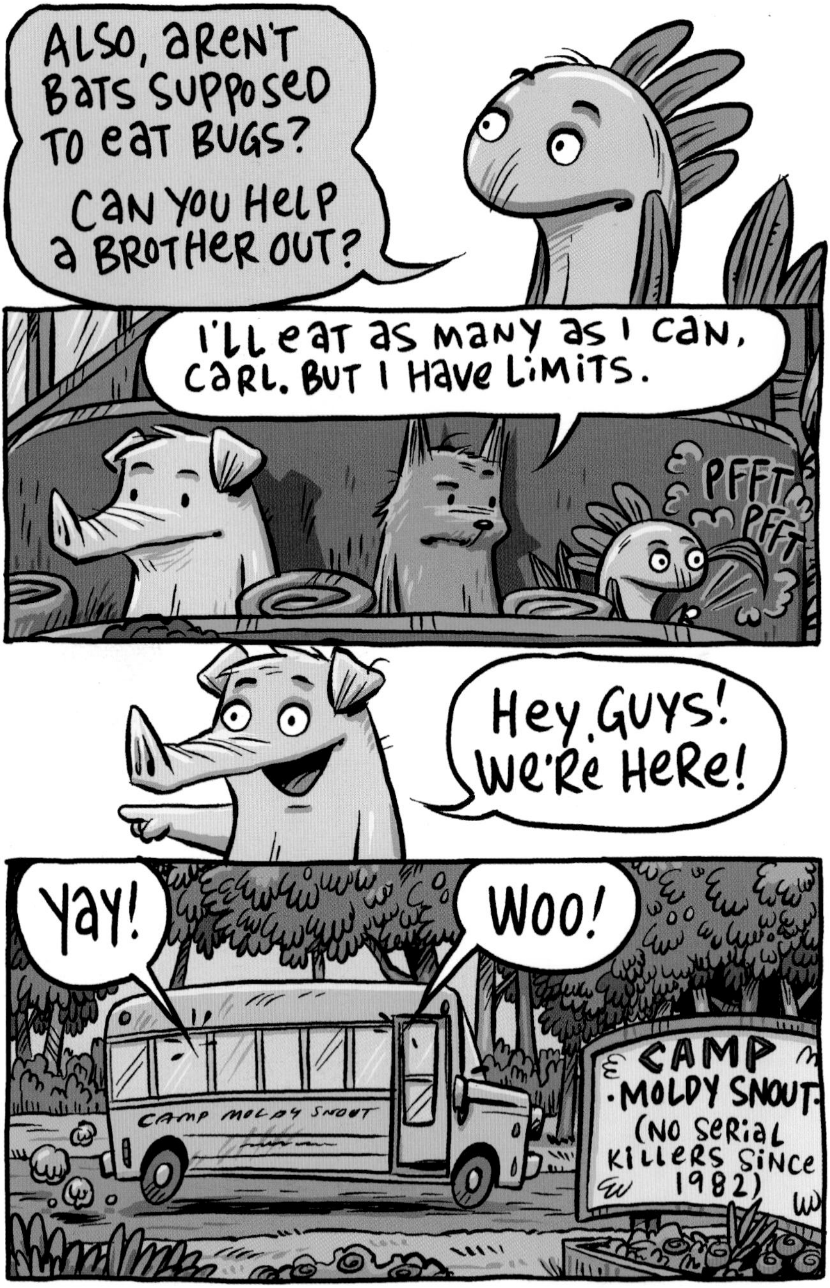
ALSO, AREN'T BATS SUPPOSED TO EAT BUGS?
CAN YOU HELP A BROTHER OUT?
I'LL EAT AS MANY AS I CAN, CARL. BUT I HAVE LIMITS.
PFFT PFFT
HEY, GUYS! WE'RE HERE!
YAY!
WOO!
CAMP MOLDY SNOUT
CAMP MOLDY SNOUT (NO SERIAL KILLERS SINCE 1982)

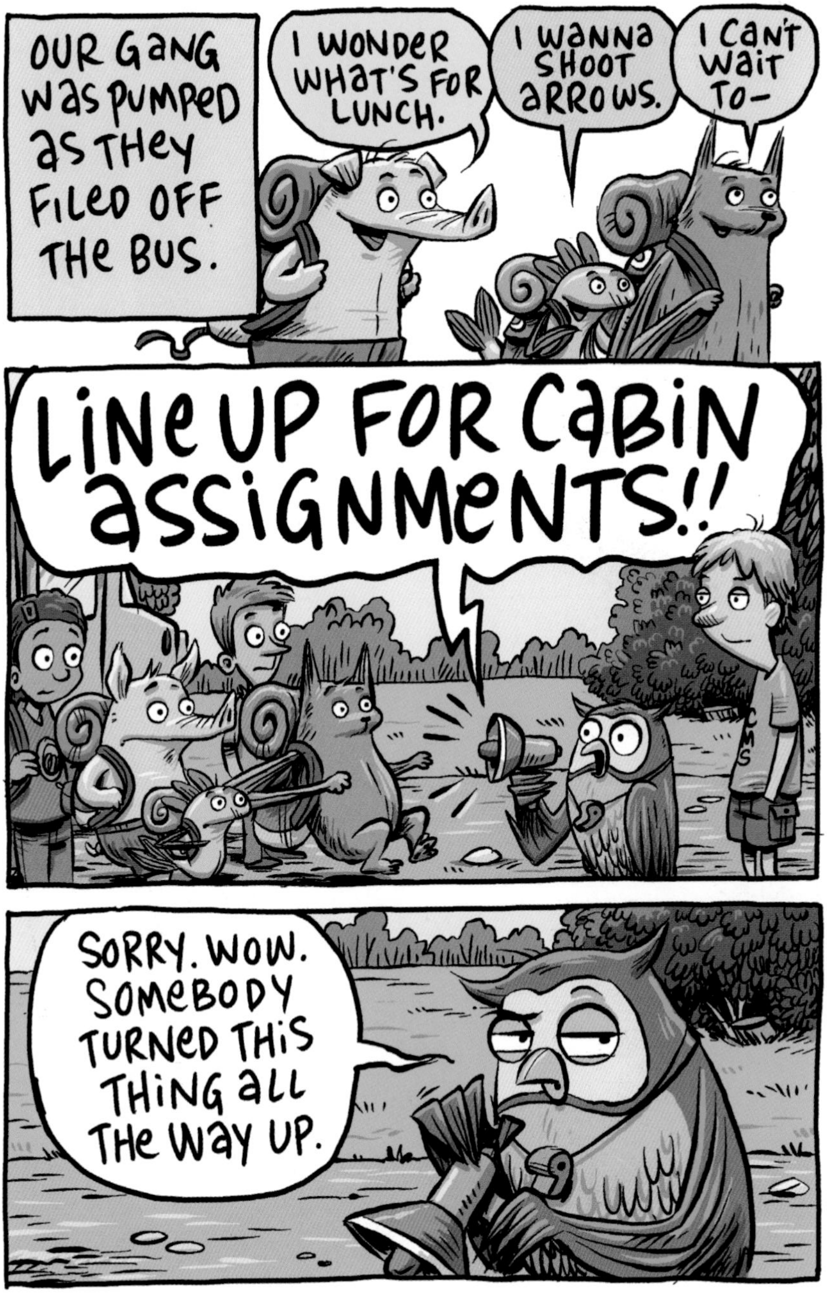
OUR GANG WAS PUMPED AS THEY FILED OFF THE BUS.
I WONDER WHAT'S FOR LUNCH.
I WANNA SHOOT ARROWS.
I CAN'T WAIT TO—
LINE UP FOR CABIN ASSIGNMENTS!!
SORRY. WOW. SOMEBODY TURNED THIS THING ALL THE WAY UP.

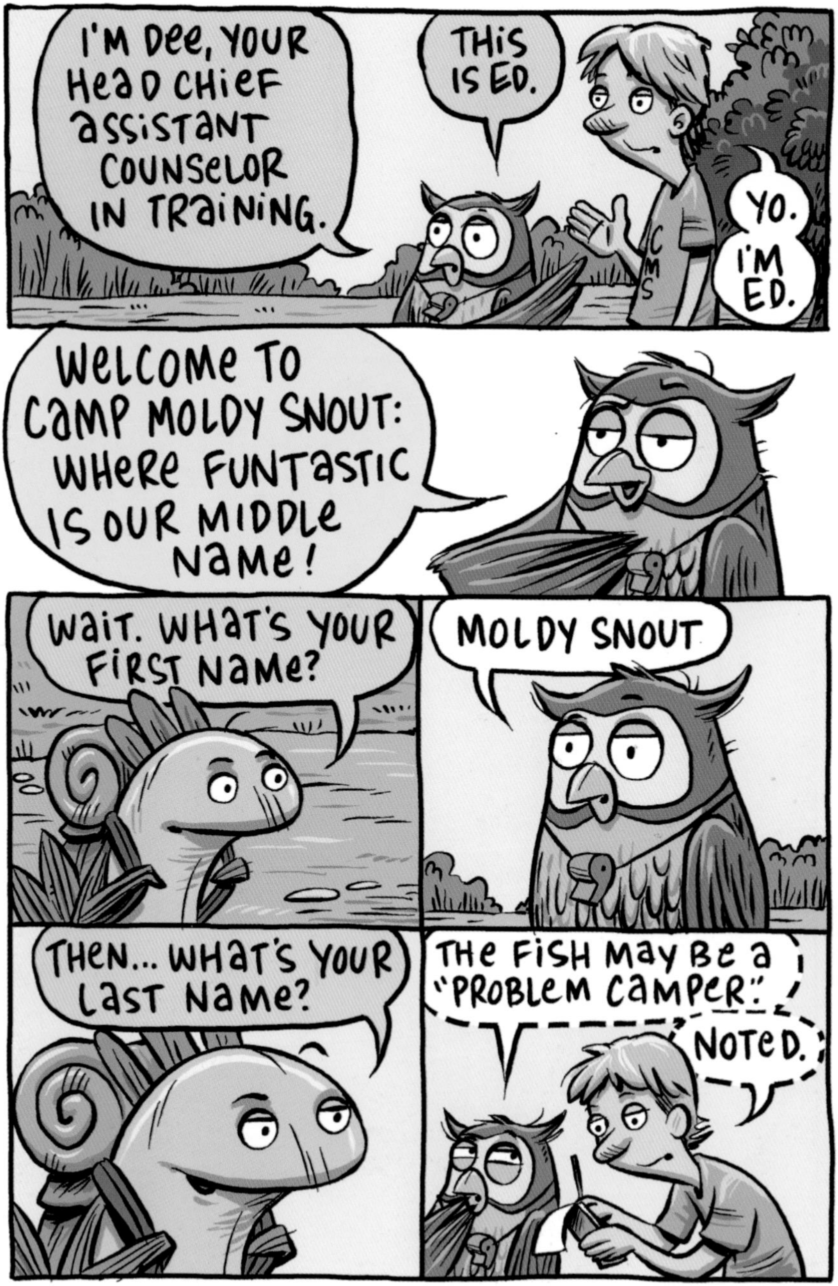
I'M DEE, YOUR HEAD CHIEF ASSISTANT COUNSELOR IN TRAINING.
THIS IS ED.
YO. I'M ED.
WELCOME TO CAMP MOLDY SNOUT: WHERE FUNTASTIC IS OUR MIDDLE NAME!
WAIT. WHAT'S YOUR FIRST NAME?
MOLDY SNOUT
THEN... WHAT'S YOUR LAST NAME?
THE FISH MAY BE A "PROBLEM CAMPER."
NOTED.

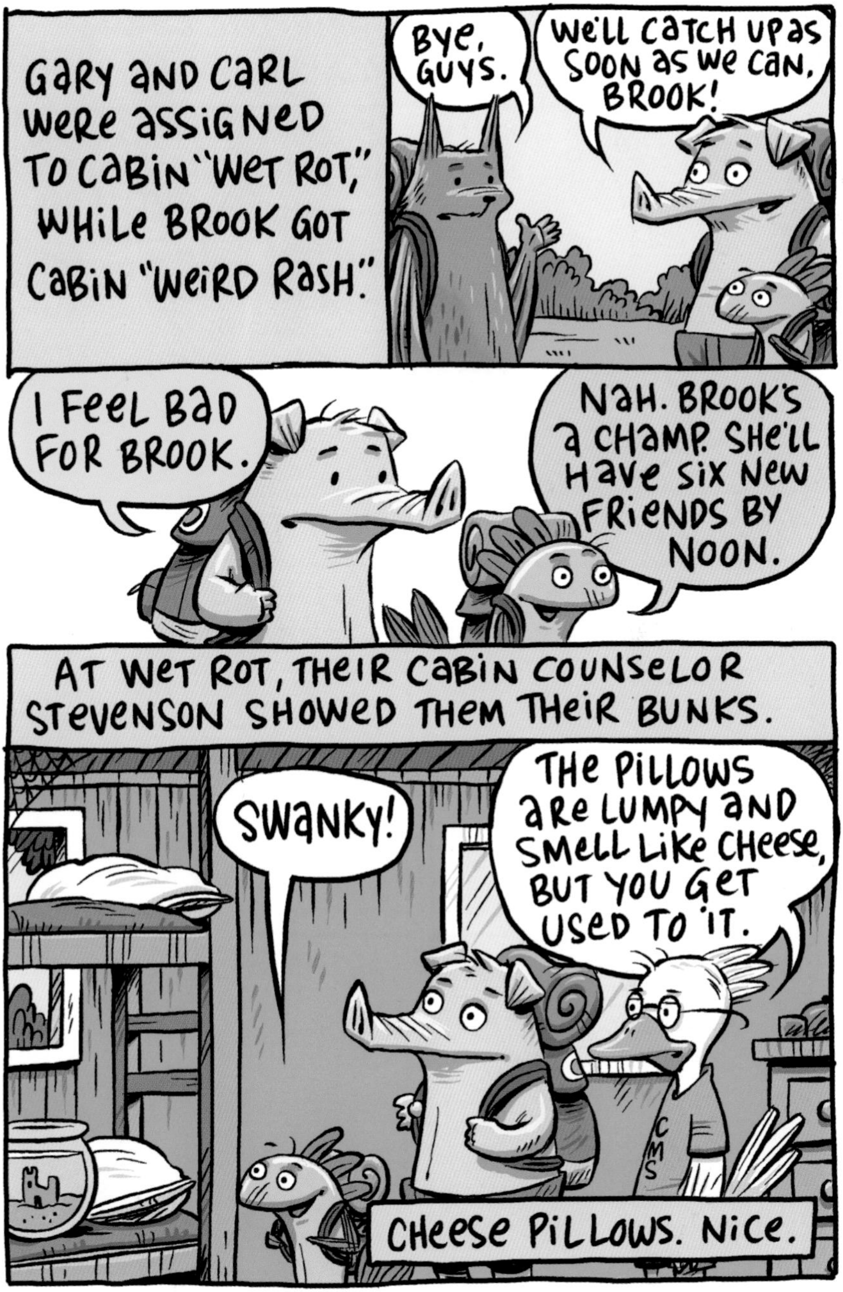

Gary and Carl were assigned to cabin "Wet Rot," while Brook got cabin "Weird Rash."
Bye, guys.
We'll catch up as soon as we can, Brook!
I feel bad for Brook.
Nah. Brook's a champ. She'll have six new friends by noon.
At Wet Rot, their cabin counselor Stevenson showed them their bunks.
Swanky!
The pillows are lumpy and smell like cheese, but you get used to it.
CMS
Cheese pillows. Nice.

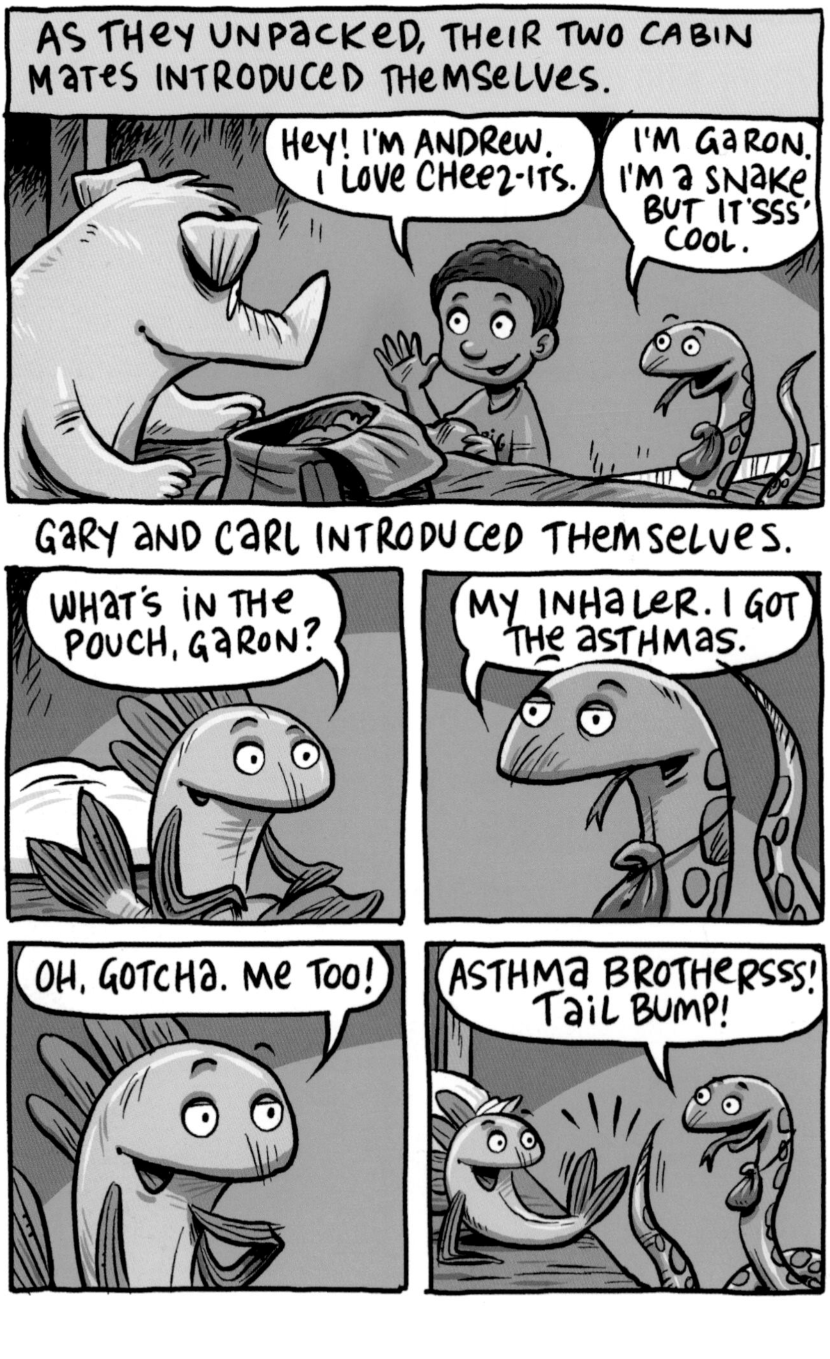
AS THEY UNPACKED, THEIR TWO CABIN MATES INTRODUCED THEMSELVES.
HEY! I'M ANDREW. I LOVE CHEEZ-ITS.
I'M GARON. I'M A SNAKE BUT IT'SSS' COOL.
GARY AND CARL INTRODUCED THEMSELVES.
WHAT'S IN THE POUCH, GARON?
MY INHALER. I GOT THE ASTHMAS.
OH, GOTCHA. ME TOO!
ASTHMA BROTHERSSS! TAIL BUMP!

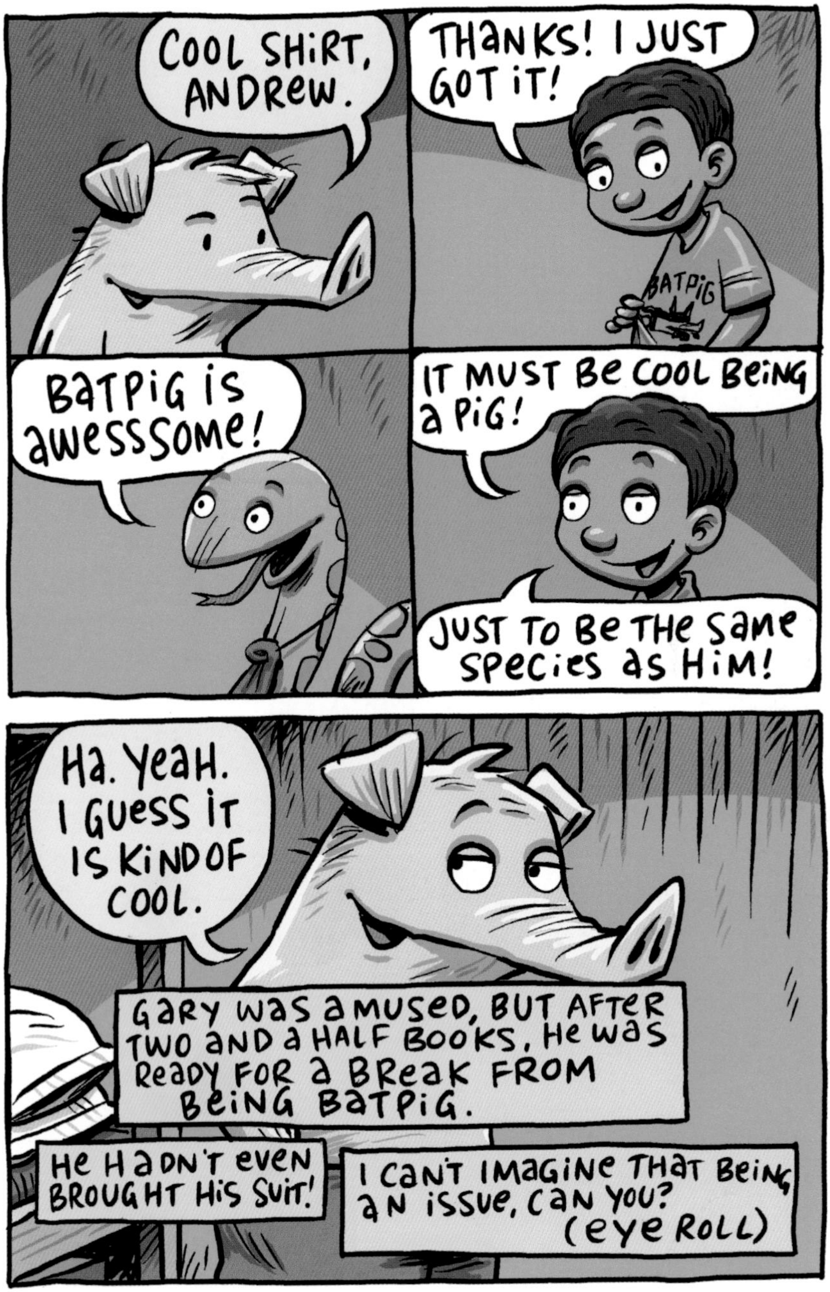
COOL SHIRT, ANDREW.
THANKS! I JUST GOT IT!
BATPIG
BATPIG IS AWESSSOME!
IT MUST BE COOL BEING A PIG!
JUST TO BE THE SAME SPECIES AS HIM!
HA. YEAH. I GUESS IT IS KIND OF COOL.
GARY WAS AMUSED, BUT AFTER TWO AND A HALF BOOKS, HE WAS READY FOR A BREAK FROM BEING BATPIG.
HE HADN'T EVEN BROUGHT HIS SUIT!
I CAN'T IMAGINE THAT BEING AN ISSUE, CAN YOU? (EYE ROLL)

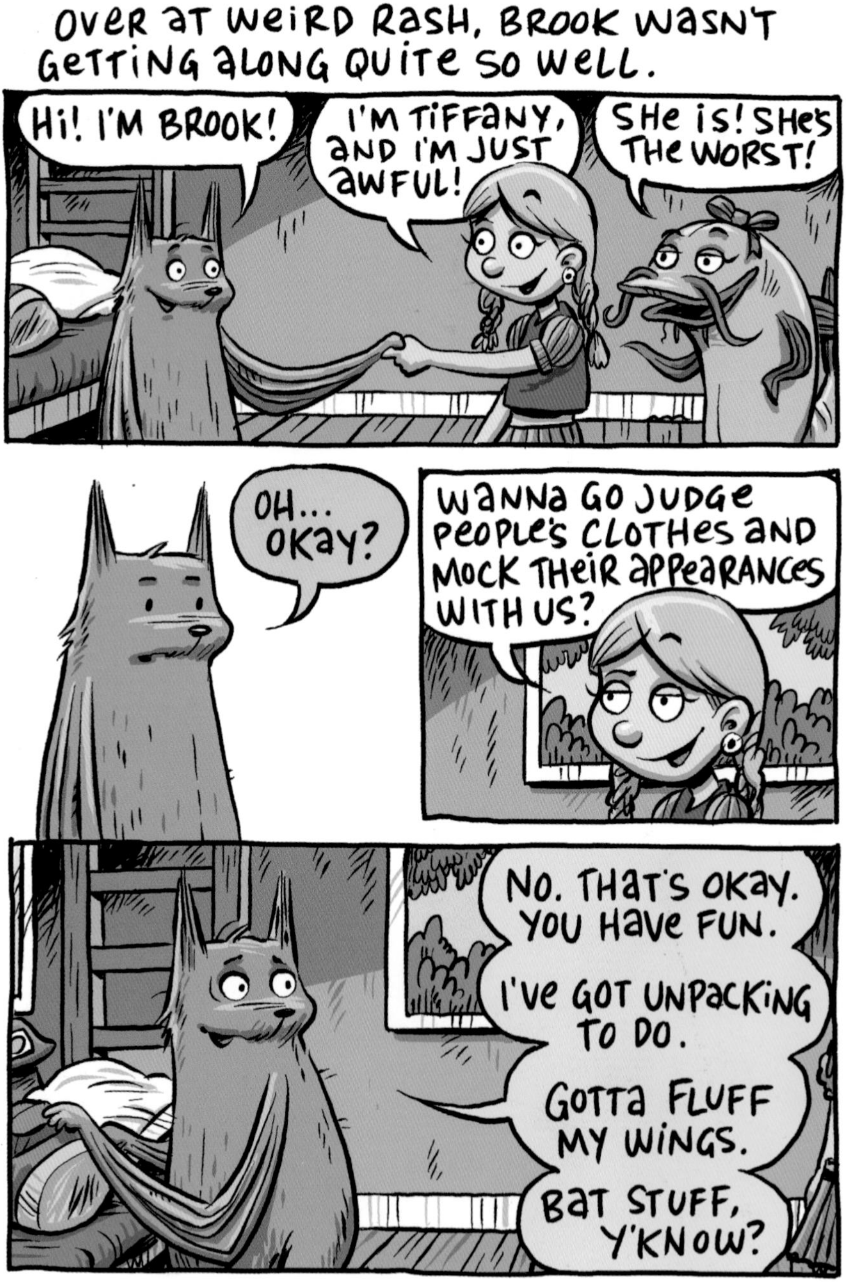
OVER AT WEIRD RASH, BROOK WASN'T GETTING ALONG QUITE SO WELL.
HI! I'M BROOK!
I'M TIFFANY, AND I'M JUST AWFUL!
SHE IS! SHE'S THE WORST!
OH... OKAY?
WANNA GO JUDGE PEOPLE'S CLOTHES AND MOCK THEIR APPEARANCES WITH US?
NO. THAT'S OKAY. YOU HAVE FUN.
I'VE GOT UNPACKING TO DO.
GOTTA FLUFF MY WINGS.
BAT STUFF, Y'KNOW?

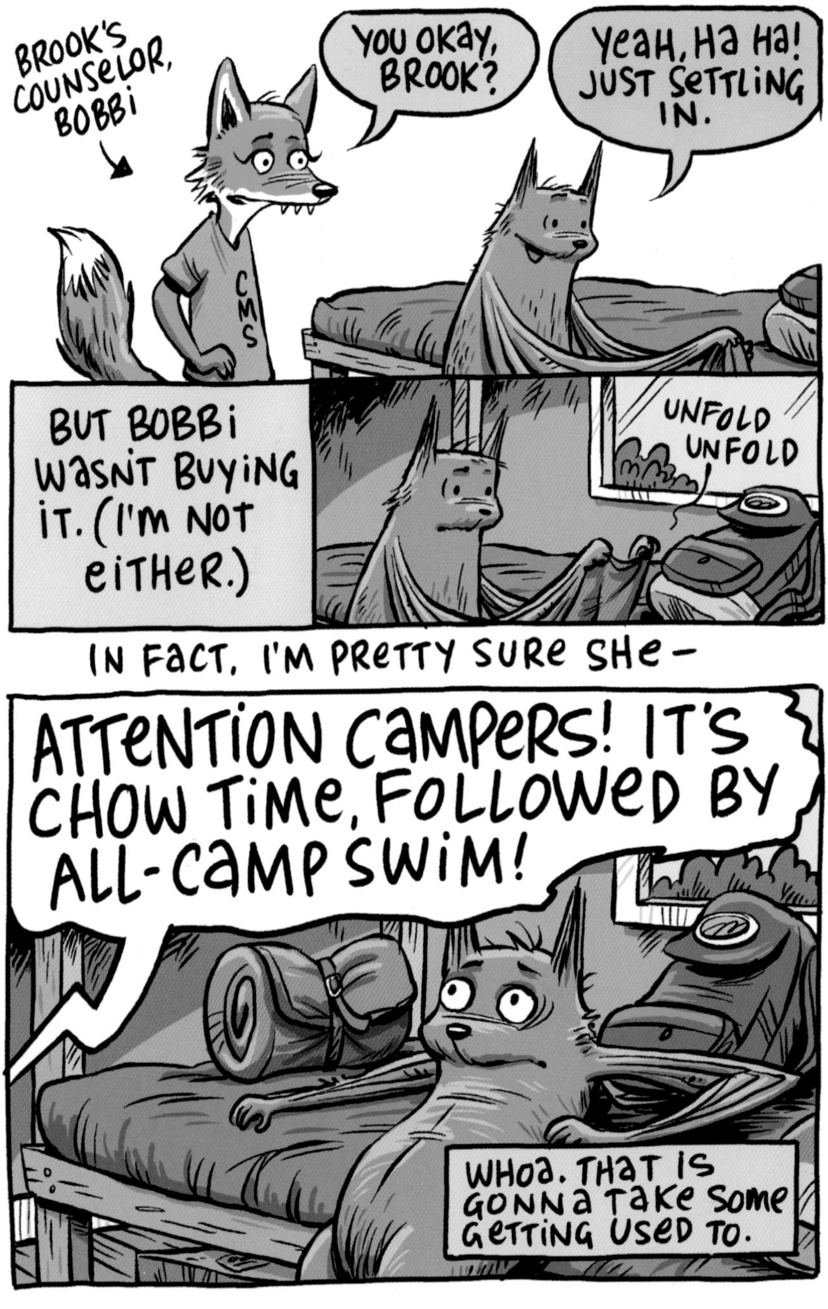
BROOK'S COUNSELOR, BOBBI
YOU OKAY, BROOK?
YEAH, HA HA! JUST SETTLING IN.
BUT BOBBI WASNT BUYING IT. (I'M NOT EITHER.)
UNFOLD UNFOLD
IN FACT, I'M PRETTY SURE SHE—
ATTENTION CAMPERS! IT'S CHOW TIME, FOLLOWED BY ALL-CAMP SWIM!
WHOA. THAT IS GONNA TAKE SOME GETTING USED TO.

CHAPTER TWO

OH, YEAH.
THAT'S THE
STUFF.

"SPLISH SPLASH"

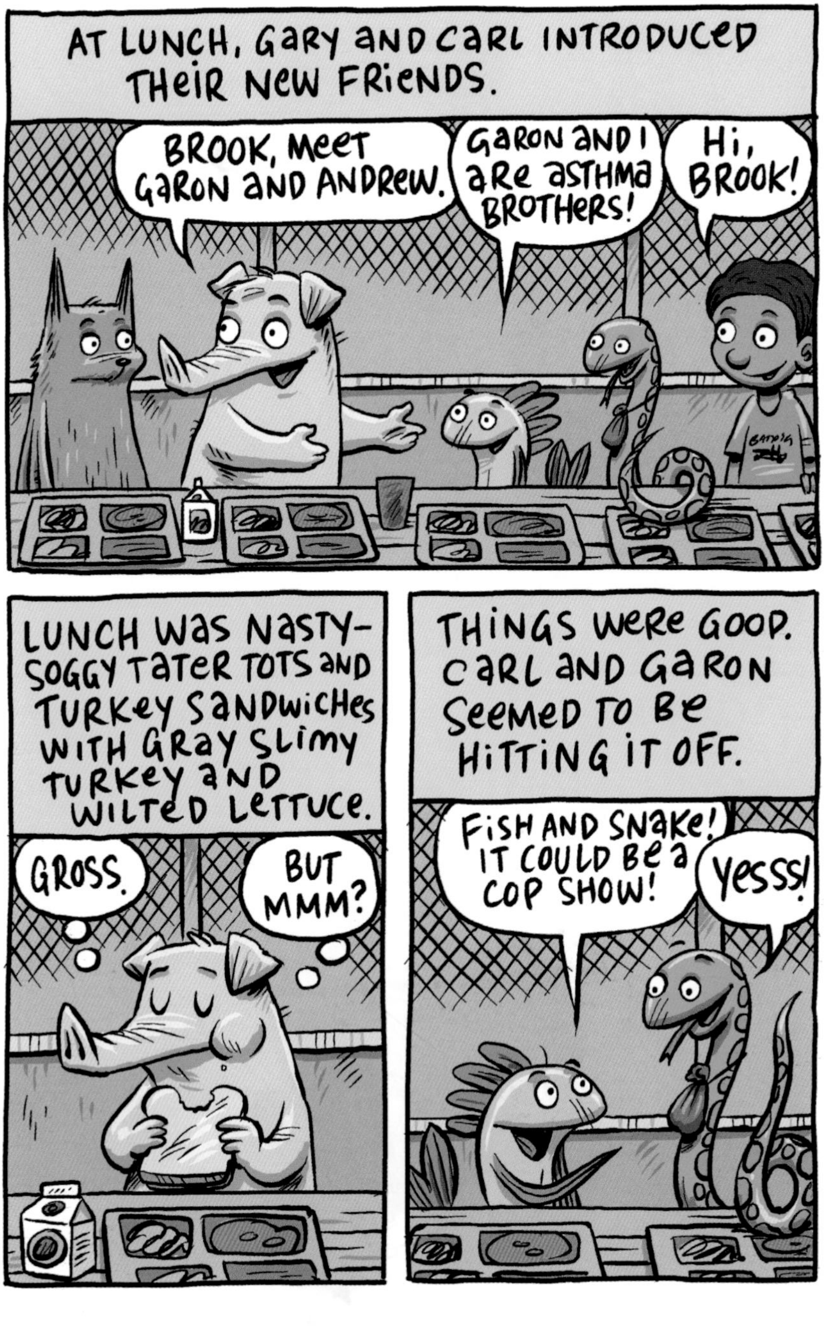
AT LUNCH, GARY AND CARL INTRODUCED THEIR NEW FRIENDS.
BROOK, MEET GARON AND ANDREW.
GARON AND I ARE ASTHMA BROTHERS!
HI, BROOK!
LUNCH WAS NASTY-SOGGY TATER TOTS AND TURKEY SANDWICHES WITH GRAY SLIMY TURKEY AND WILTED LETTUCE.
GROSS.
BUT MMM?
THINGS WERE GOOD. CARL AND GARON SEEMED TO BE HITTING IT OFF.
FISH AND SNAKE! IT COULD BE A COP SHOW!
YESSS!

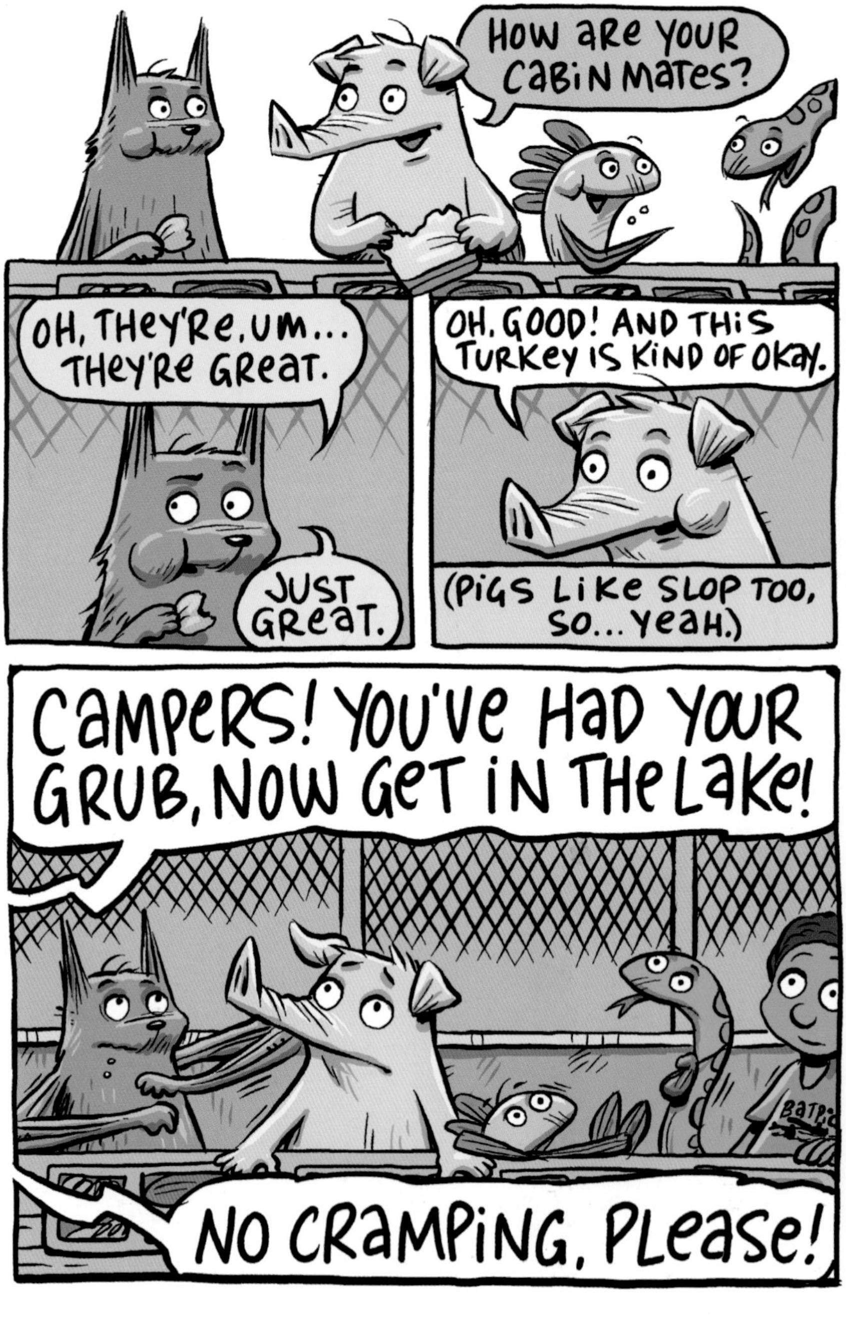
HOW ARE YOUR CABIN MATES?
OH, THEY'RE, UM... THEY'RE GREAT.
JUST GREAT.
OH. GOOD! AND THIS TURKEY IS KIND OF OKAY.
(PIGS LIKE SLOP TOO, SO... YEAH.)
CAMPERS! YOU'VE HAD YOUR GRUB, NOW GET IN THE LAKE!
NO CRAMPING, PLEASE!

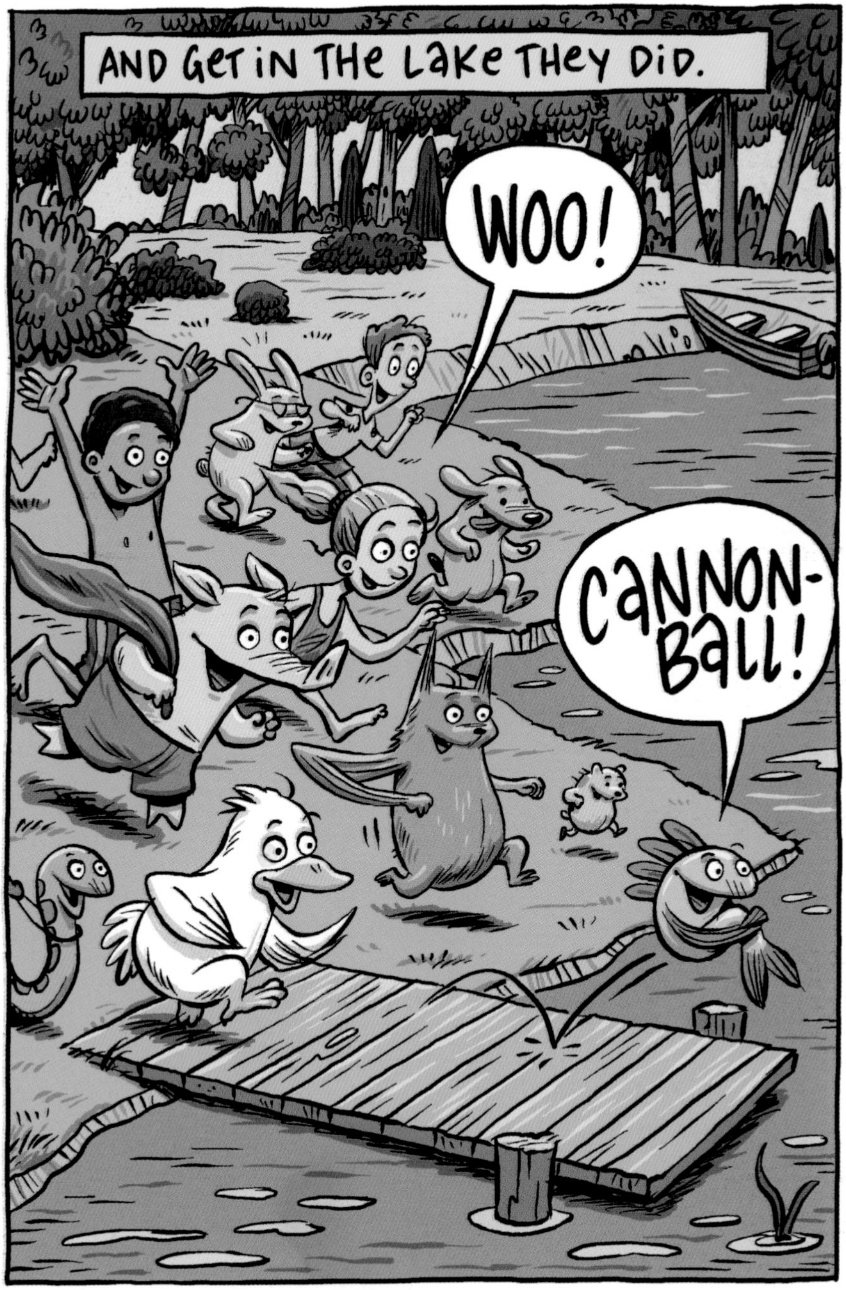
AND GET IN THE LAKE THEY DID.
WOO!
CANNON-BALL!

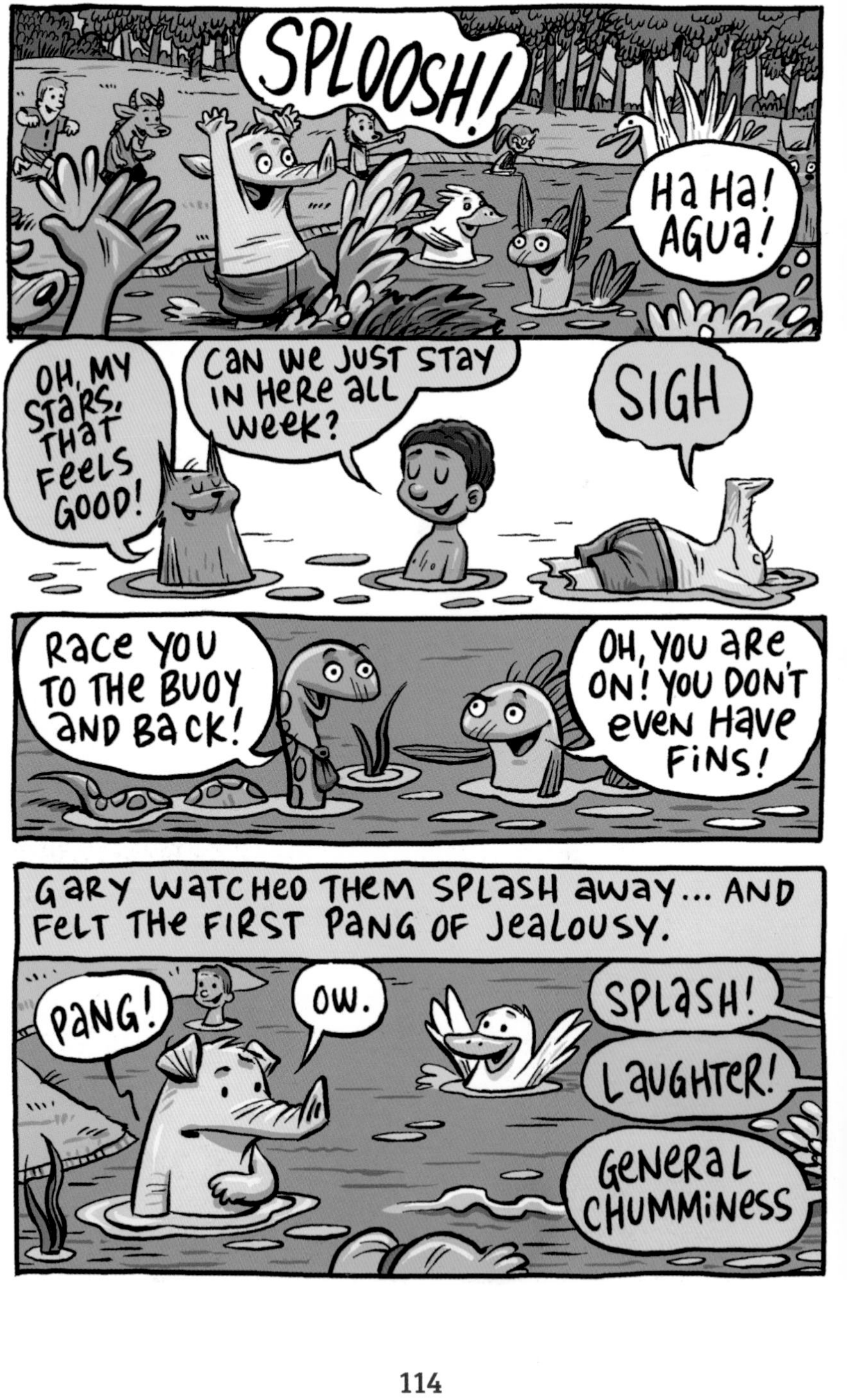
SPLOOSH!
Ha Ha! AGUA!
OH, MY STARS, THAT FEELS GOOD!
CAN WE JUST STAY IN HERE ALL WEEK?
SIGH
RACE YOU TO THE BUOY AND BACK!
OH, YOU ARE ON! YOU DON'T EVEN HAVE FINS!
GARY WATCHED THEM SPLASH AWAY... AND FELT THE FIRST PANG OF JEALOUSY.
PANG!
OW.
SPLASH!
LAUGHTER!
GENERAL CHUMMINESS

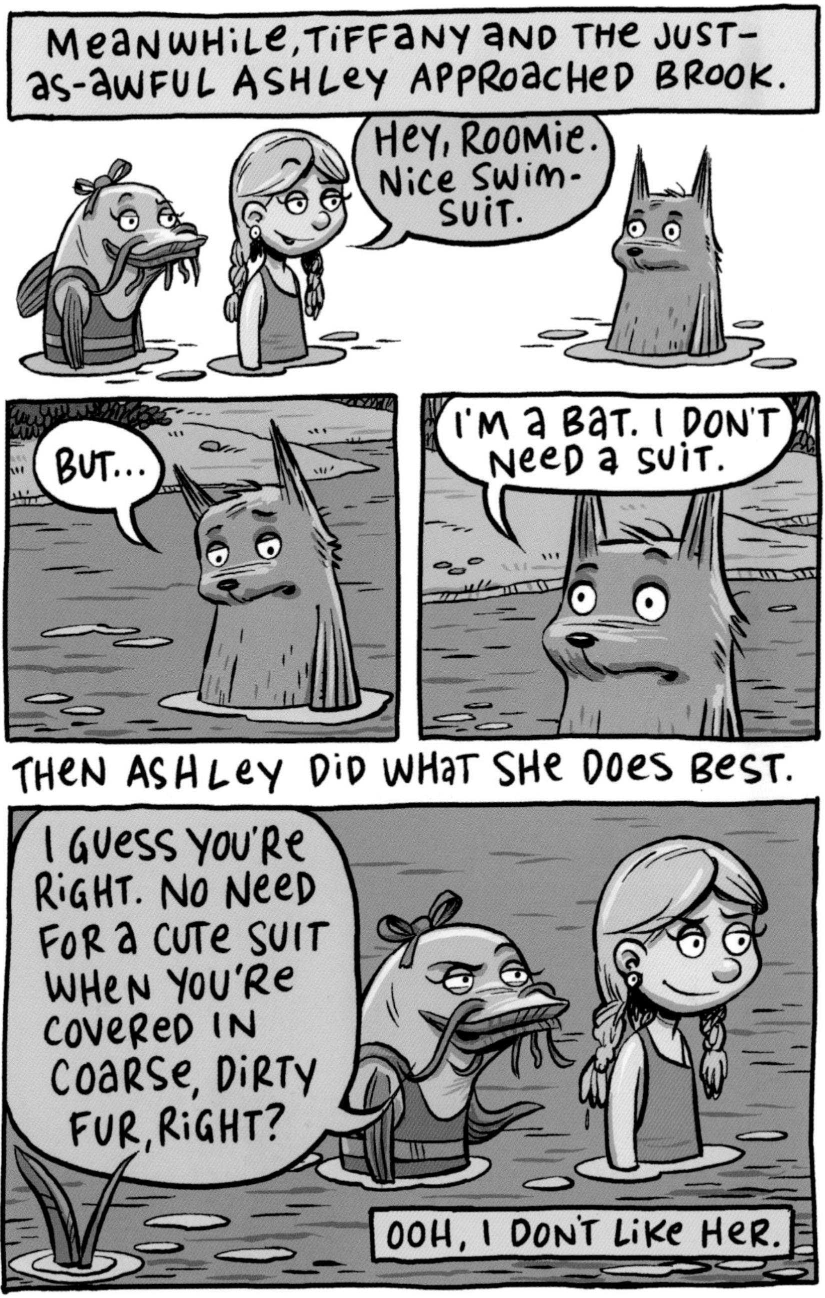
MEANWHILE, TIFFANY AND THE JUST-AS-AWFUL ASHLEY APPROACHED BROOK.
HEY, ROOMIE. NICE SWIM-SUIT.
BUT...
I'M A BAT. I DON'T NEED A SUIT.
THEN ASHLEY DID WHAT SHE DOES BEST.
I GUESS YOU'RE RIGHT. NO NEED FOR A CUTE SUIT WHEN YOU'RE COVERED IN COARSE, DIRTY FUR, RIGHT?
OOH, I DON'T LIKE HER.

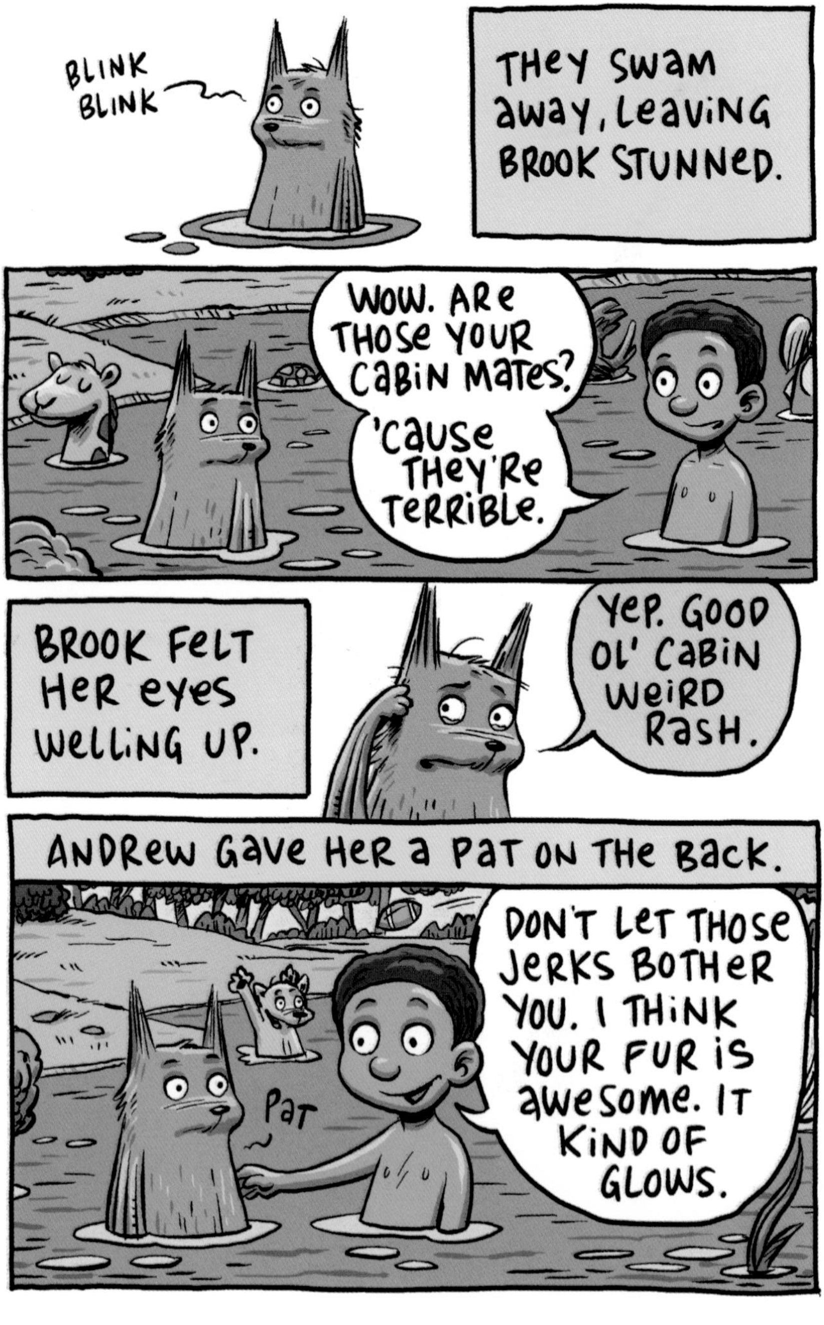
BLINK BLINK
THEY SWAM AWAY, LEAVING BROOK STUNNED.
WOW. ARE THOSE YOUR CABIN MATES?
'CAUSE THEY'RE TERRIBLE.
BROOK FELT HER EYES WELLING UP.
YEP. GOOD OL' CABIN WEIRD RASH.
ANDREW GAVE HER A PAT ON THE BACK.
PAT
DON'T LET THOSE JERKS BOTHER YOU. I THINK YOUR FUR IS AWESOME. IT KIND OF GLOWS.

THEN SOMETHING HAPPENED.

BROOK BLUSHED.

YOU COULD BARELY
SEE IT UNDER ALL
THAT BEAUTIFUL FUR.

BUT TRUST ME.
IT WAS A BLUSH.

CHAPTER THREE

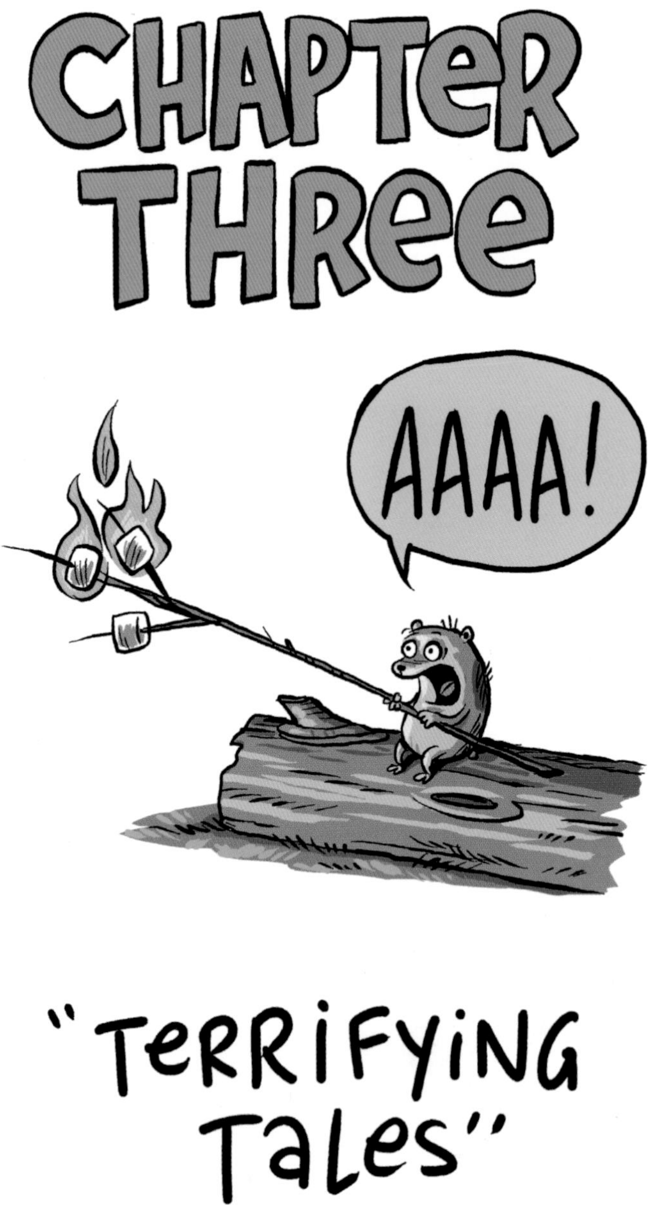
AAAA!

"TERRIFYING TALES"

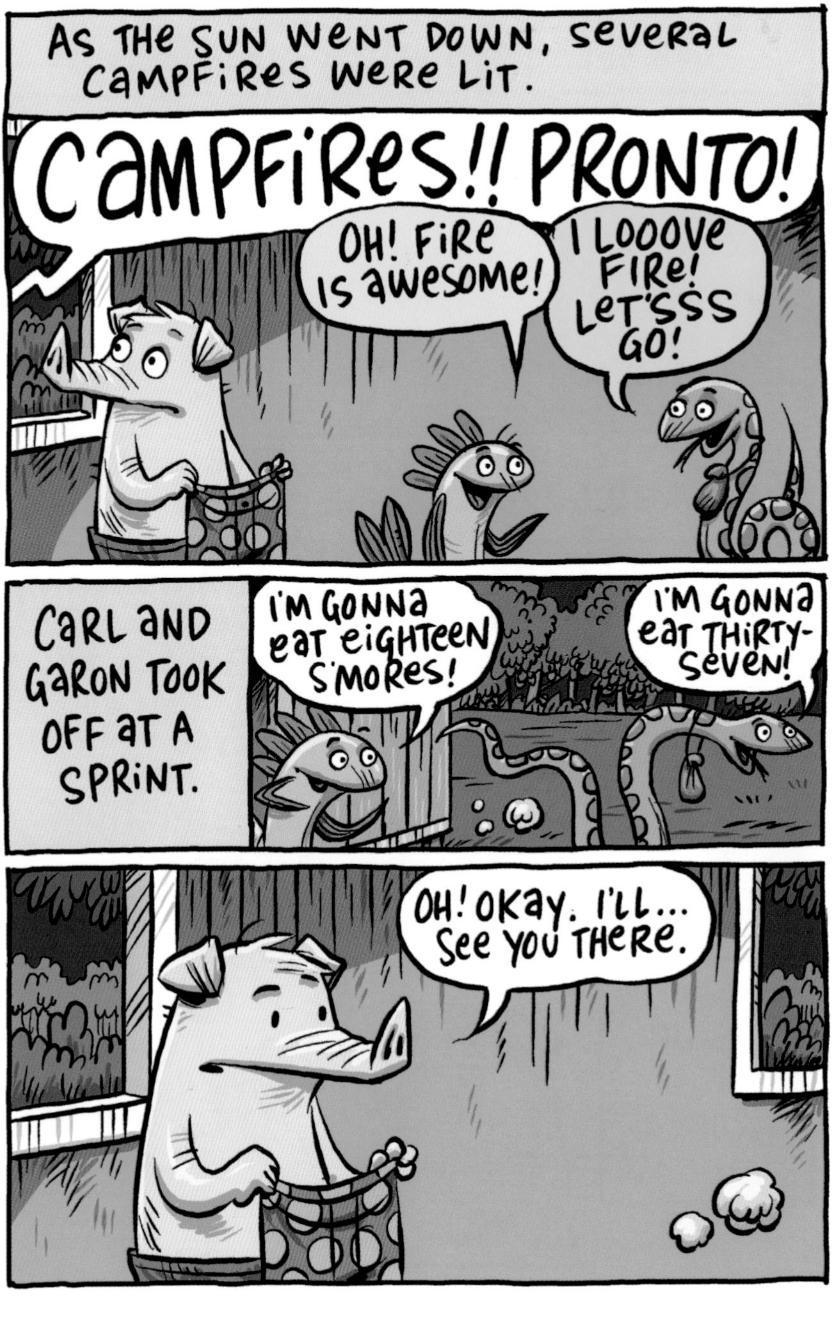
AS THE SUN WENT DOWN, SEVERAL CAMPFIRES WERE LIT.
CAMPFIRES!! PRONTO!
OH! FIRE IS AWESOME!
I LOOOVE FIRE! LET'SSS GO!
CARL AND GARON TOOK OFF AT A SPRINT.
I'M GONNA EAT EIGHTEEN S'MORES!
I'M GONNA EAT THIRTY-SEVEN!
OH! OKAY. I'LL... SEE YOU THERE.

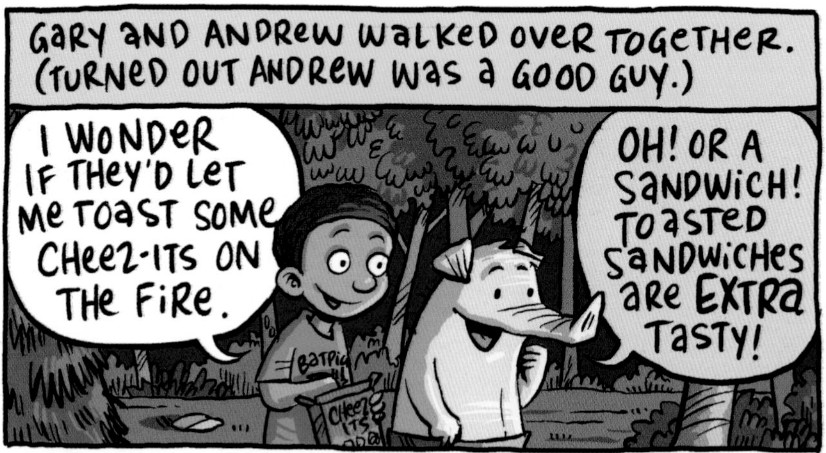
GARY AND ANDREW WALKED OVER TOGETHER. (TURNED OUT ANDREW WAS A GOOD GUY.)
I WONDER IF THEY'D LET ME TOAST SOME CHEEZ-ITS ON THE FIRE.
OH! OR A SANDWICH! TOASTED SANDWICHES ARE EXTRA TASTY!

BROOK'S CABIN WAS AT THE SAME FIRE, AND GARY WAS EXCITED TO SEE HER.

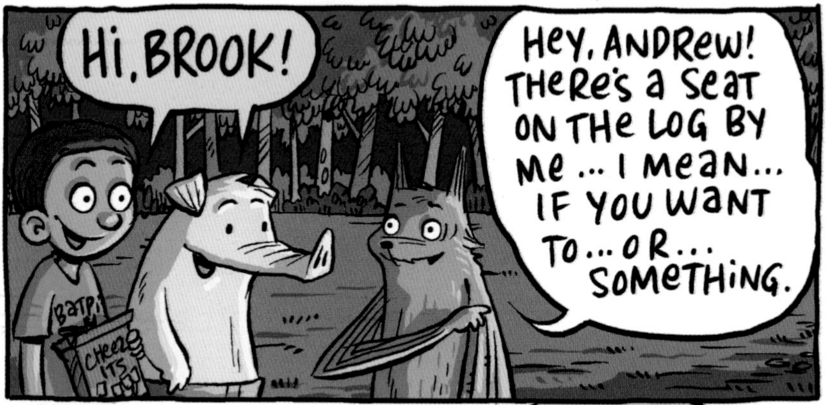
HI, BROOK!
HEY, ANDREW! THERE'S A SEAT ON THE LOG BY ME ... I MEAN... IF YOU WANT TO... OR... SOMETHING.

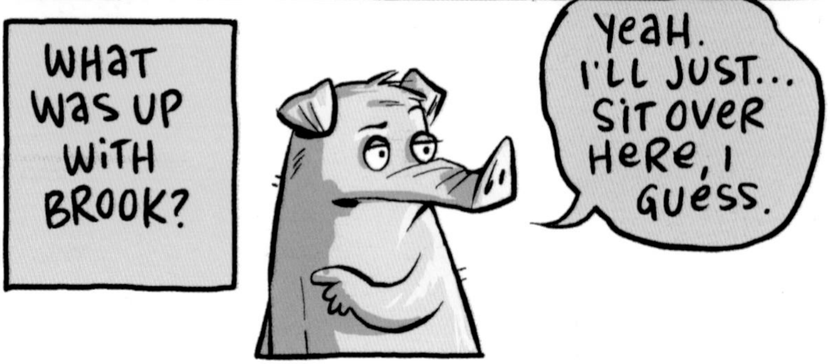
WHAT WAS UP WITH BROOK?
YEAH. I'LL JUST... SIT OVER HERE, I GUESS.

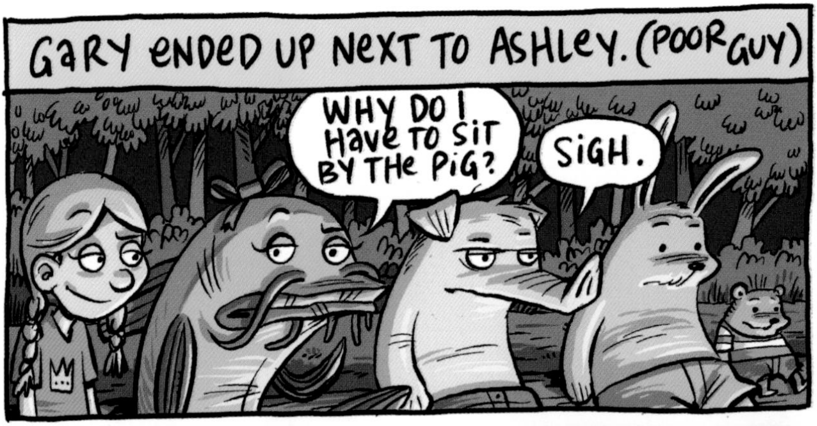
GARY ENDED UP NEXT TO ASHLEY. (POOR GUY)
WHY DO I HAVE TO SIT BY THE PIG?
SIGH.

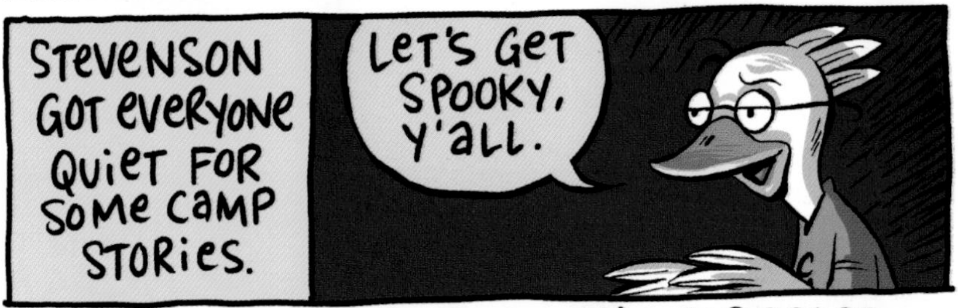
STEVENSON GOT EVERYONE QUIET FOR SOME CAMP STORIES.
LET'S GET SPOOKY, Y'ALL.

HE TOLD A FEW OF THE CLASSICS.

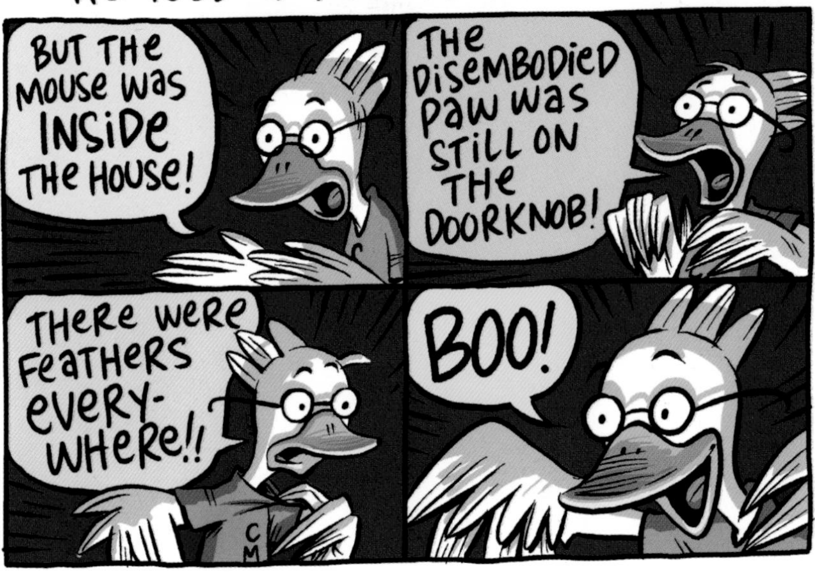
BUT THE MOUSE WAS INSIDE THE HOUSE!
THE DISEMBODIED PAW WAS STILL ON THE DOORKNOB!
THERE WERE FEATHERS EVERY-WHERE!!
BOO!

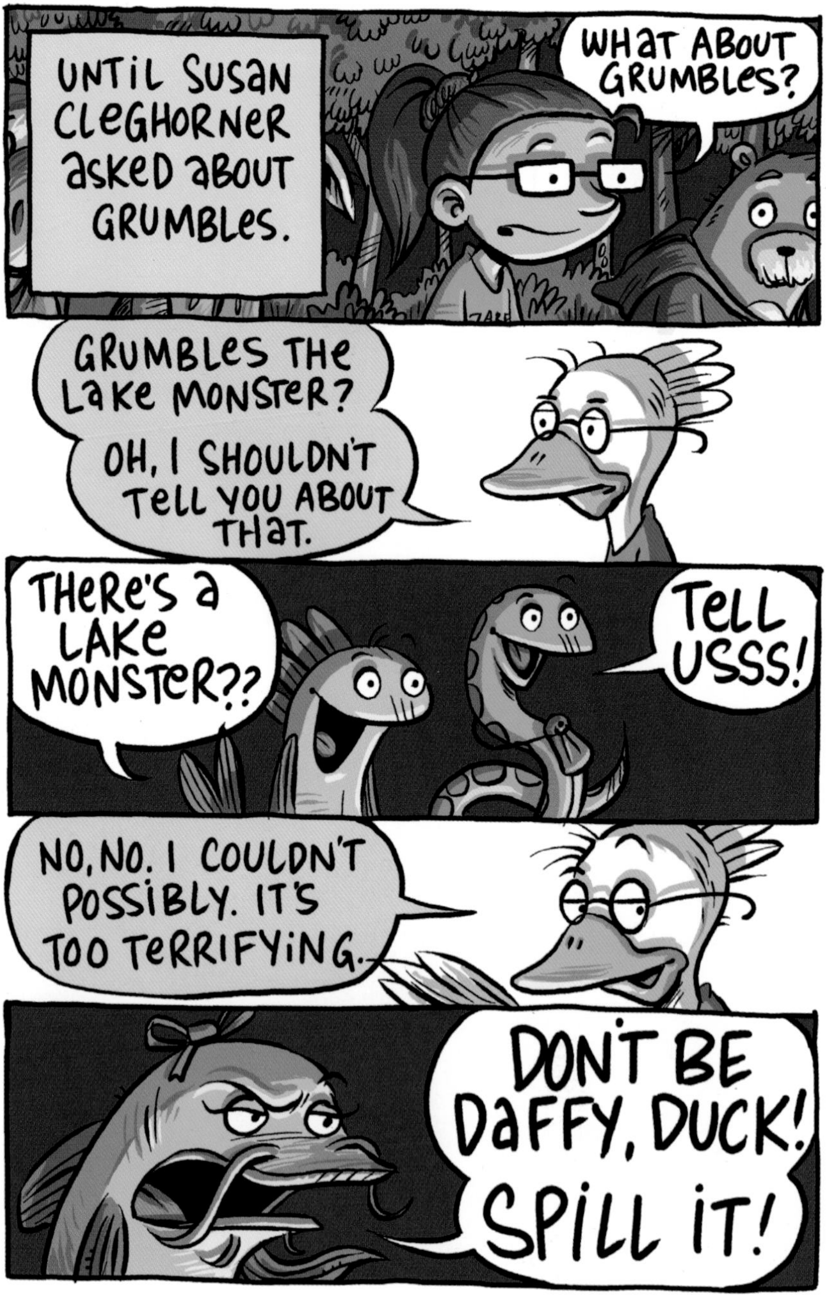
UNTIL SUSAN CLEGHORNER ASKED ABOUT GRUMBLES.
WHAT ABOUT GRUMBLES?
GRUMBLES THE LAKE MONSTER?
OH, I SHOULDN'T TELL YOU ABOUT THAT.
THERE'S A LAKE MONSTER??
TELL USSS!
NO, NO. I COULDN'T POSSIBLY. IT'S TOO TERRIFYING.
DON'T BE DAFFY, DUCK!
SPILL IT!

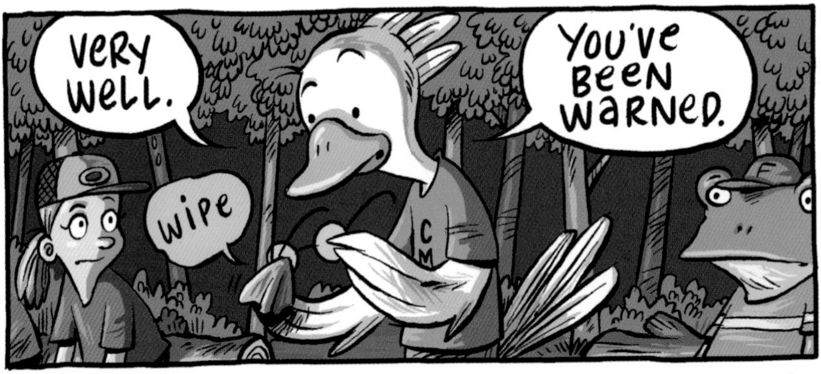
Very well.
wipe
You've been warned.

STORY IN A STORY WARNING!

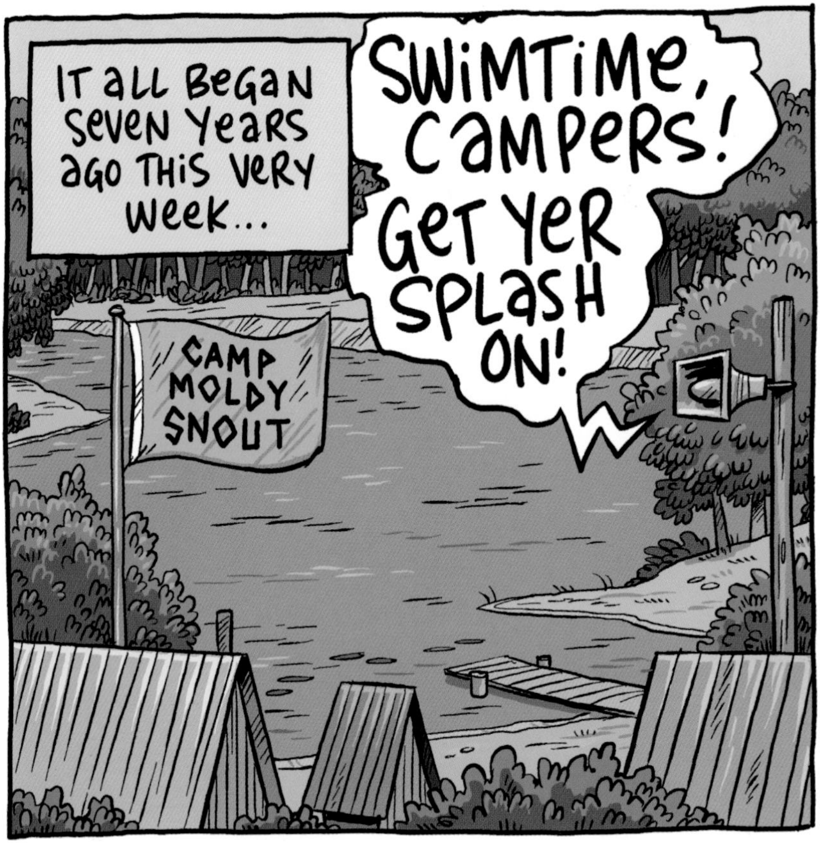
It all began seven years ago this very week...
SWIMTIME, CAMPERS! GET YER SPLASH ON!
CAMP MOLDY SNOUT

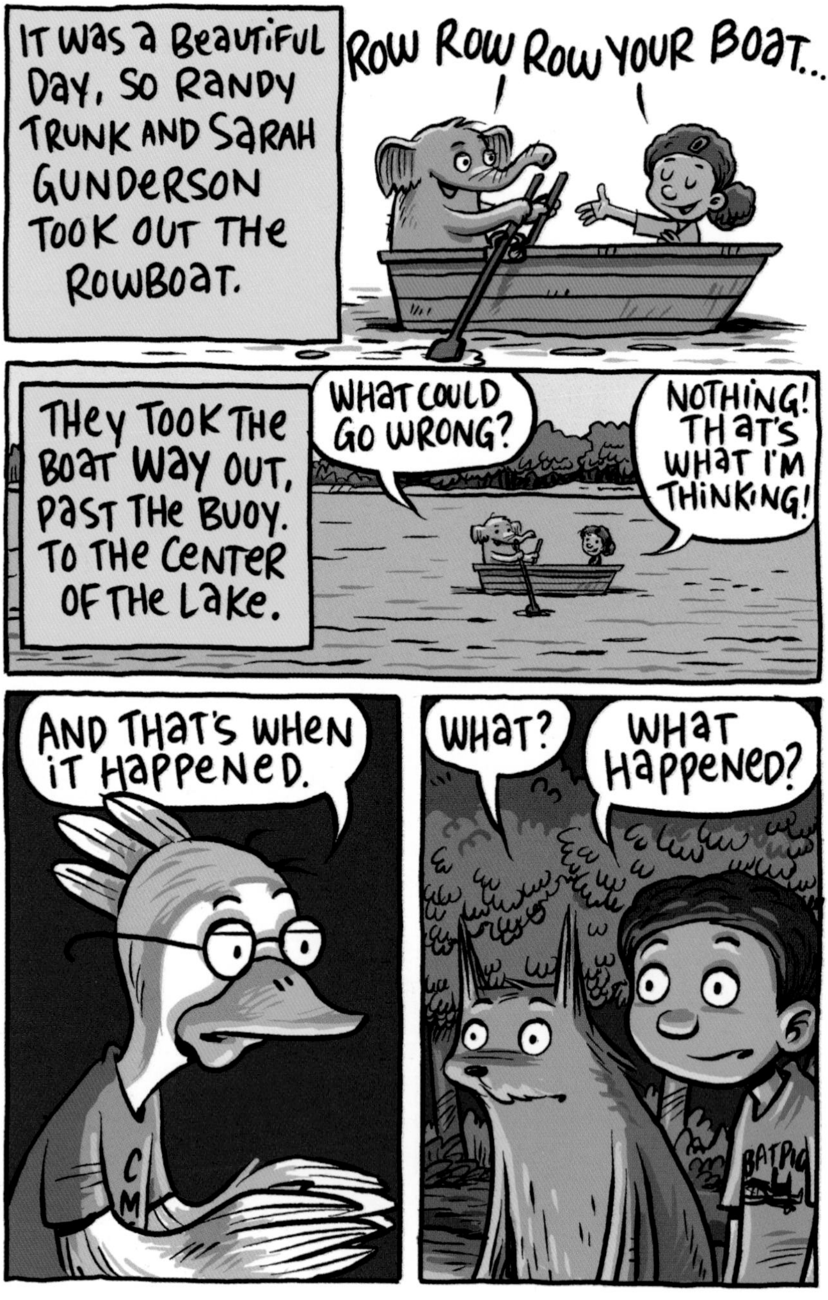
IT WAS A BEAUTIFUL DAY, SO RANDY TRUNK AND SARAH GUNDERSON TOOK OUT THE ROWBOAT.
ROW ROW ROW YOUR BOAT...
THEY TOOK THE BOAT WAY OUT, PAST THE BUOY. TO THE CENTER OF THE LAKE.
WHAT COULD GO WRONG?
NOTHING! THAT'S WHAT I'M THINKING!
AND THAT'S WHEN IT HAPPENED.
WHAT?
WHAT HAPPENED?

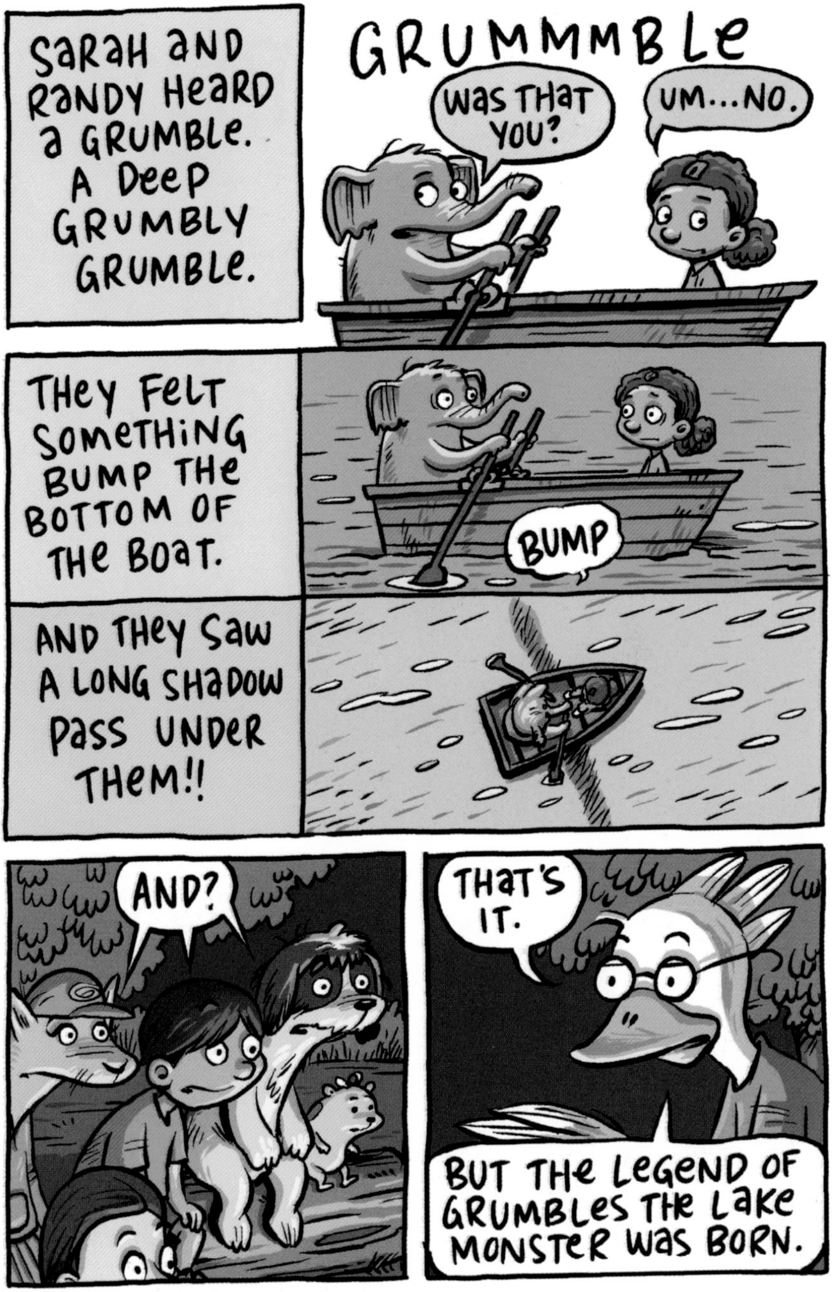
SARAH AND RANDY HEARD A GRUMBLE. A DEEP GRUMBLY GRUMBLE.
GRUMMMMBLE
WAS THAT YOU?
UM...NO.
THEY FELT SOMETHING BUMP THE BOTTOM OF THE BOAT.
BUMP
AND THEY SAW A LONG SHADOW PASS UNDER THEM!!
AND?
THAT'S IT.
BUT THE LEGEND OF GRUMBLES THE LAKE MONSTER WAS BORN.

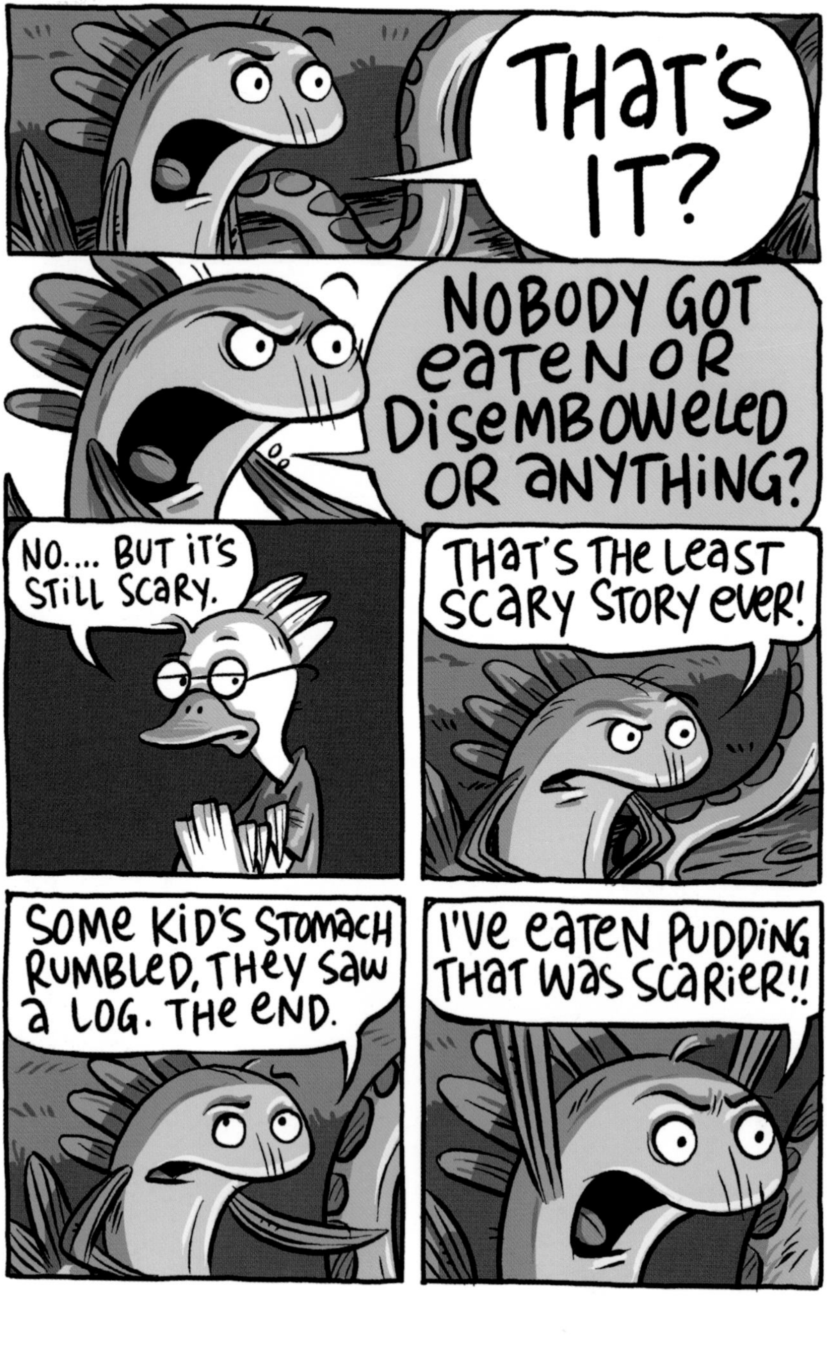
THAT'S IT?
NOBODY GOT EATEN OR DISEMBOWELED OR ANYTHING?
NO.... BUT IT'S STILL SCARY.
THAT'S THE LEAST SCARY STORY EVER!
SOME KID'S STOMACH RUMBLED, THEY SAW A LOG. THE END.
I'VE EATEN PUDDING THAT WAS SCARIER!!

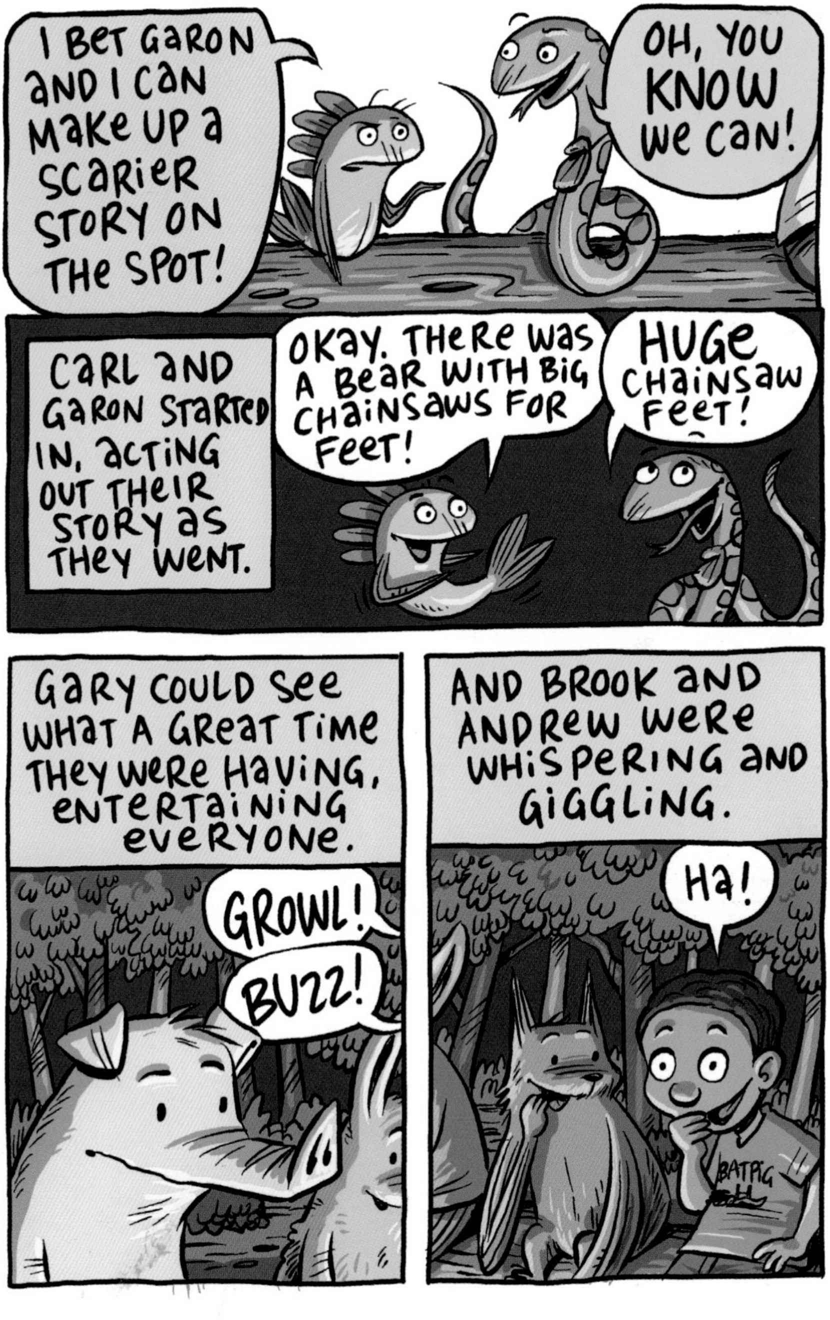
I BET GARON AND I CAN MAKE UP A SCARIER STORY ON THE SPOT!
OH, YOU KNOW WE CAN!
CARL AND GARON STARTED IN, ACTING OUT THEIR STORY AS THEY WENT.
OKAY. THERE WAS A BEAR WITH BIG CHAINSAWS FOR FEET!
HUGE CHAINSAW FEET!
GARY COULD SEE WHAT A GREAT TIME THEY WERE HAVING, ENTERTAINING EVERYONE.
GROWL!
BUZZ!
AND BROOK AND ANDREW WERE WHISPERING AND GIGGLING.
HA!
BATPIG

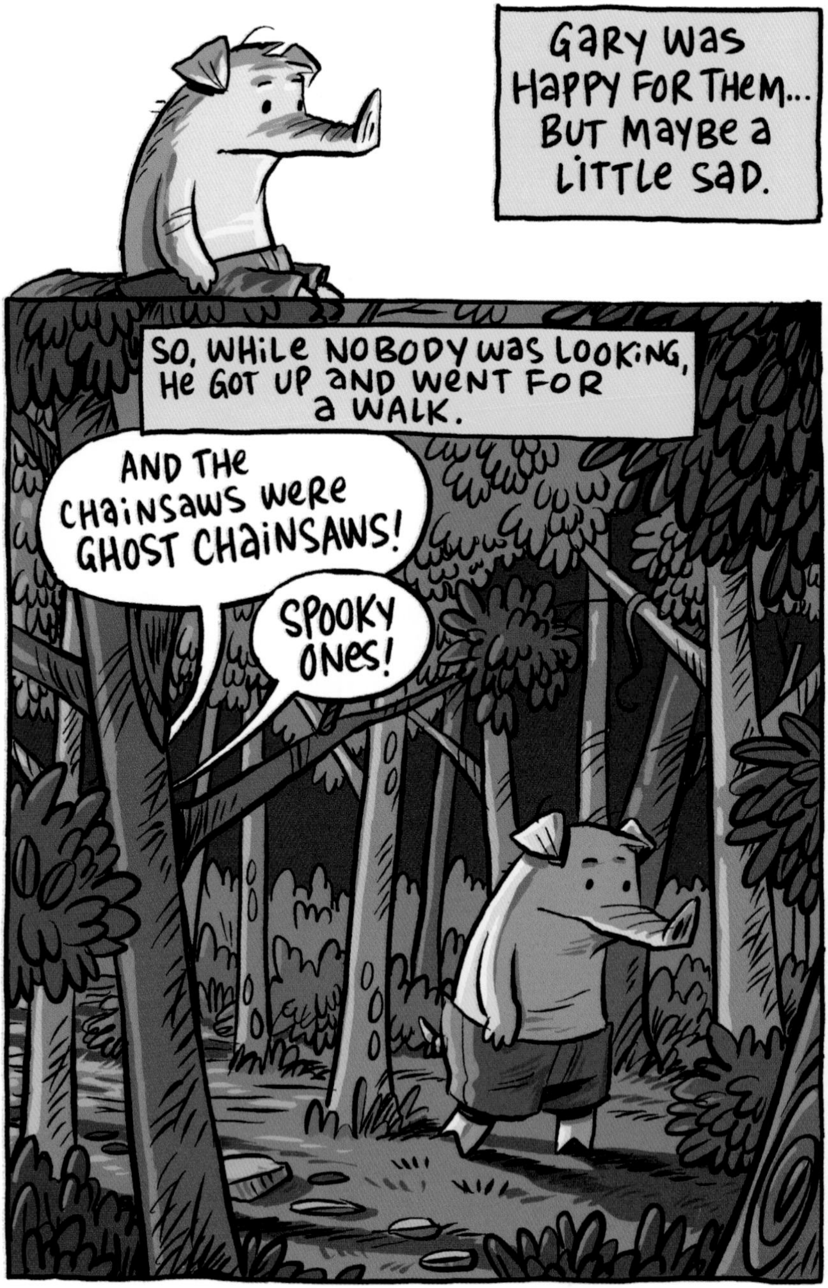
Gary was
Happy for them...
But maybe a
little sad.
So, while nobody was looking,
he got up and went for
a walk.
And the
chainsaws were
ghost chainsaws!
Spooky
ones!

CHAPTER FOUR

"LAKESIDE BY MOONLIGHT"

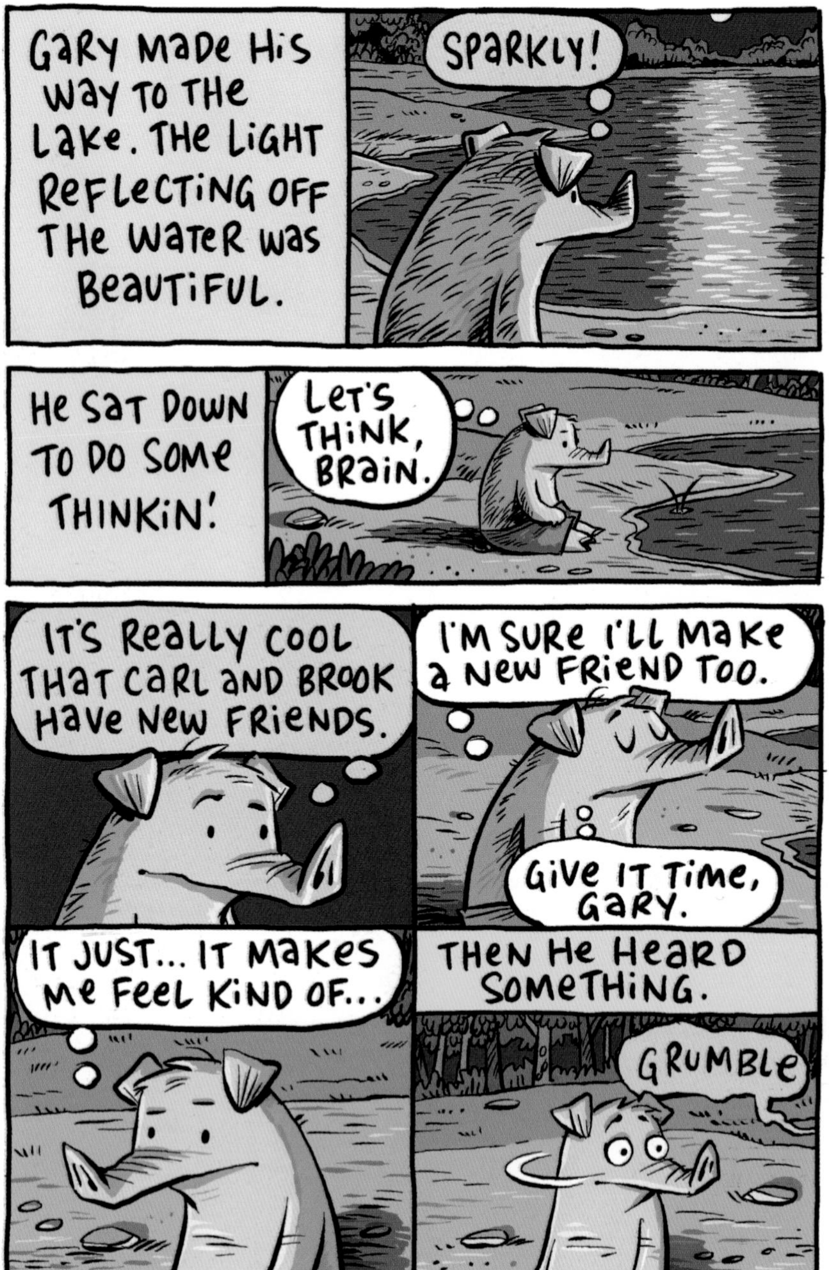
GARY MADE HIS WAY TO THE LAKE. THE LIGHT REFLECTING OFF THE WATER WAS BEAUTIFUL.
SPARKLY!
HE SAT DOWN TO DO SOME THINKIN'.
LET'S THINK, BRAIN.
IT'S REALLY COOL THAT CARL AND BROOK HAVE NEW FRIENDS.
I'M SURE I'LL MAKE A NEW FRIEND TOO.
GIVE IT TIME, GARY.
IT JUST... IT MAKES ME FEEL KIND OF...
THEN HE HEARD SOMETHING.
GRUMBLE

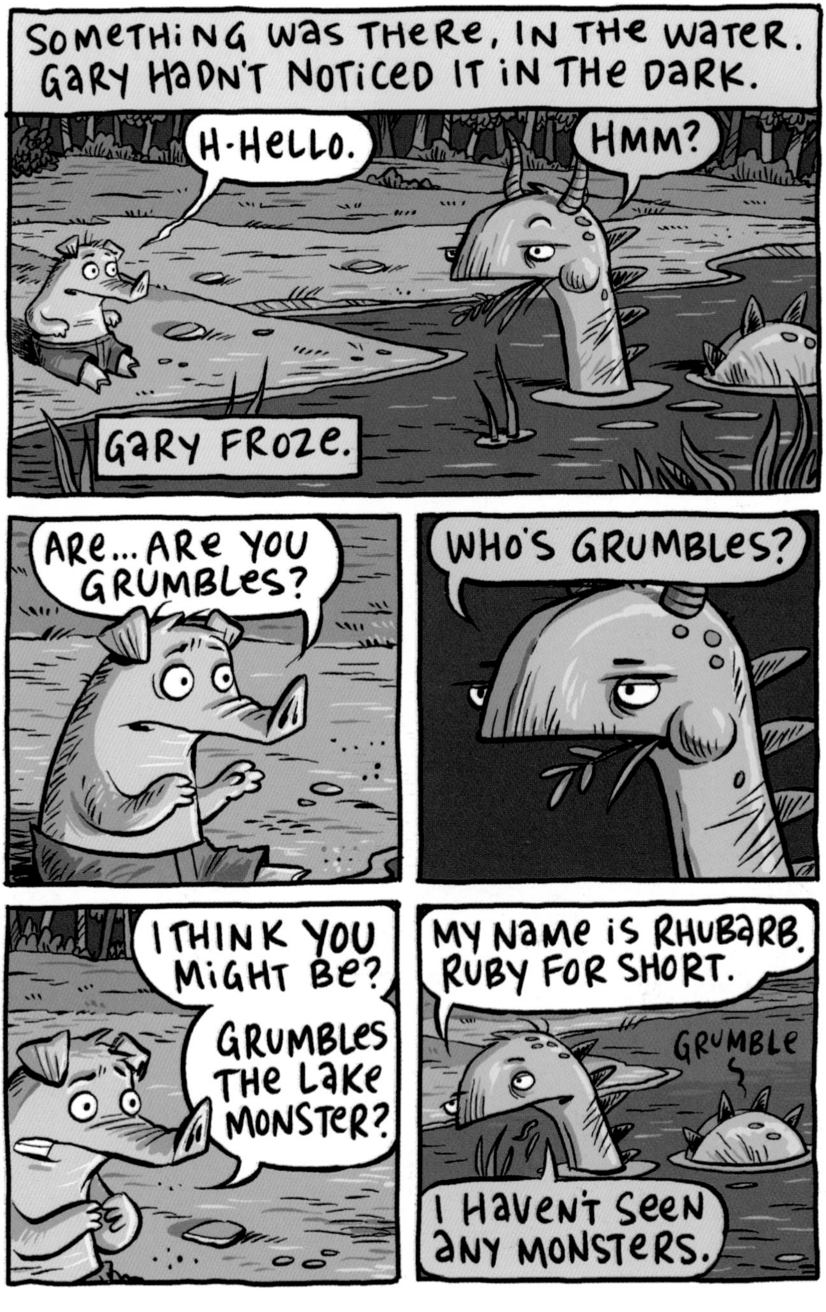
SOMETHING WAS THERE, IN THE WATER. GARY HADN'T NOTICED IT IN THE DARK.
H-HELLO.
HMM?
GARY FROZE.
ARE... ARE YOU GRUMBLES?
WHO'S GRUMBLES?
I THINK YOU MIGHT BE?
GRUMBLES THE LAKE MONSTER?
MY NAME IS RHUBARB. RUBY FOR SHORT.
GRUMBLE
I HAVEN'T SEEN ANY MONSTERS.

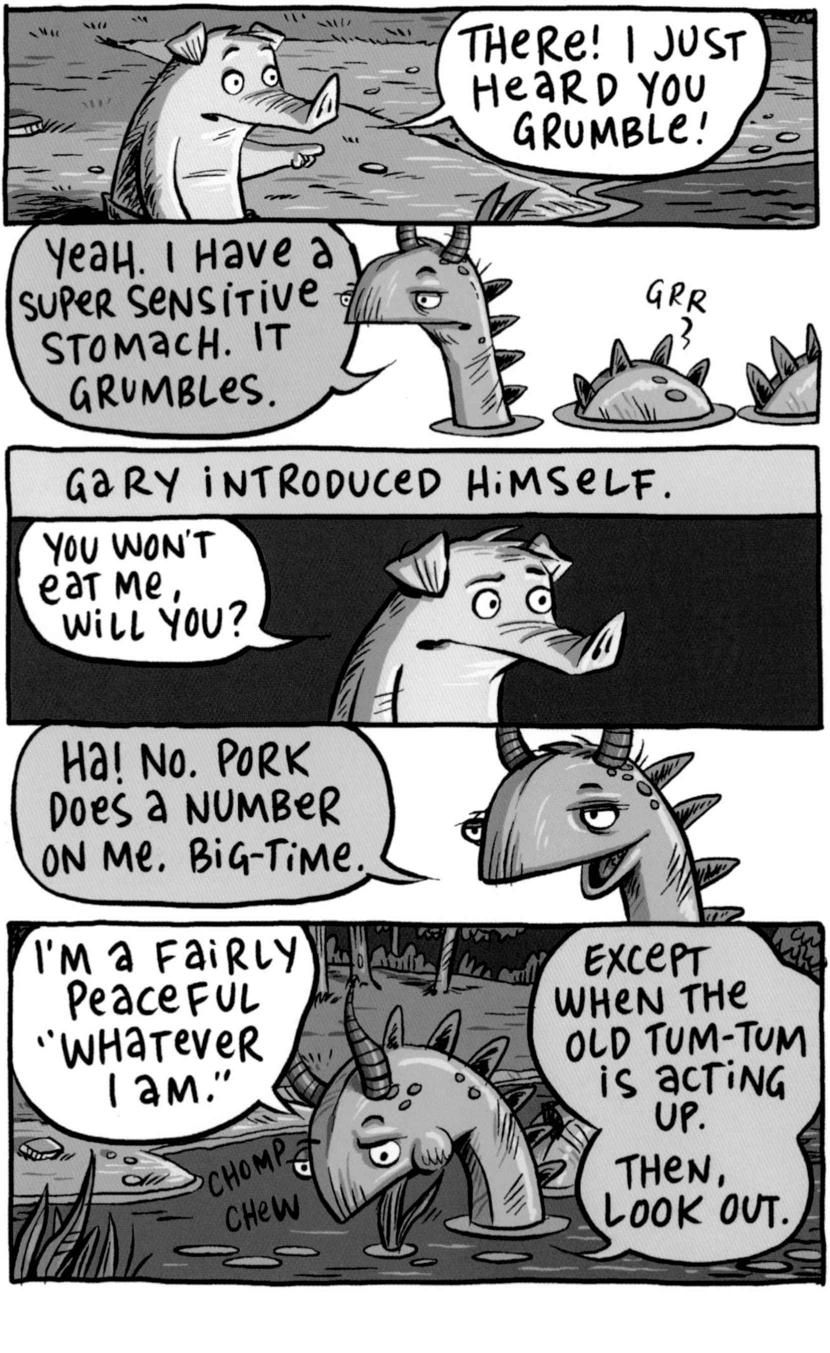
THERE! I JUST HEARD YOU GRUMBLE!
YEAH. I HAVE A SUPER SENSITIVE STOMACH. IT GRUMBLES.
GRR
GARY INTRODUCED HIMSELF.
YOU WON'T EAT ME, WILL YOU?
HA! NO. PORK DOES A NUMBER ON ME. BIG-TIME.
I'M A FAIRLY PEACEFUL "WHATEVER I AM."
CHOMP
CHEW
EXCEPT WHEN THE OLD TUM-TUM IS ACTING UP.
THEN, LOOK OUT.

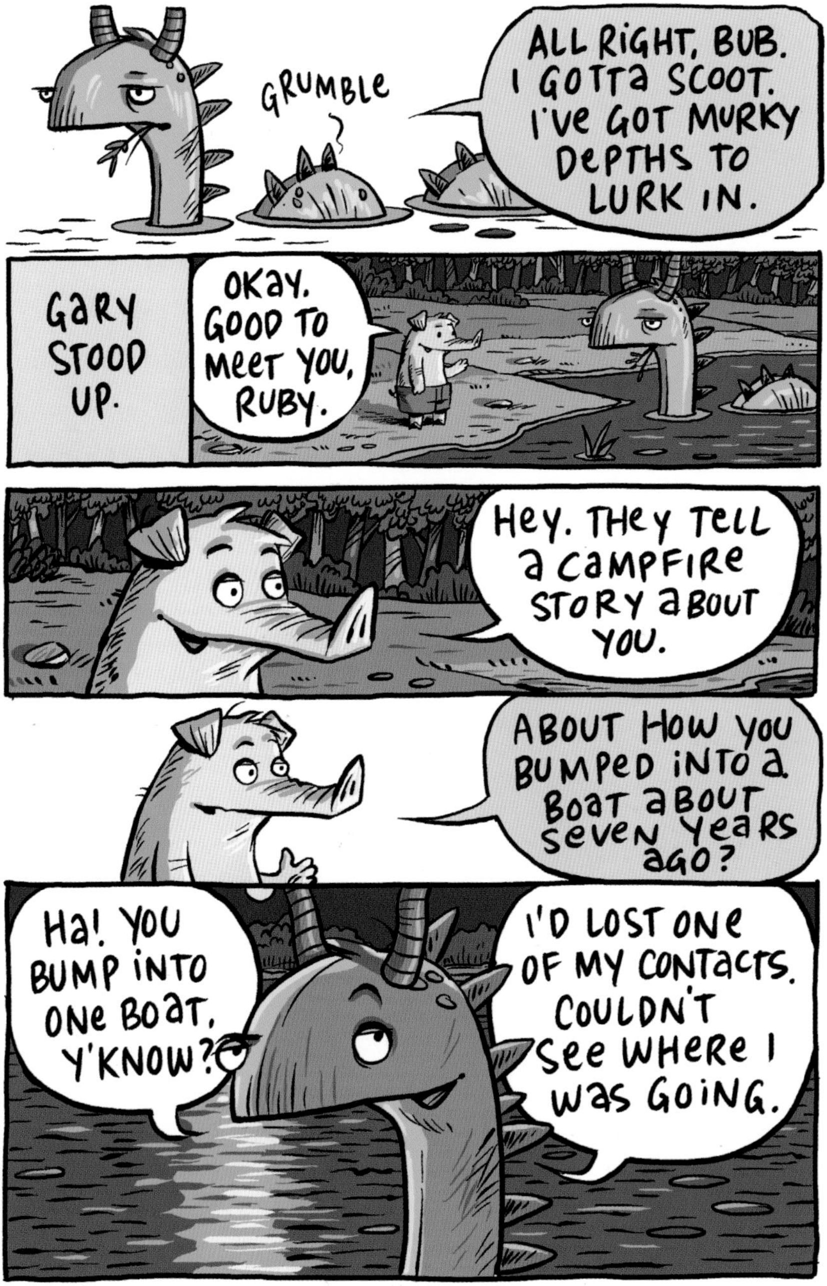
GRUMBLE
ALL RIGHT, BUB. I GOTTA SCOOT. I'VE GOT MURKY DEPTHS TO LURK IN.
GARY STOOD UP.
OKAY. GOOD TO MEET YOU, RUBY.
HEY. THEY TELL A CAMPFIRE STORY ABOUT YOU.
ABOUT HOW YOU BUMPED INTO A BOAT ABOUT SEVEN YEARS AGO?
HA! YOU BUMP INTO ONE BOAT, Y'KNOW?
I'D LOST ONE OF MY CONTACTS. COULDN'T SEE WHERE I WAS GOING.

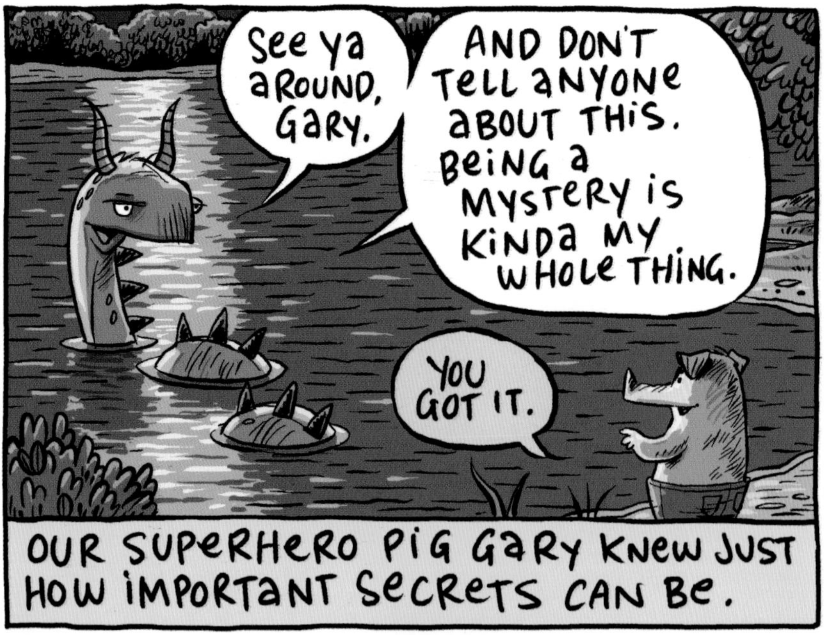
See ya around, Gary.
AND DON'T TELL ANYONE ABOUT THIS. BEING A MYSTERY IS KINDA MY WHOLE THING.
YOU GOT IT.
OUR SUPERHERO PIG GARY KNEW JUST HOW IMPORTANT SECRETS CAN BE.

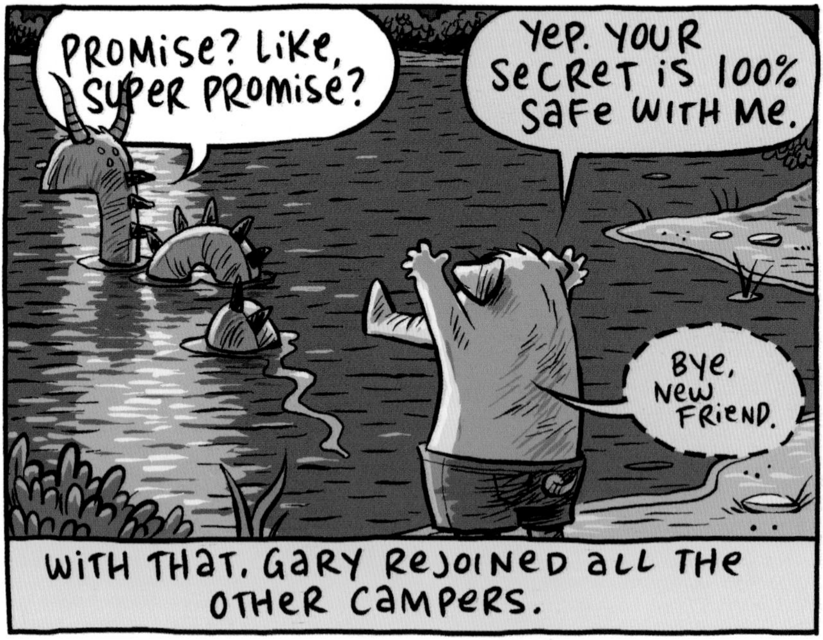
PROMISE? LIKE, SUPER PROMISE?
YEP. YOUR SECRET IS 100% SAFE WITH ME.
BYE, NEW FRIEND.
WITH THAT, GARY REJOINED ALL THE OTHER CAMPERS.

CHAPTER FIVE

PYRAMI
FISH
DEODORA
(FOR
FISH)

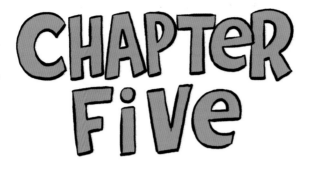

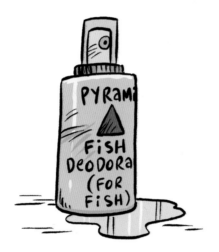

"FISH OIL"

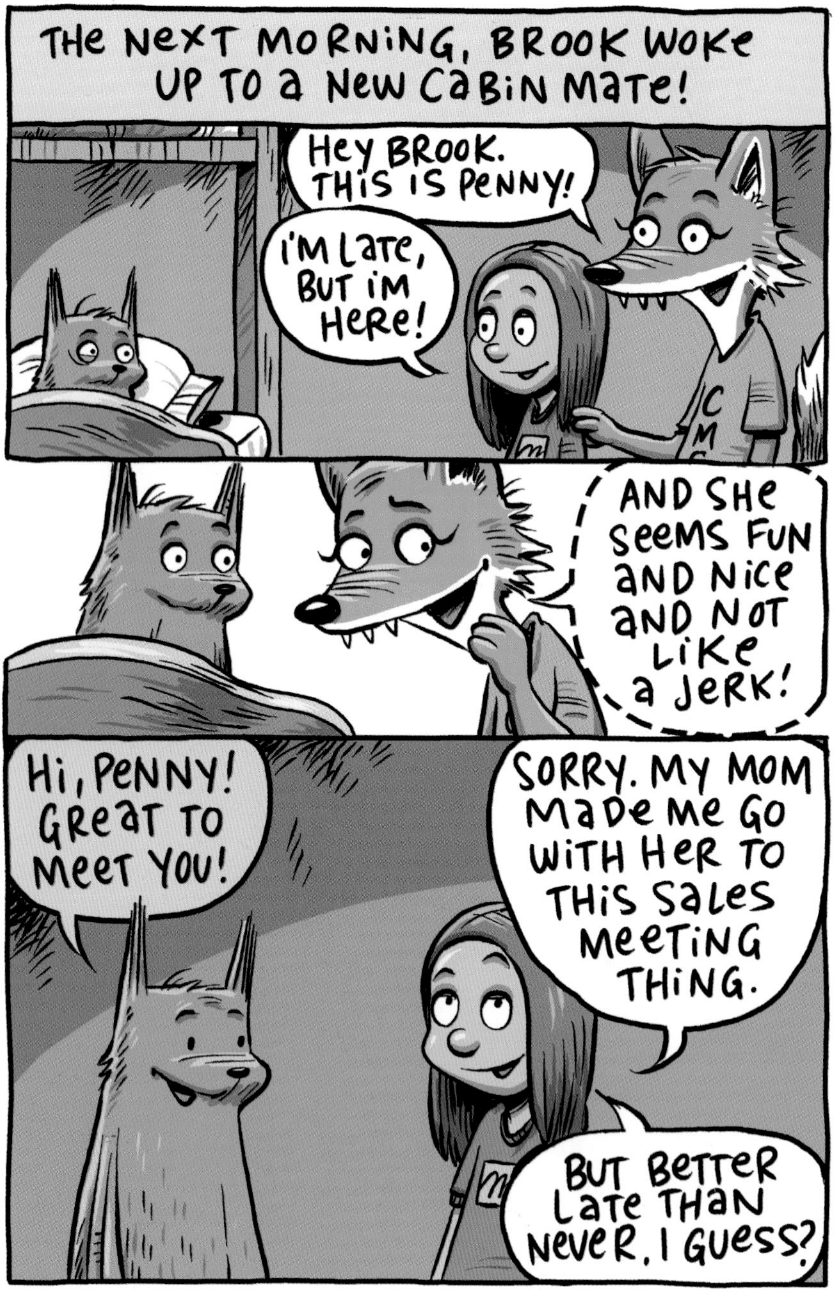
THE NEXT MORNING, BROOK WOKE UP TO A NEW CABIN MATE!
HEY BROOK. THIS IS PENNY!
I'M LATE, BUT IM HERE!
AND SHE SEEMS FUN AND NICE AND NOT LIKE A JERK!
HI, PENNY! GREAT TO MEET YOU!
SORRY. MY MOM MADE ME GO WITH HER TO THIS SALES MEETING THING.
BUT BETTER LATE THAN NEVER, I GUESS?

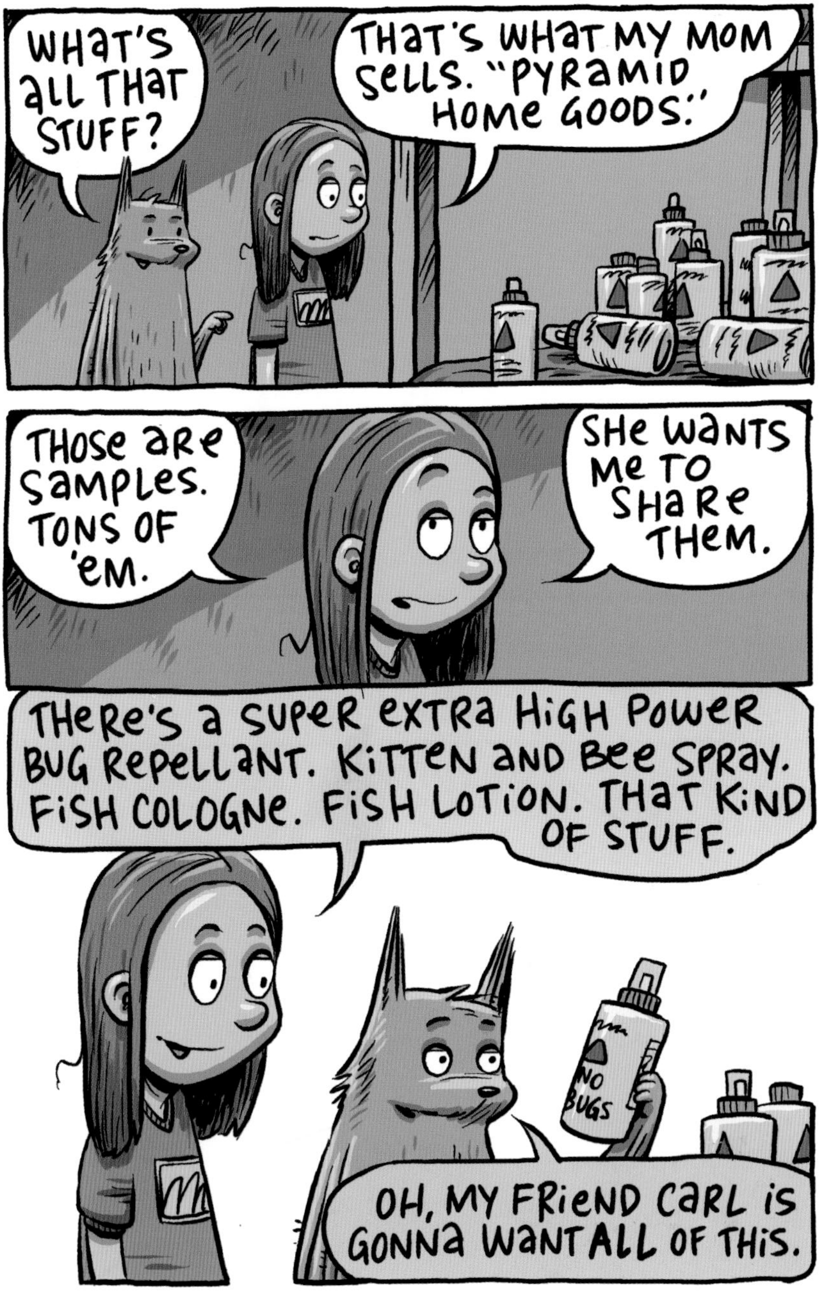
WHAT'S ALL THAT STUFF?
THAT'S WHAT MY MOM SELLS. "PYRAMID HOME GOODS."
THOSE ARE SAMPLES. TONS OF 'EM.
SHE WANTS ME TO SHARE THEM.
THERE'S A SUPER EXTRA HIGH POWER BUG REPELLANT. KITTEN AND BEE SPRAY. FISH COLOGNE. FISH LOTION. THAT KIND OF STUFF.
NO BUGS
OH, MY FRIEND CARL IS GONNA WANT ALL OF THIS.

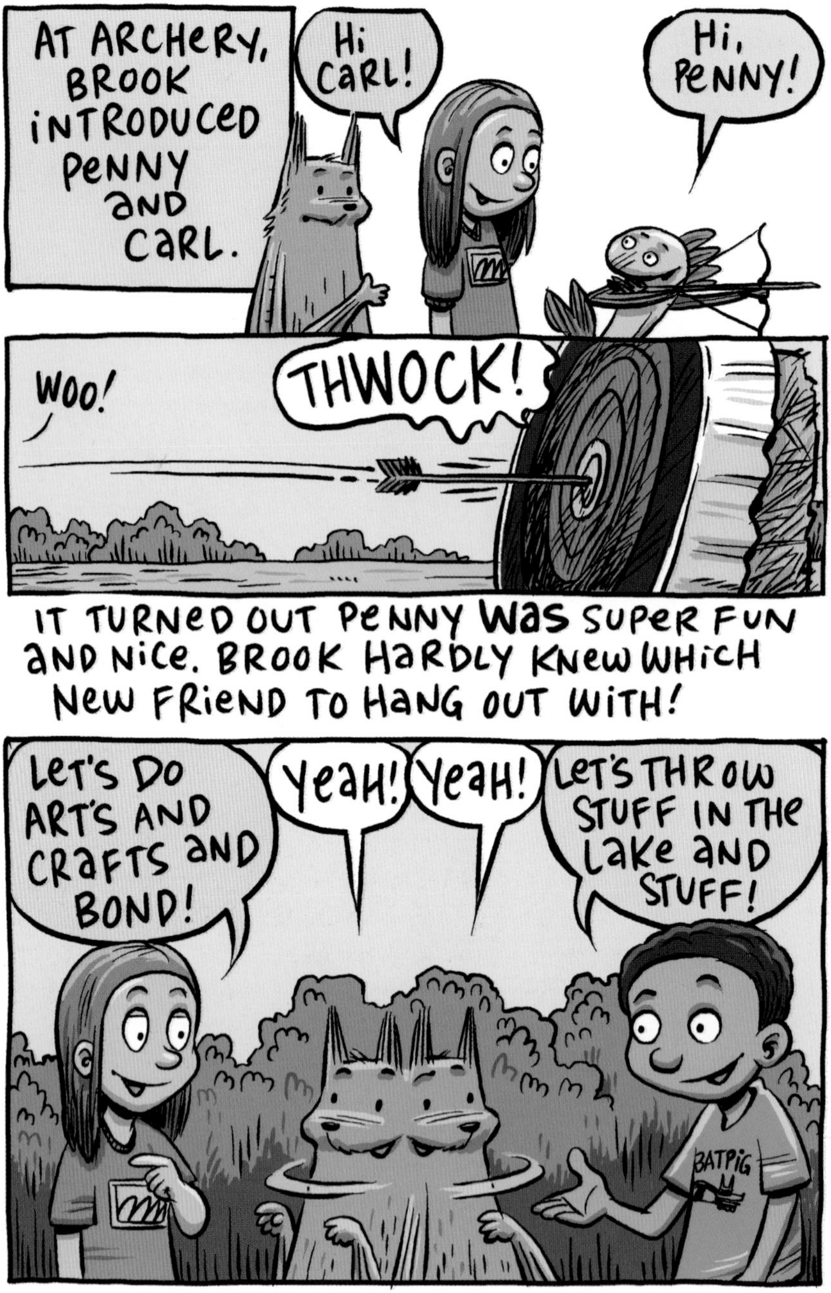
AT ARCHERY, BROOK INTRODUCED PENNY AND CARL.
Hi CARL!
Hi, PENNY!
WOO!
THWOCK!
IT TURNED OUT PENNY WAS SUPER FUN AND NICE. BROOK HARDLY KNEW WHICH NEW FRIEND TO HANG OUT WITH!
LET'S DO ART'S AND CRAFTS AND BOND!
YEAH!
YEAH!
LET'S THROW STUFF IN THE LAKE AND STUFF!
BATPIG

AFTER LUNCH, PENNY SHOWED CARL AND GARY ALL THE SPRAYS AND LOTIONS.

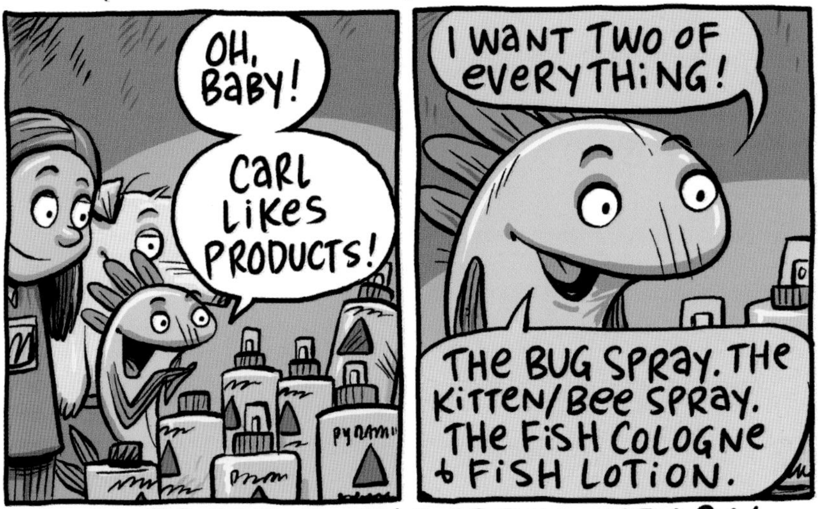
OH, BABY!
CARL LIKES PRODUCTS!
I WANT TWO OF EVERYTHING!
THE BUG SPRAY. THE KITTEN/BEE SPRAY. THE FISH COLOGNE + FISH LOTION.

CARL RACED TO THE CABIN WITH ALL HIS NEW STUFF. HE WAS SUPER JAZZED.

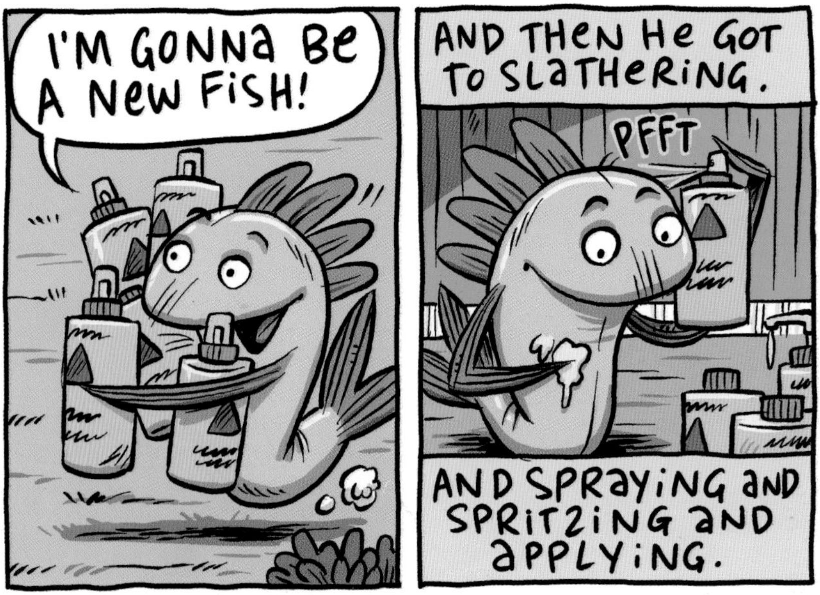
I'M GONNA BE A NEW FISH!
AND THEN HE GOT TO SLATHERING.
PFFT
AND SPRAYING AND SPRITZING AND APPLYING.

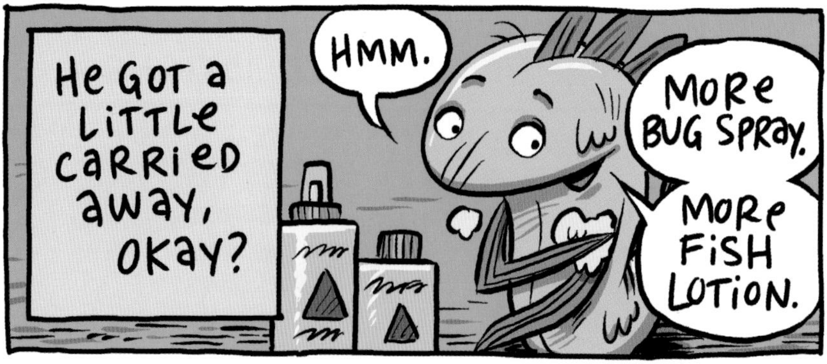
He got a little carried away, okay?
HMM.
More bug spray.
More fish lotion.

BY THE TIME HE WAS DONE, HE HAD, LIKE, HALF AN INCH OF GOO OVER HIS WHOLE BODY. IT WAS NASTY.

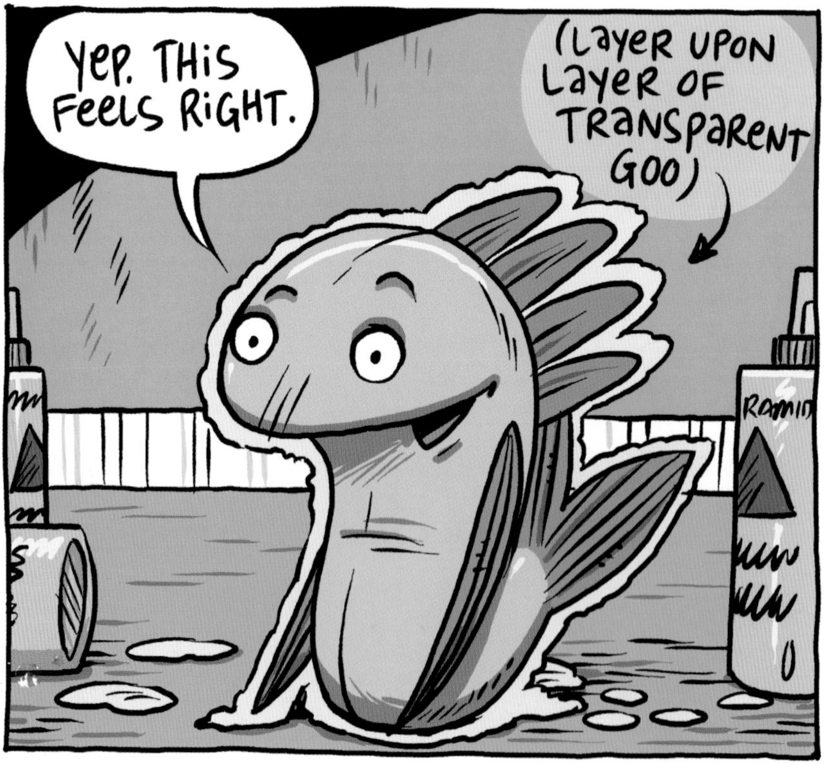
Yep. This feels right.
(Layer upon layer of transparent goo)

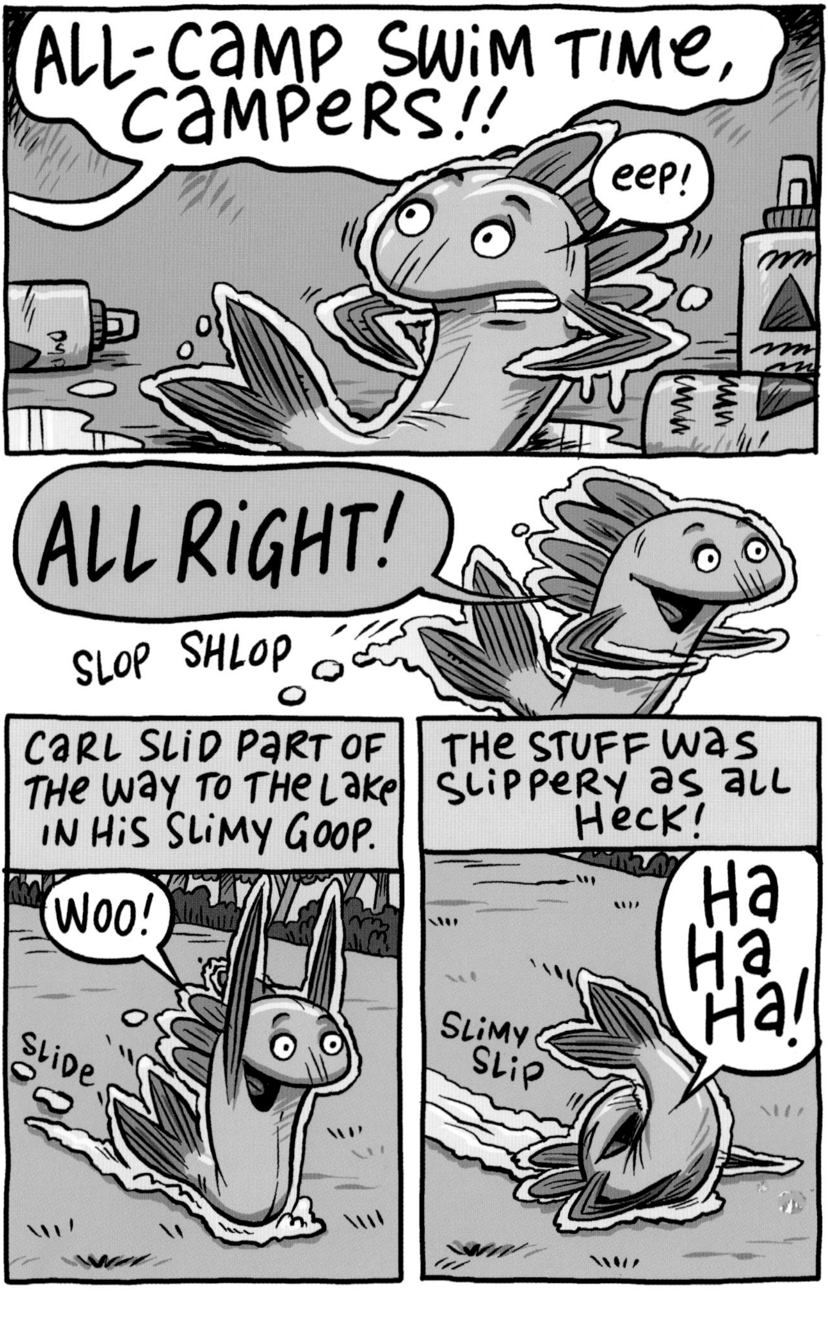
ALL-CAMP SWIM TIME, CAMPERS!!
eep!
ALL RIGHT!
SLOP SHLOP
CARL SLID PART OF THE WAY TO THE LAKE IN HIS SLIMY GOOP.
WOO!
SLIDE
THE STUFF WAS SLIPPERY AS ALL HECK!
HA HA HA!
SLIMY SLIP

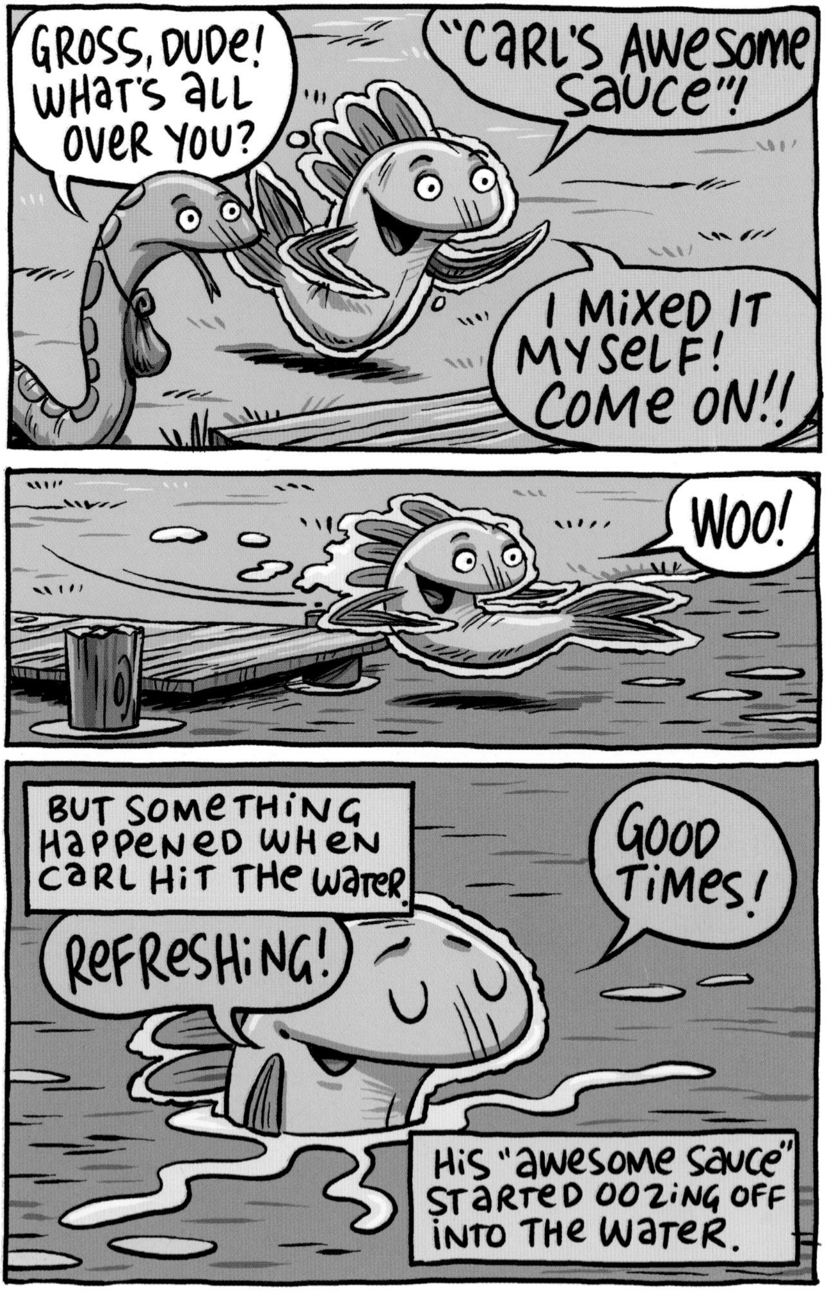
GROSS, DUDE! WHAT'S ALL OVER YOU?
"CARL'S AWESOME SAUCE"!
I MIXED IT MYSELF! COME ON!!
WOO!
BUT SOMETHING HAPPENED WHEN CARL HIT THE WATER.
GOOD TIMES!
REFRESHING!
HIS "AWESOME SAUCE" STARTED OOZING OFF INTO THE WATER.

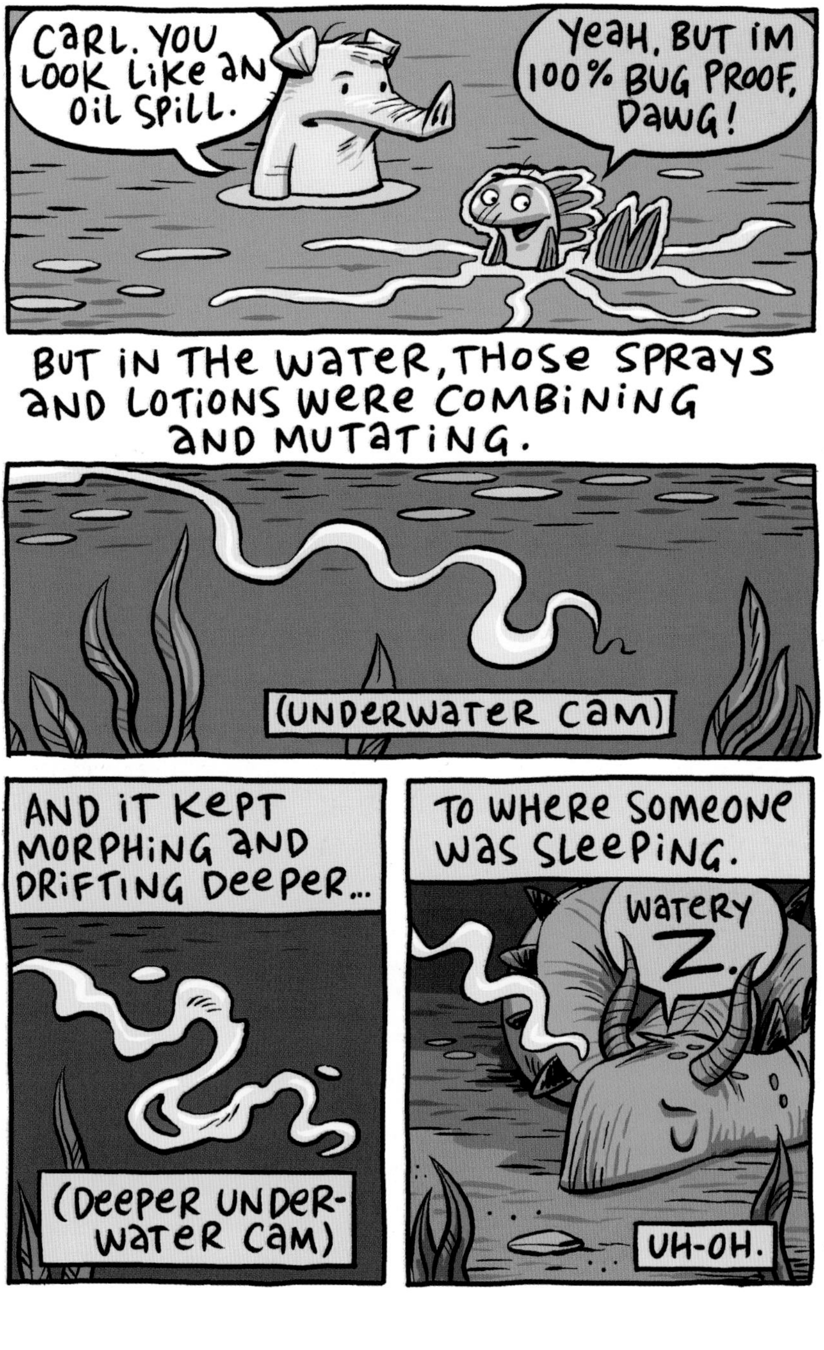
CARL. YOU LOOK LIKE AN OIL SPILL.
YEAH, BUT IM 100% BUG PROOF, DAWG!
BUT IN THE WATER, THOSE SPRAYS AND LOTIONS WERE COMBINING AND MUTATING.
(UNDERWATER CAM)
AND IT KEPT MORPHING AND DRIFTING DEEPER...
(DEEPER UNDER-WATER CAM)
TO WHERE SOMEONE WAS SLEEPING.
WATERY Z.
UH-OH.

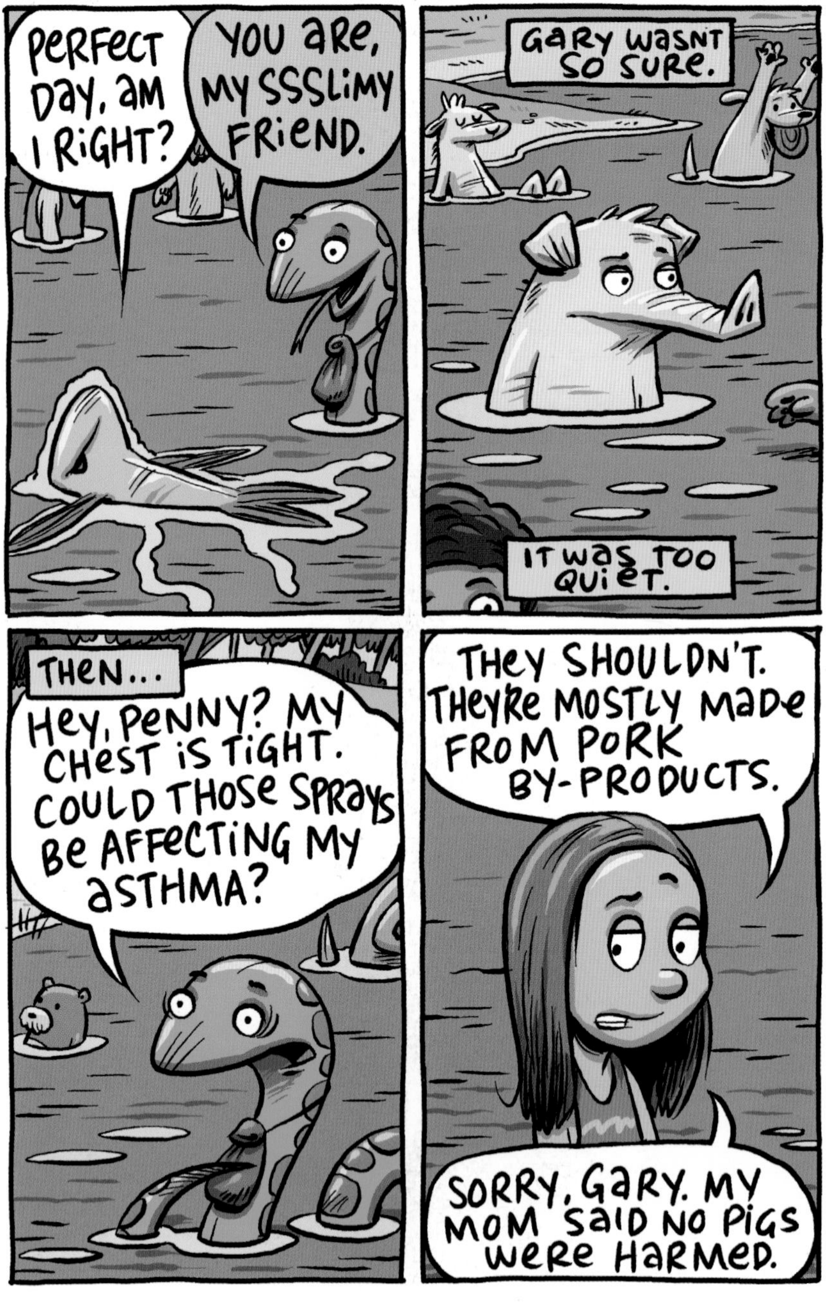
PERFECT DAY, AM I RIGHT?
YOU ARE, MY SSSLIMY FRIEND.
GARY WASN'T SO SURE.
IT WAS TOO QUIET.
THEN...
HEY, PENNY? MY CHEST IS TIGHT. COULD THOSE SPRAYS BE AFFECTING MY ASTHMA?
THEY SHOULDN'T. THEY'RE MOSTLY MADE FROM PORK BY-PRODUCTS.
SORRY, GARY. MY MOM SAID NO PIGS WERE HARMED.

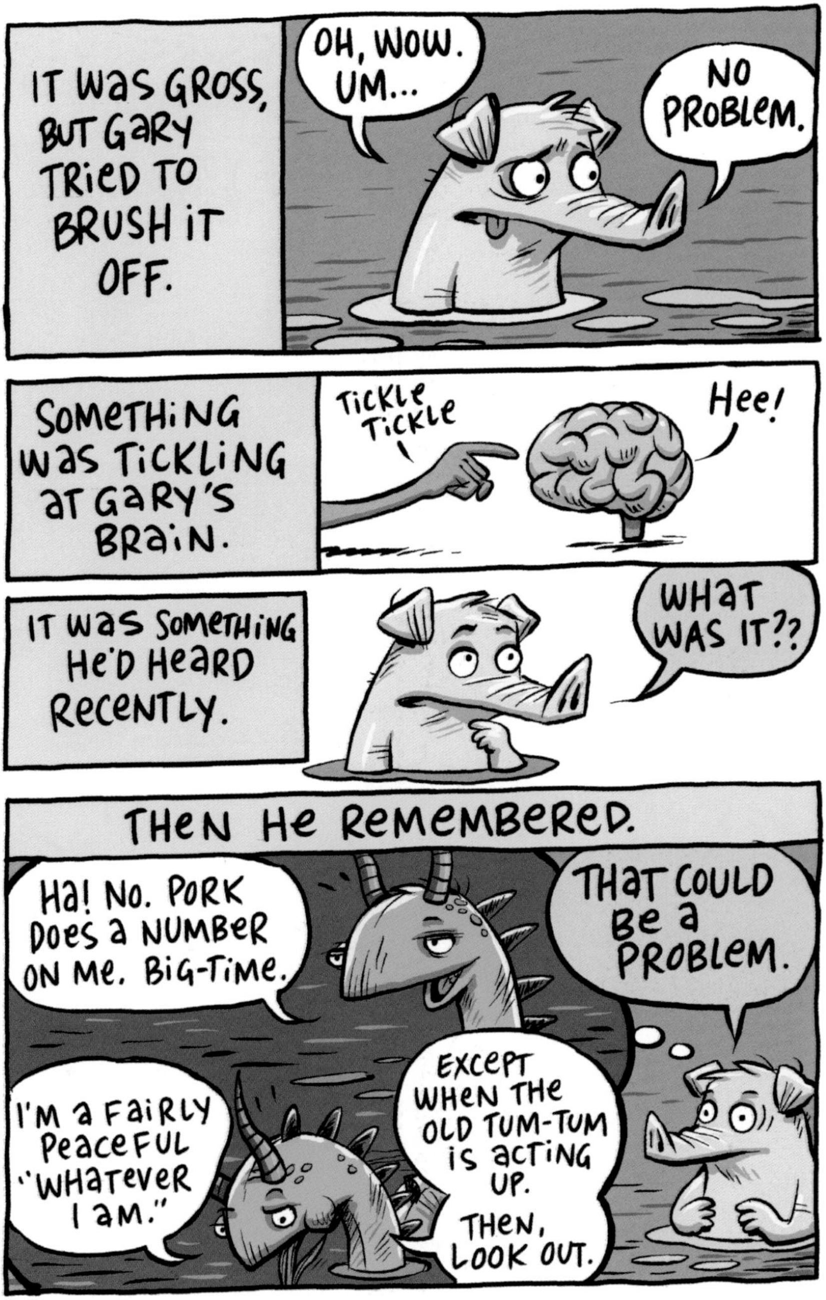
IT WAS GROSS, BUT GARY TRIED TO BRUSH IT OFF.
OH, WOW. UM...
NO PROBLEM.
SOMETHING WAS TICKLING AT GARY'S BRAIN.
TICKLE TICKLE
HEE!
IT WAS SOMETHING HE'D HEARD RECENTLY.
WHAT WAS IT??
THEN HE REMEMBERED.
HA! NO. PORK DOES A NUMBER ON ME. BIG-TIME.
THAT COULD BE A PROBLEM.
I'M A FAIRLY PEACEFUL "WHATEVER I AM."
EXCEPT WHEN THE OLD TUM-TUM IS ACTING UP.
THEN, LOOK OUT.

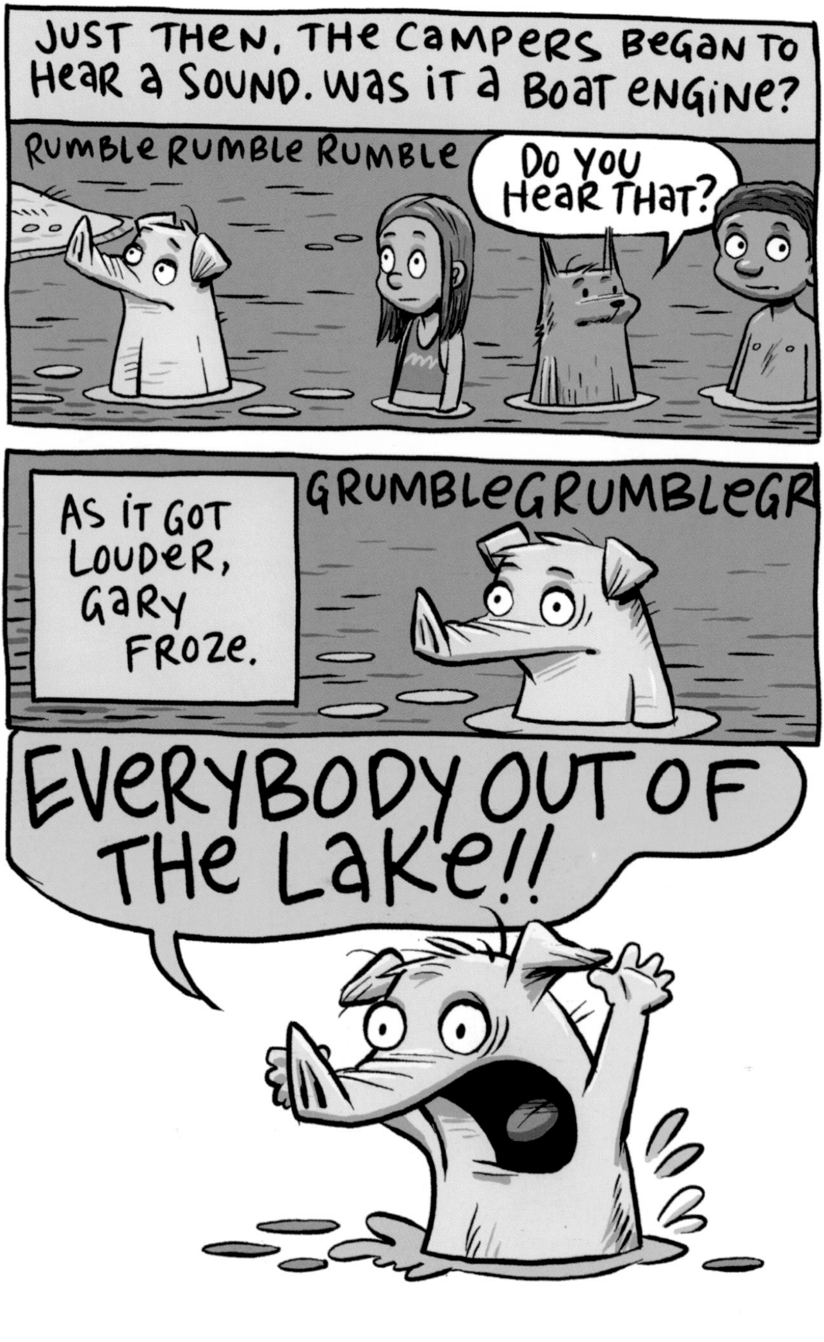
JUST THEN, THE CAMPERS BEGAN TO HEAR A SOUND. WAS IT A BOAT ENGINE?
RUMBLE RUMBLE RUMBLE
DO YOU HEAR THAT?
AS IT GOT LOUDER, GARY FROZE.
GRUMBLEGRUMBLEGR
EVERYBODY OUT OF THE LAKE!!

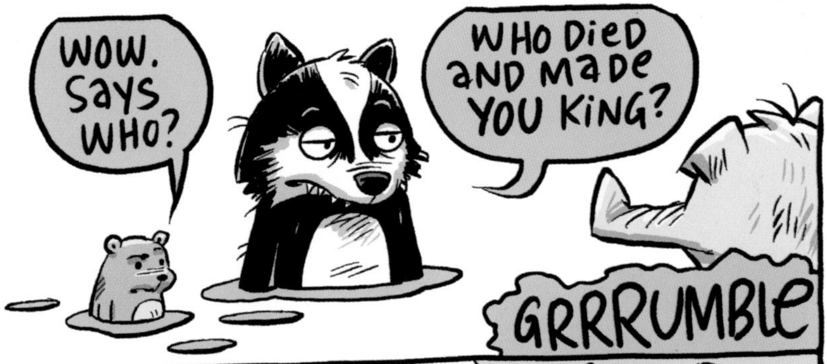
WOW. SAYS WHO?
WHO DIED AND MADE YOU KING?
GRRRUMBLE

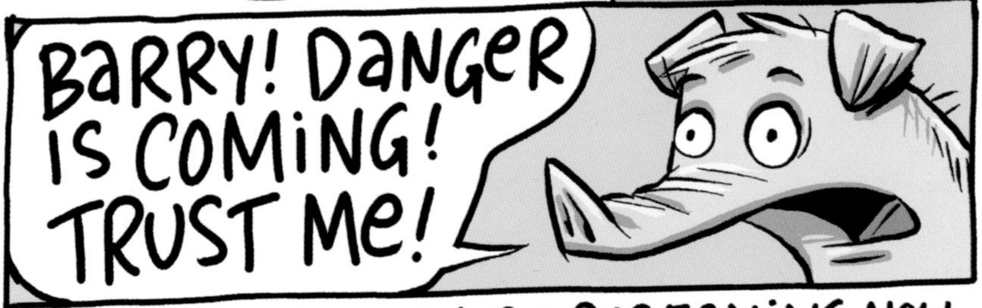
BARRY! DANGER IS COMING! TRUST ME!

THE GRUMBLING WAS DEAFENING NOW, SHAKING THE GROUND AND MAKING THE WATER CHOPPY.

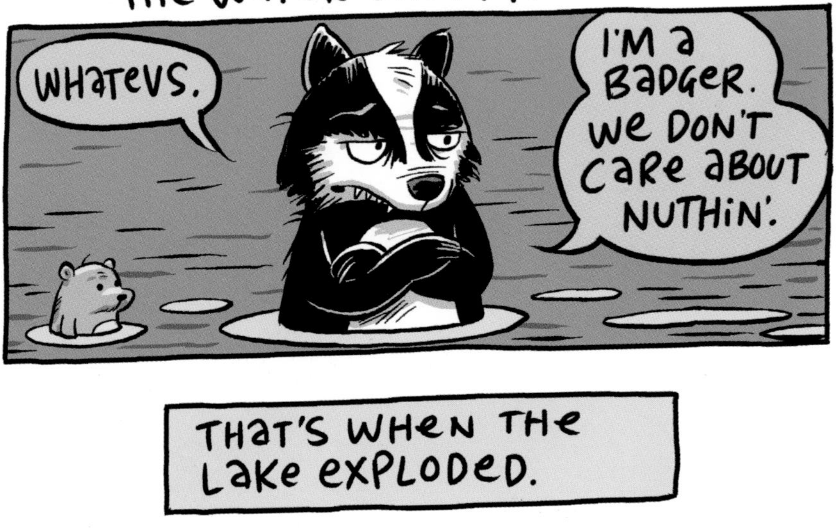
WHATEVS.
I'M A BADGER. WE DON'T CARE ABOUT NUTHIN'.

THAT'S WHEN THE LAKE EXPLODED.

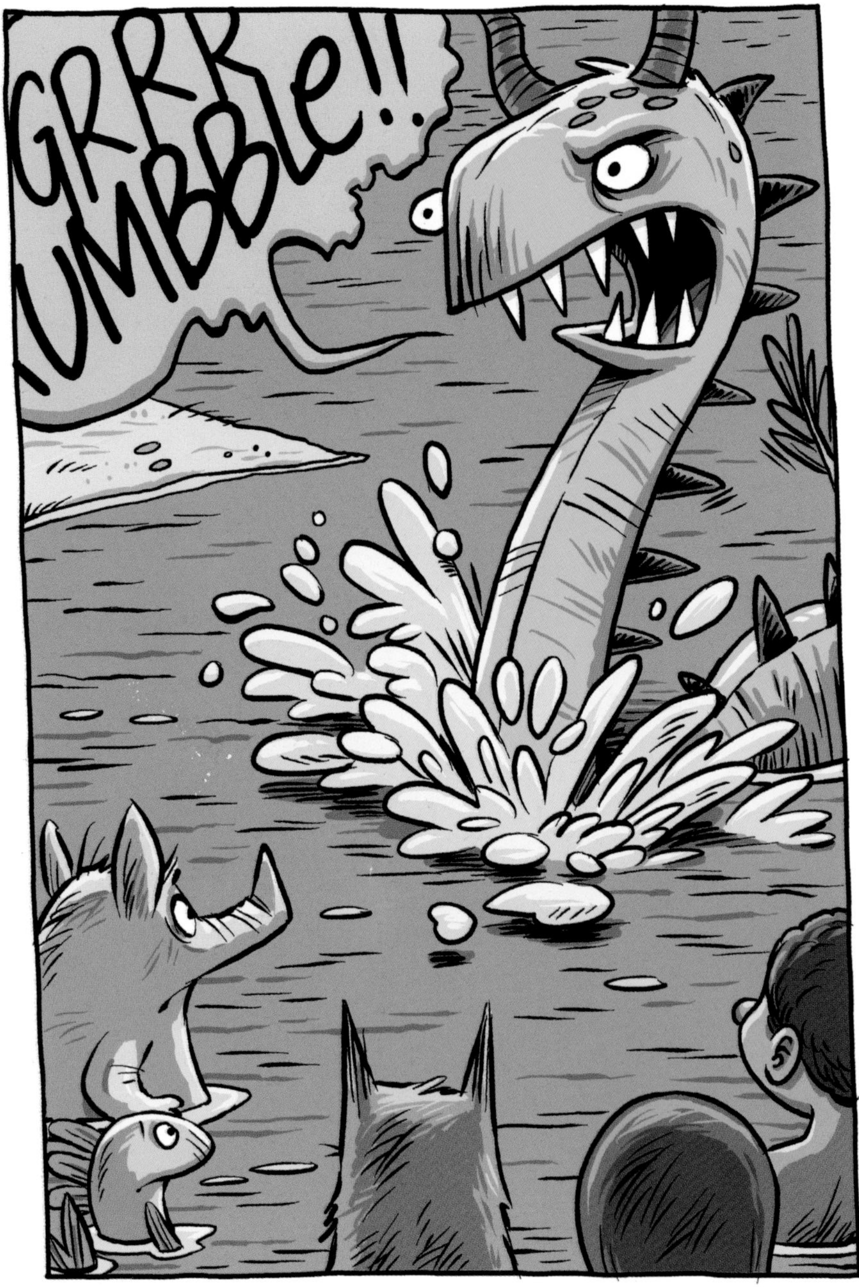
GRRR
UMBBLE!!

CHAPTER SIX

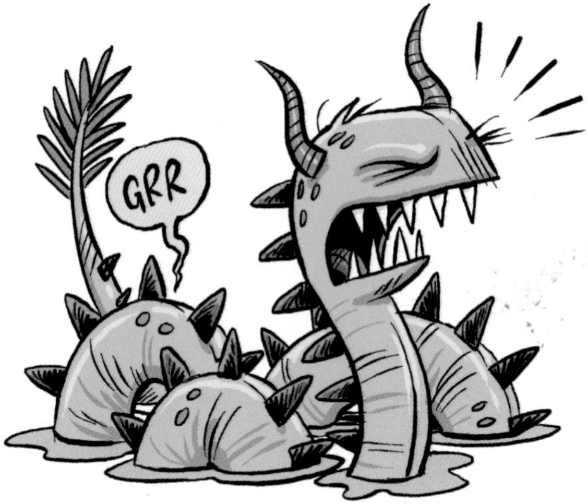
GRR

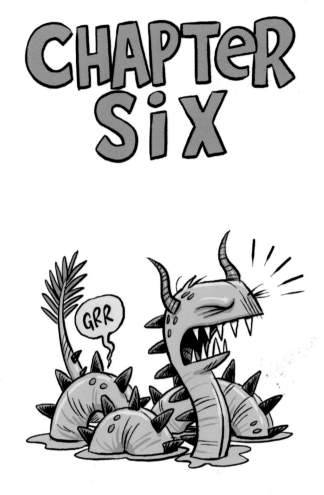

"BAD GRUMBLES"

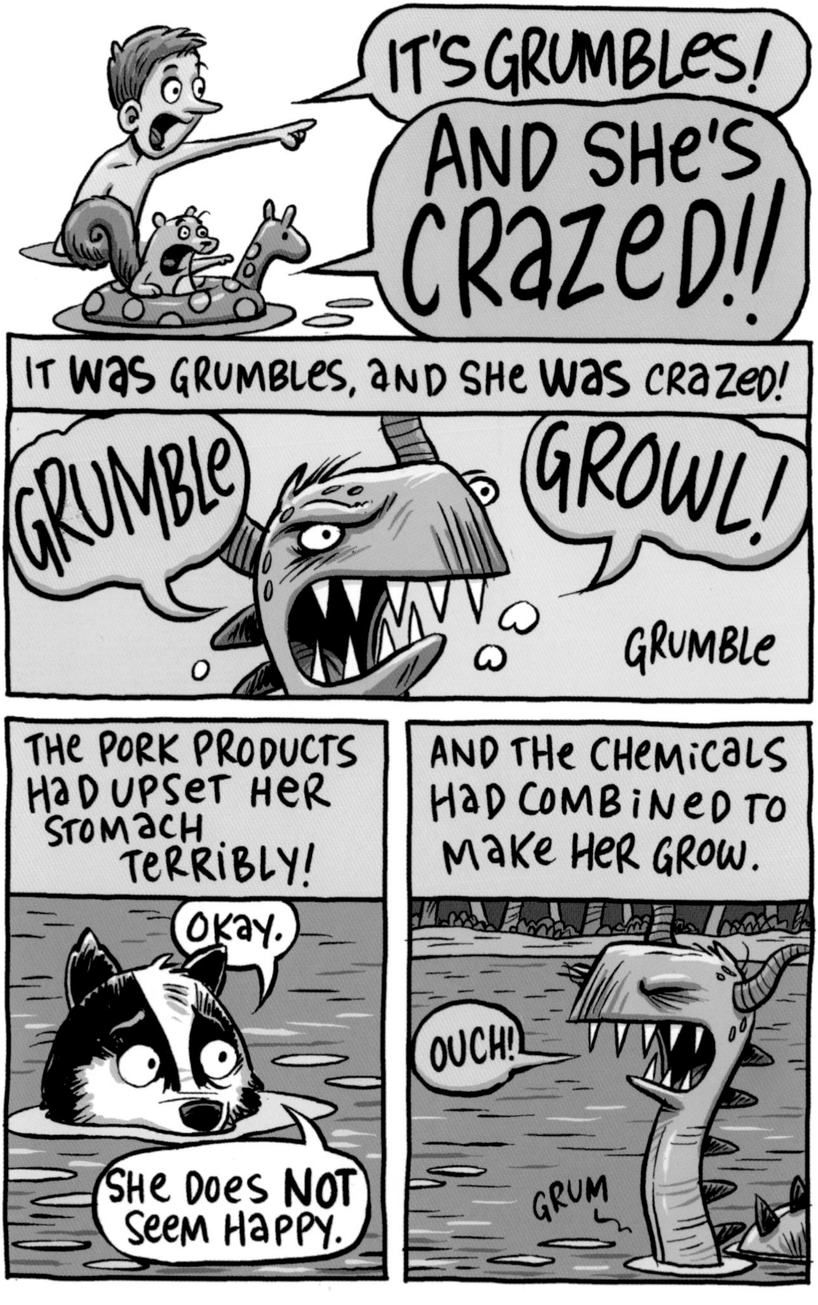
IT'S GRUMBLES!
AND SHE'S CRAZED!!
IT WAS GRUMBLES, AND SHE WAS CRAZED!
GRUMBLE
GROWL!
GRUMBLE
THE PORK PRODUCTS HAD UPSET HER STOMACH TERRIBLY!
OKAY.
SHE DOES NOT SEEM HAPPY.
AND THE CHEMICALS HAD COMBINED TO MAKE HER GROW.
OUCH!
GRUM

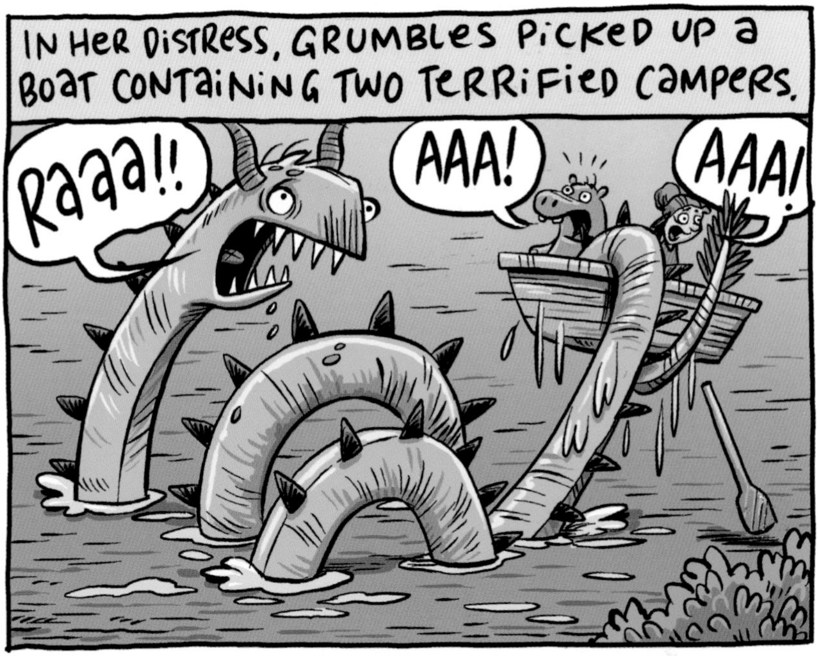
IN HER DISTRESS, GRUMBLES PICKED UP A BOAT CONTAINING TWO TERRIFIED CAMPERS.
RAAAA!!
AAA!
AAA!

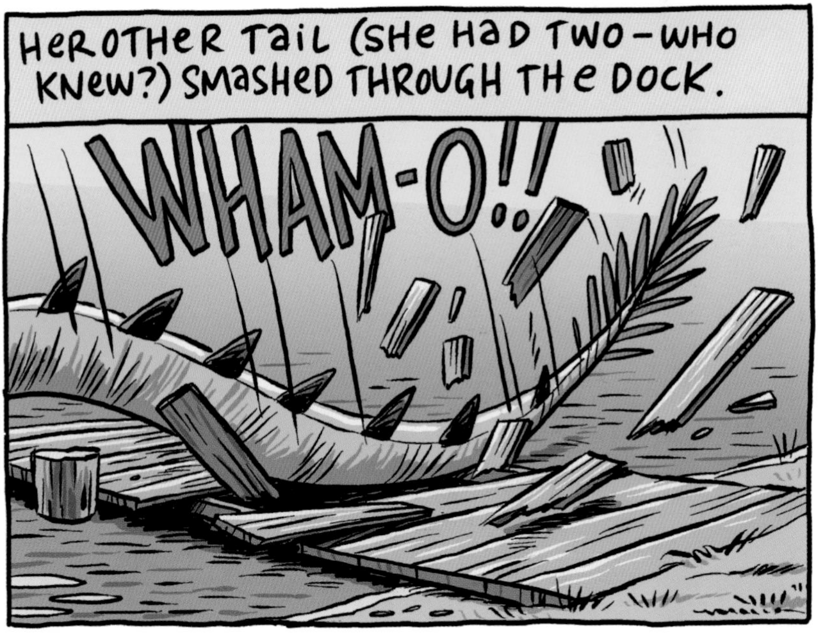
HER OTHER TAIL (SHE HAD TWO–WHO KNEW?) SMASHED THROUGH THE DOCK.
WHAM-O!!

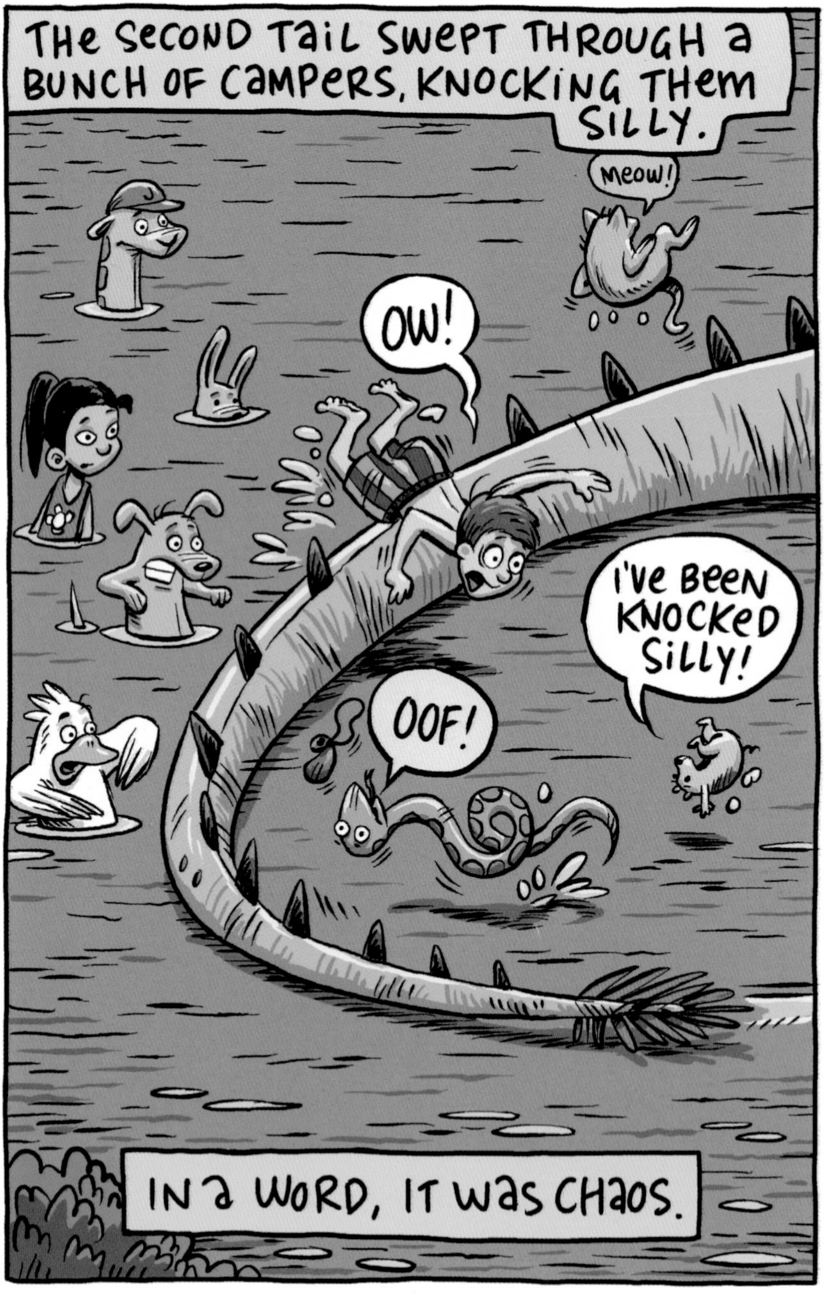
THE SECOND TAIL SWEPT THROUGH A BUNCH OF CAMPERS, KNOCKING THEM SILLY.
MEOW!
OW!
I'VE BEEN KNOCKED SILLY!
OOF!
IN A WORD, IT WAS CHAOS.

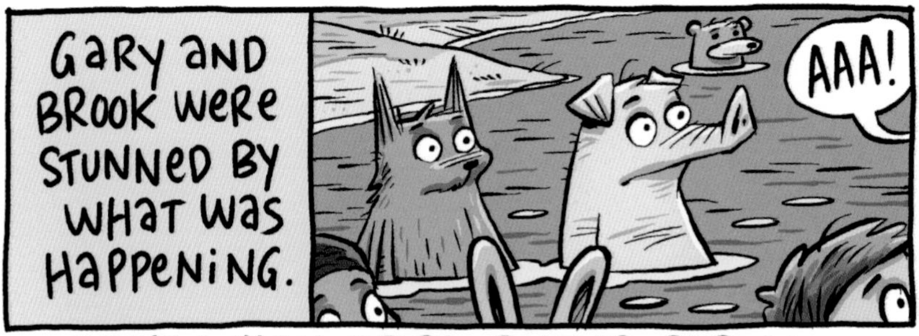
GARY AND BROOK WERE STUNNED BY WHAT WAS HAPPENING.
AAA!

THAT'S WHEN CARL FOUND GARON, DAZED AND GASPING FOR AIR.

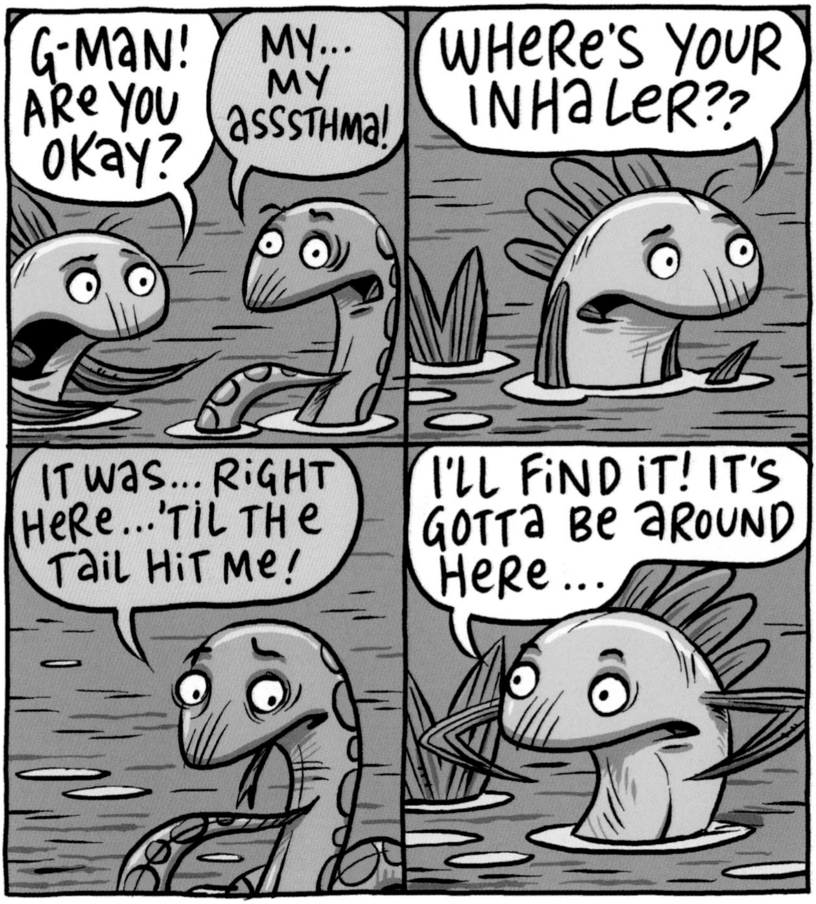
G-MAN! ARE YOU OKAY?
MY... MY ASSSTHMA!
WHERE'S YOUR INHALER??
IT WAS... RIGHT HERE...'TIL THE TAIL HIT ME!
I'LL FIND IT! IT'S GOTTA BE AROUND HERE...

HELP!!
GARON'S INHALER
...SOMEWHERE.
OH NO!

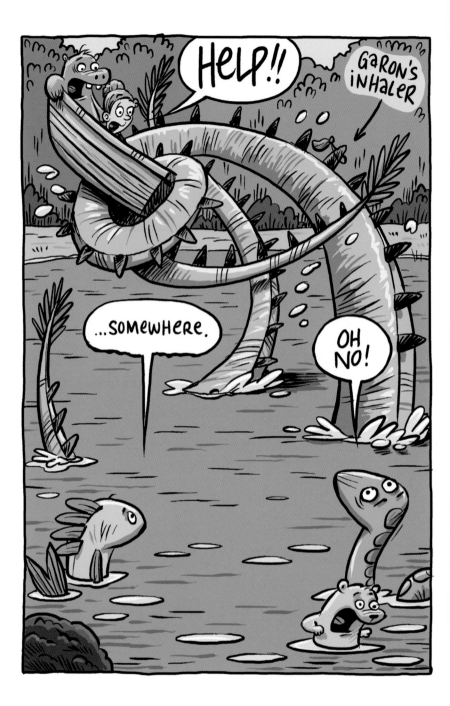

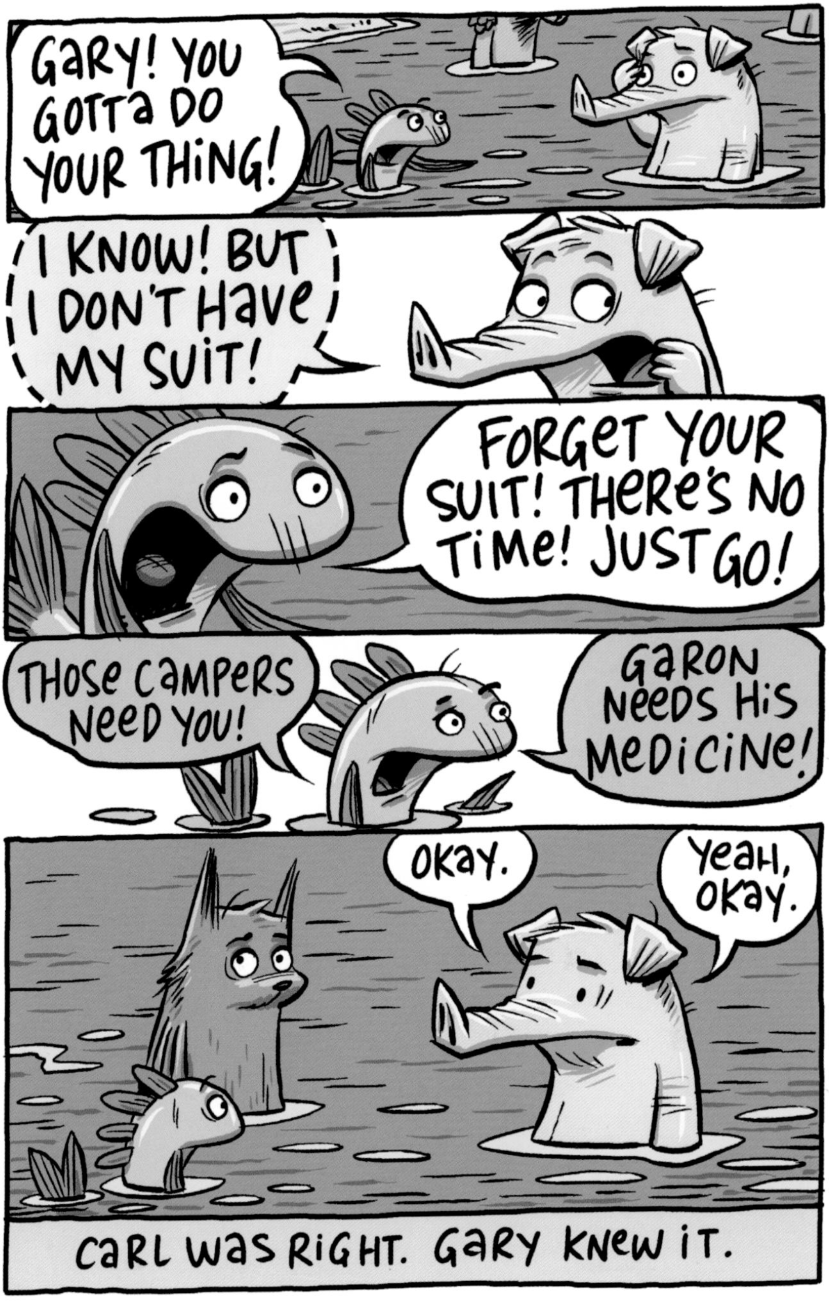
GaRY! YOU GOTTa DO YOUR THiNG!
I KNOW! BUT I DON'T Have MY SUiT!
FORGeT YOUR SUIT! THeRe'S NO TiMe! JUST GO!
THOSe CaMPeRS NeeD YOU!
GaRON NeeDS HiS MeDiCiNe!
OKaY.
YeaH, OKaY.
CaRL WaS RiGHT. GaRY KNeW iT.

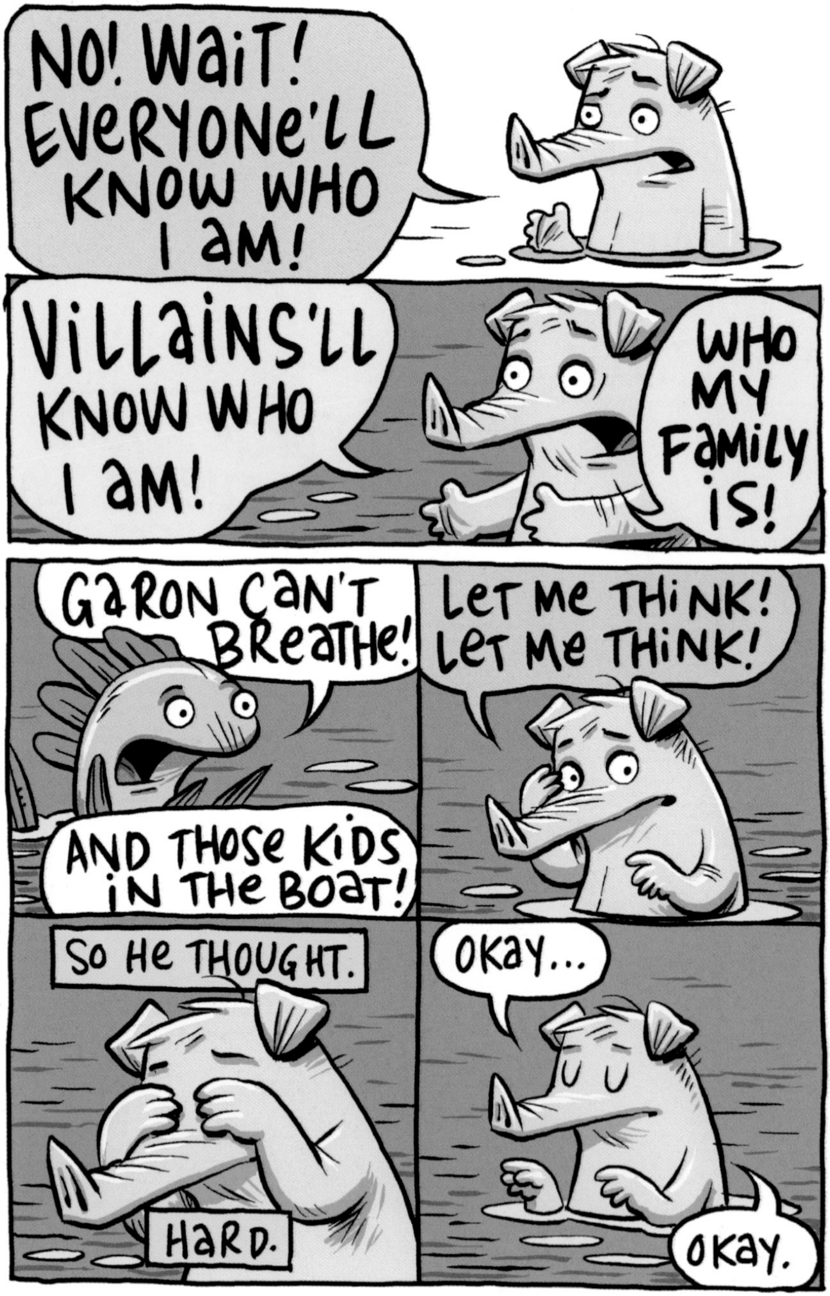
NO! WAIT! EVERYONE'LL KNOW WHO I AM!
VILLAINS'LL KNOW WHO I AM!
WHO MY FAMILY IS!
GARON CAN'T BREATHE!
AND THOSE KIDS IN THE BOAT!
LET ME THINK! LET ME THINK!
SO HE THOUGHT.
HARD.
OKAY...
OKAY.

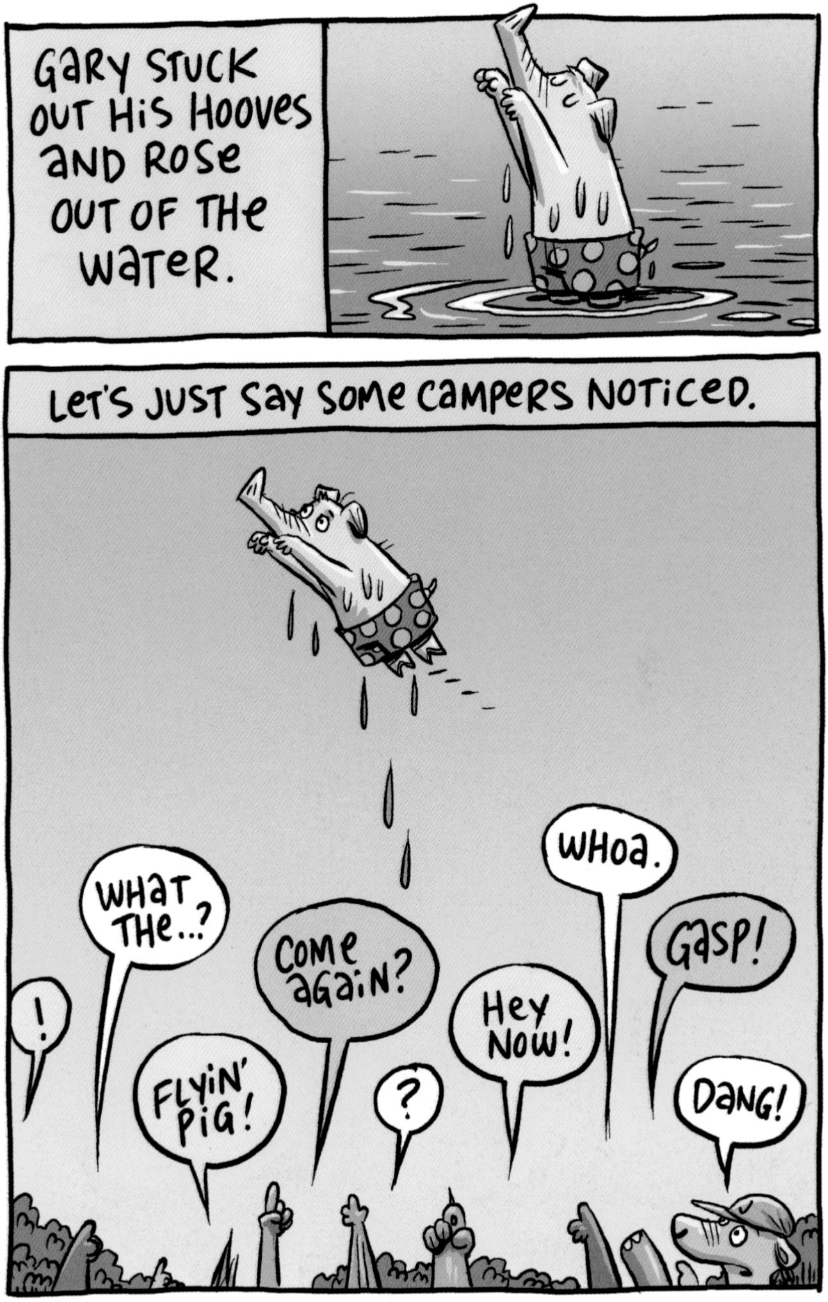
GARY STUCK OUT HIS HOOVES AND ROSE OUT OF THE WATER.
LET'S JUST SAY SOME CAMPERS NOTICED.
!
WHAT THE..?
FLYIN' PIG!
COME AGAIN?
?
HEY NOW!
WHOA.
GASP!
DANG!

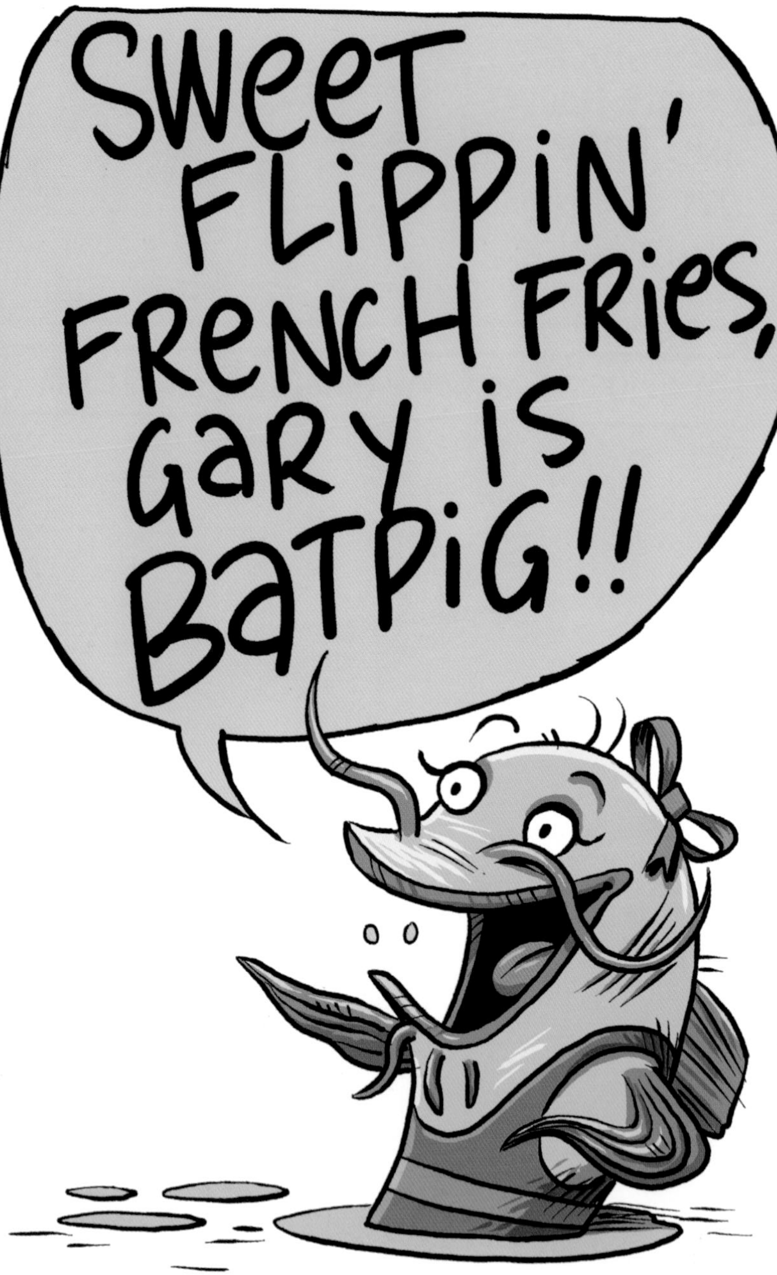
SWEET FLIPPIN' FRENCH FRIES, GARY IS BATPIG!!

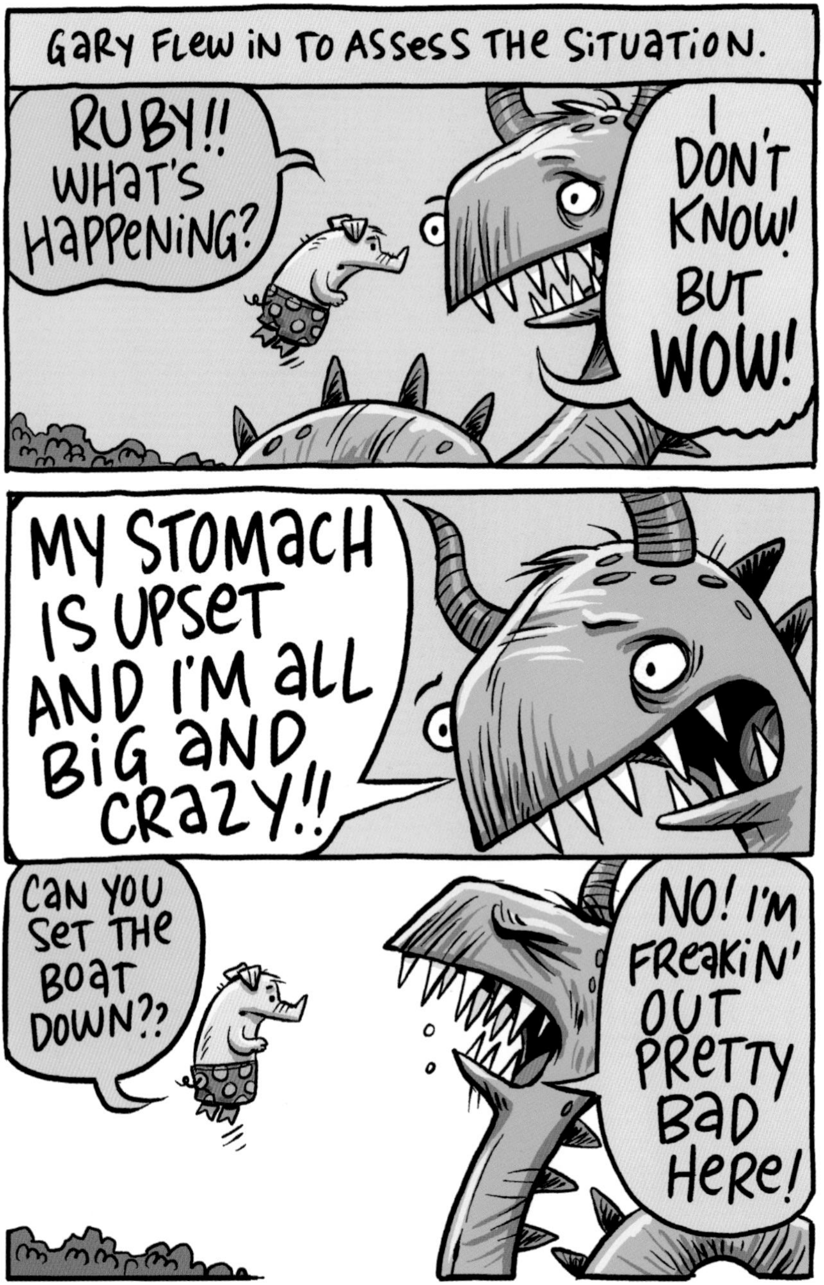
GARY FLEW IN TO ASSESS THE SITUATION.
RUBY!! WHAT'S HAPPENING?
I DON'T KNOW! BUT WOW!
MY STOMACH IS UPSET AND I'M ALL BIG AND CRAZY!!
CAN YOU SET THE BOAT DOWN??
NO! I'M FREAKIN' OUT PRETTY BAD HERE!

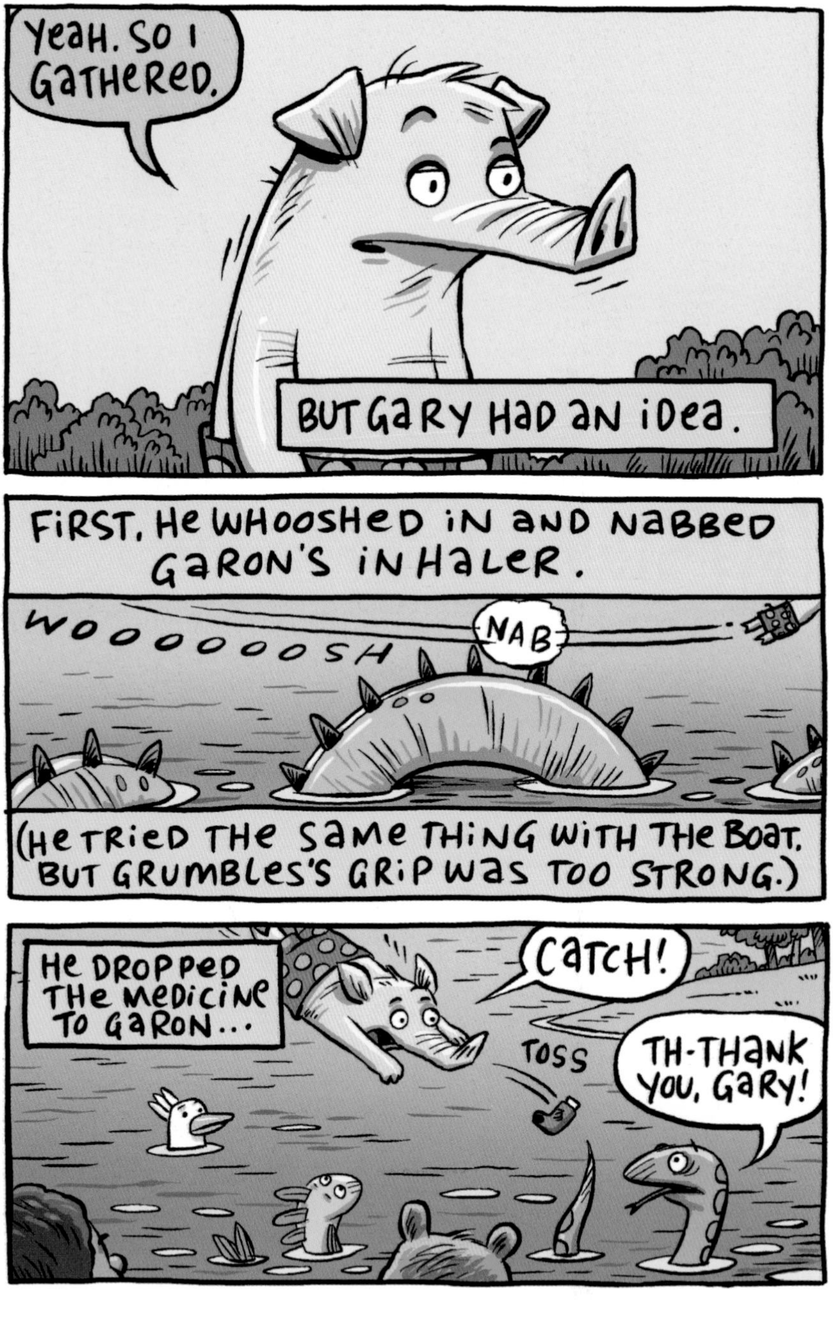
YEAH. SO I GATHERED.
BUT GARY HAD AN IDEA.
FIRST, HE WHOOSHED IN AND NABBED GARON'S INHALER.
WOOOOOOOSH
NAB
(HE TRIED THE SAME THING WITH THE BOAT, BUT GRUMBLES'S GRIP WAS TOO STRONG.)
HE DROPPED THE MEDICINE TO GARON...
CATCH!
TOSS
TH-THANK YOU, GARY!

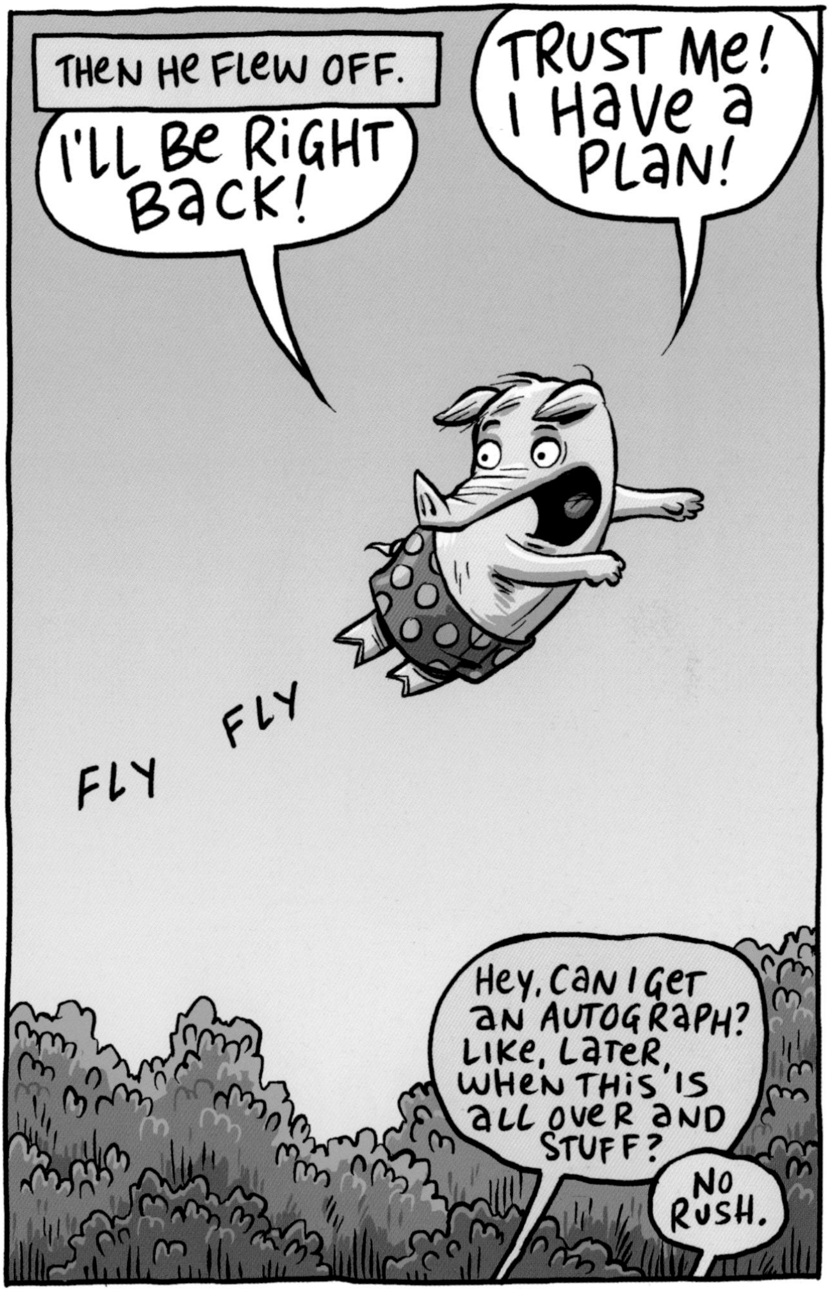
THEN HE FLEW OFF.
I'LL BE RIGHT BACK!
TRUST ME! I HAVE A PLAN!
FLY
FLY
HEY, CAN I GET AN AUTOGRAPH? LIKE, LATER, WHEN THIS IS ALL OVER AND STUFF?
NO RUSH.

CHAPTER SEVEN

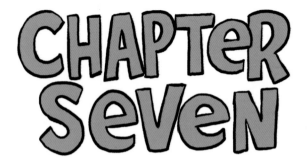

"PLOP PLOP, FIZZ FIZZ"

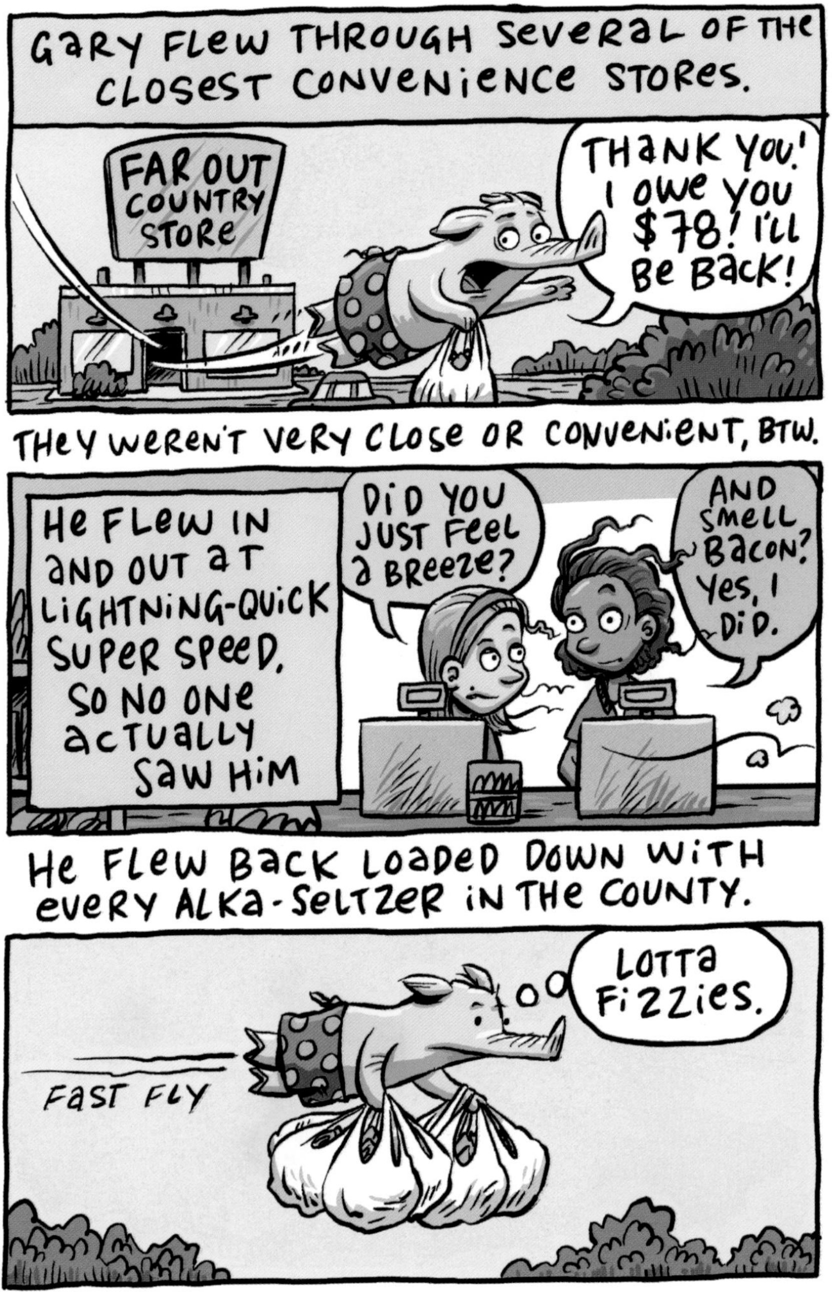
GARY FLEW THROUGH SEVERAL OF THE CLOSEST CONVENIENCE STORES.
FAR OUT COUNTRY STORE
THANK YOU! I OWE YOU $78! I'LL BE BACK!
THEY WEREN'T VERY CLOSE OR CONVENIENT, BTW.
HE FLEW IN AND OUT AT LIGHTNING-QUICK SUPER SPEED, SO NO ONE ACTUALLY SAW HIM
DID YOU JUST FEEL A BREEZE?
AND SMELL BACON? YES, I DID.
HE FLEW BACK LOADED DOWN WITH EVERY ALKA-SELTZER IN THE COUNTY.
LOTTA FIZZIES.
FAST FLY

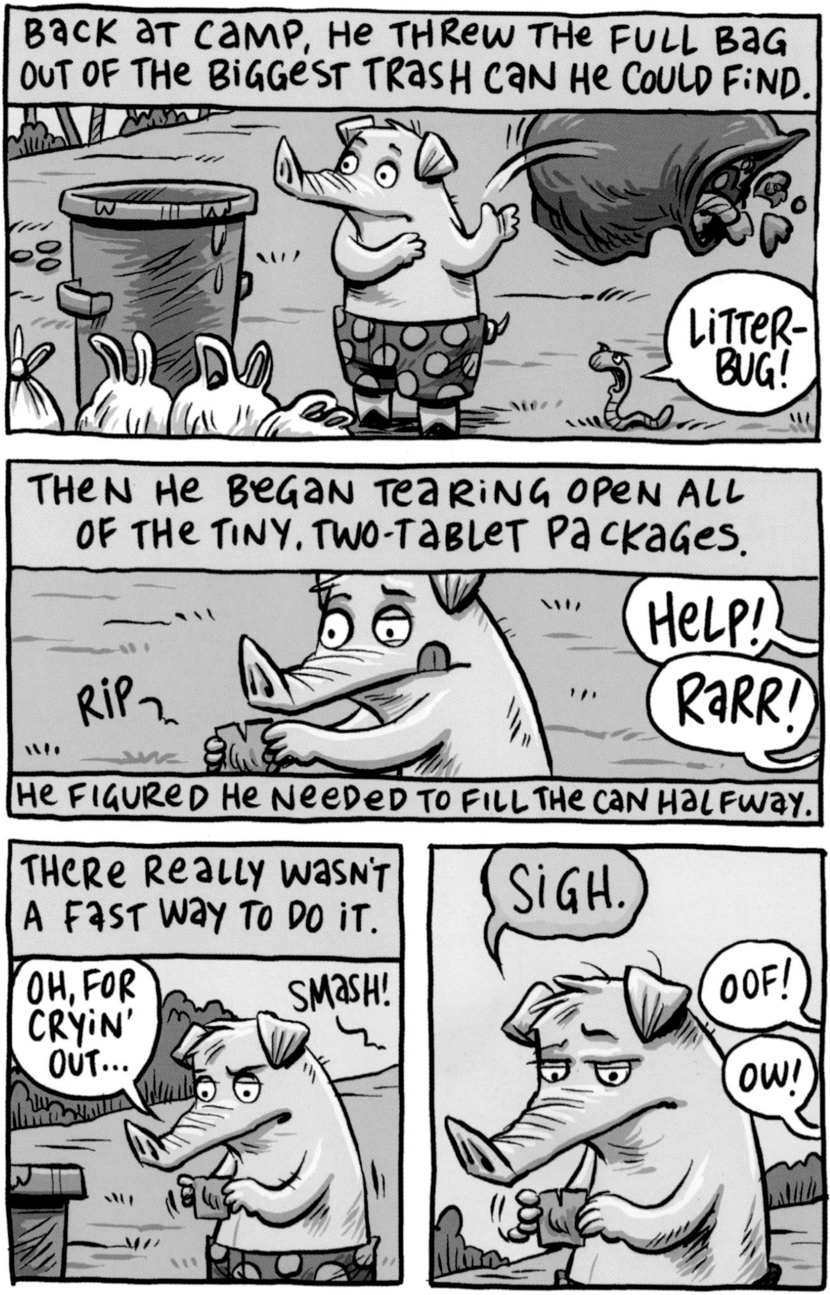
BACK AT CAMP, HE THREW THE FULL BAG OUT OF THE BIGGEST TRASH CAN HE COULD FIND.
LITTER-BUG!
THEN HE BEGAN TEARING OPEN ALL OF THE TINY, TWO-TABLET PACKAGES.
RIP
HELP!
RARR!
HE FIGURED HE NEEDED TO FILL THE CAN HALFWAY.
THERE REALLY WASN'T A FAST WAY TO DO IT.
OH, FOR CRYIN' OUT...
SMASH!
SIGH.
OOF!
OW!

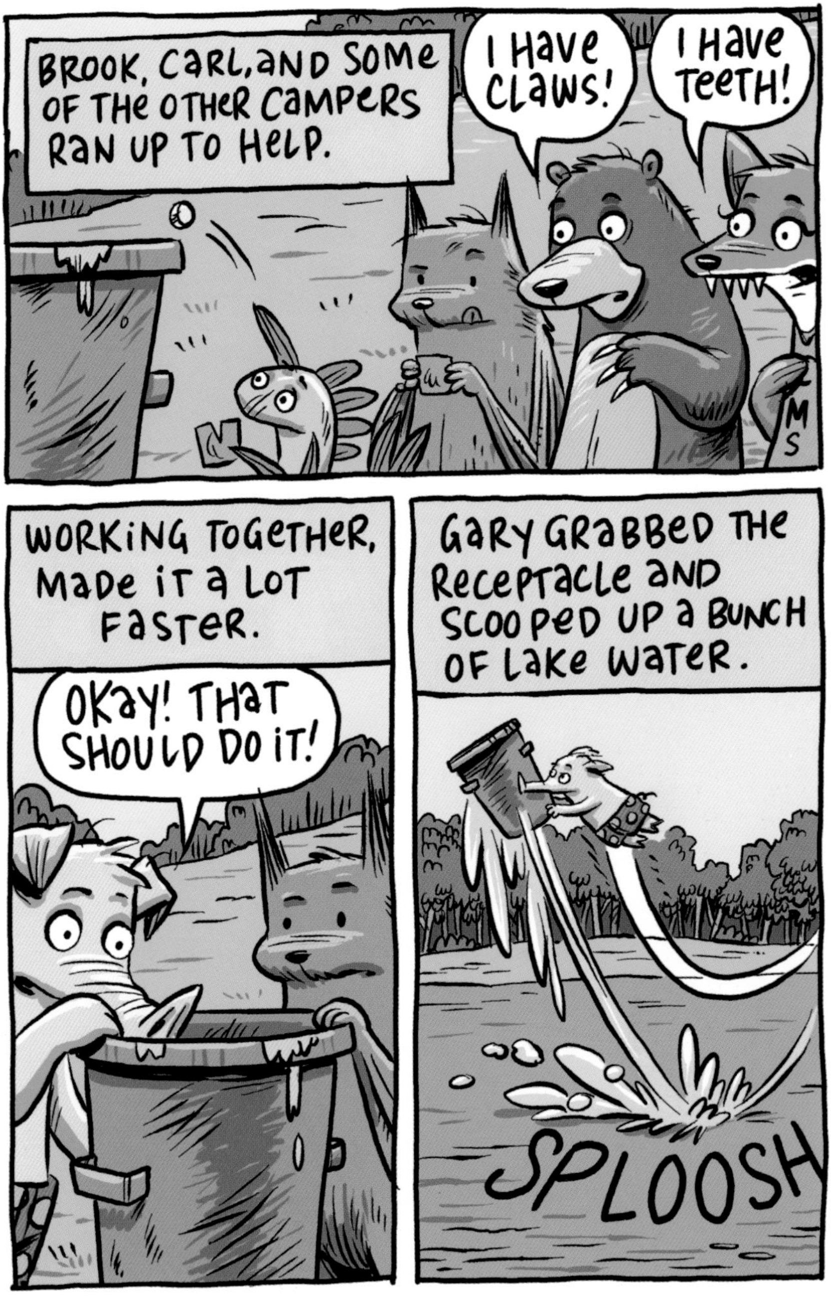
BROOK, CARL, AND SOME OF THE OTHER CAMPERS RAN UP TO HELP.
I HAVE CLAWS!
I HAVE TEETH!
MS
WORKING TOGETHER, MADE IT A LOT FASTER.
OKAY! THAT SHOULD DO IT!
GARY GRABBED THE RECEPTACLE AND SCOOPED UP A BUNCH OF LAKE WATER.
SPLOOSH

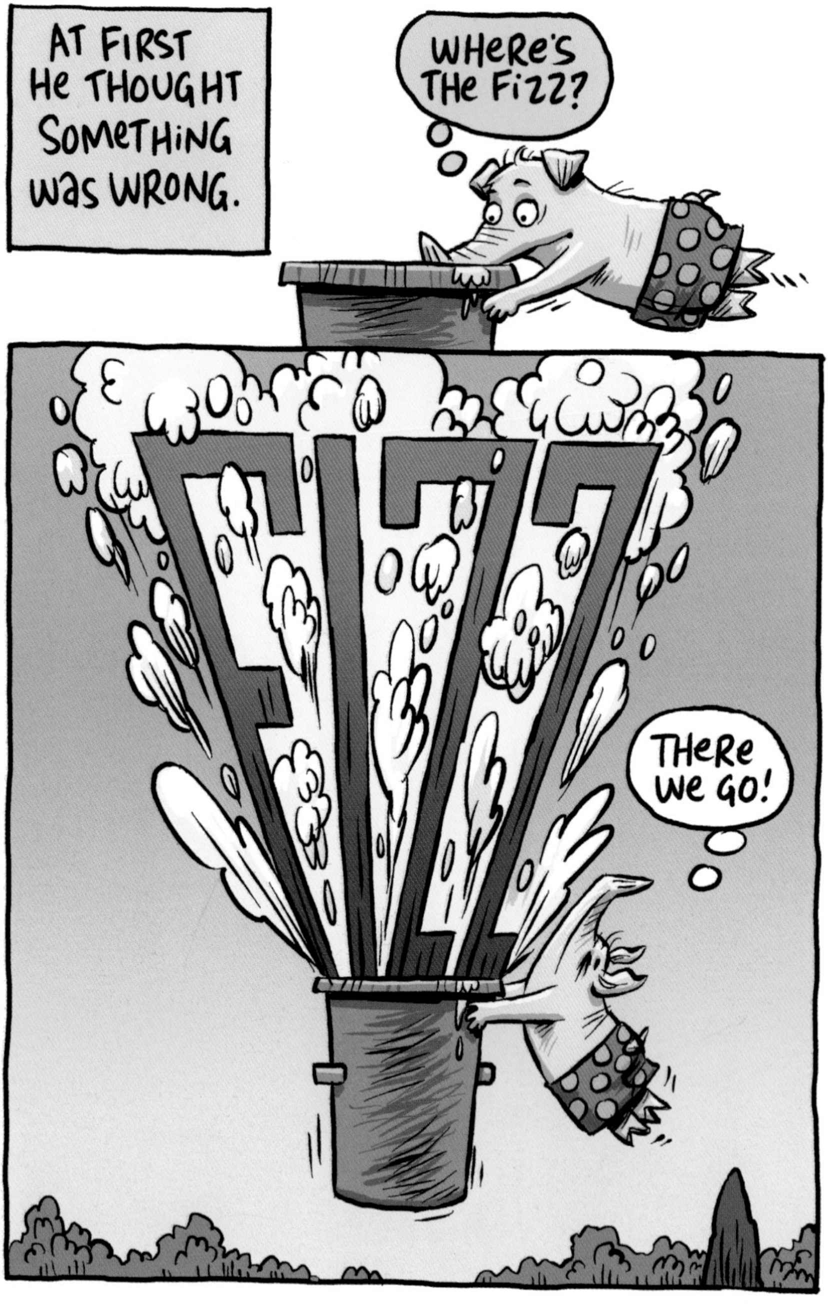
AT FIRST HE THOUGHT SOMETHING WAS WRONG.
WHERE'S THE FIZZ?
FIZZ
THERE WE GO!

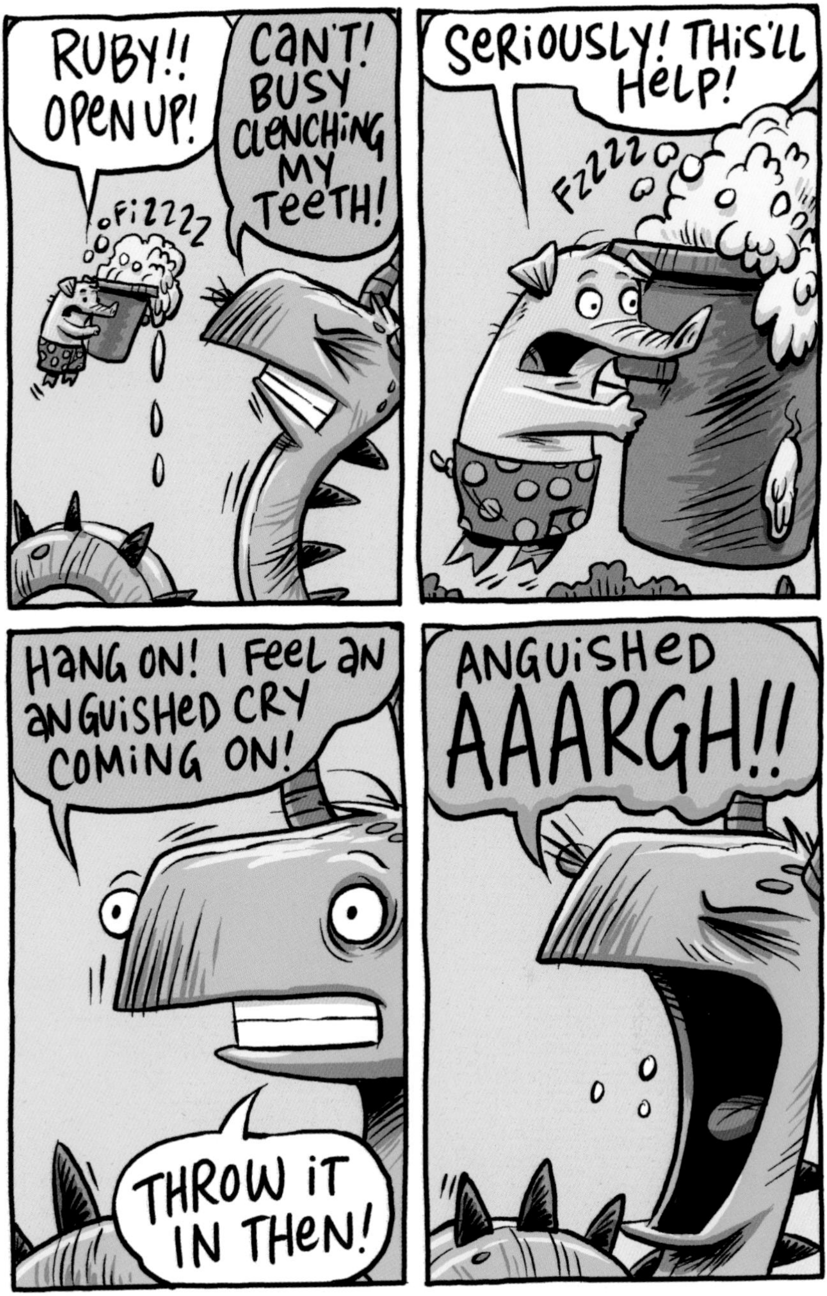
RUBY!! OPEN UP!
FIZZZZ
CAN'T! BUSY CLENCHING MY TEETH!
SERIOUSLY! THIS'LL HELP!
FZZZZ
HANG ON! I FEEL AN ANGUISHED CRY COMING ON!
THROW IT IN THEN!
ANGUISHED AAARGH!!

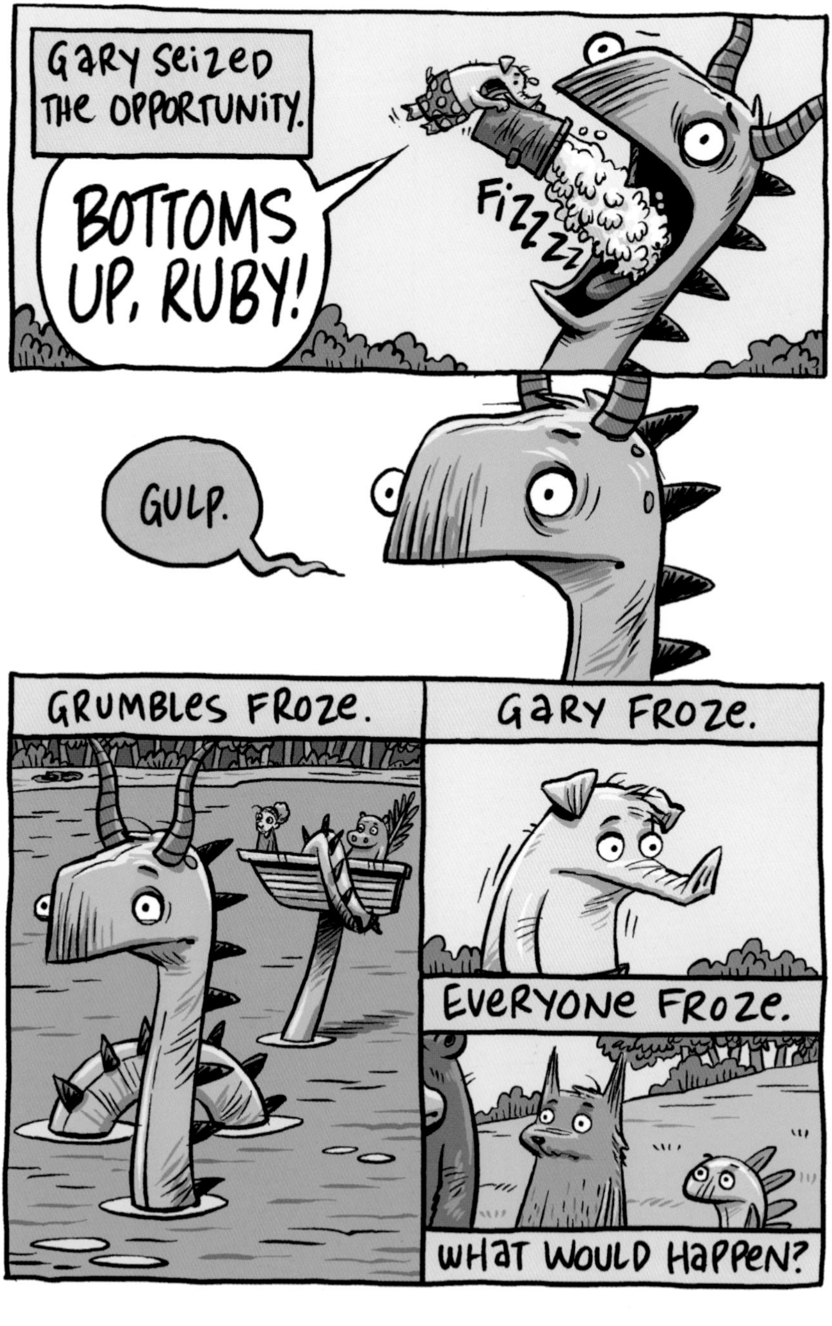

GARY SEIZED THE OPPORTUNITY.
BOTTOMS UP, RUBY!
FIZZZZZ
GULP.
GRUMBLES FROZE.
GARY FROZE.
EVERYONE FROZE.
WHAT WOULD HAPPEN?

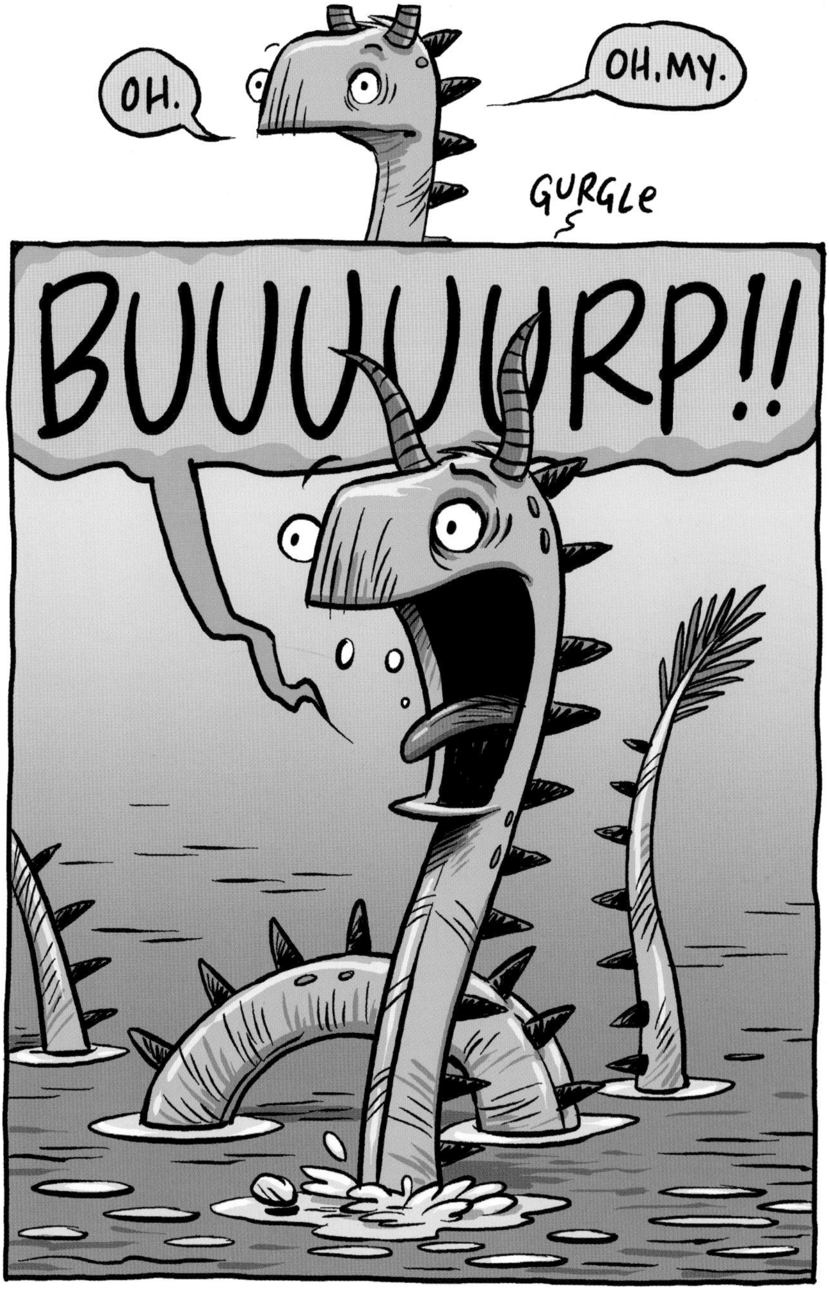
OH.
OH. MY.
GURGLE
BUUUUURP!!

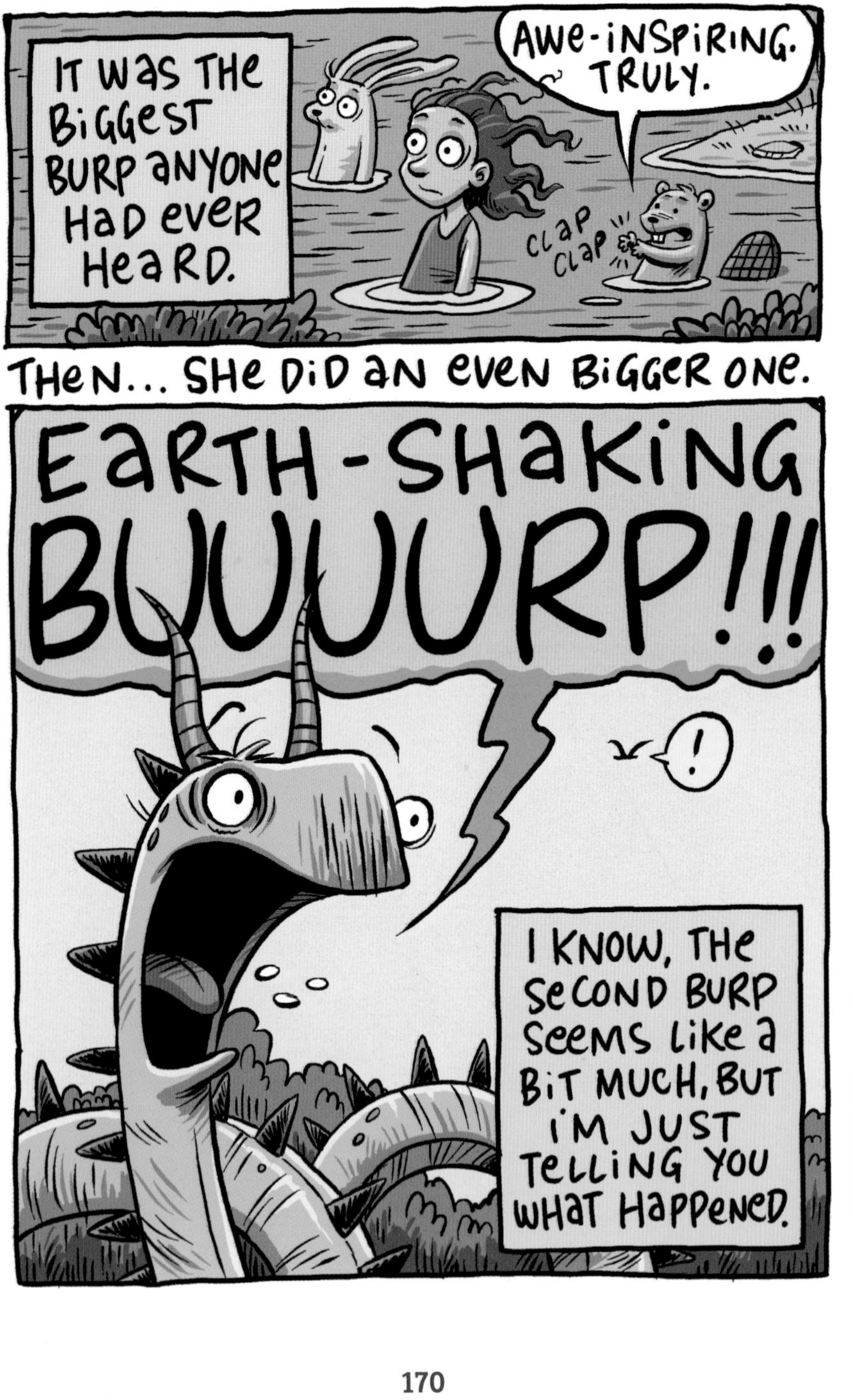
IT WAS THE BIGGEST BURP ANYONE HAD EVER HEARD.
AWE-INSPIRING. TRULY.
CLAP CLAP
THEN... SHE DID AN EVEN BIGGER ONE.
EARTH-SHAKING BUUUURP!!!
!
I KNOW, THE SECOND BURP SEEMS LIKE A BIT MUCH, BUT I'M JUST TELLING YOU WHAT HAPPENED.

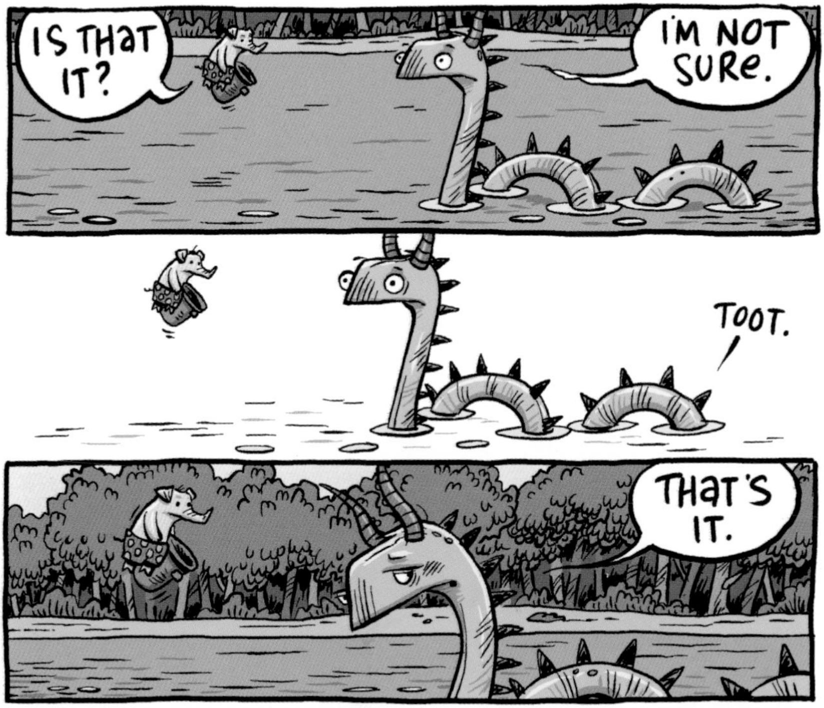
IS THAT IT?
I'M NOT SURE.
TOOT.
THAT'S IT.

AGAIN, I'M JUST REPORTING WHAT HAPPENED.

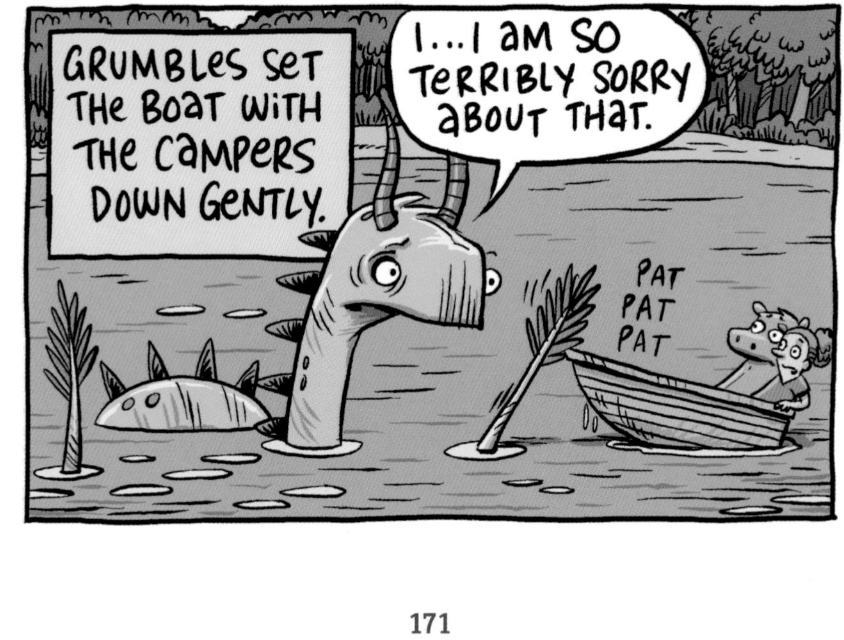
GRUMBLES SET THE BOAT WITH THE CAMPERS DOWN GENTLY.
I...I AM SO TERRIBLY SORRY ABOUT THAT.
PAT PAT PAT

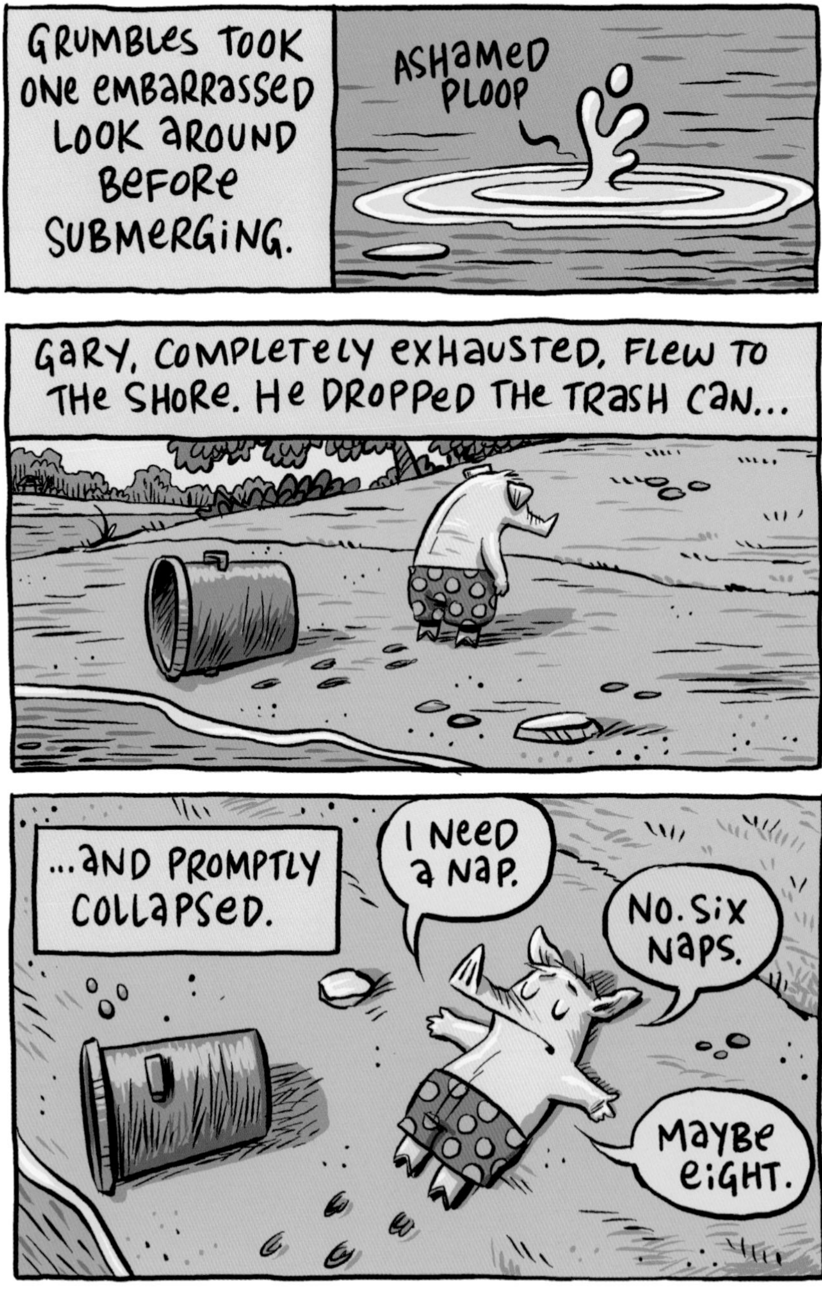
GRUMBLES TOOK ONE EMBARRASSED LOOK AROUND BEFORE SUBMERGING.
ASHAMED PLOOP
GARY, COMPLETELY EXHAUSTED, FLEW TO THE SHORE. HE DROPPED THE TRASH CAN...
...AND PROMPTLY COLLAPSED.
I NEED A NAP.
NO. SIX NAPS.
MAYBE EIGHT.

CHAPTER EIGHT

"A STAR IS BORN"

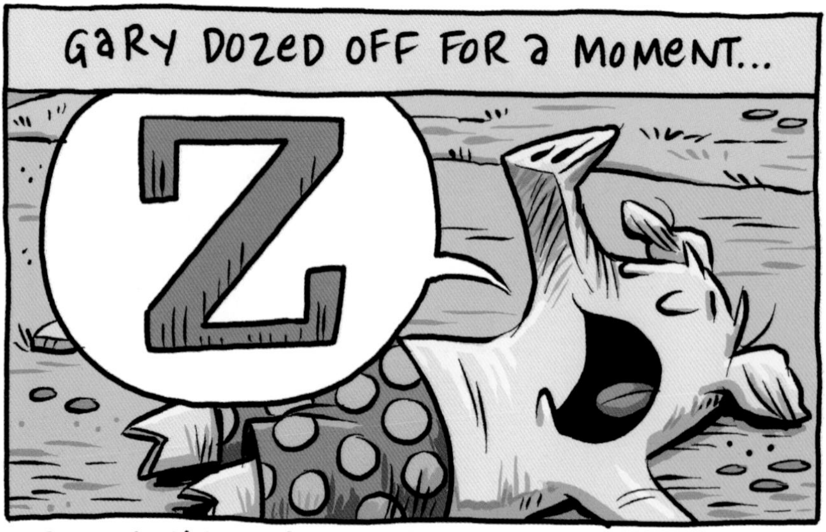
GARY DOZED OFF FOR A MOMENT...
Z

BUT WHEN HE WOKE, HE COULD FEEL HIMSELF BEING LIFTED UP.

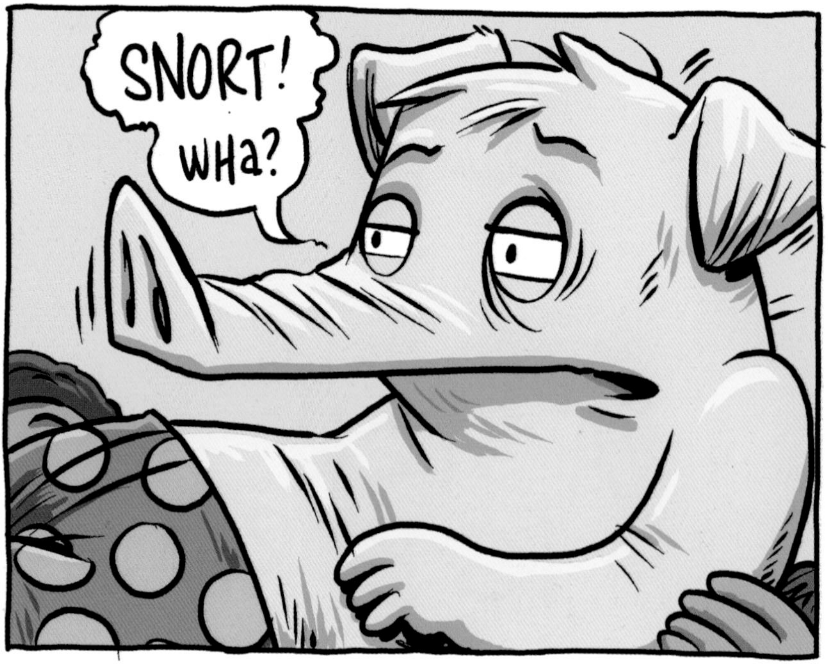
SNORT! WHA?

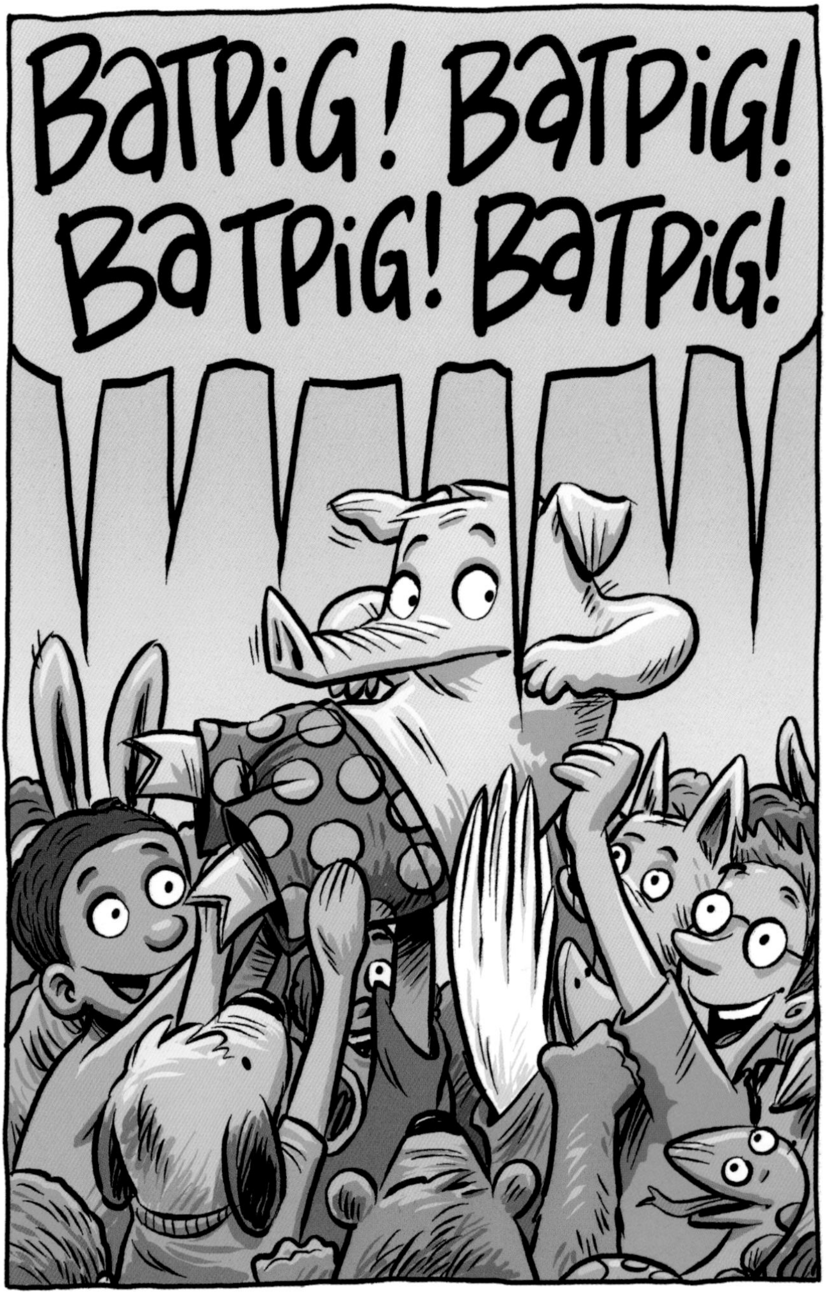
BATPIG! BATPIG! BATPIG! BATPIG!

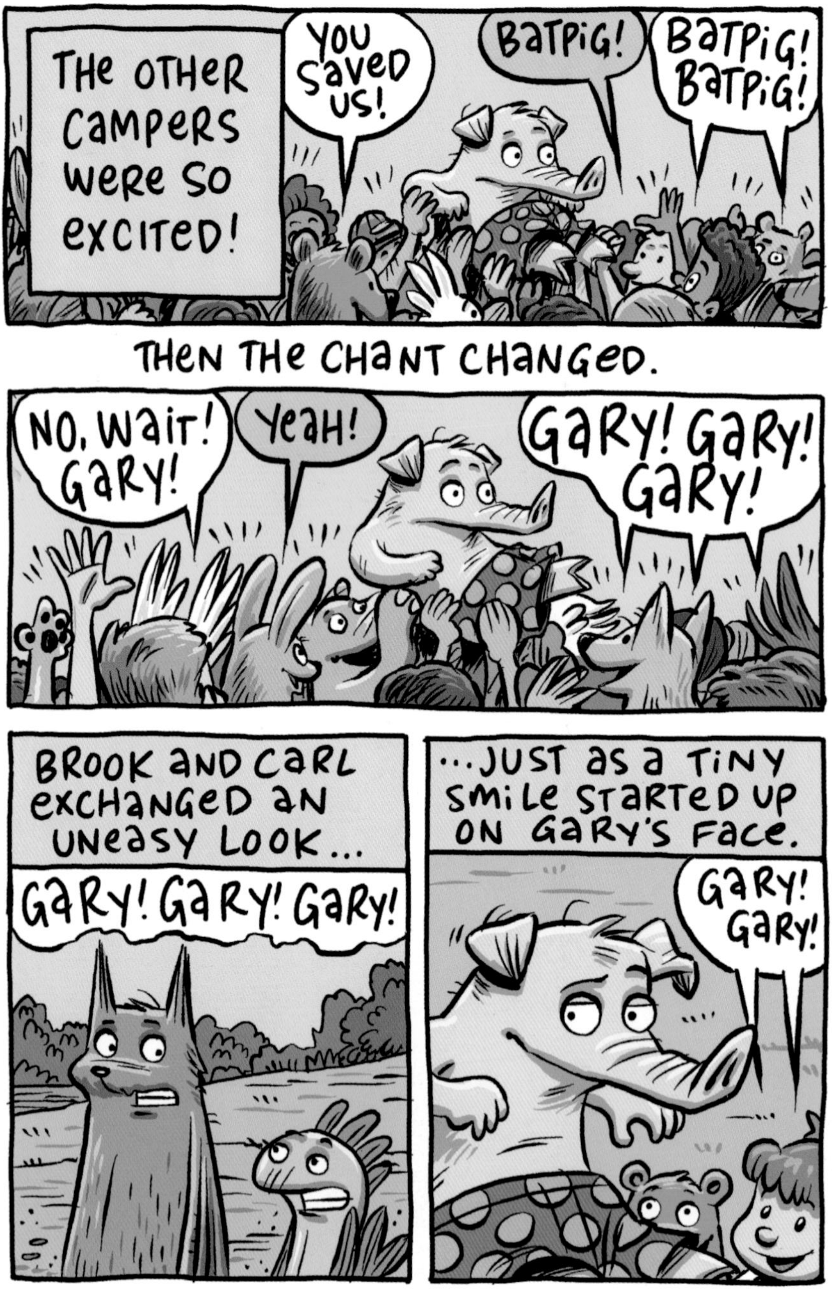
THE OTHER CAMPERS WERE SO EXCITED!
YOU SAVED US!
BATPIG!
BATPIG! BATPIG!
THEN THE CHANT CHANGED.
NO, WAIT! GARY!
YEAH!
GARY! GARY! GARY!
BROOK AND CARL EXCHANGED AN UNEASY LOOK...
GARY! GARY! GARY!
...JUST AS A TINY SMILE STARTED UP ON GARY'S FACE.
GARY! GARY!

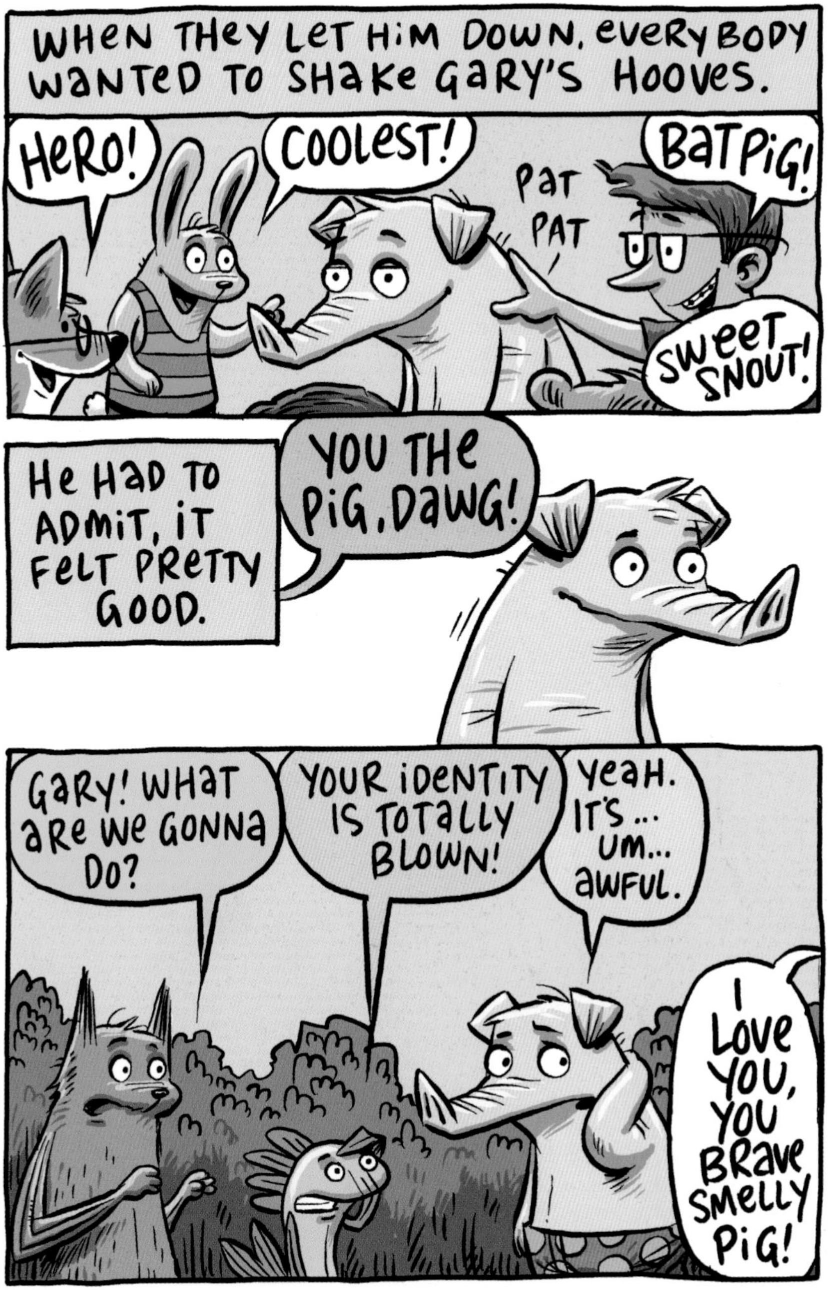

WHEN THEY LET HIM DOWN, EVERYBODY WANTED TO SHAKE GARY'S HOOVES.
HERO!
COOLEST!
PAT PAT
BATPIG!
SWEET SNOUT!
HE HAD TO ADMIT, IT FELT PRETTY GOOD.
YOU THE PIG, DAWG!
GARY! WHAT ARE WE GONNA DO?
YOUR IDENTITY IS TOTALLY BLOWN!
YEAH. IT'S... UM... AWFUL.
I LOVE YOU, YOU BRAVE SMELLY PIG!

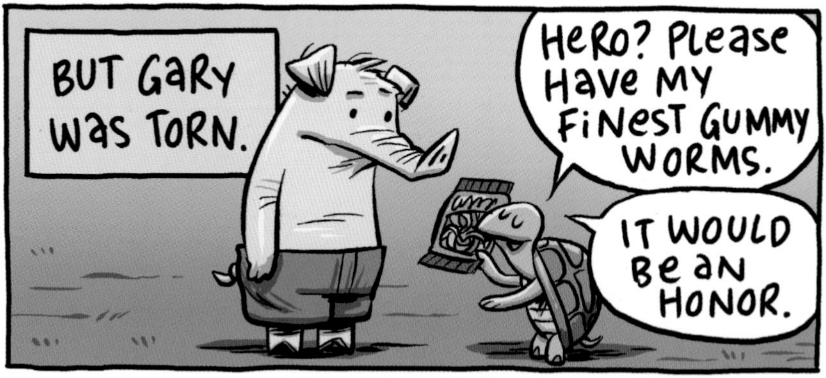
BUT GARY WAS TORN.
HERO? PLEASE HAVE MY FINEST GUMMY WORMS.
IT WOULD BE AN HONOR.

AT LUNCH, HE'D NEVER BEEN SO POPULAR.

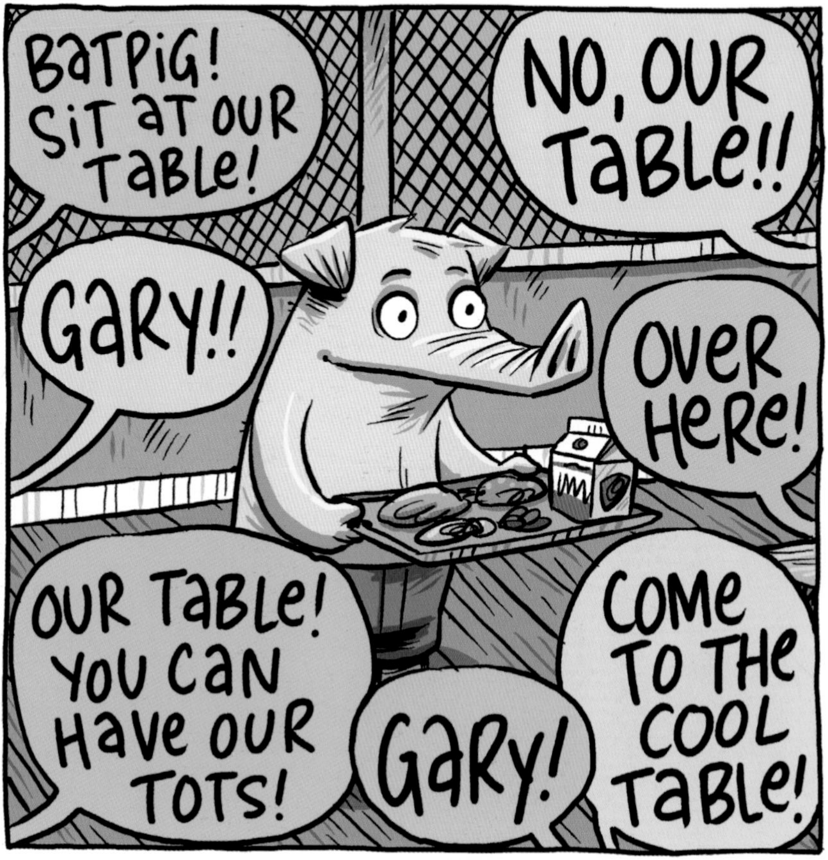
BATPIG! SIT AT OUR TABLE!
NO, OUR TABLE!!
GARY!!
OVER HERE!
OUR TABLE! YOU CAN HAVE OUR TOTS!
GARY!
COME TO THE COOL TABLE!

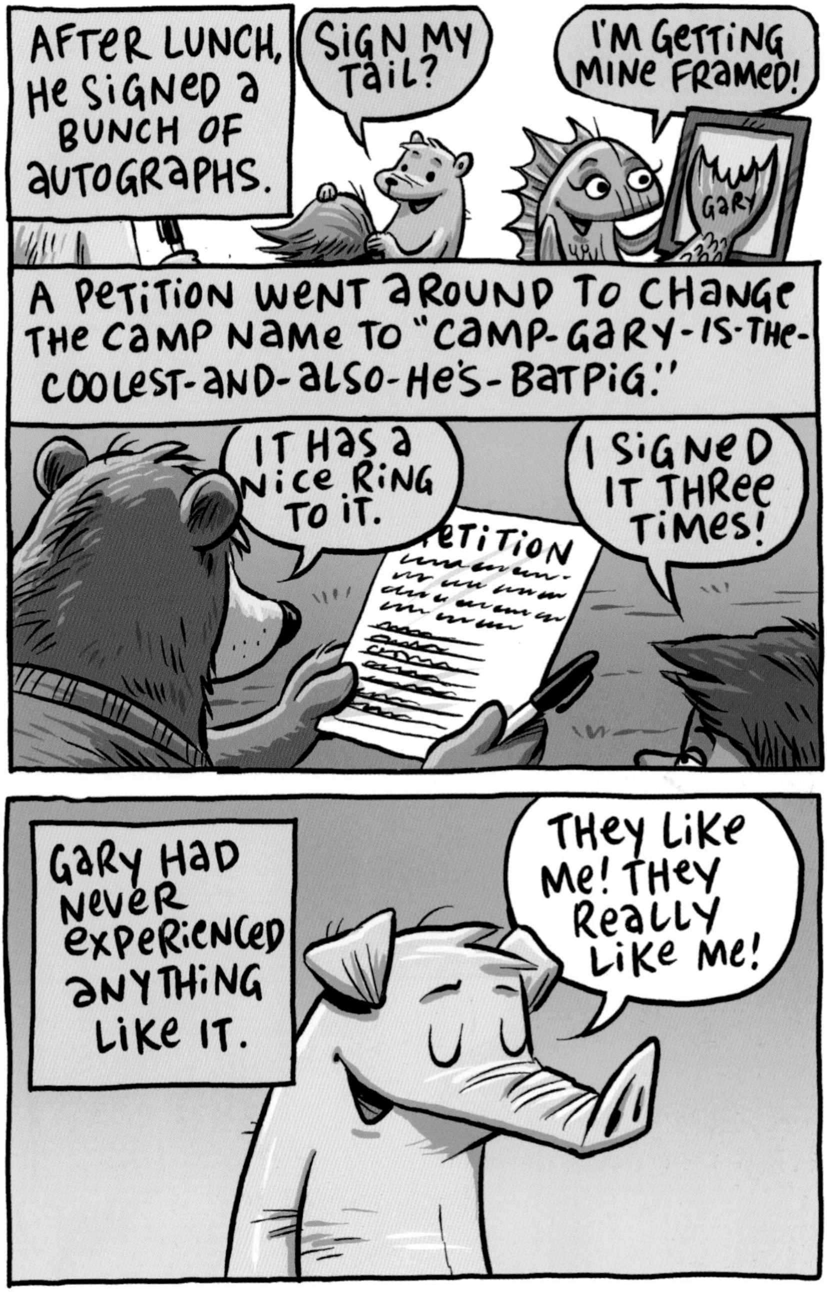
AFTER LUNCH, HE SIGNED A BUNCH OF AUTOGRAPHS.
SIGN MY TAIL?
I'M GETTING MINE FRAMED!
GARY
A PETITION WENT AROUND TO CHANGE THE CAMP NAME TO "CAMP-GARY-IS-THE-COOLEST-AND-ALSO-HE'S-BATPIG."
IT HAS A NICE RING TO IT.
PETITION
I SIGNED IT THREE TIMES!
GARY HAD NEVER EXPERIENCED ANYTHING LIKE IT.
THEY LIKE ME! THEY REALLY LIKE ME!

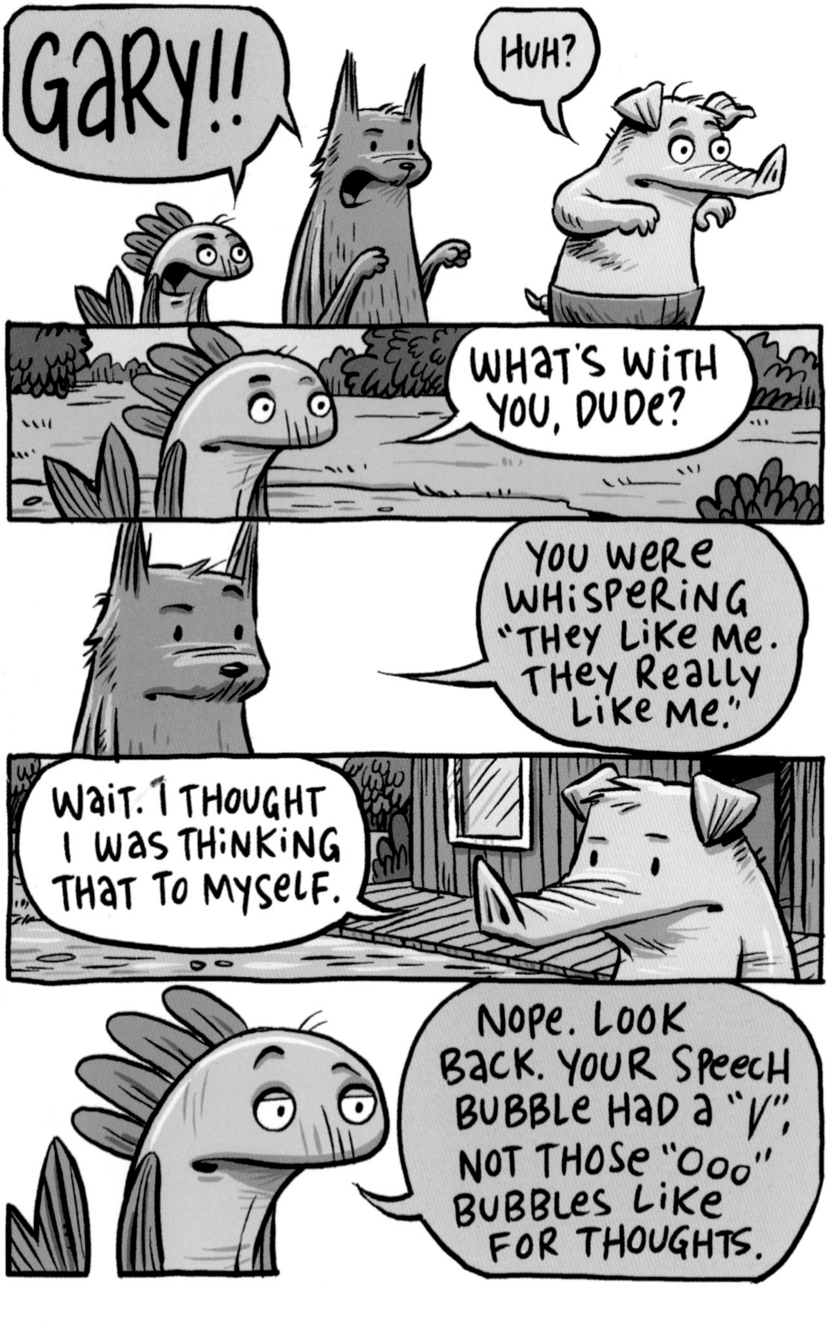
GARY!!
HUH?
WHAT'S WITH YOU, DUDE?
YOU WERE WHISPERING "THEY LIKE ME. THEY REALLY LIKE ME."
WAIT. I THOUGHT I WAS THINKING THAT TO MYSELF.
NOPE. LOOK BACK. YOUR SPEECH BUBBLE HAD A "V", NOT THOSE "OOO" BUBBLES LIKE FOR THOUGHTS.

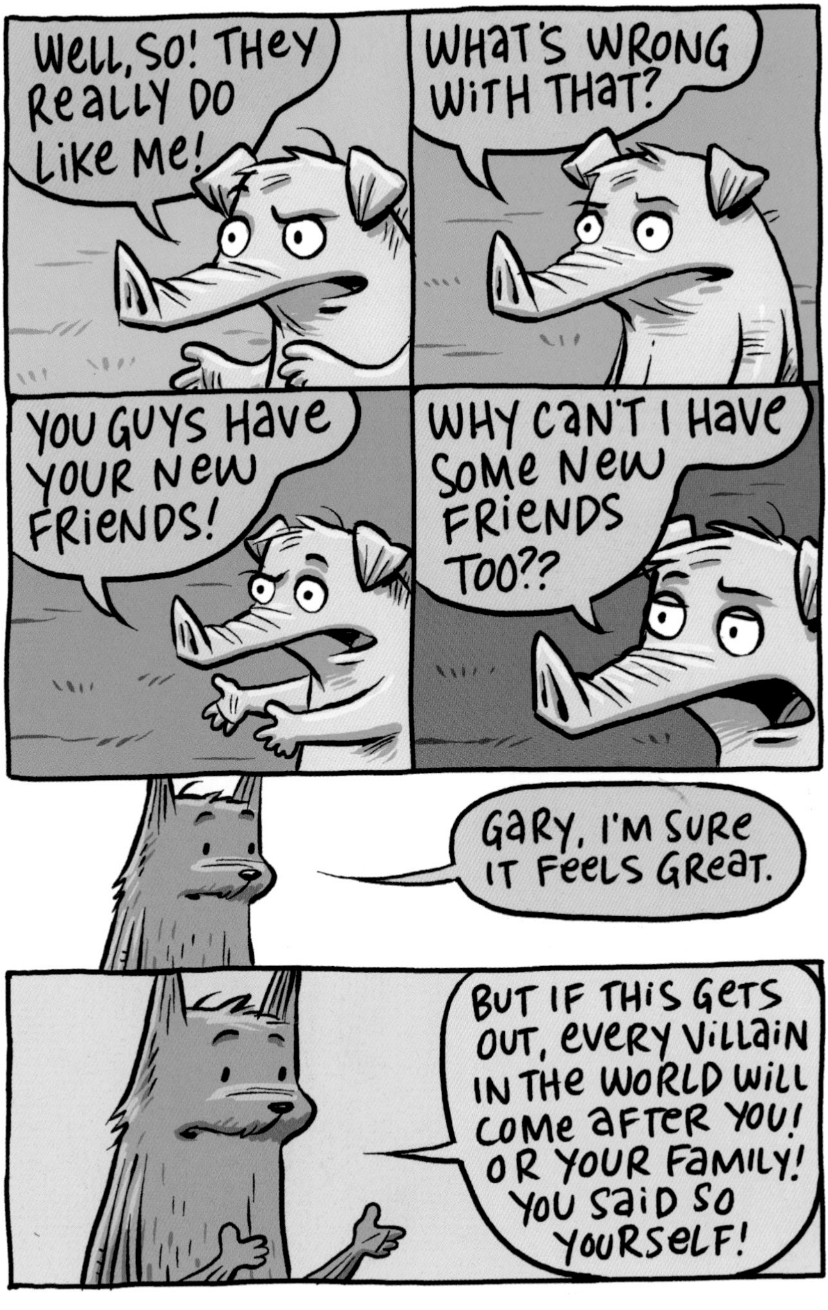
WELL, SO! THEY REALLY DO LIKE ME!
WHAT'S WRONG WITH THAT?
YOU GUYS HAVE YOUR NEW FRIENDS!
WHY CAN'T I HAVE SOME NEW FRIENDS TOO??
GARY, I'M SURE IT FEELS GREAT.
BUT IF THIS GETS OUT, EVERY VILLAIN IN THE WORLD WILL COME AFTER YOU! OR YOUR FAMILY! YOU SAID SO YOURSELF!

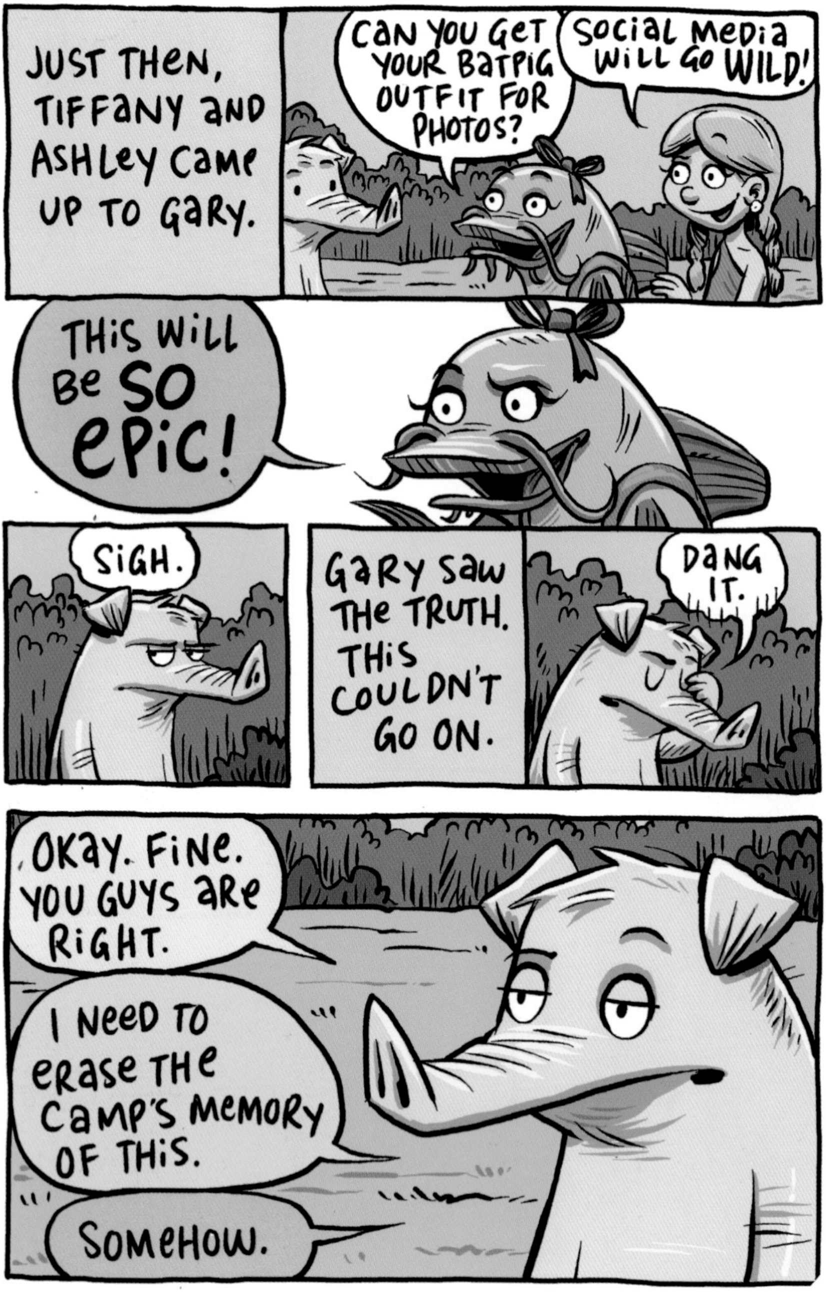
JUST THEN, TIFFANY AND ASHLEY CAME UP TO GARY.
CAN YOU GET YOUR BATPIG OUTFIT FOR PHOTOS?
SOCIAL MEDIA WILL GO WILD!
THIS WILL BE SO EPIC!
SIGH.
GARY SAW THE TRUTH. THIS COULDN'T GO ON.
DANG IT.
OKAY. FINE. YOU GUYS ARE RIGHT.
I NEED TO ERASE THE CAMP'S MEMORY OF THIS.
SOMEHOW.

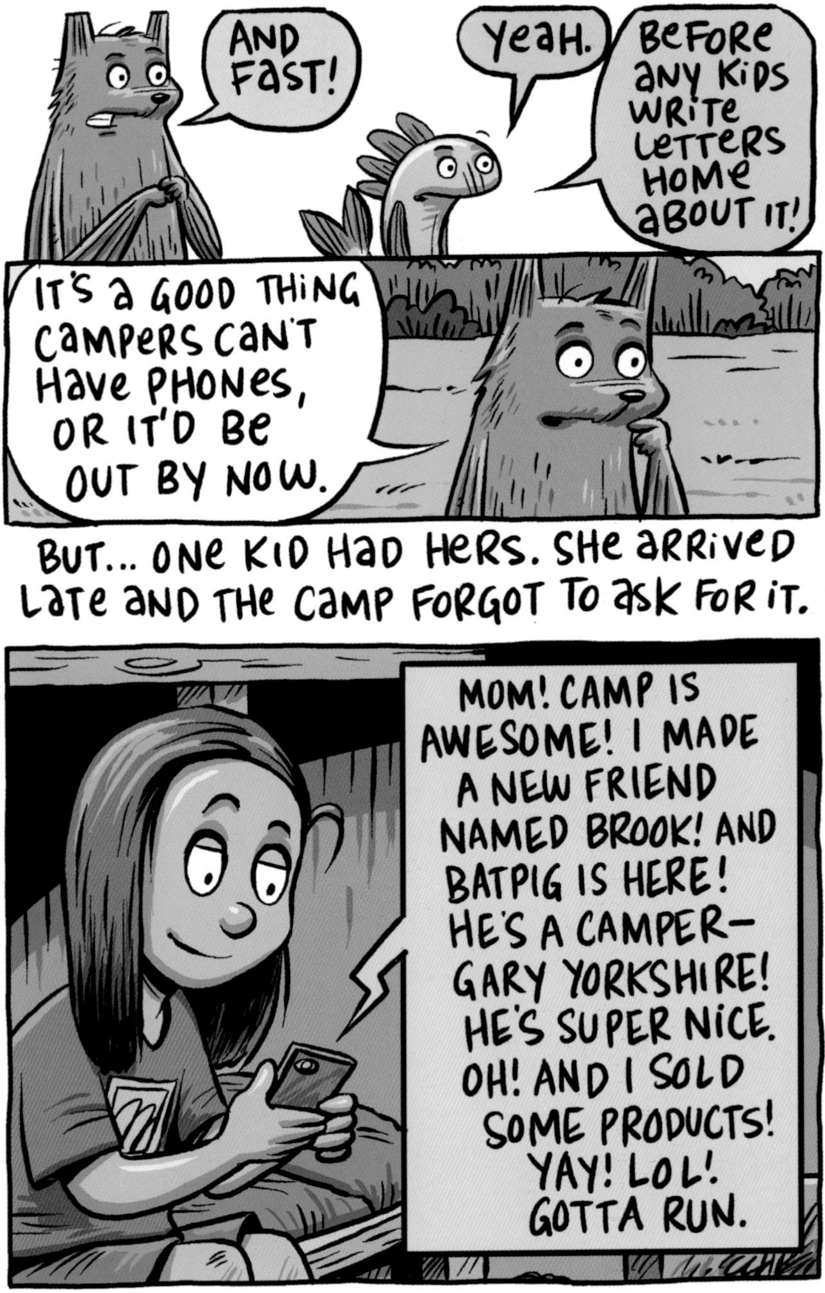
AND FAST!
YeaH.
BeFoRe any KiDS WRiTe LeTTeRS HoMe aBOUT IT!
IT'S a GOOD THiNG CamPeRS CaN'T Have PHONeS, OR IT'D Be OUT BY NOW.
BUT... ONe KID HaD HeRS. SHe aRRiveD Late aND THe CamP FORGOT To ask FoR iT.
MOM! CAMP IS AWESOME! I MADE A NEW FRIEND NAMED BROOK! AND BATPIG IS HERE! HE'S A CAMPER- GARY YORKSHIRE! HE'S SUPER NICE. OH! AND I SOLD SOME PRODUCTS! YAY! LOL! GOTTA RUN.

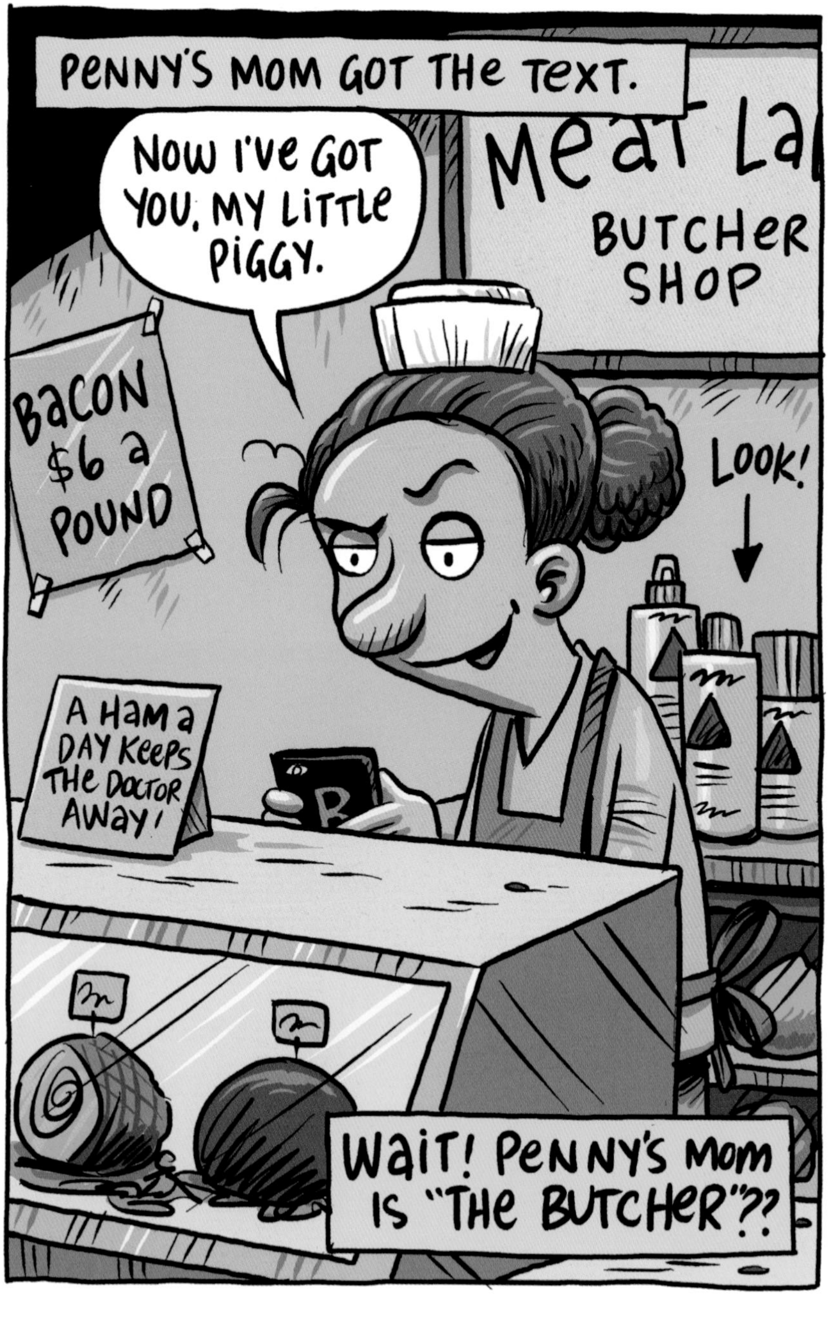
PENNY'S MOM GOT THE TEXT.
NOW I'VE GOT YOU, MY LITTLE PIGGY.
MEAT LA
BUTCHER SHOP
BACON $6 A POUND
LOOK!
A HAM A DAY KEEPS THE DOCTOR AWAY!
WAIT! PENNY'S MOM IS "THE BUTCHER"??

CHAPTER NINE

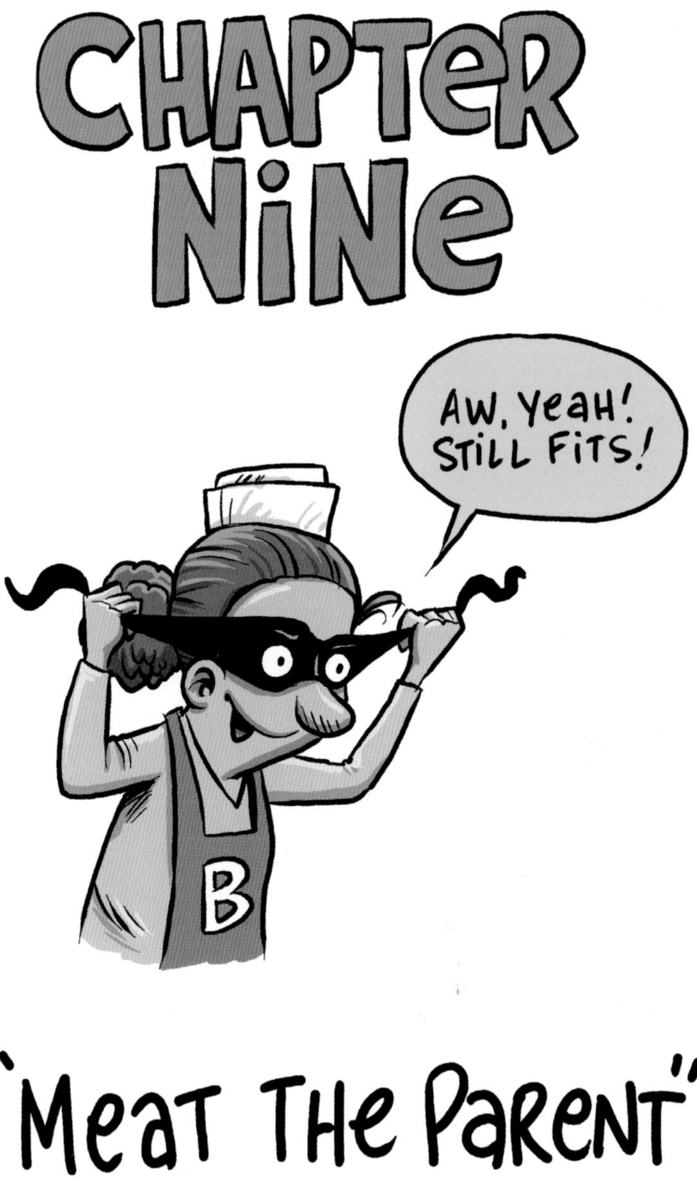
AW, YEAH! STILL FITS!

"MEAT THE PARENT"

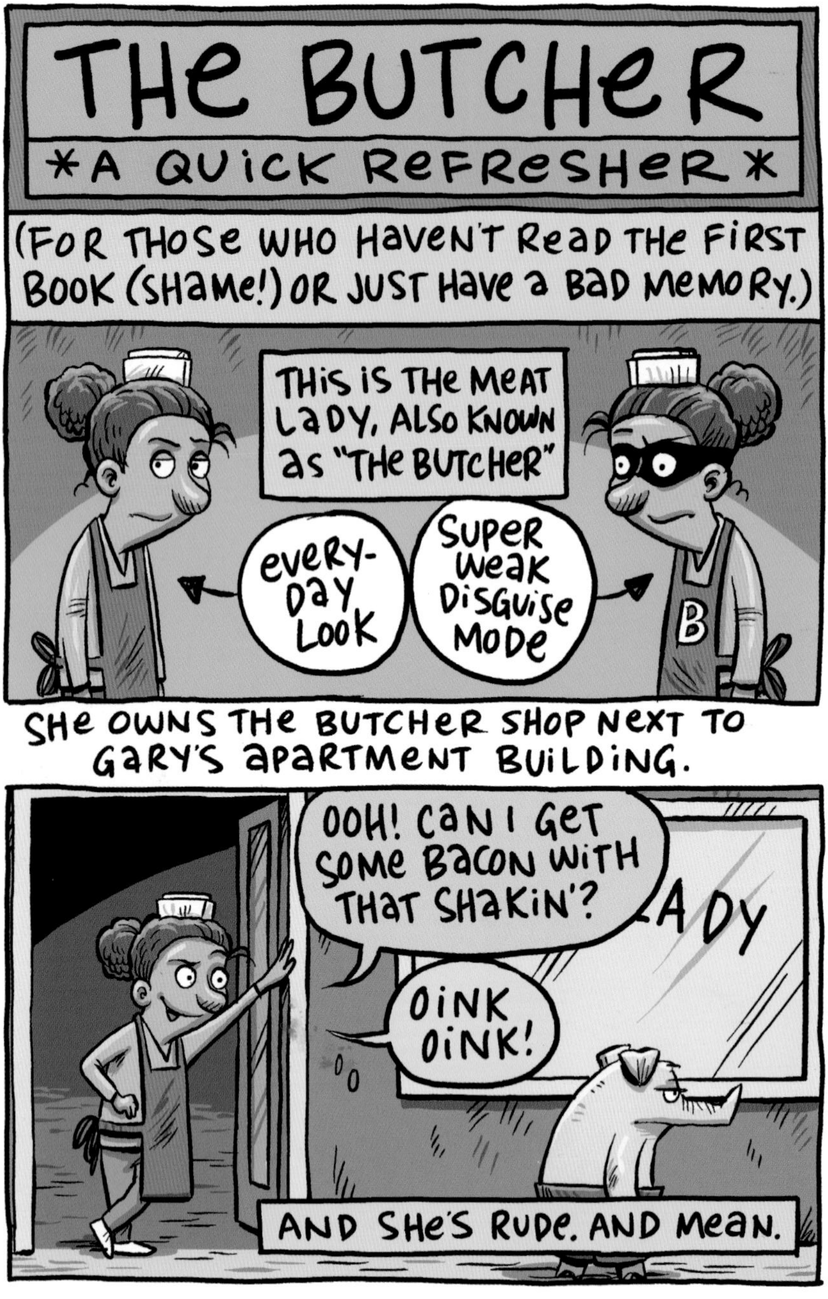
THE BUTCHER
A QUICK REFRESHER
(FOR THOSE WHO HAVEN'T READ THE FIRST BOOK (SHAME!) OR JUST HAVE A BAD MEMORY.)
THIS IS THE MEAT LADY, ALSO KNOWN AS "THE BUTCHER"
EVERY-DAY LOOK
SUPER WEAK DISGUISE MODE
B
SHE OWNS THE BUTCHER SHOP NEXT TO GARY'S APARTMENT BUILDING.
OOH! CAN I GET SOME BACON WITH THAT SHAKIN'?
OINK OINK!
AND SHE'S RUDE. AND MEAN.

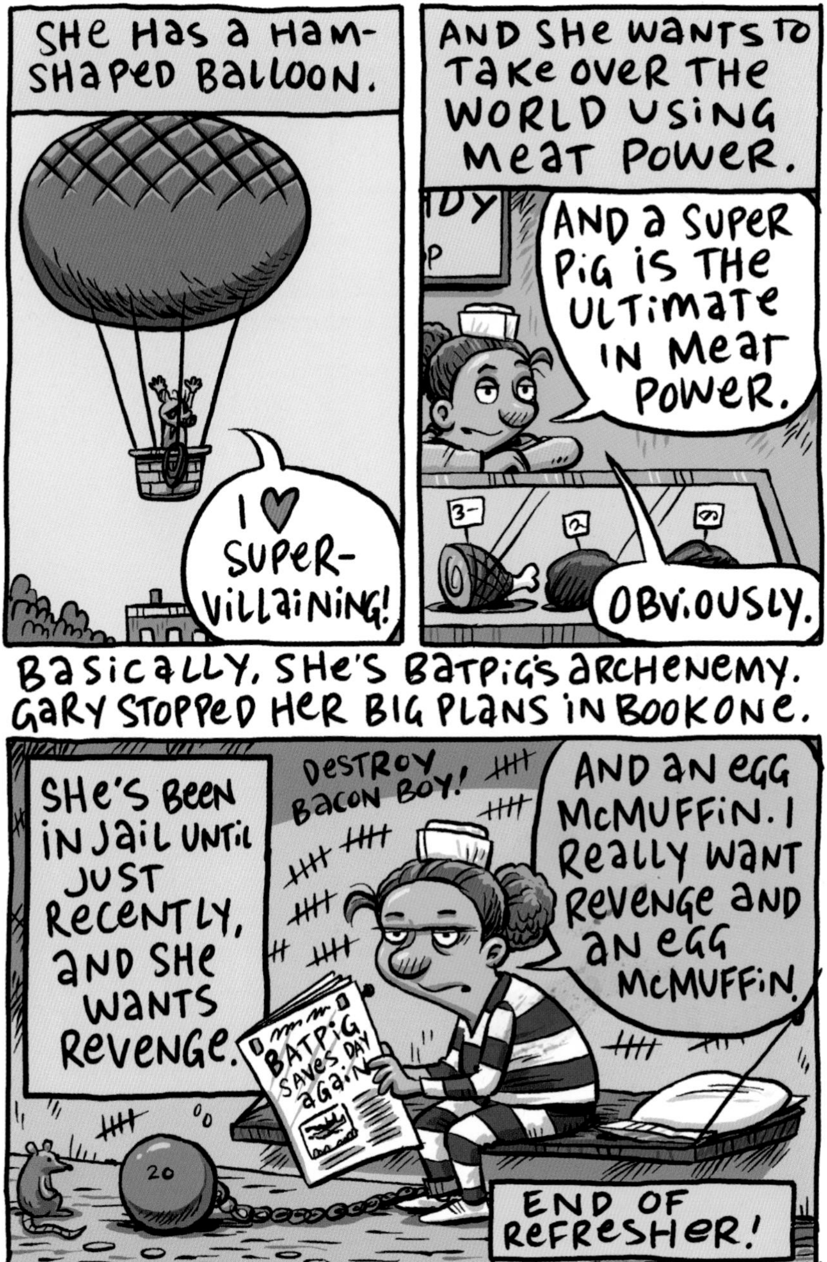
SHE HAS A HAM-SHAPED BALLOON.
I ♥ SUPER-VILLAINING!
AND SHE WANTS TO TAKE OVER THE WORLD USING MEAT POWER.
AND A SUPER PIG IS THE ULTIMATE IN MEAT POWER.
OBVIOUSLY.
BASICALLY, SHE'S BATPIG'S ARCHENEMY. GARY STOPPED HER BIG PLANS IN BOOK ONE.
SHE'S BEEN IN JAIL UNTIL JUST RECENTLY, AND SHE WANTS REVENGE.
DESTROY BACON BOY!
AND AN EGG MCMUFFIN. I REALLY WANT REVENGE AND AN EGG MCMUFFIN.
BATPIG SAVES DAY AGAIN
END OF REFRESHER!

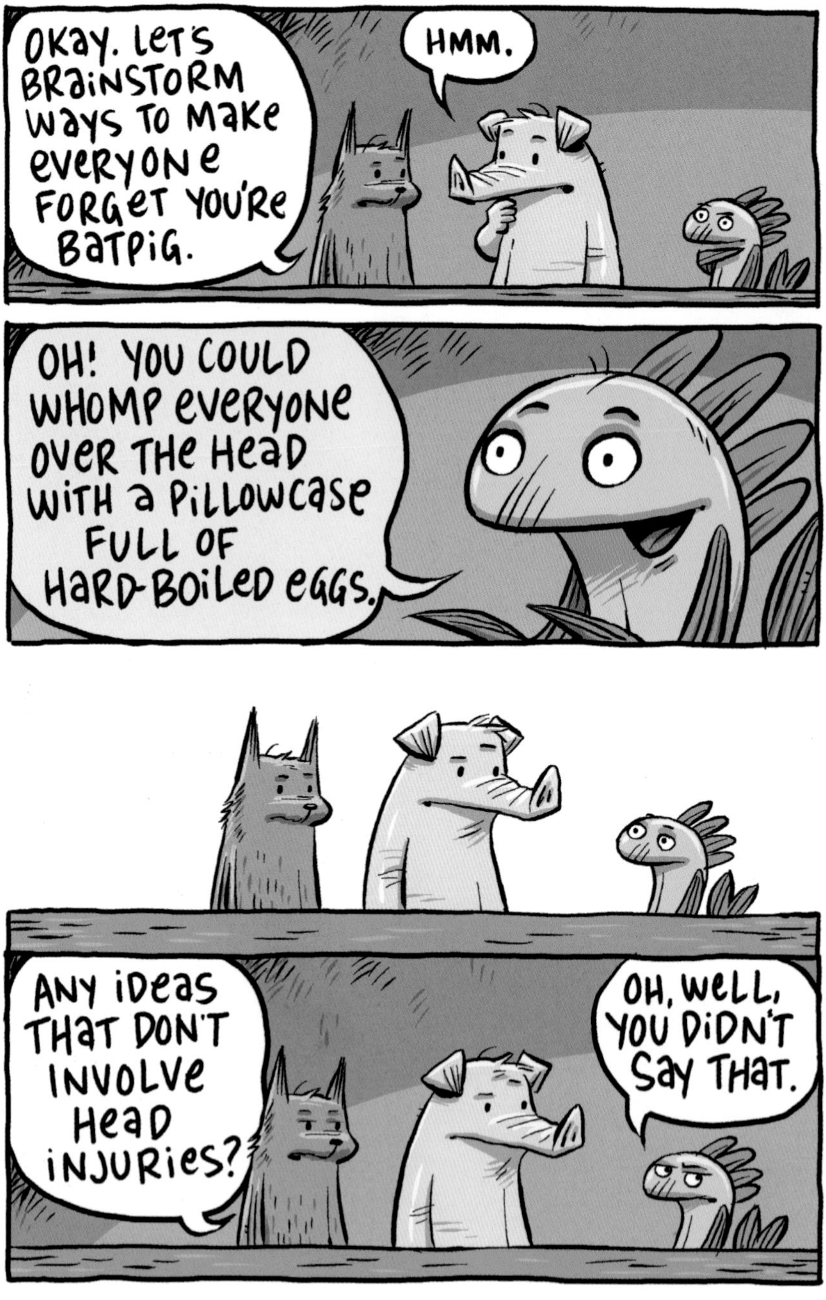
OKAY. LET'S BRAINSTORM WAYS TO MAKE EVERYONE FORGET YOU'RE BATPIG.
HMM.
OH! YOU COULD WHOMP EVERYONE OVER THE HEAD WITH A PILLOWCASE FULL OF HARD-BOILED EGGS.
ANY IDEAS THAT DON'T INVOLVE HEAD INJURIES?
OH, WELL, YOU DIDN'T SAY THAT.

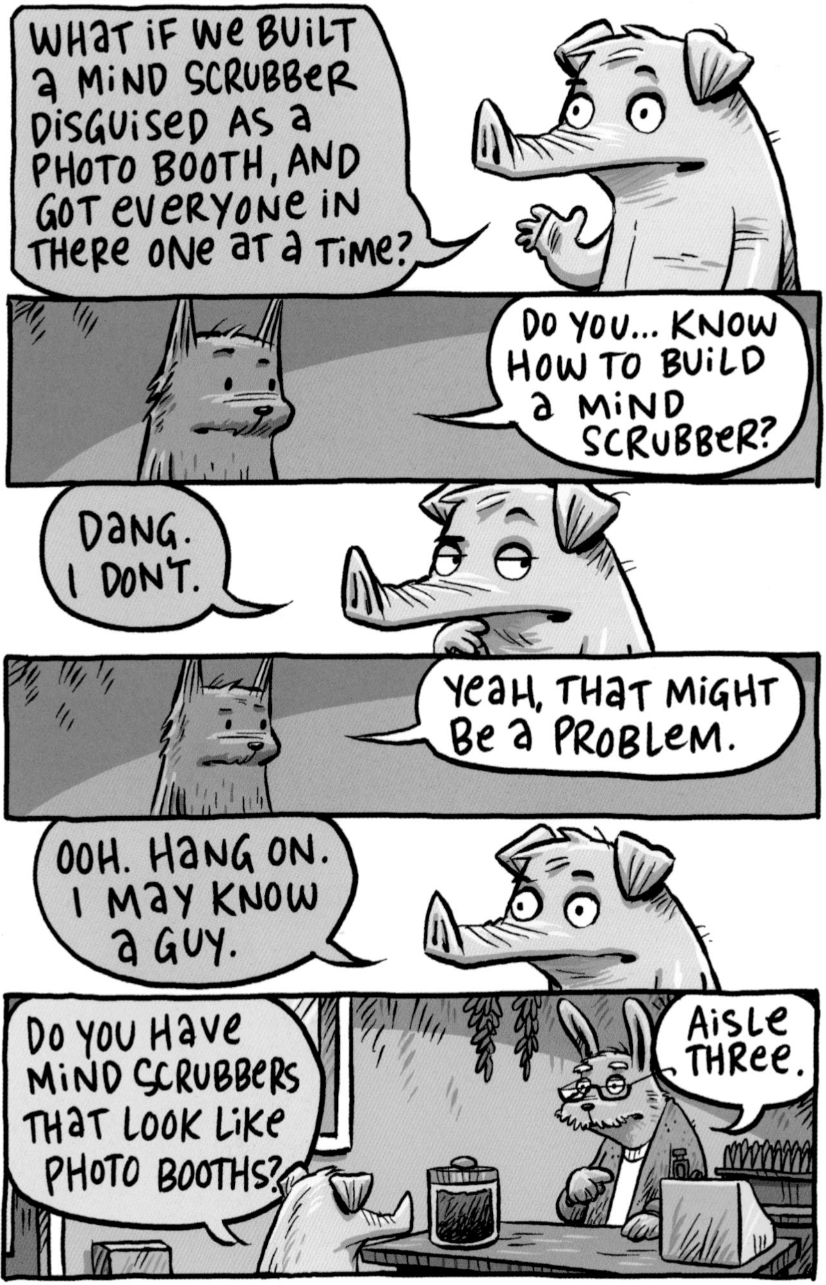
WHAT iF WE BUILT a MIND SCRUBBER DISGUISED AS a PHOTO BOOTH, AND GOT EVERYONE IN THERE ONE AT a TIME?
DO YOU... KNOW HOW TO BUILD a MIND SCRUBBER?
DANG. I DON'T.
YEAH, THAT MIGHT BE a PROBLEM.
OOH. HANG ON. I MAY KNOW a GUY.
DO YOU HAVE MIND SCRUBBERS THAT LOOK LIKE PHOTO BOOTHS?
AISLE THREE.

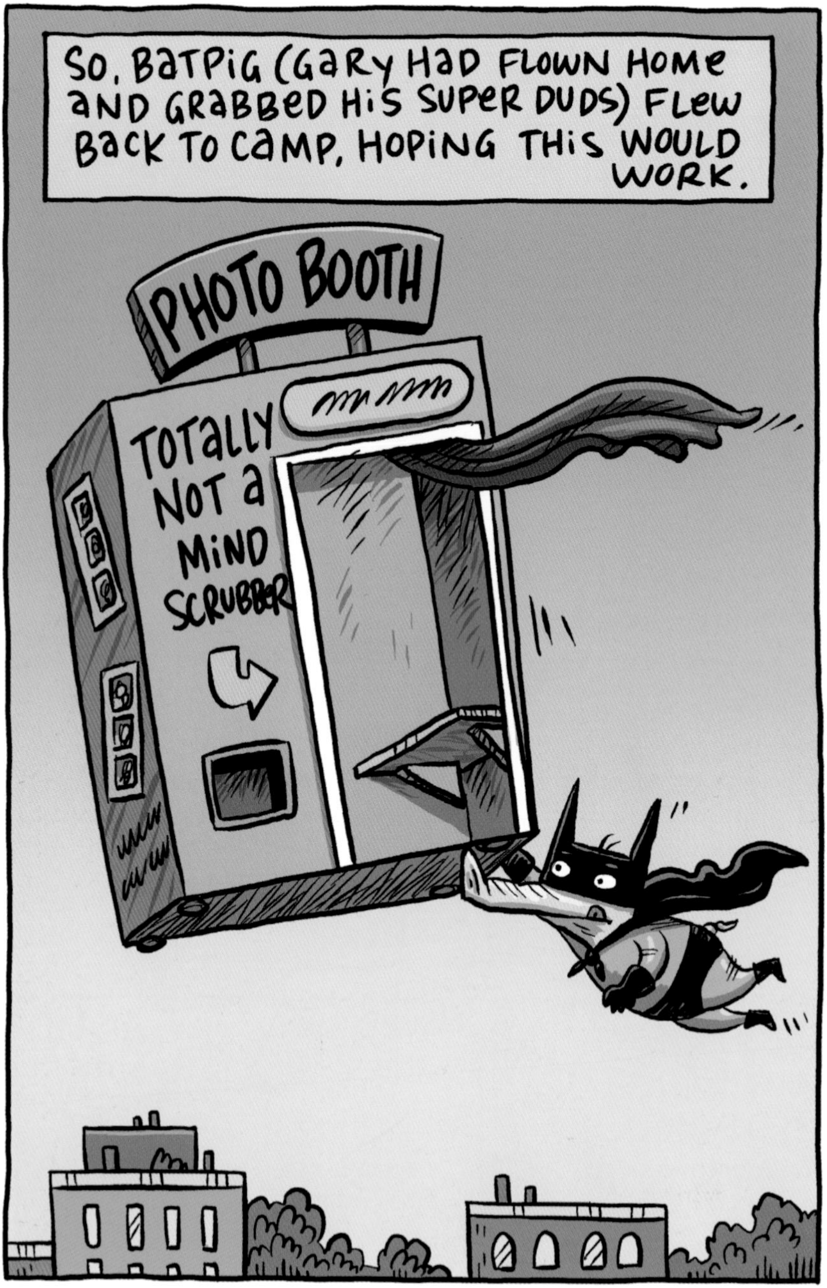
SO, BATPIG (GARY HAD FLOWN HOME AND GRABBED HIS SUPER DUDS) FLEW BACK TO CAMP, HOPING THIS WOULD WORK.
PHOTO BOOTH
TOTALLY NOT A MIND SCRUBBER

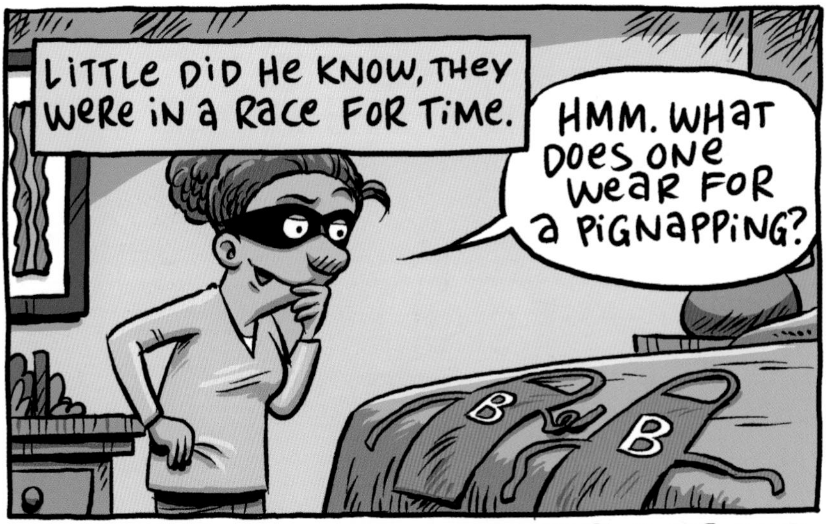
LITTLE DID HE KNOW, THEY WERE IN A RACE FOR TIME.
HMM. WHAT DOES ONE WEAR FOR A PIGNAPPING?
B
B

THE HAM BALLOON WAS FIRED UP AND THE BUTCHER WAS READY TO GO.

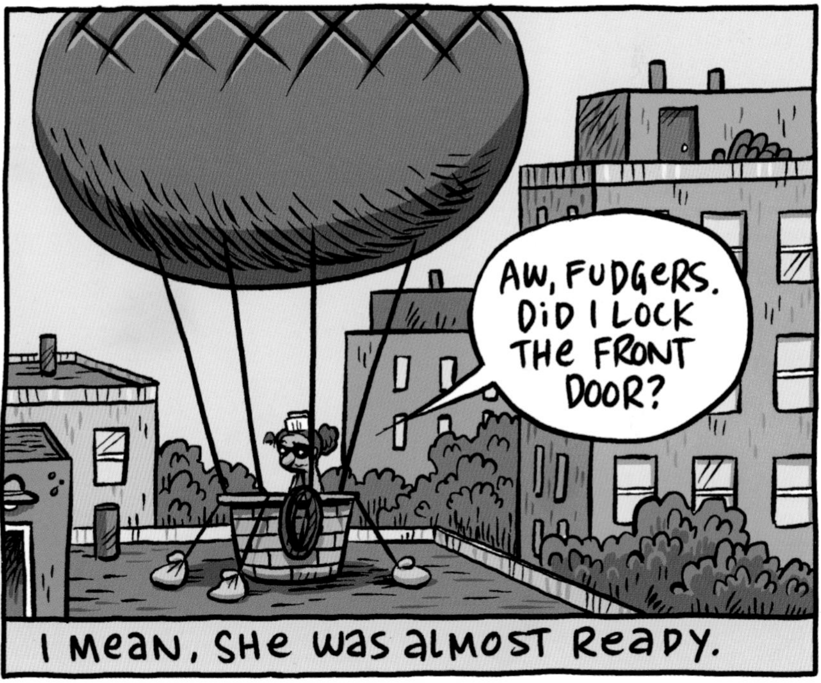
AW, FUDGERS. DID I LOCK THE FRONT DOOR?
I MEAN, SHE WAS ALMOST READY.

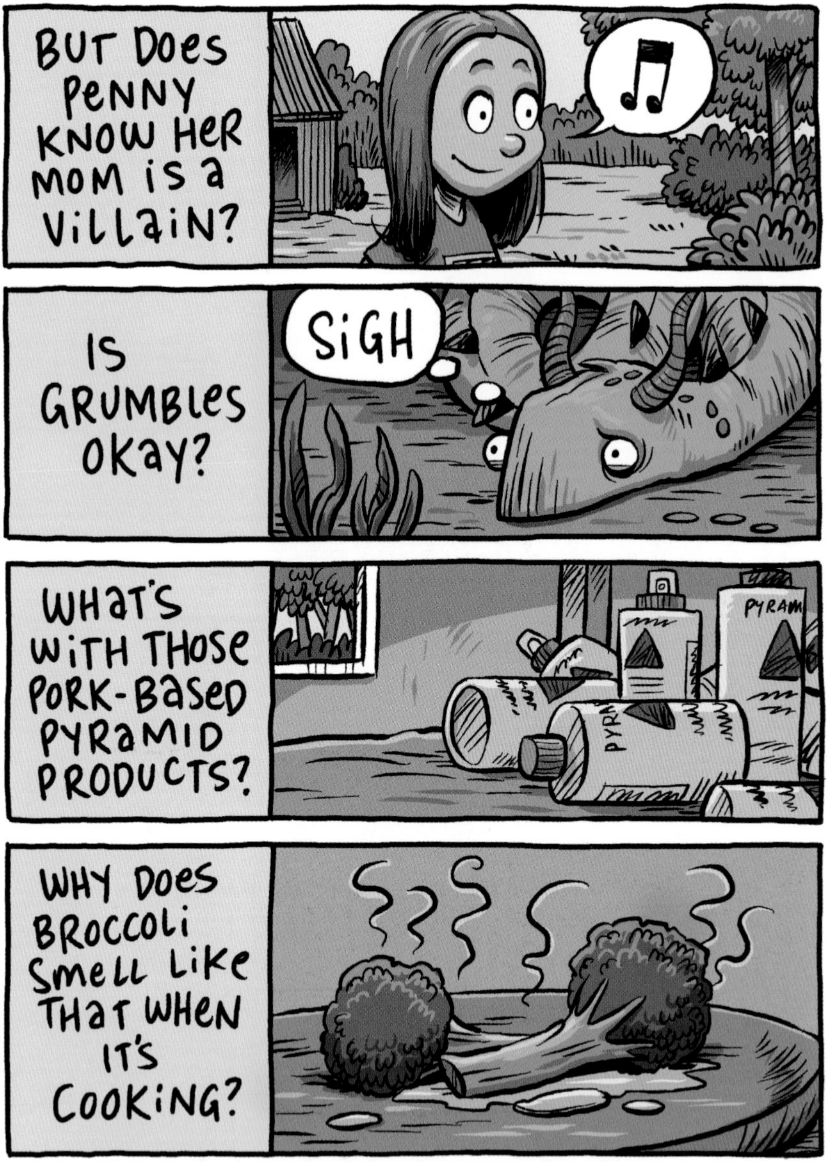
BUT DOES PENNY KNOW HER MOM IS A VILLAIN?
IS GRUMBLES OKAY?
SIGH
WHAT'S WITH THOSE PORK-BASED PYRAMID PRODUCTS?
PYRAM
PYRA
WHY DOES BROCCOLI SMELL LIKE THAT WHEN IT'S COOKING?

WELL, KEEP READING! THAT'S HOW BOOKS WORK!

CHAPTER TEN

BRAIN
(FRESHLY
CLEANED)

"SCRUB-a-DUB-DUB"

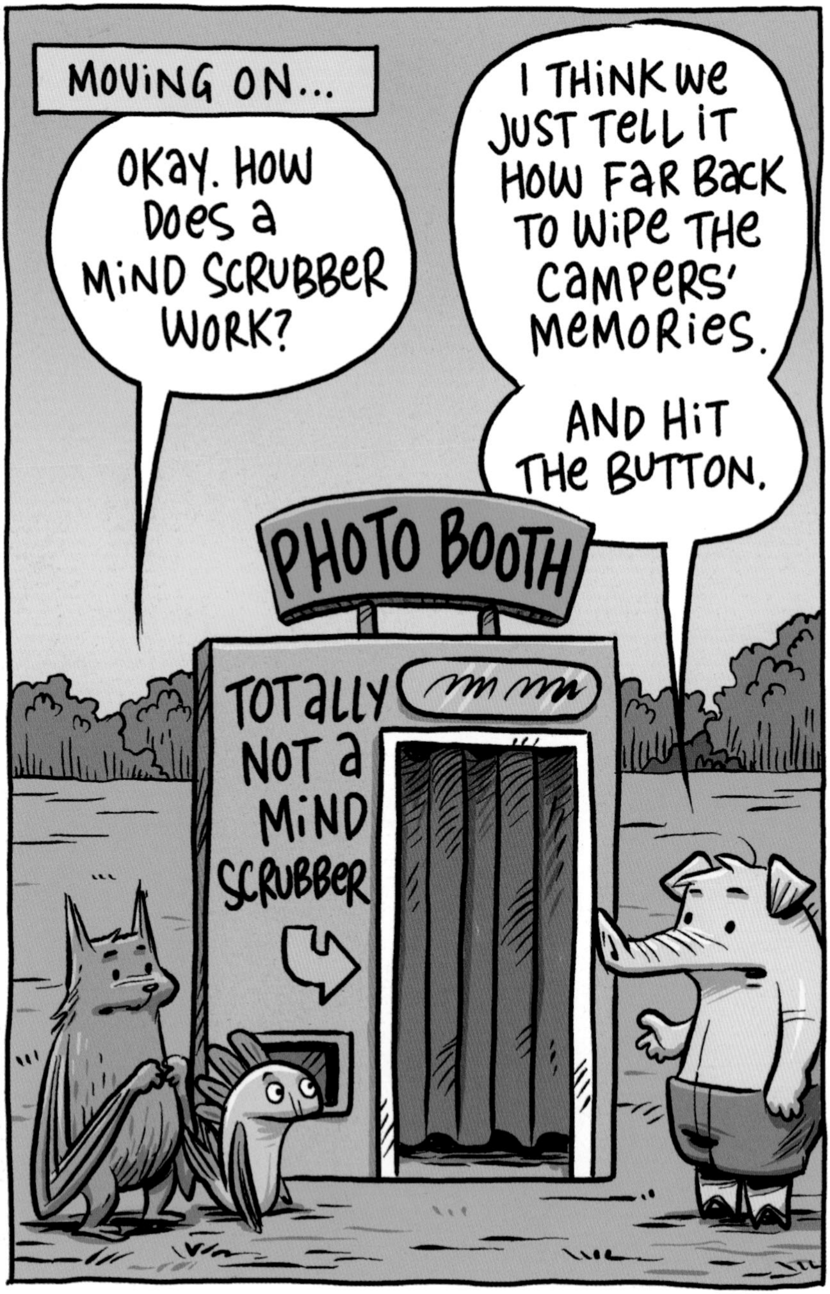
MOVING ON...
OKAY. HOW DOES A MIND SCRUBBER WORK?
I THINK WE JUST TELL IT HOW FAR BACK TO WIPE THE CAMPERS' MEMORIES.
AND HIT THE BUTTON.
PHOTO BOOTH
TOTALLY NOT A MIND SCRUBBER

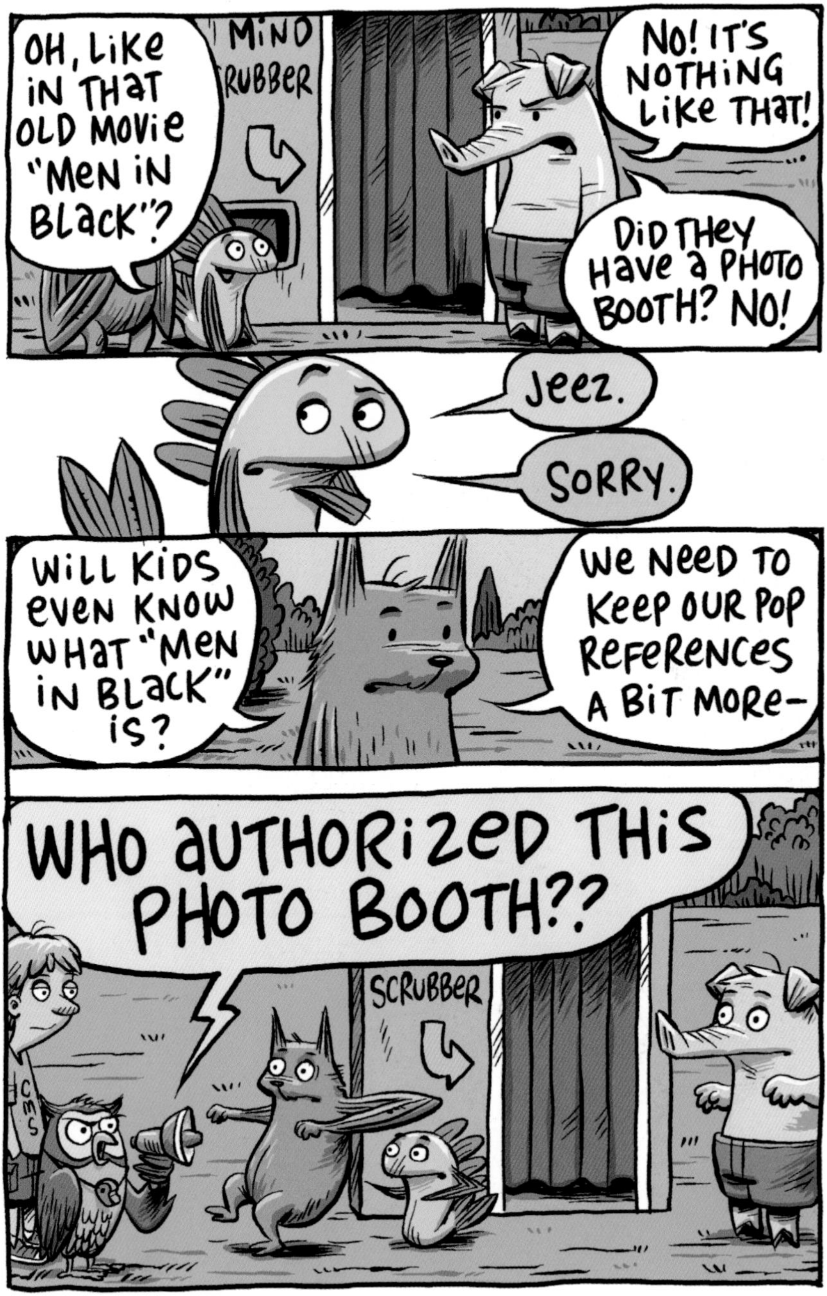
OH, LIKE IN THAT OLD MOVIE "MEN IN BLACK"?
MIND RUBBER
NO! IT'S NOTHING LIKE THAT!
DID THEY HAVE A PHOTO BOOTH? NO!
JEEZ.
SORRY.
WILL KIDS EVEN KNOW WHAT "MEN IN BLACK" IS?
WE NEED TO KEEP OUR POP REFERENCES A BIT MORE-
WHO AUTHORIZED THIS PHOTO BOOTH??
SCRUBBER
CMS

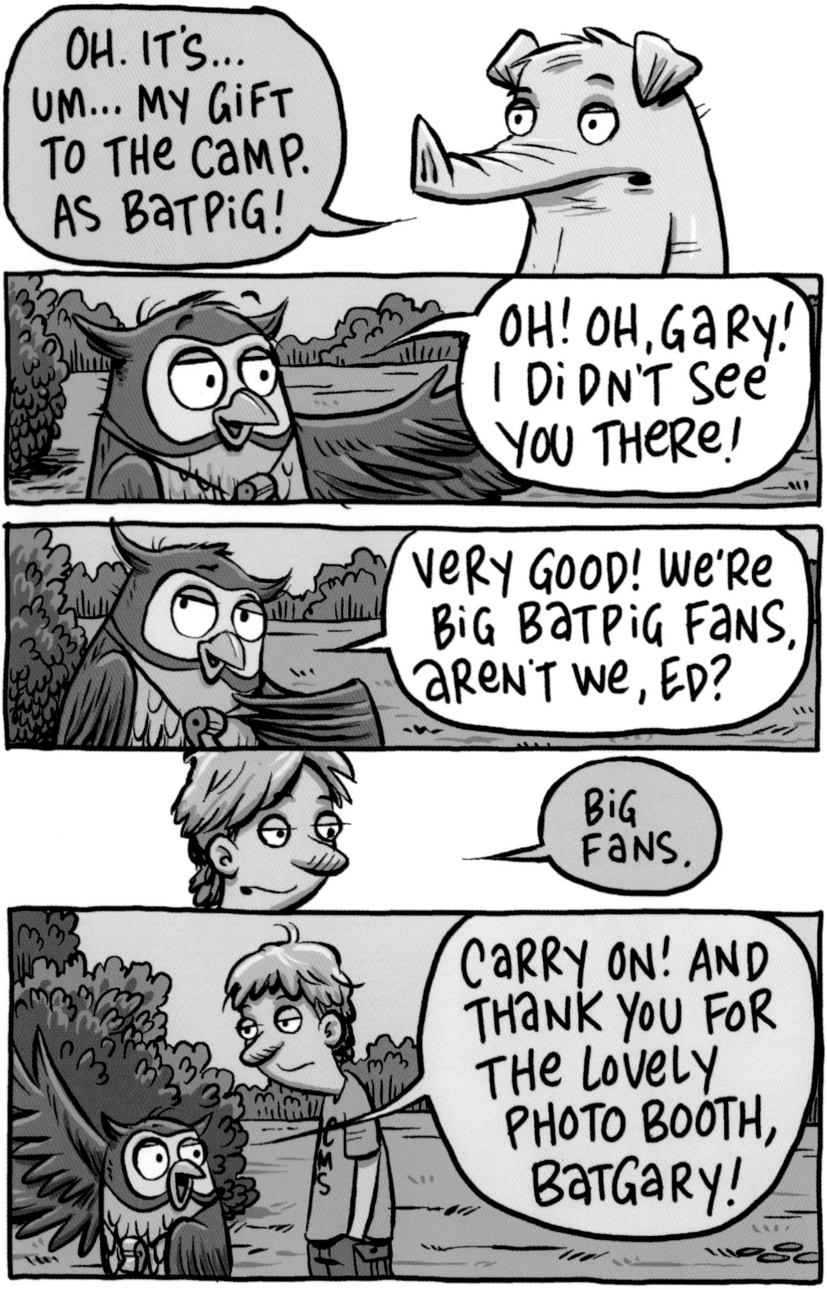
OH. IT'S... UM... MY GIFT TO THE CAMP. AS BATPIG!
OH! OH, GARY! I DIDN'T SEE YOU THERE!
VERY GOOD! WE'RE BIG BATPIG FANS, AREN'T WE, ED?
BIG FANS.
CARRY ON! AND THANK YOU FOR THE LOVELY PHOTO BOOTH, BATGARY!
CMS

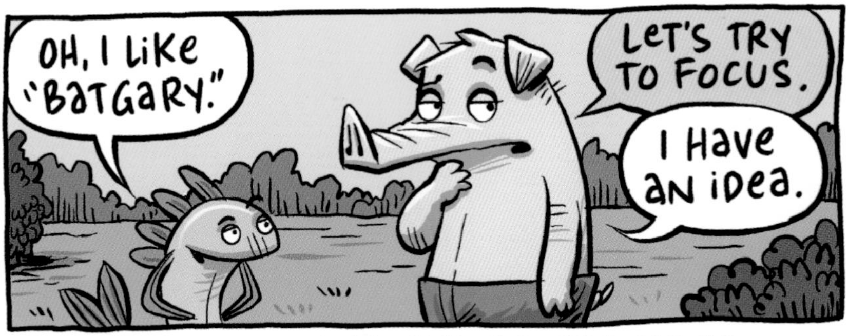
OH, I LIKE "BATGARY."
LET'S TRY TO FOCUS.
I HAVE AN IDEA.

GARY MADE FLYERS AS THE NEXT PHASE OF HIS (SO-CALLED) PLAN.

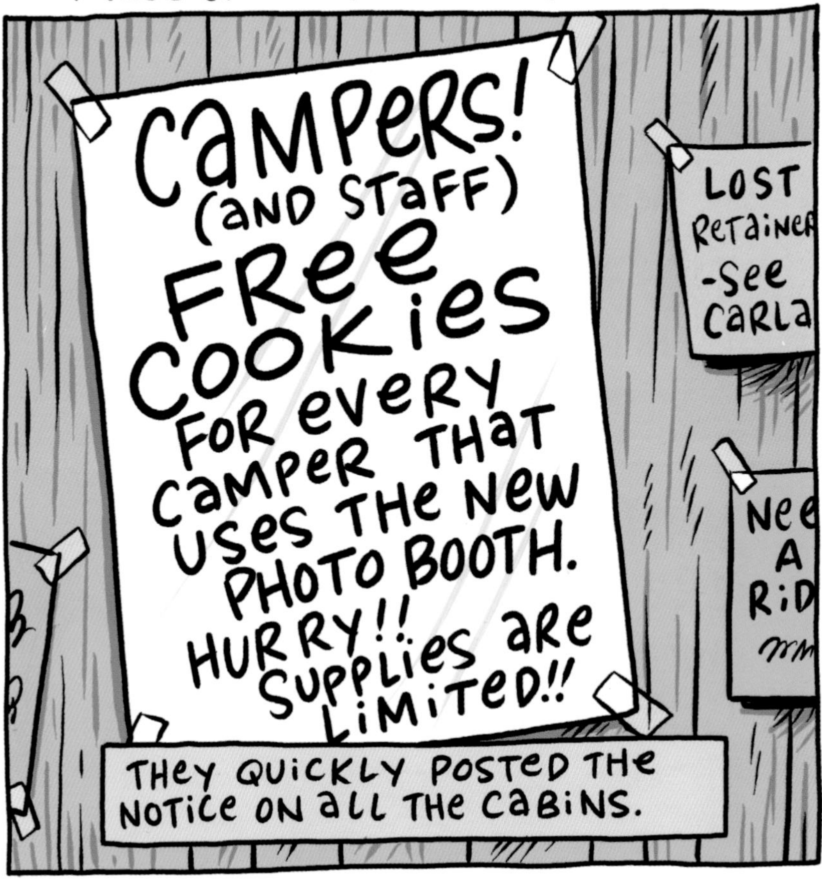
CAMPERS! (AND STAFF) FREE COOKIES FOR EVERY CAMPER THAT USES THE NEW PHOTO BOOTH. HURRY!! SUPPLIES ARE LIMITED!!
LOST
-SEE CARLA
THEY QUICKLY POSTED THE NOTICE ON ALL THE CABINS.

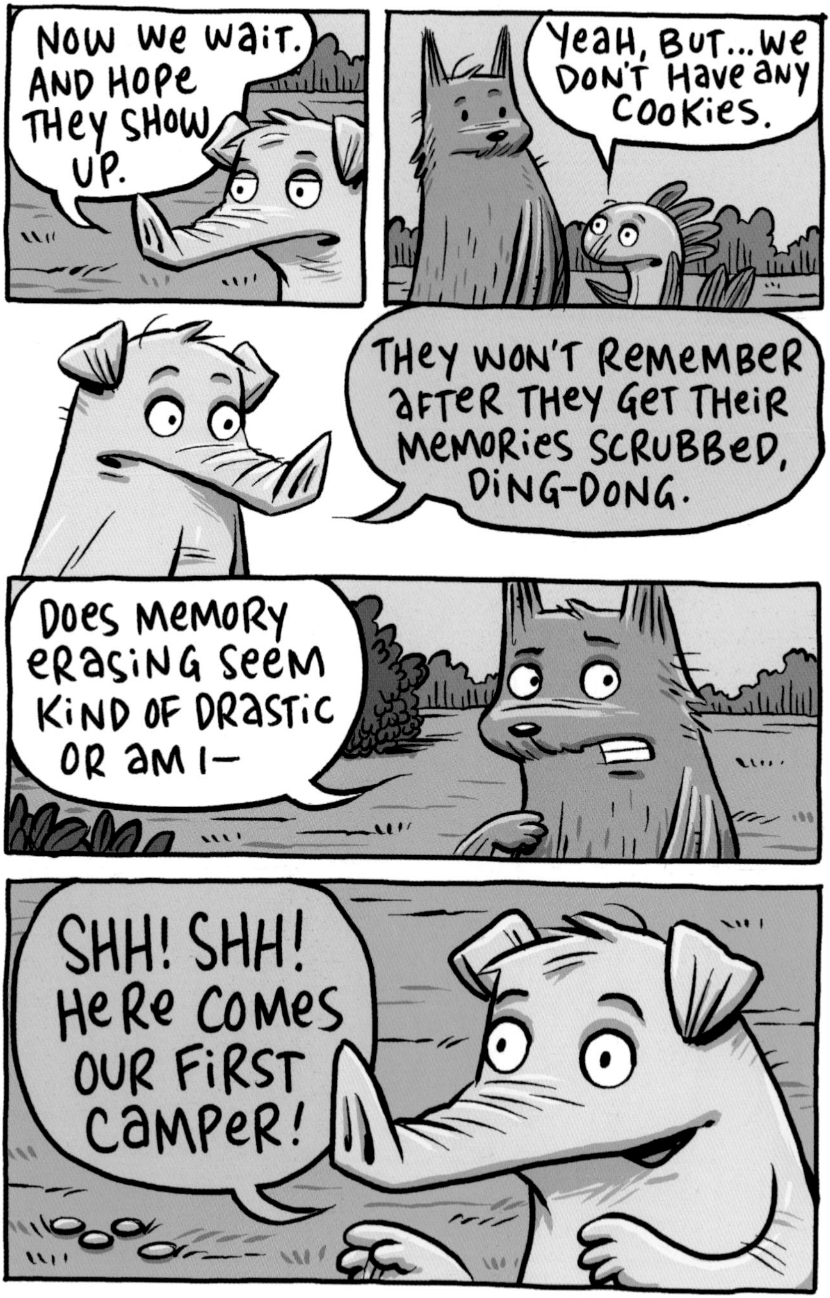
NOW WE WAIT. AND HOPE THEY SHOW UP.
YEAH, BUT...WE DON'T HAVE ANY COOKIES.
THEY WON'T REMEMBER AFTER THEY GET THEIR MEMORIES SCRUBBED, DING-DONG.
DOES MEMORY ERASING SEEM KIND OF DRASTIC OR AM I—
SHH! SHH! HERE COMES OUR FIRST CAMPER!

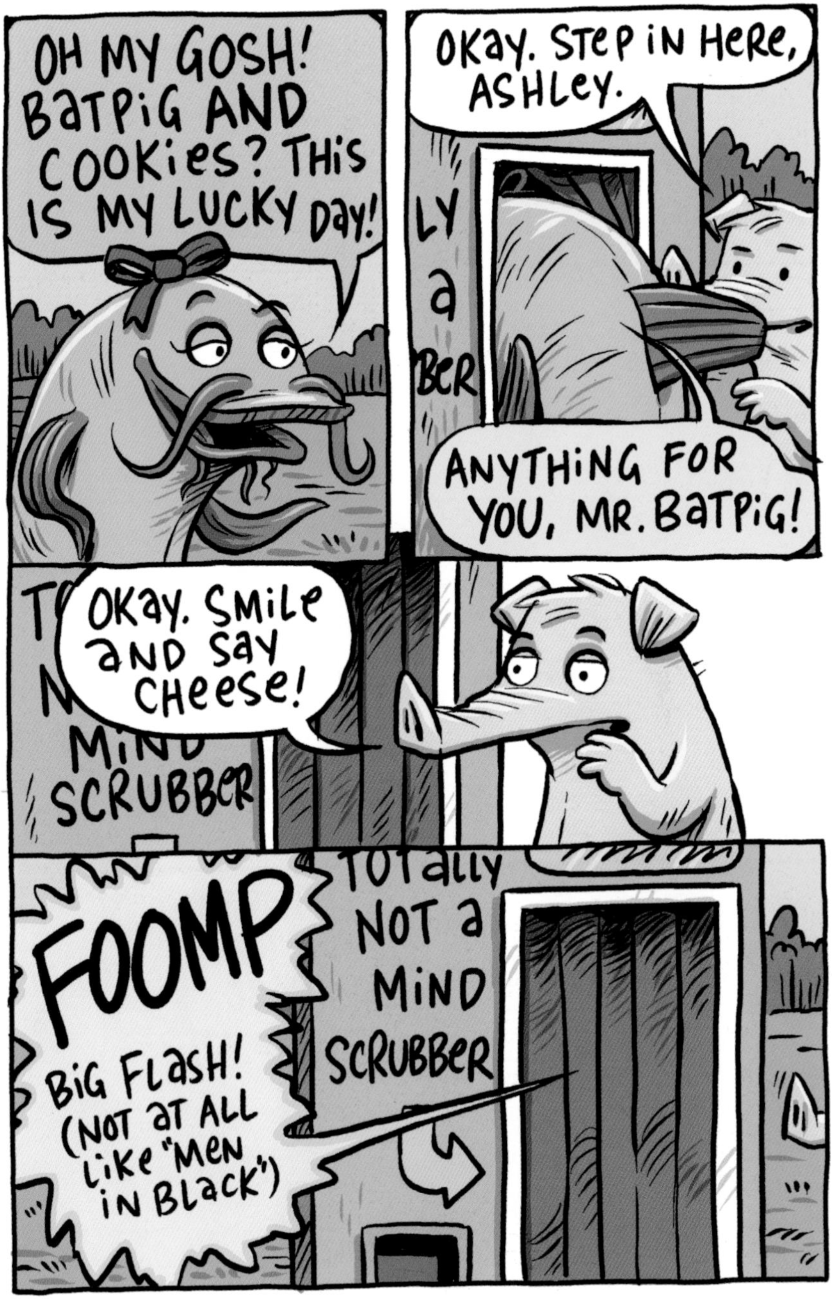
OH MY GOSH! BaTPiG AND COOKies? THIS IS MY LUCKY Day!
OKay. STeP iN HeRe, ASHLey.
ANYTHiNG FOR YOU, MR. BaTPiG!
OKay. SMiLe aND Say CHeese!
SCRUBBeR
FOOMP
TOTaLLy NOT a MiND SCRUBBeR
BiG FLasH! (NOT aT ALL Like "MeN iN BLack")

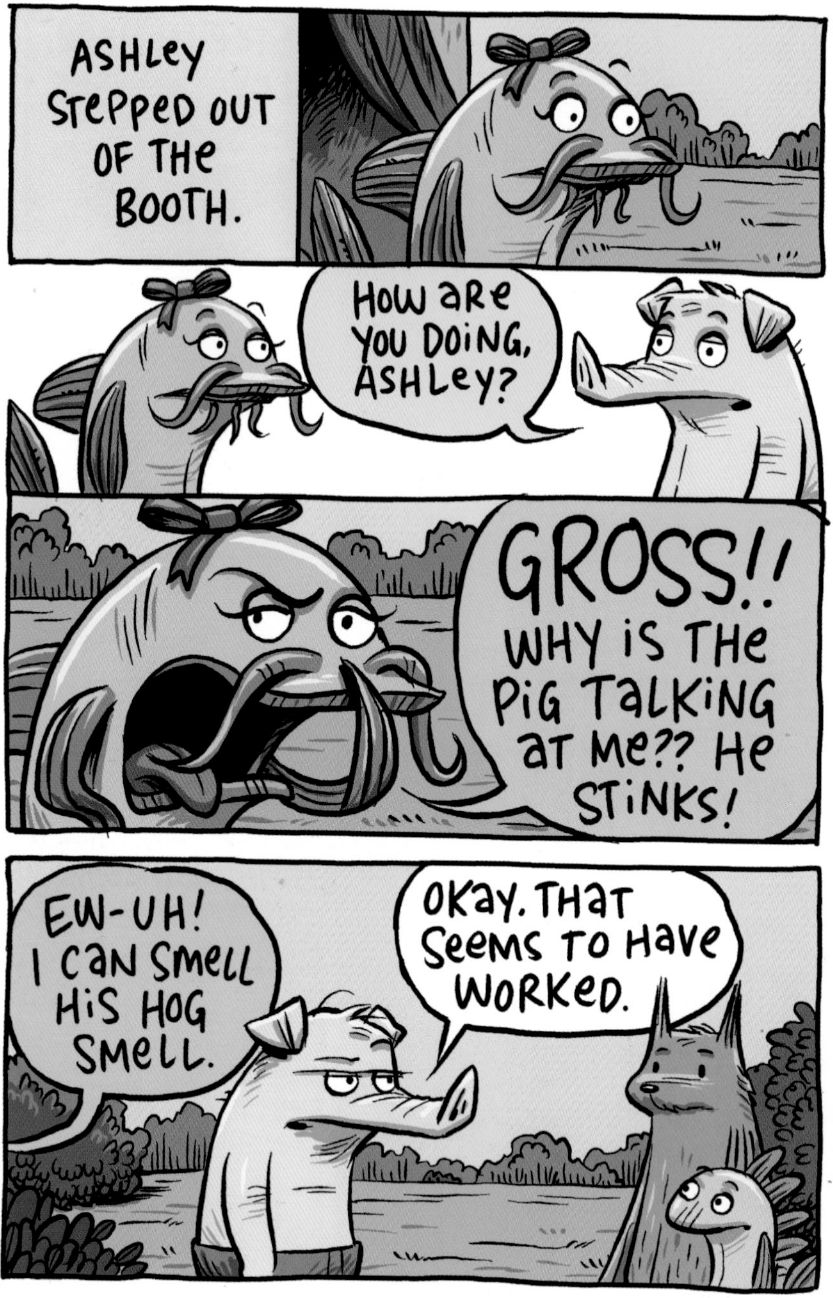
ASHLEY STEPPED OUT OF THE BOOTH.
HOW ARE YOU DOING, ASHLEY?
GROSS!! WHY IS THE PIG TALKING AT ME?? HE STINKS!
EW-UH! I CAN SMELL HIS HOG SMELL.
OKAY. THAT SEEMS TO HAVE WORKED.

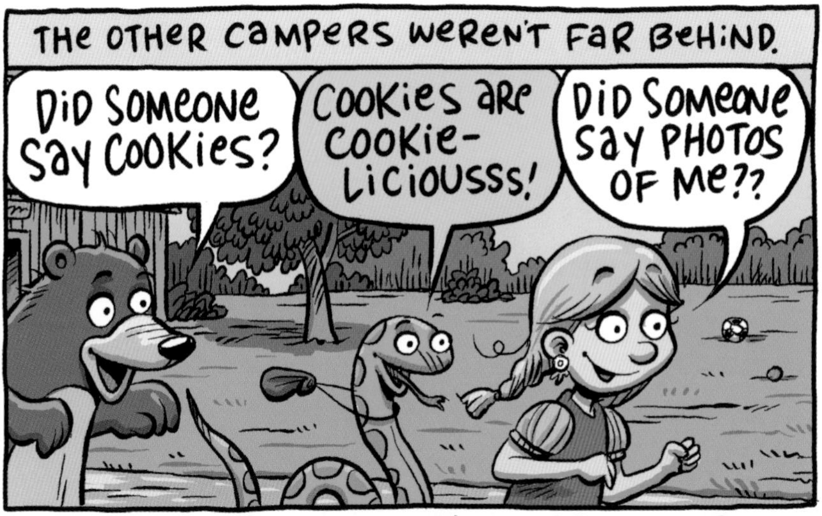
THE OTHER CAMPERS WEREN'T FAR BEHIND.
DID SOMEONE SAY COOKIES?
COOKIES ARE COOKIE-LICIOUSSS!
DID SOMEONE SAY PHOTOS OF ME??

PRETTY SOON, THE WHOLE CAMP WAS LINED UP AND THINGS WERE GETTING BACK TO NORMAL.

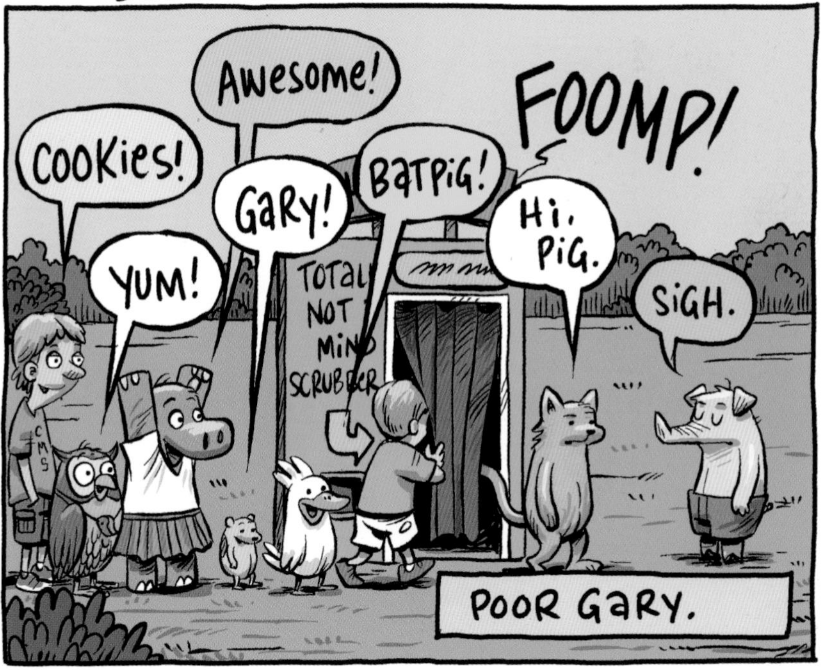
COOKIES!
AWESOME!
YUM!
GARY!
BATPIG!
FOOMP!
HI, PIG.
SIGH.
POOR GARY.

CHAPTER ELEVEN

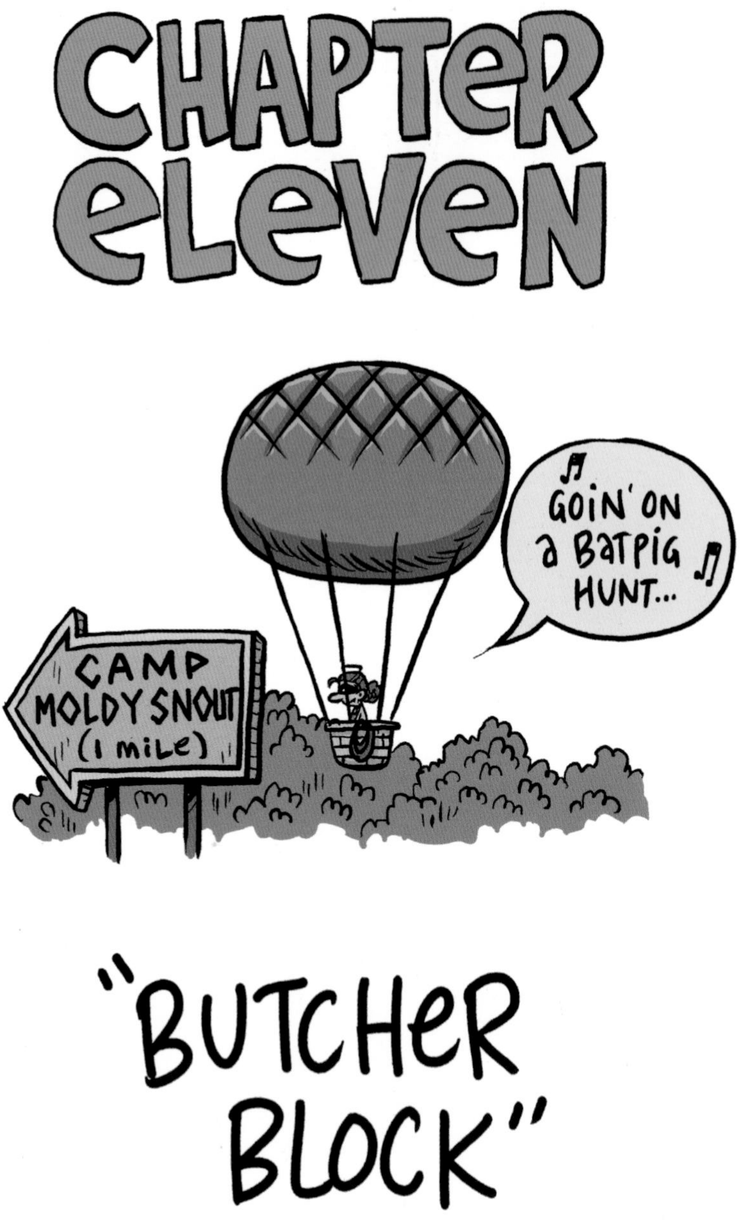
GOIN' ON a BATPIG HUNT...
CAMP MOLDY SNOUT (1 MILE)

"BUTCHER BLOCK"

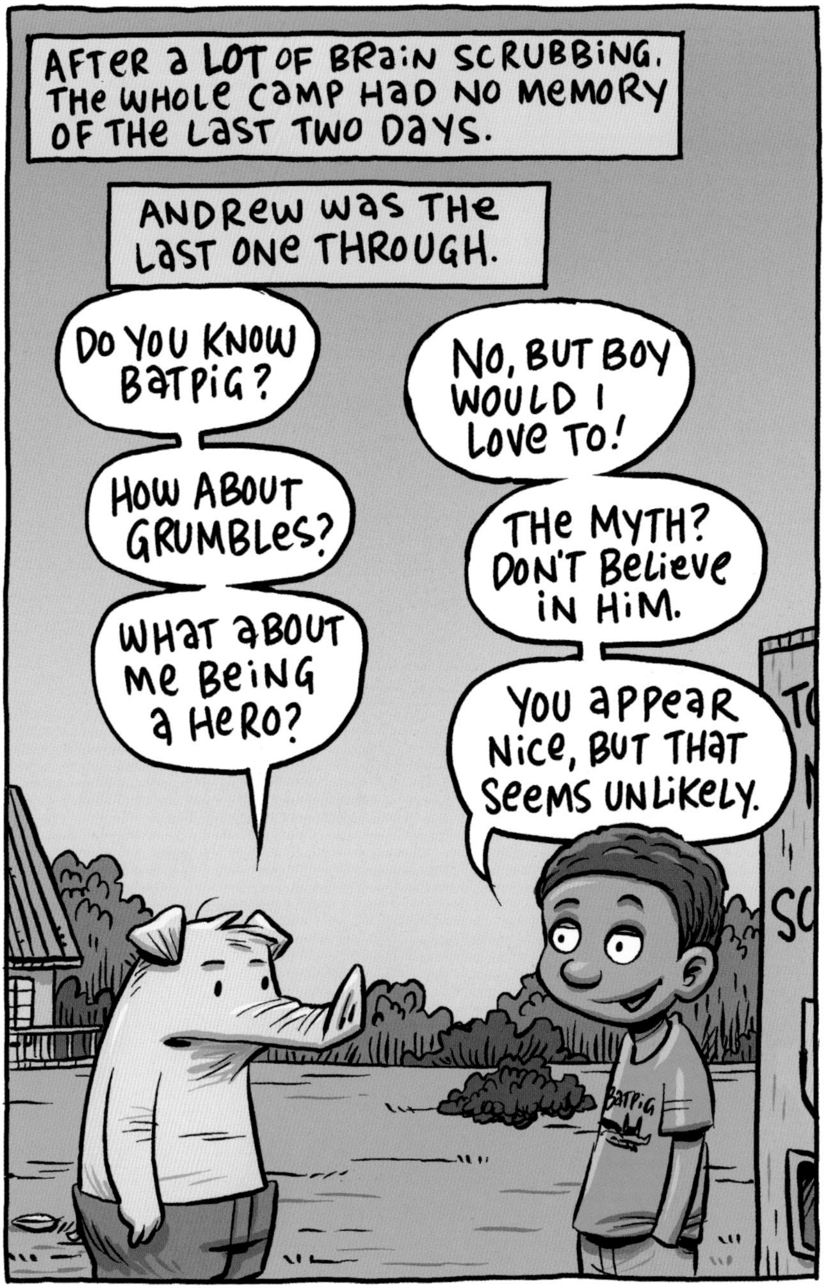
AFTER A LOT OF BRAIN SCRUBBING, THE WHOLE CAMP HAD NO MEMORY OF THE LAST TWO DAYS.
ANDREW WAS THE LAST ONE THROUGH.
DO YOU KNOW BATPIG?
NO, BUT BOY WOULD I LOVE TO!
HOW ABOUT GRUMBLES?
THE MYTH? DON'T BELIEVE IN HIM.
WHAT ABOUT ME BEING A HERO?
YOU APPEAR NICE, BUT THAT SEEMS UNLIKELY.
BATPIG

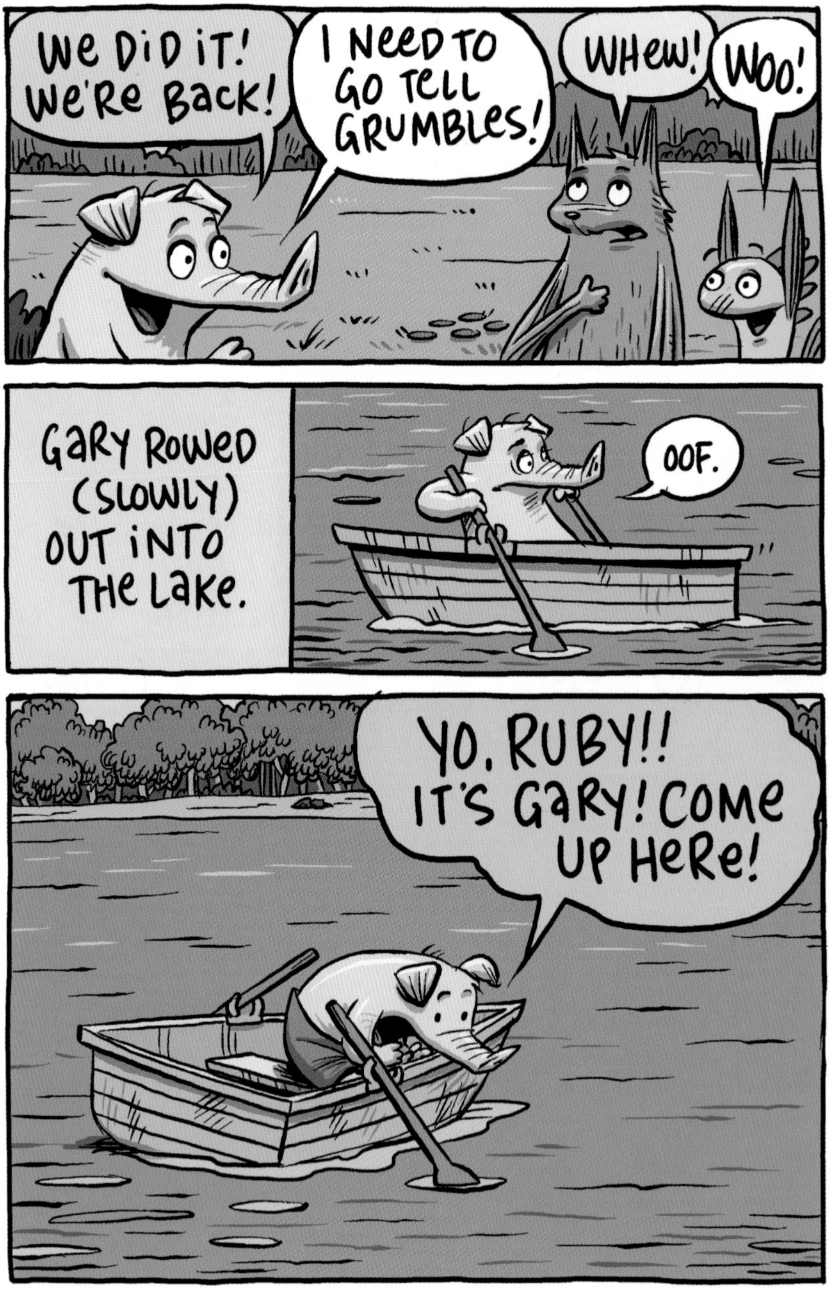
WE DID IT! WE'RE BACK!
I NEED TO GO TELL GRUMBLES!
WHEW!
WOO!
GARY ROWED (SLOWLY) OUT INTO THE LAKE.
OOF.
YO, RUBY!! IT'S GARY! COME UP HERE!

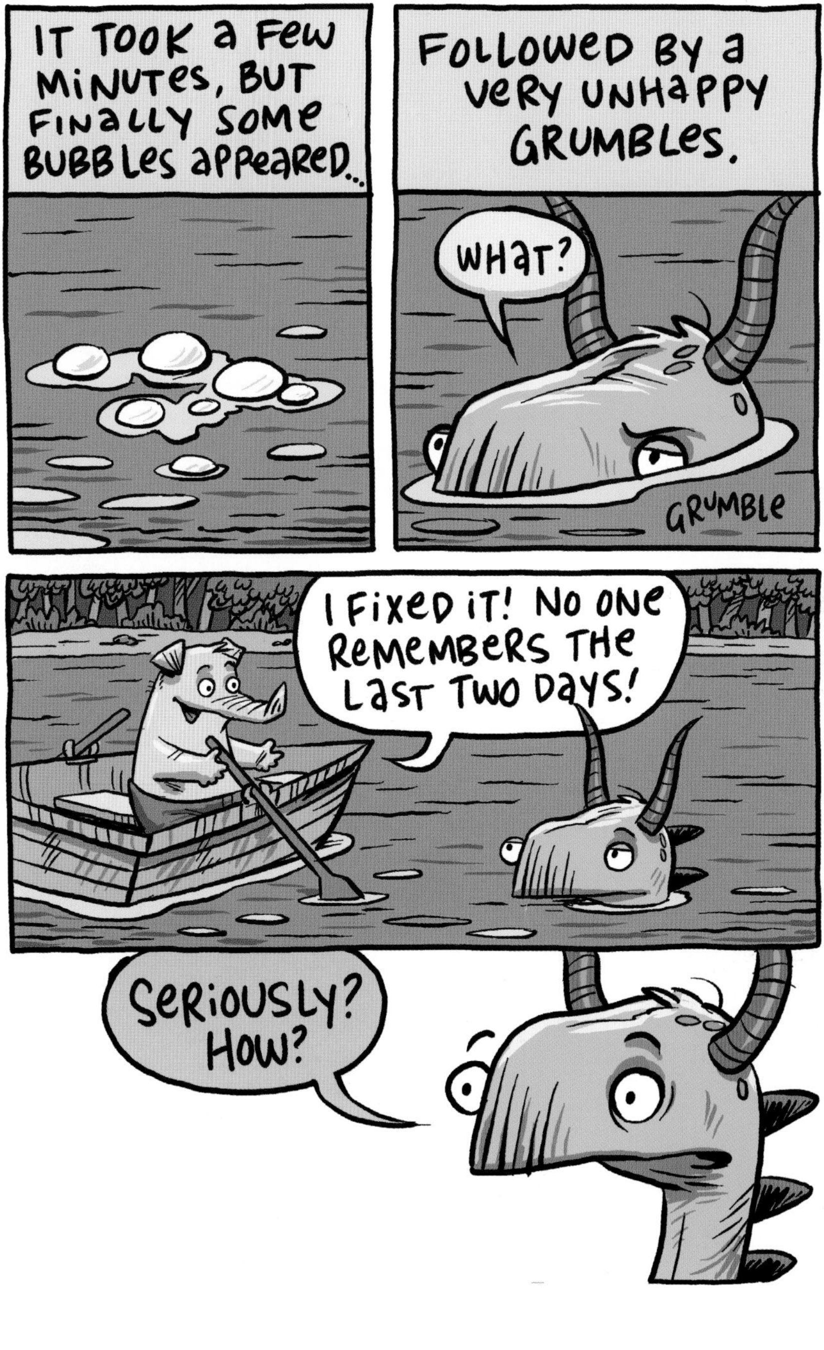
IT TOOK a FEW MINUTES, BUT FINALLY SOME BUBBLES APPEARED...
FOLLOWED BY a VERY UNHAPPY GRUMBLES.
WHAT?
GRUMBLE
I FIXED IT! NO ONE REMEMBERS THE LAST TWO DAYS!
SERIOUSLY? HOW?

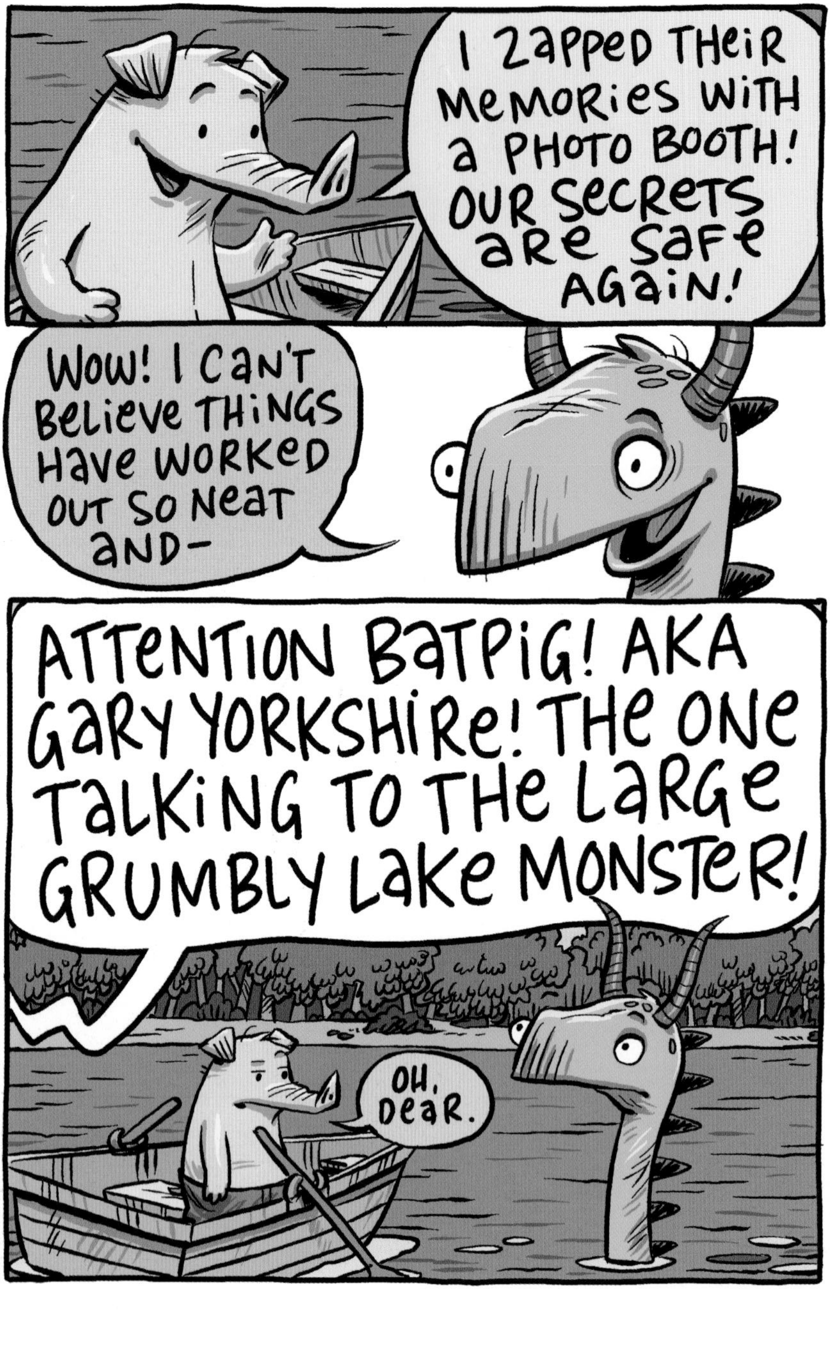
I ZAPPED THEIR MEMORIES WITH A PHOTO BOOTH! OUR SECRETS ARE SAFE AGAIN!
WOW! I CAN'T BELIEVE THINGS HAVE WORKED OUT SO NEAT AND-
ATTENTION BATPIG! AKA GARY YORKSHIRE! THE ONE TALKING TO THE LARGE GRUMBLY LAKE MONSTER!
OH, DEAR.

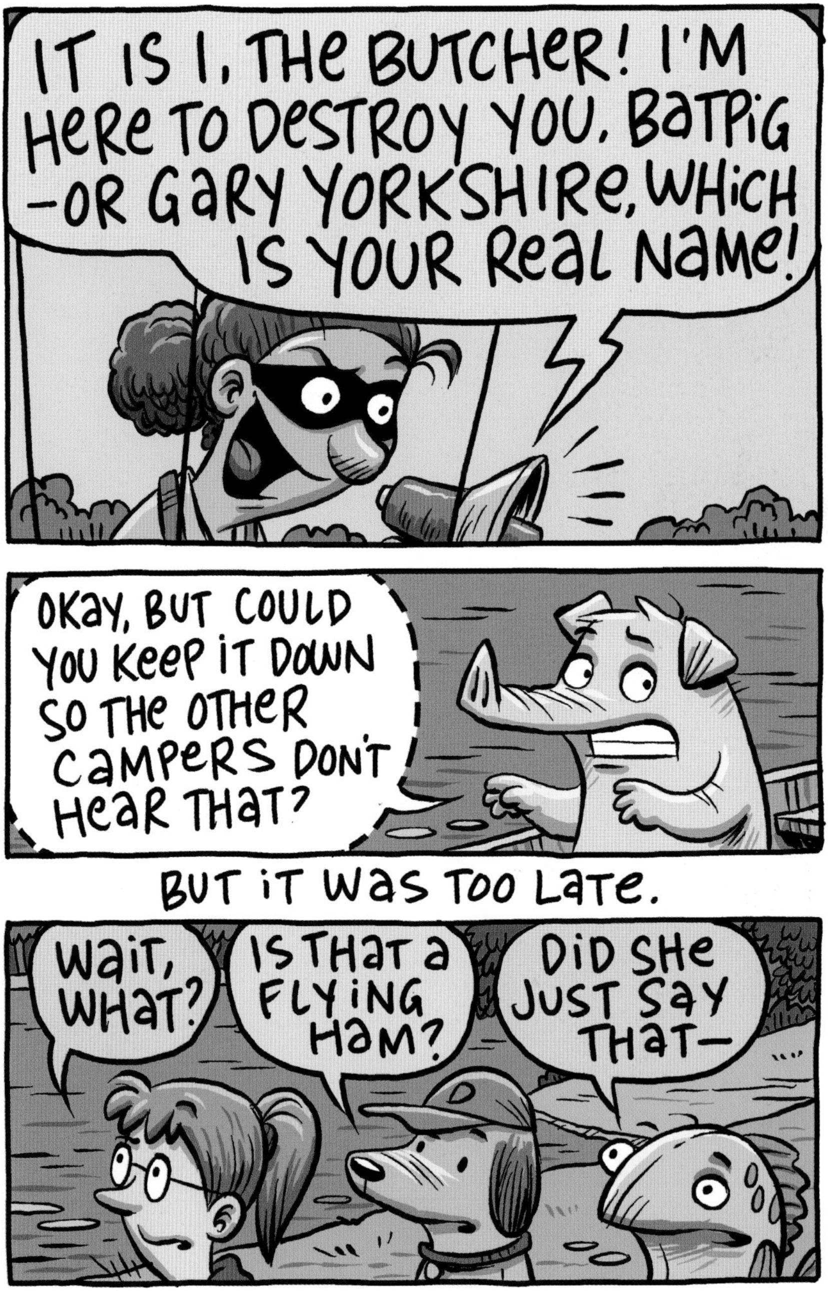
IT IS I, THE BUTCHER! I'M HERE TO DESTROY YOU, BATPIG -OR GARY YORKSHIRE, WHICH IS YOUR REAL NAME!
OKAY, BUT COULD YOU KEEP IT DOWN SO THE OTHER CAMPERS DON'T HEAR THAT?
BUT IT WAS TOO LATE.
WAIT, WHAT?
IS THAT A FLYING HAM?
DID SHE JUST SAY THAT—

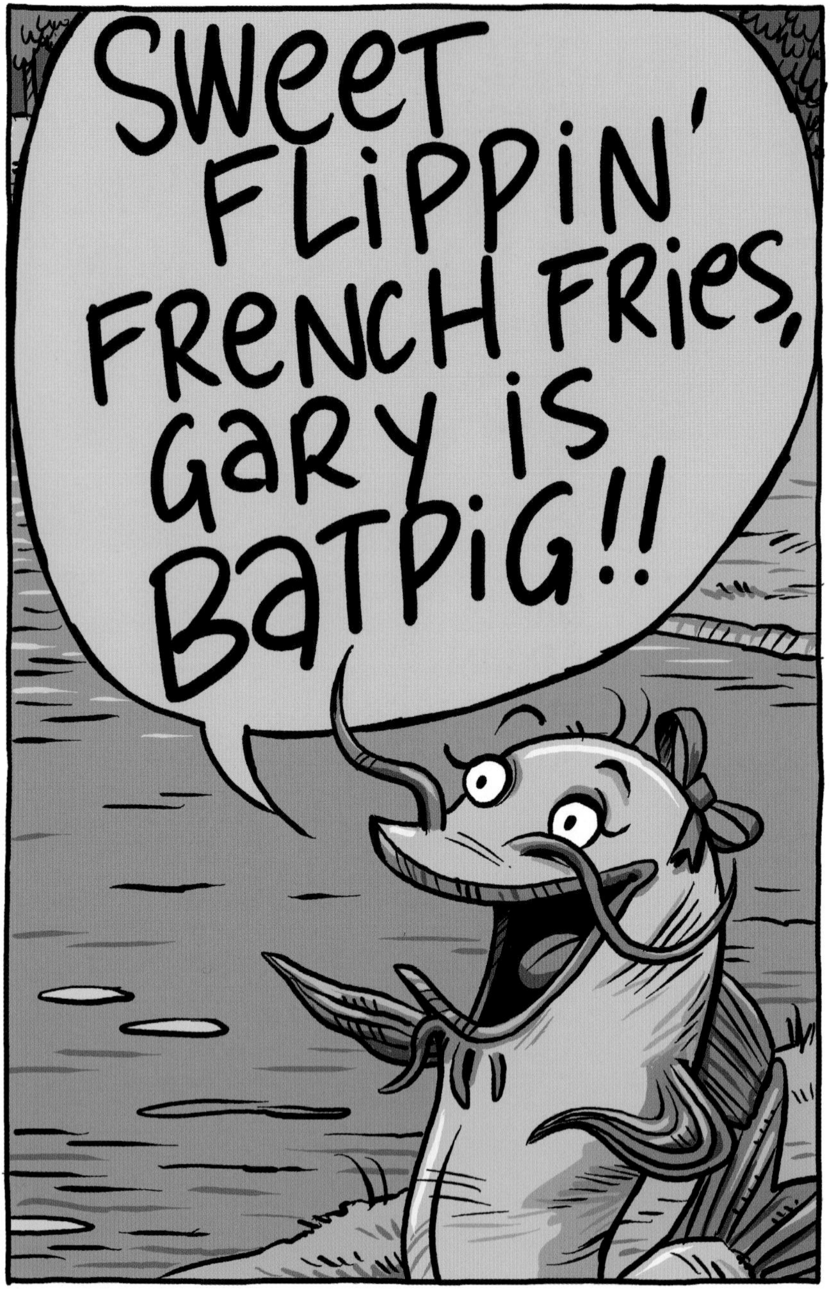
SWEET FLIPPIN' FRENCH FRIES, GARY IS BATPIG!!

CHAPTER TWELVE

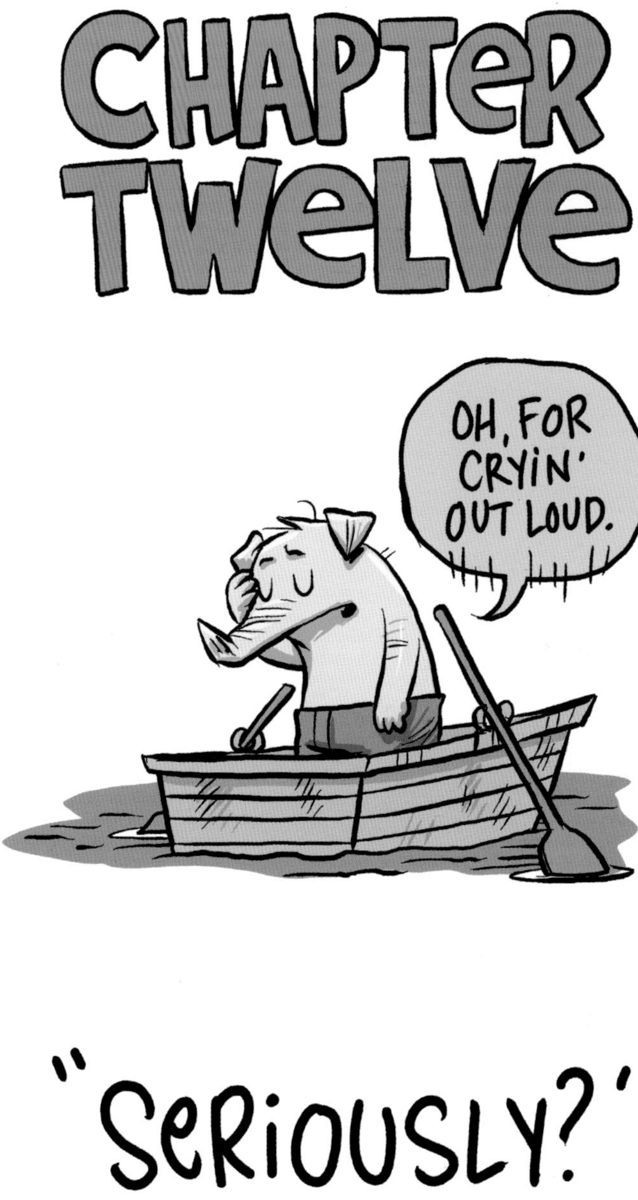
OH, FOR CRYIN' OUT LOUD.

"SERIOUSLY?"

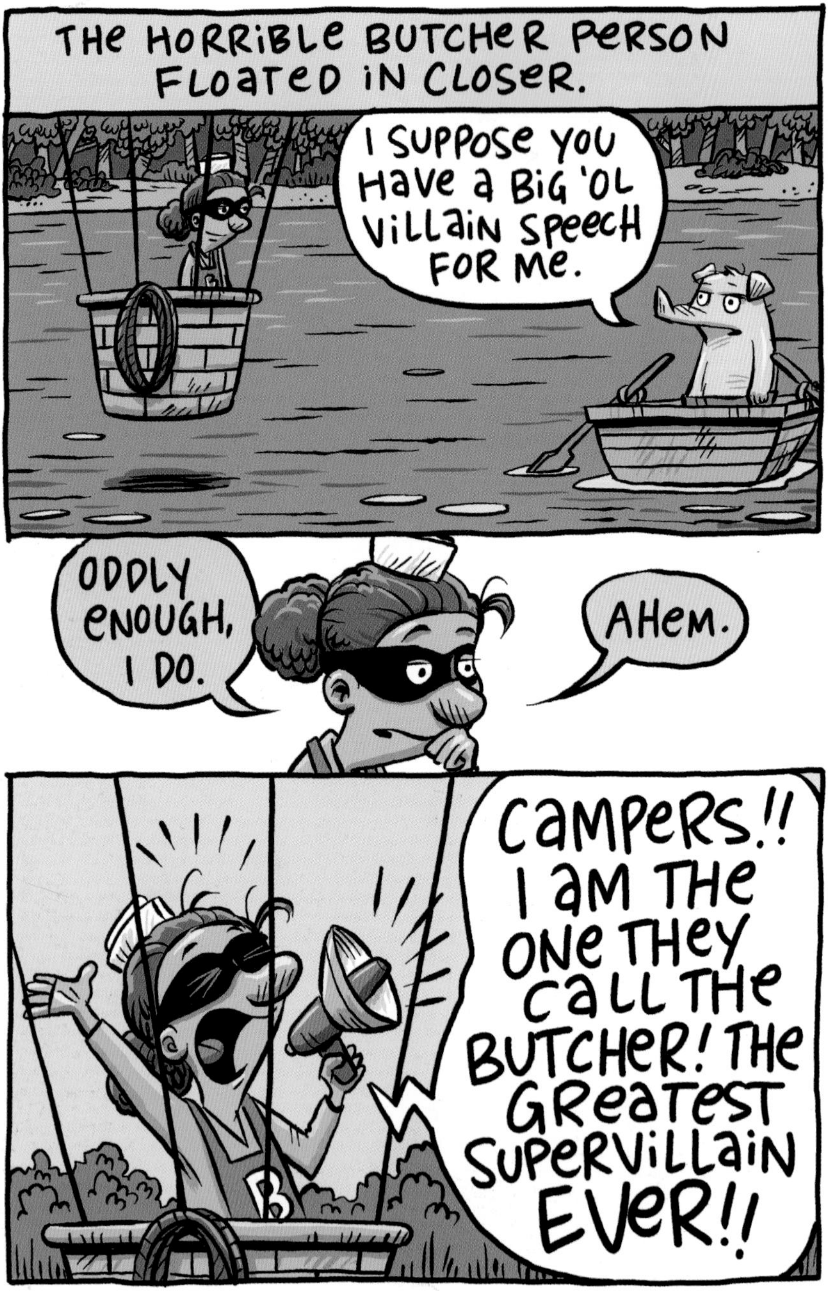
THE HORRIBLE BUTCHER PERSON FLOATED IN CLOSER.
I SUPPOSE YOU HAVE A BIG 'OL VILLAIN SPEECH FOR ME.
ODDLY ENOUGH, I DO.
AHEM.
CAMPERS!! I AM THE ONE THEY CALL THE BUTCHER! THE GREATEST SUPERVILLAIN EVER!!

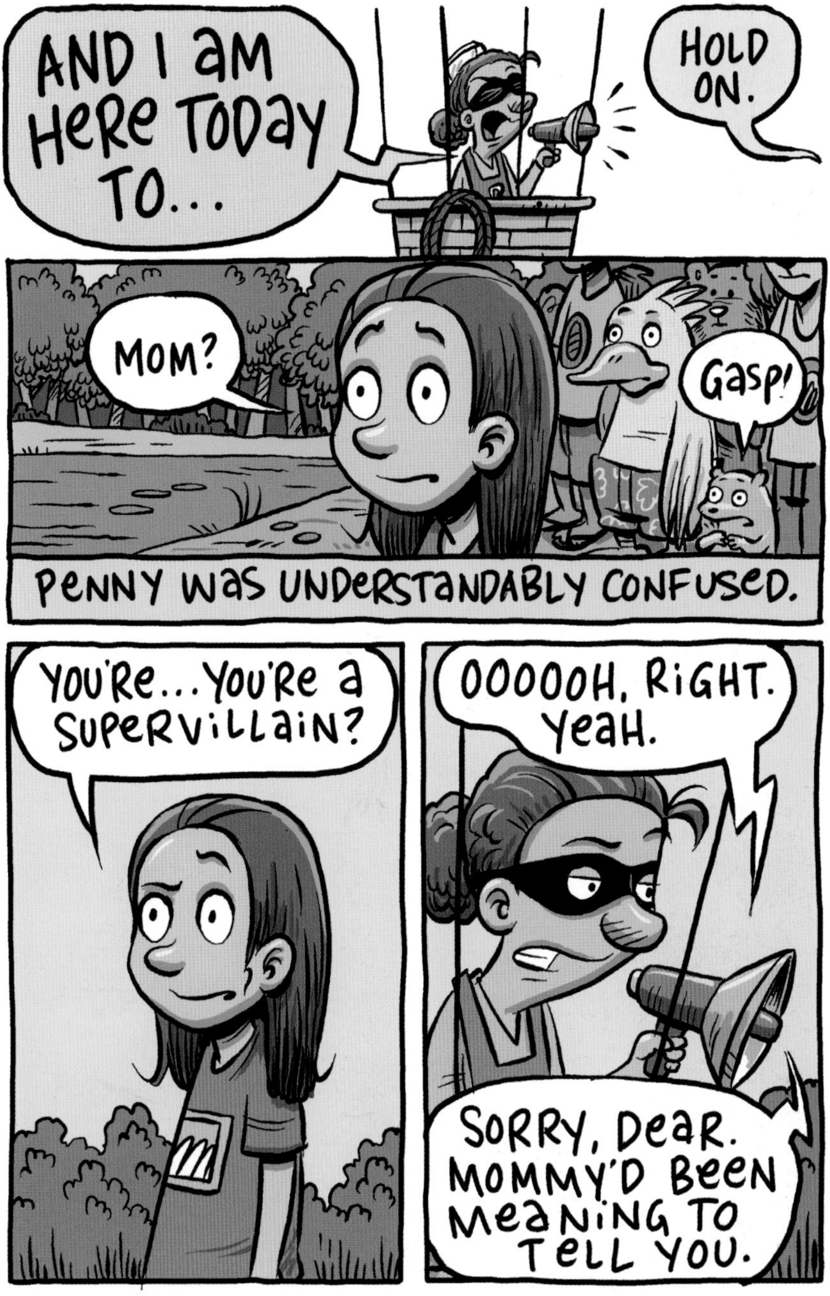
AND I AM HERE TODAY TO...
HOLD ON.
MOM?
GASP!
PENNY WAS UNDERSTANDABLY CONFUSED.
YOU'RE... YOU'RE A SUPERVILLAIN?
OOOOOH, RIGHT. YEAH.
SORRY, DEAR. MOMMY'D BEEN MEANING TO TELL YOU.

YEAH. WOW.

WITH A BIG HAM BALLOON AND EVERYTHING.

I KNOW.

IT'S PROBABLY A LOT TO TAKE IN, HUH?

MAYBE LATER WE GO FOR FRO-YO? TALK ABOUT IT?

THEY'D DRIFTED CLOSE ENOUGH THAT THE BUTCHER DIDN'T NEED THE MEGAPHONE.

"FRO-YO MAKES EVERYTHING BETTER." REMEMBER?

IN HER DEFENSE, FRO-YO IS AWESOME.

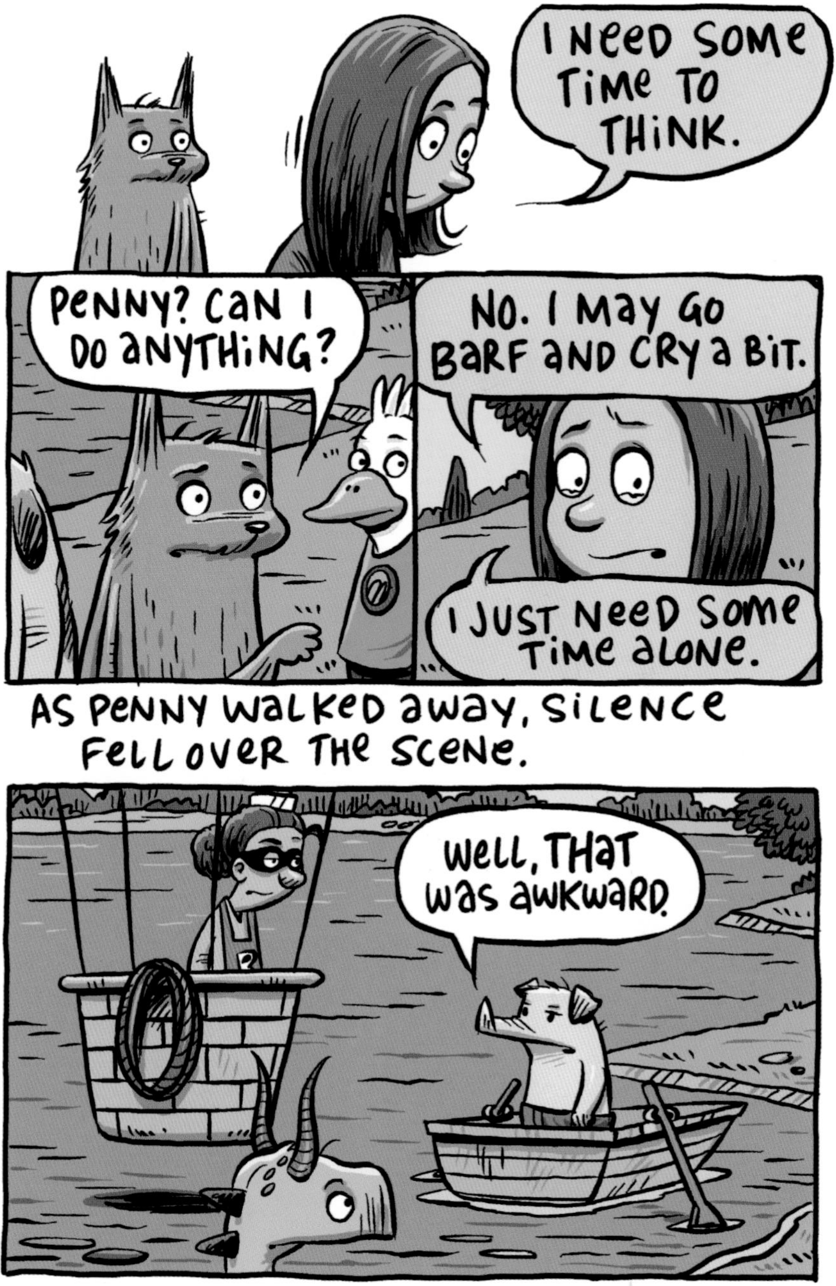
I NEED SOME TIME TO THINK.
PENNY? CAN I DO ANYTHING?
NO. I MAY GO BARF AND CRY A BIT.
I JUST NEED SOME TIME ALONE.
AS PENNY WALKED AWAY, SILENCE FELL OVER THE SCENE.
WELL, THAT WAS AWKWARD.

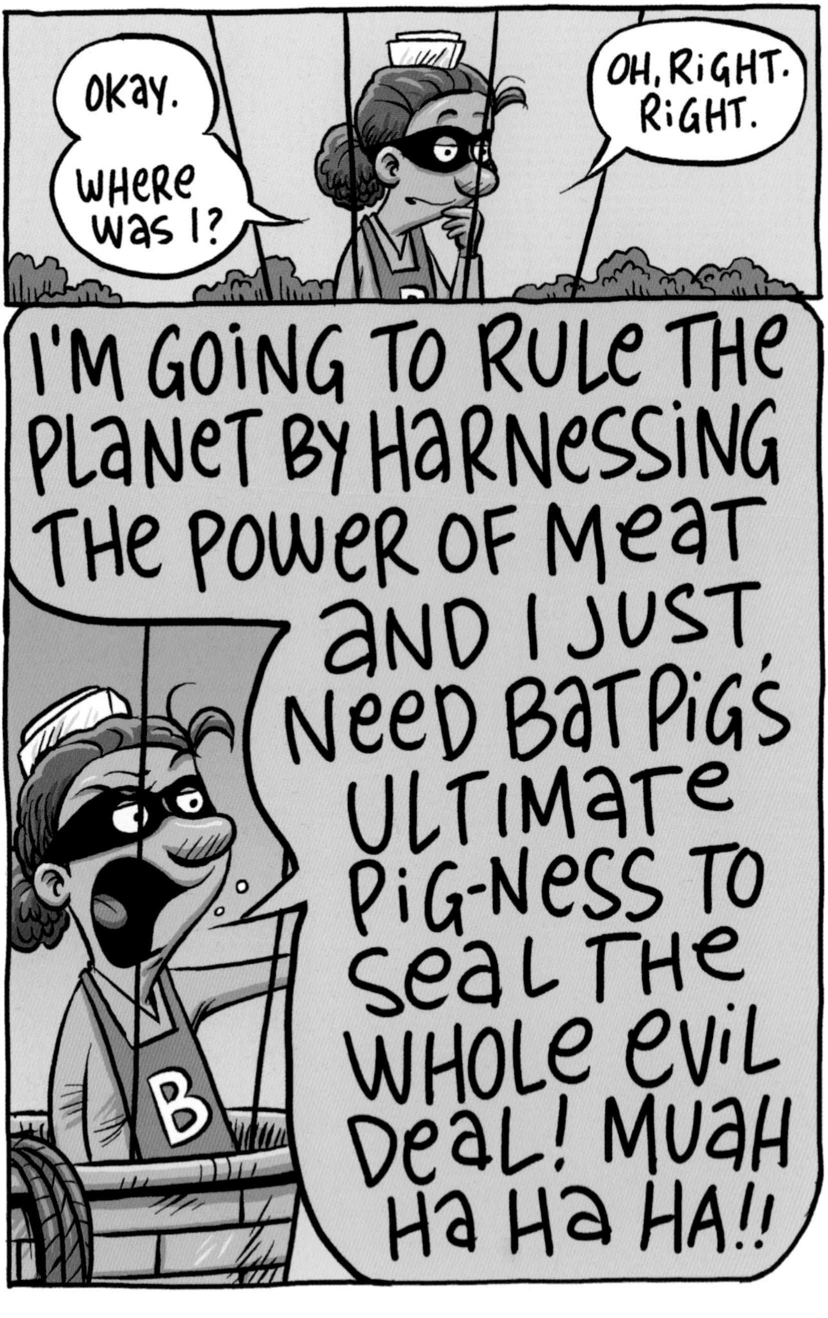
OKAY.
WHERE WAS I?
OH, RIGHT. RIGHT.
I'M GOING TO RULE THE PLANET BY HARNESSING THE POWER OF MEAT AND I JUST NEED BATPIG'S ULTIMATE PIG-NESS TO SEAL THE WHOLE EVIL DEAL! MUAH HA HA HA!!

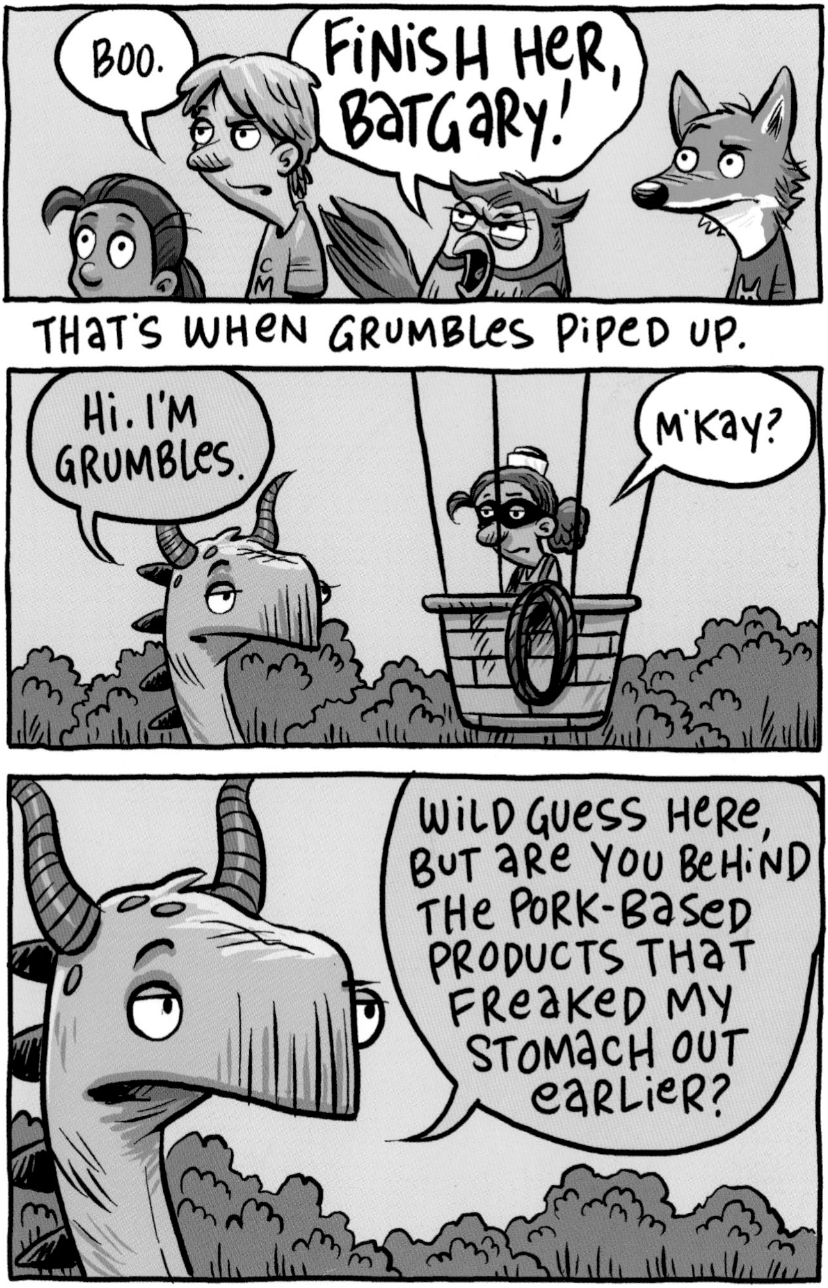
BOO.
FINISH HER, BATGARY!
THAT'S WHEN GRUMBLES PIPED UP.
HI. I'M GRUMBLES.
M'KAY?
WILD GUESS HERE, BUT ARE YOU BEHIND THE PORK-BASED PRODUCTS THAT FREAKED MY STOMACH OUT EARLIER?

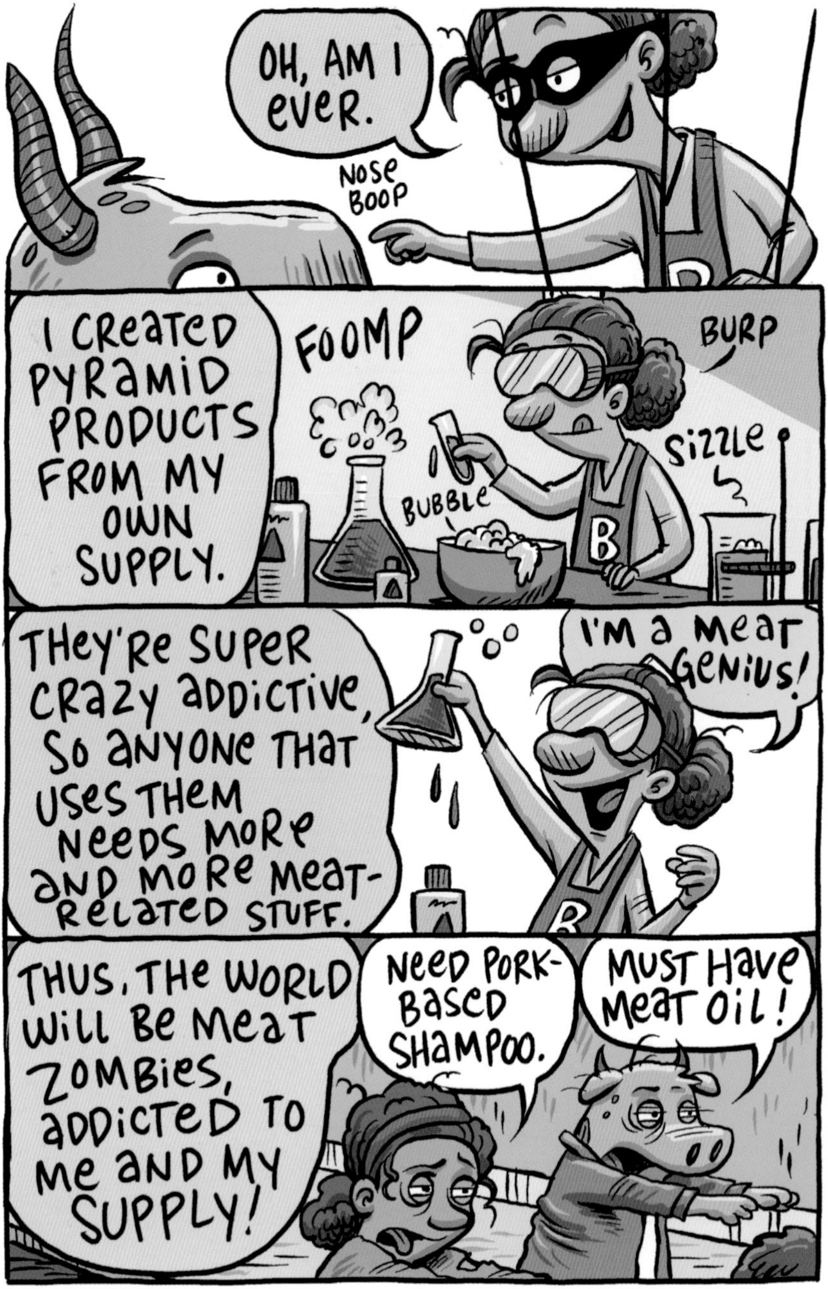
OH, AM I EVER.
NOSE BOOP
I CREATED PYRAMID PRODUCTS FROM MY OWN SUPPLY.
FOOMP
BURP
SIZZLE
BUBBLE
THEY'RE SUPER CRAZY ADDICTIVE, SO ANYONE THAT USES THEM NEEDS MORE AND MORE MEAT-RELATED STUFF.
I'M A MEAT GENIUS!
THUS, THE WORLD WILL BE MEAT ZOMBIES, ADDICTED TO ME AND MY SUPPLY!
NEED PORK-BASED SHAMPOO.
MUST HAVE MEAT OIL!

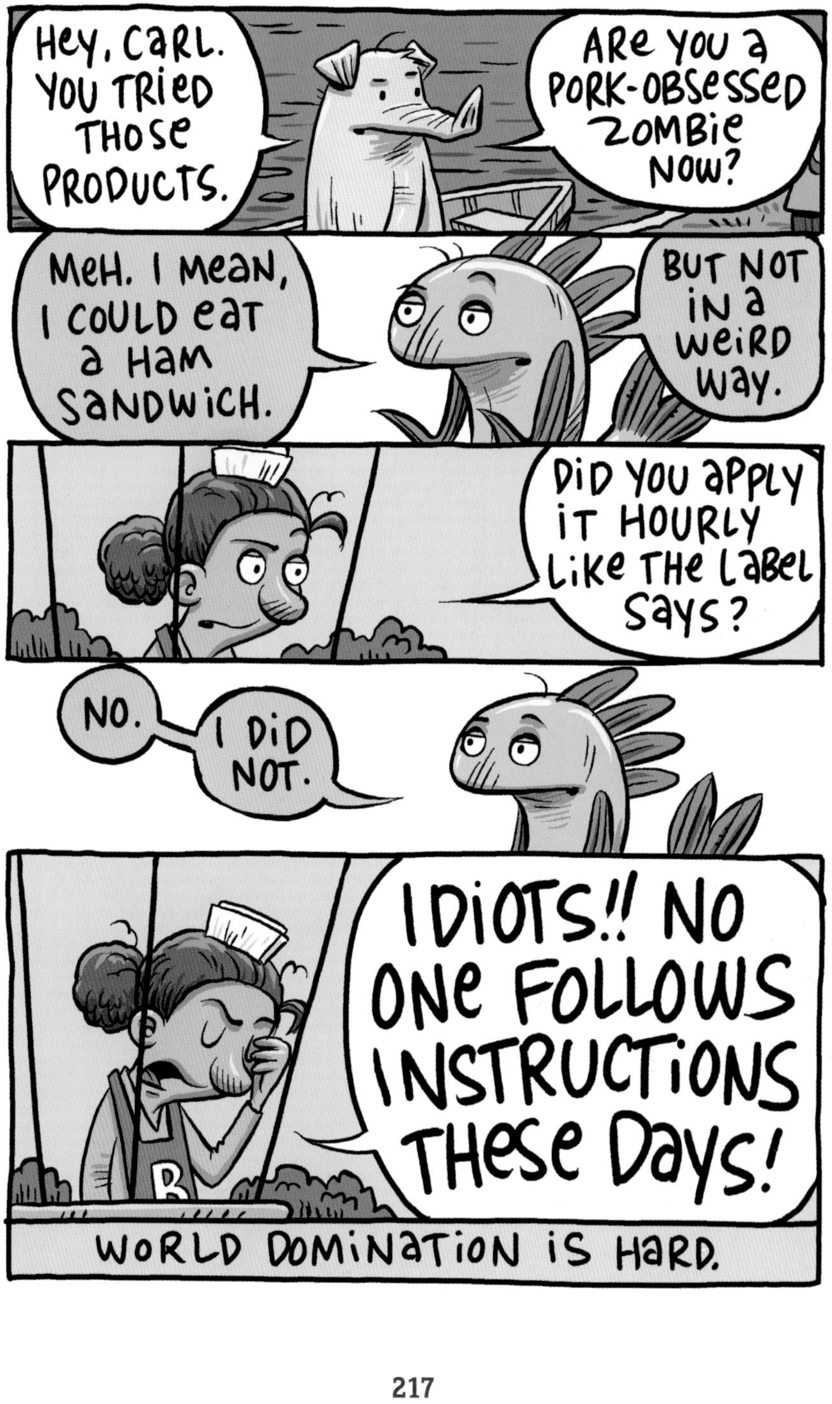
HEY, CARL. YOU TRIED THOSE PRODUCTS.
ARE YOU A PORK-OBSESSED ZOMBIE NOW?
MEH. I MEAN, I COULD EAT A HAM SANDWICH.
BUT NOT IN A WEIRD WAY.
DID YOU APPLY IT HOURLY LIKE THE LABEL SAYS?
NO.
I DID NOT.
IDIOTS!! NO ONE FOLLOWS INSTRUCTIONS THESE DAYS!
B
WORLD DOMINATION IS HARD.

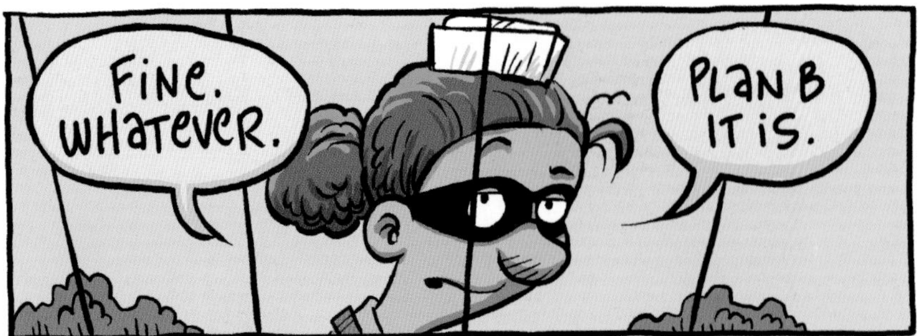
FINE. WHATEVER.
PLAN B IT IS.

WITH THAT, THE BUTCHER THREW A BIG 'OL NET OUT OVER GARY.

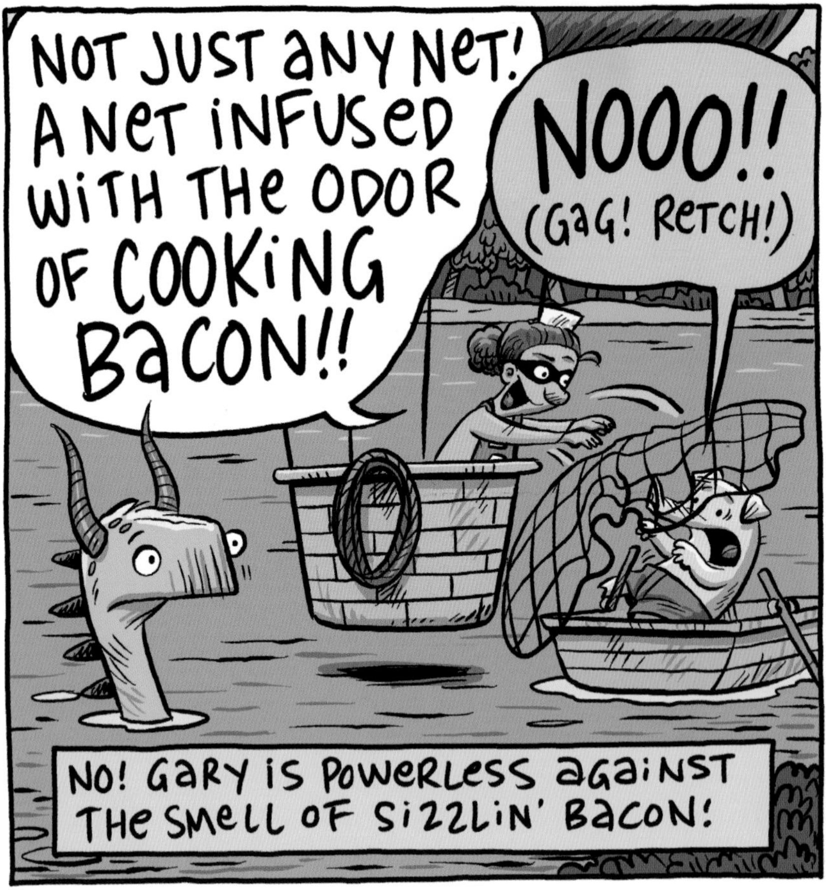
NOT JUST ANY NET! A NET INFUSED WITH THE ODOR OF COOKING BACON!!
NOOO!! (GAG! RETCH!)
NO! GARY IS POWERLESS AGAINST THE SMELL OF SIZZLIN' BACON!

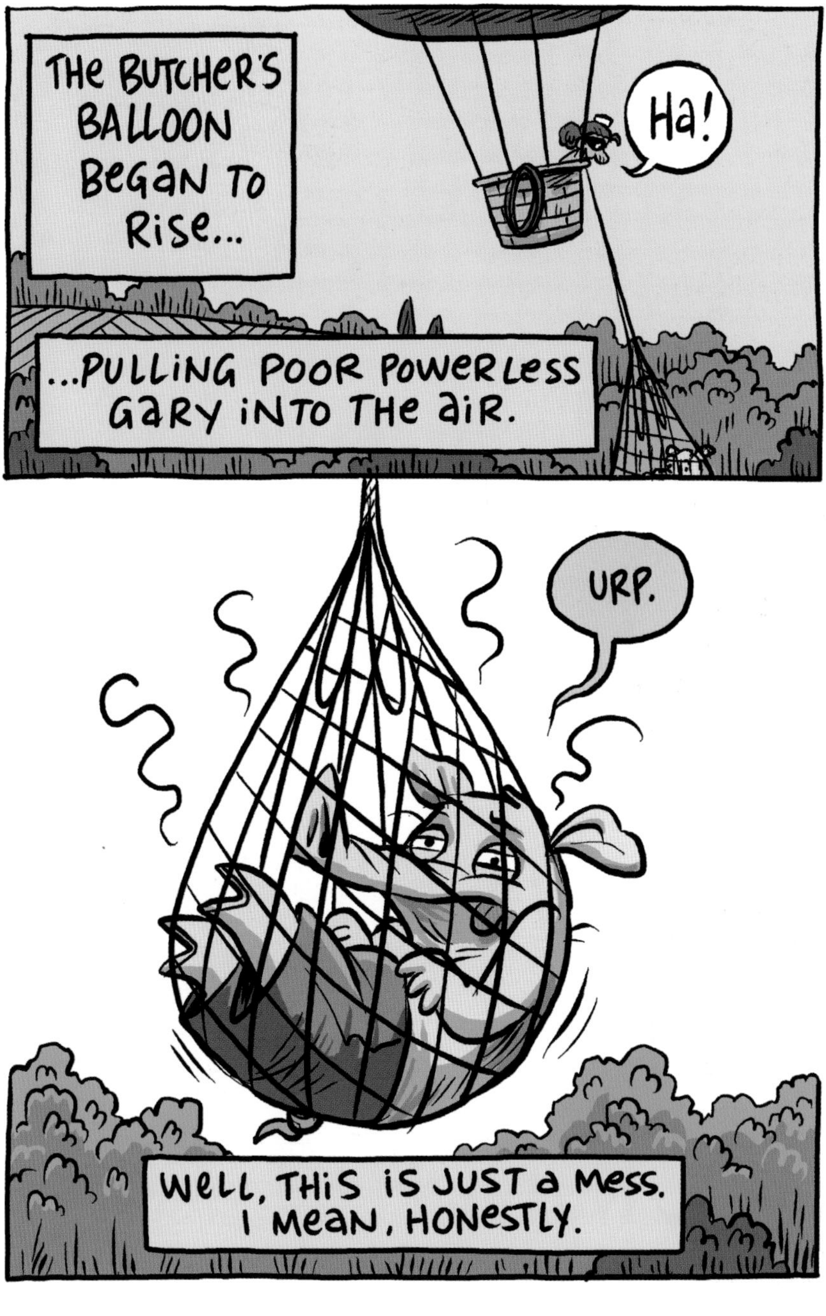
THE BUTCHER'S BALLOON BEGAN TO RISE...
Ha!
...PULLING POOR POWERLESS GARY INTO THE AIR.
URP.
WELL, THIS IS JUST A MESS. I MEAN, HONESTLY.

CHAPTER THIRTEEN

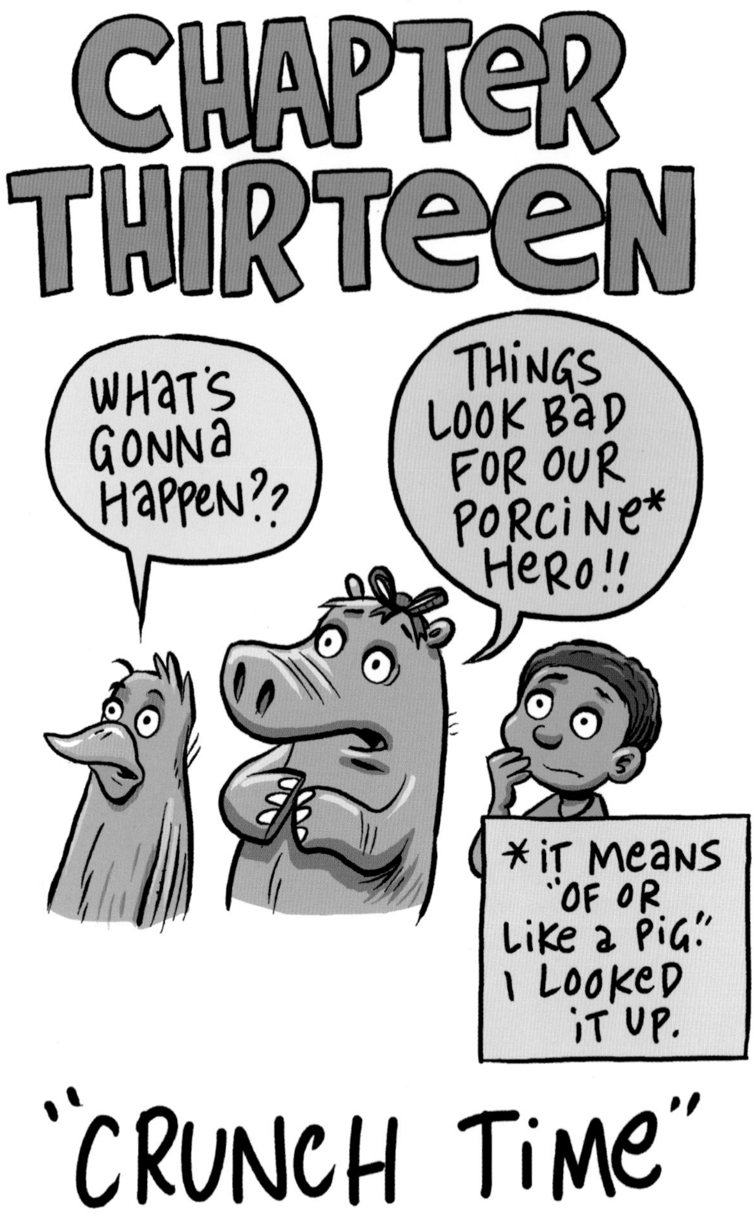
WHAT'S GONNA HAPPEN??
THINGS LOOK BAD FOR OUR PORCINE* HERO!!
*IT MEANS "OF OR LIKE A PIG." I LOOKED IT UP.

"CRUNCH TIME"

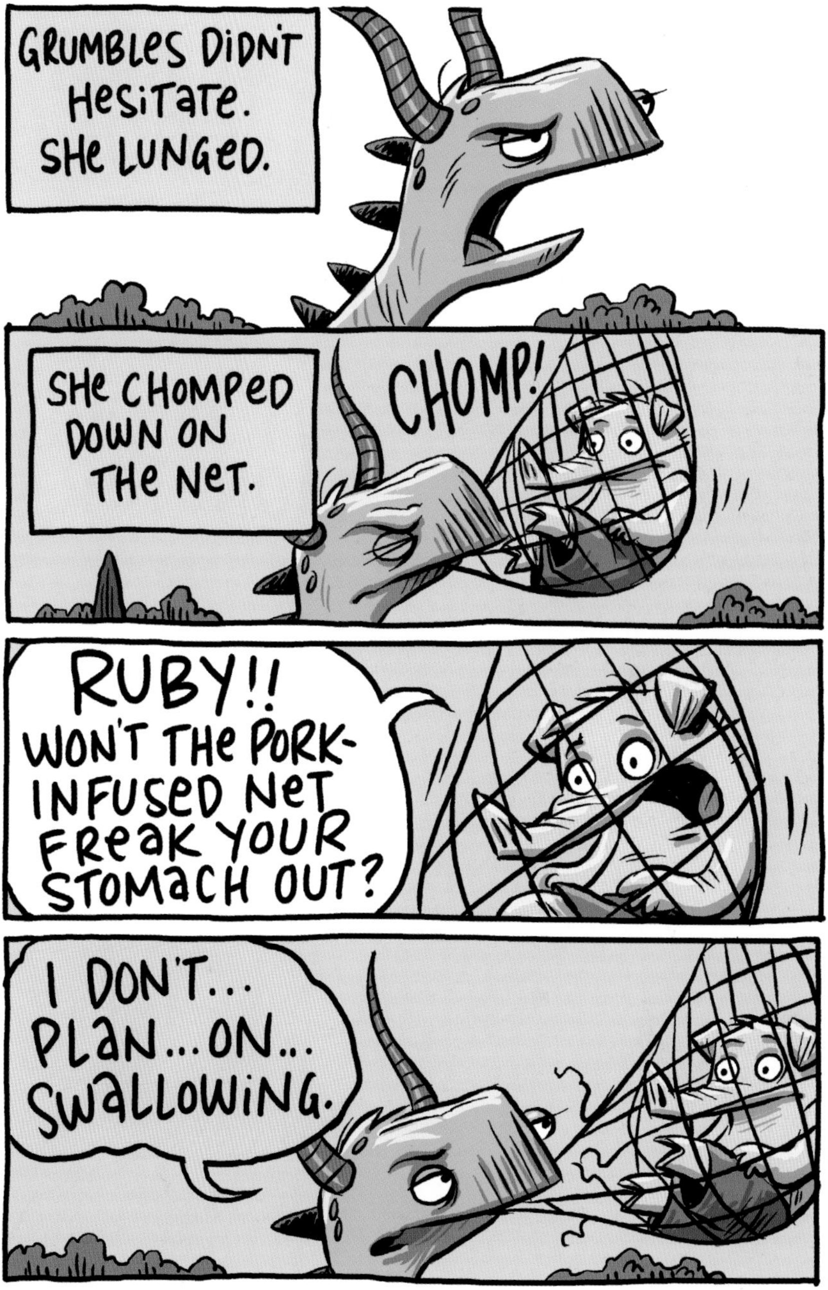
GRUMBLES DIDN'T HESITATE. SHE LUNGED.
SHE CHOMPED DOWN ON THE NET.
CHOMP!
RUBY!! WON'T THE PORK-INFUSED NET FREAK YOUR STOMACH OUT?
I DON'T... PLAN...ON... SWALLOWING.

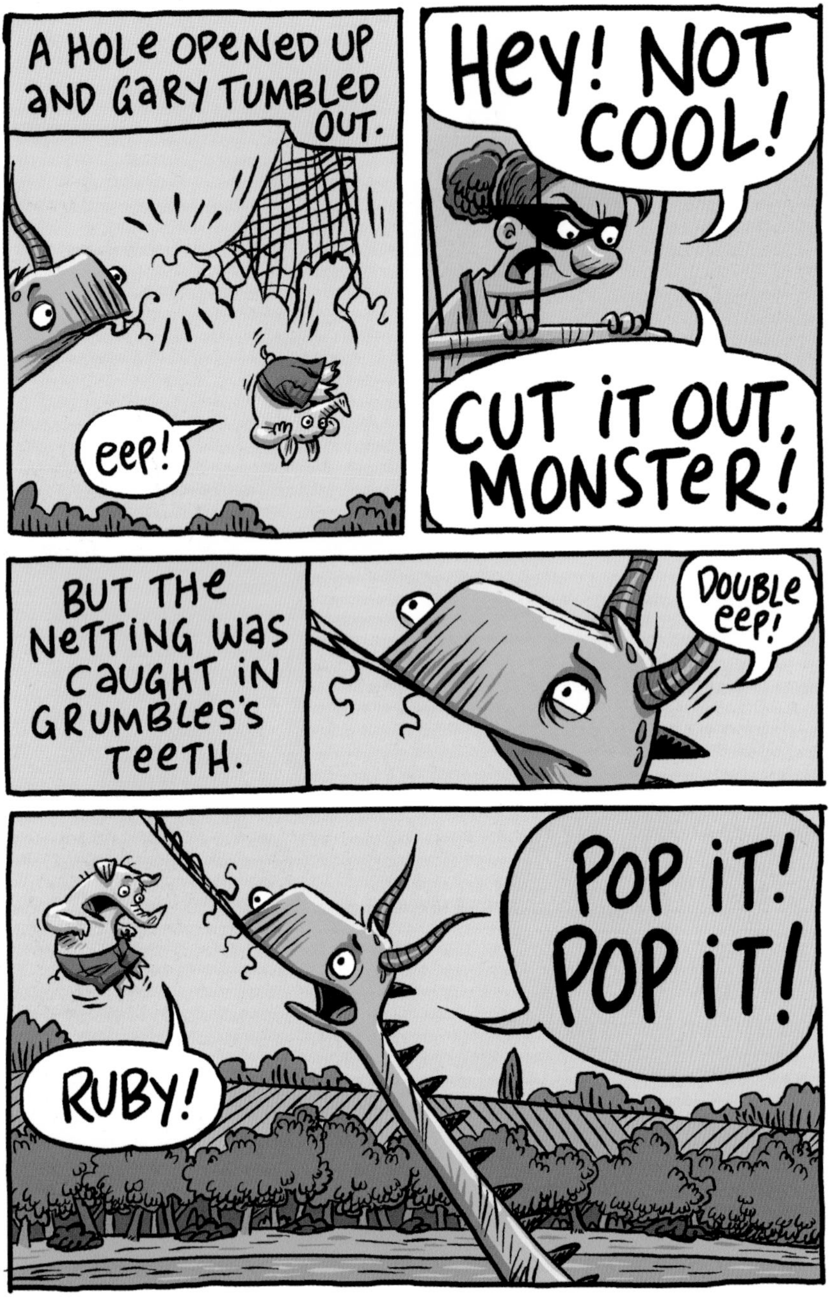
A HOLE OPENED UP AND GARY TUMBLED OUT.
eep!
HEY! NOT COOL!
CUT IT OUT, MONSTER!
BUT THE NETTING WAS CAUGHT IN GRUMBLES'S TEETH.
DOUBLE EEP!
POP IT! POP IT!
RUBY!

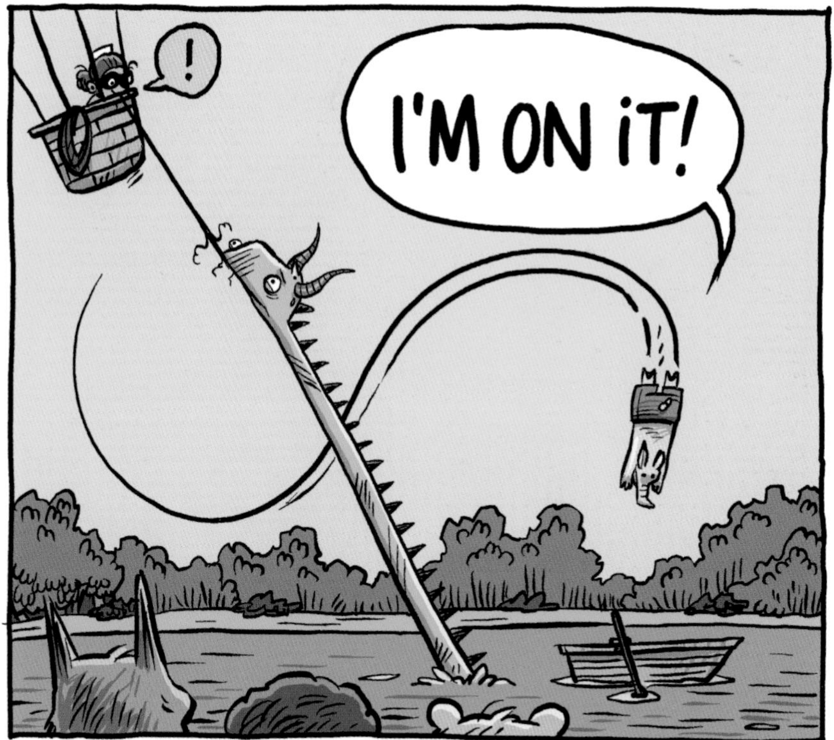
!
I'M ON IT!

THE CROWD WATCHED AS GARY SCOOPED UP A BOAT AND TOOK TO THE AIR.

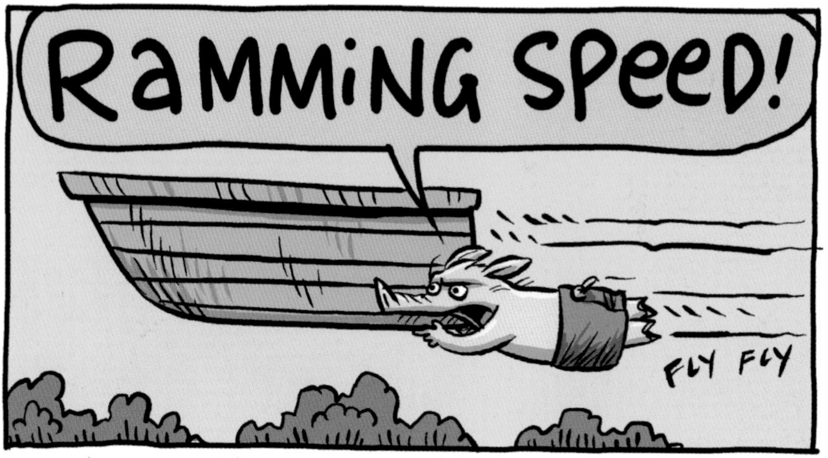
RAMMING SPEED!
FLY FLY

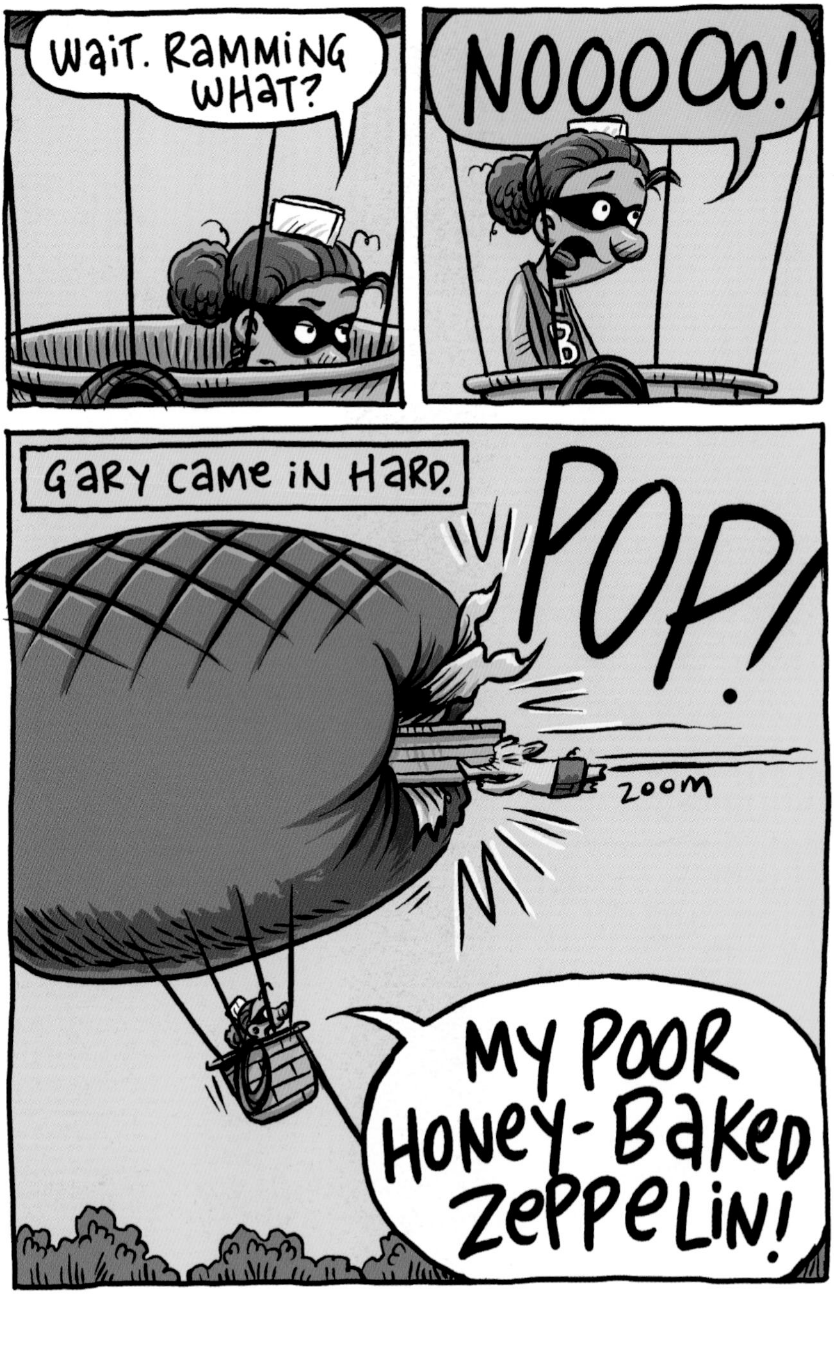
WAIT. RAMMING WHAT?
NOOOOOO!
GARY CAME IN HARD.
POP!
ZOOM
MY POOR HONEY-BAKED ZEPPELIN!

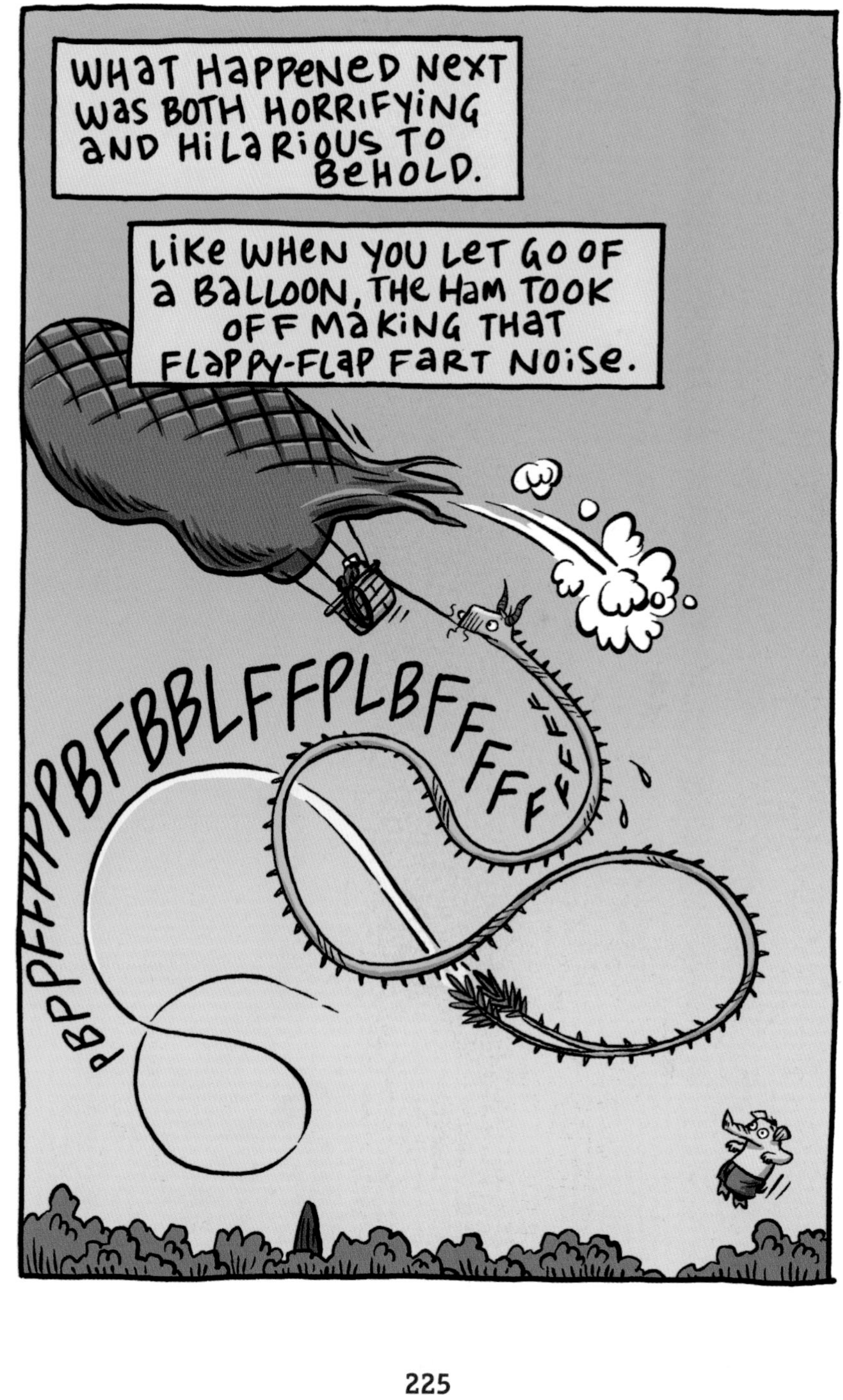
WHAT HAPPENED NEXT WAS BOTH HORRIFYING AND HILARIOUS TO BEHOLD.
LIKE WHEN YOU LET GO OF A BALLOON, THE HAM TOOK OFF MAKING THAT FLAPPY-FLAP FART NOISE.
PBPPPFFFPPPBFBBLFFPLBFFFFFFFFFFFF

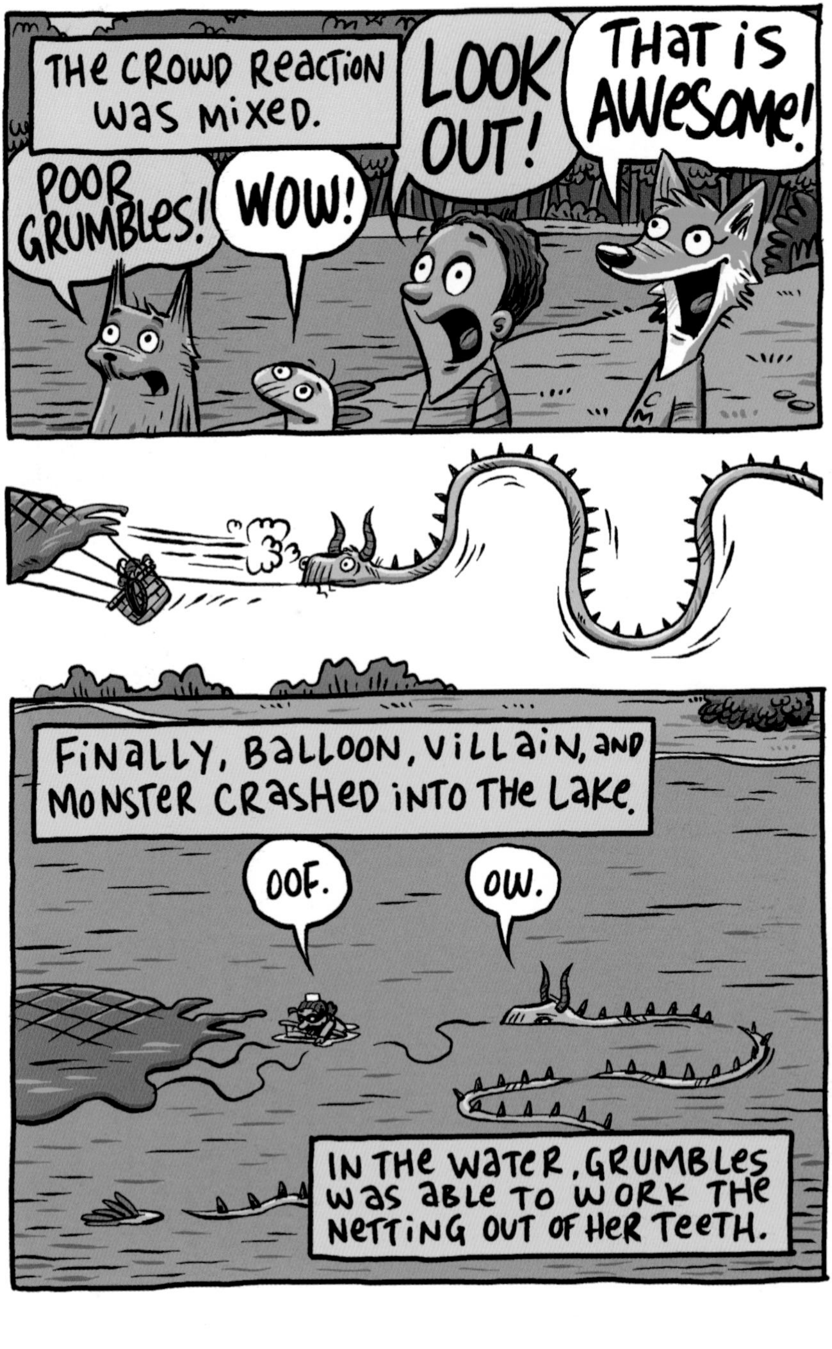
THE CROWD REACTION WAS MIXED.
POOR GRUMBLES!
WOW!
LOOK OUT!
THAT IS AWESOME!
FINALLY, BALLOON, VILLAIN, AND MONSTER CRASHED INTO THE LAKE.
OOF.
OW.
IN THE WATER, GRUMBLES WAS ABLE TO WORK THE NETTING OUT OF HER TEETH.

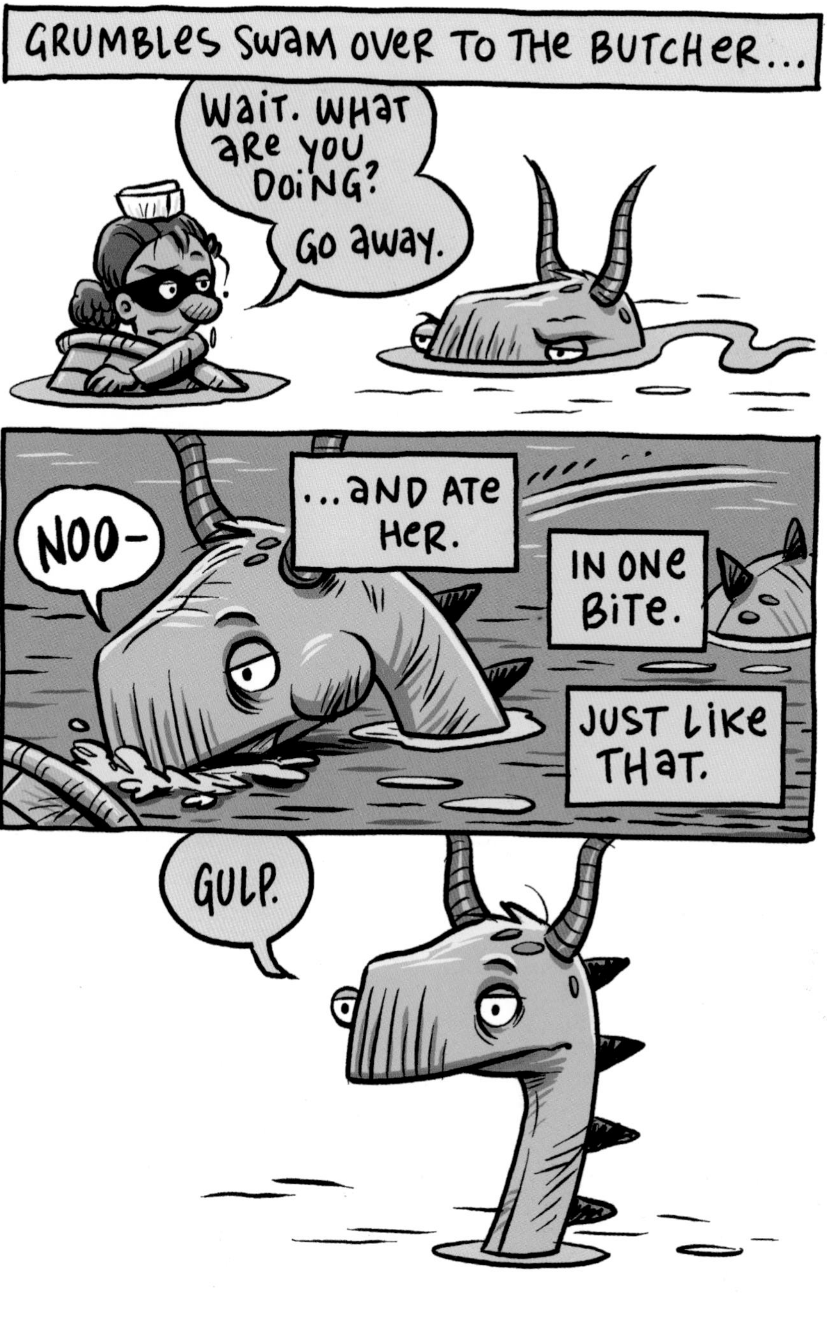
GRUMBLES SWAM OVER TO THE BUTCHER...
WAIT. WHAT ARE YOU DOING?
GO AWAY.
...AND ATE HER.
NOO-
IN ONE BITE.
JUST LIKE THAT.
GULP.

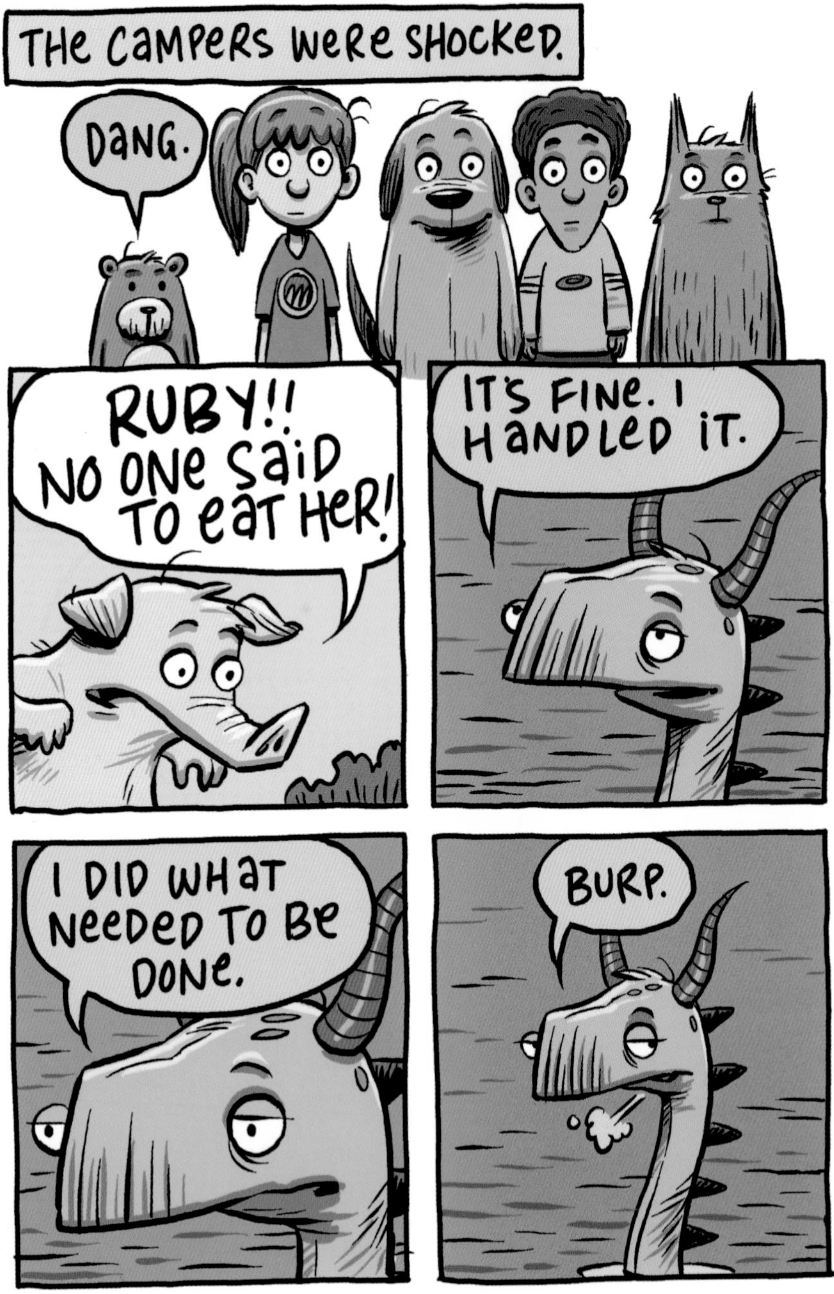
THE CAMPERS WERE SHOCKED.
DANG.
RUBY!! NO ONE SAID TO EAT HER!
IT'S FINE. I HANDLED IT.
I DID WHAT NEEDED TO BE DONE.
BURP.

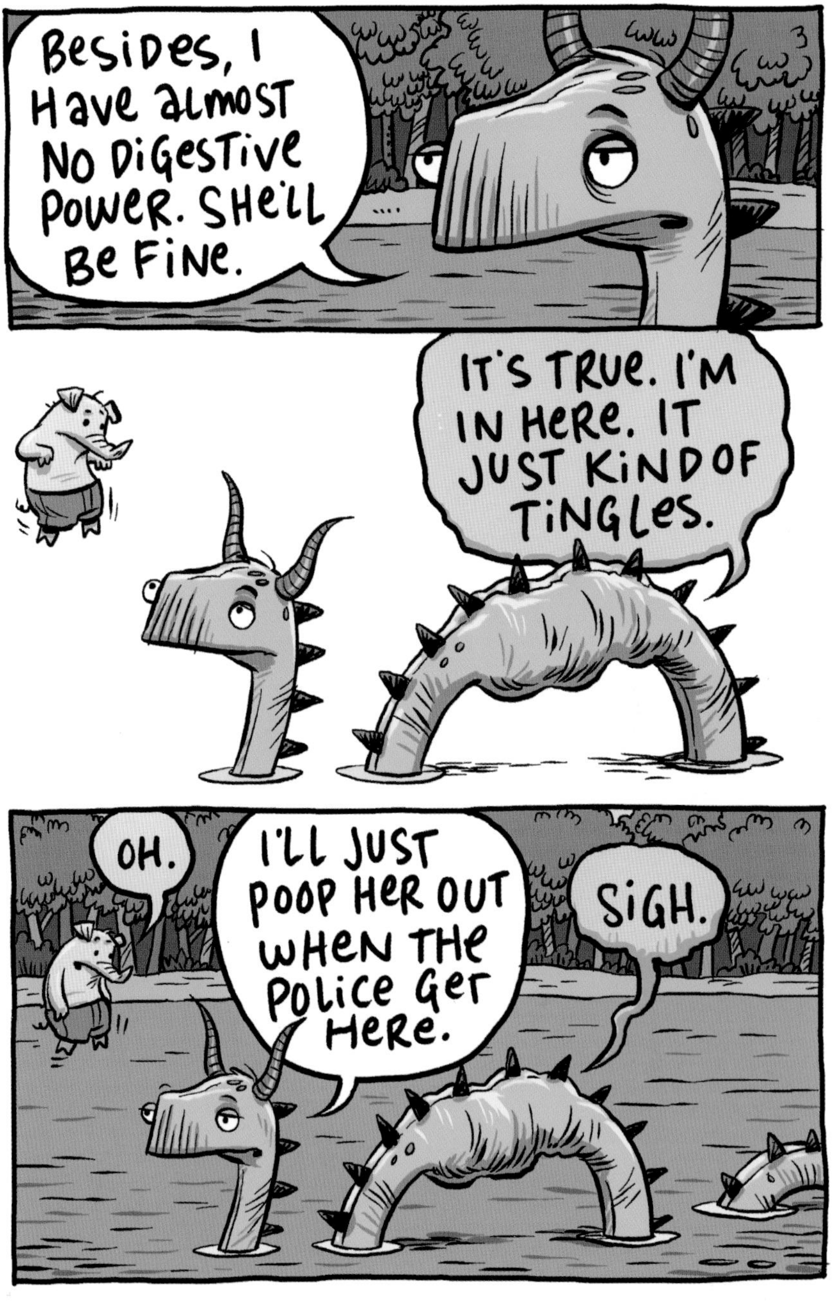
BESIDES, I HAVE ALMOST NO DIGESTIVE POWER. SHE'LL BE FINE.
IT'S TRUE. I'M IN HERE. IT JUST KIND OF TINGLES.
OH.
I'LL JUST POOP HER OUT WHEN THE POLICE GET HERE.
SIGH.

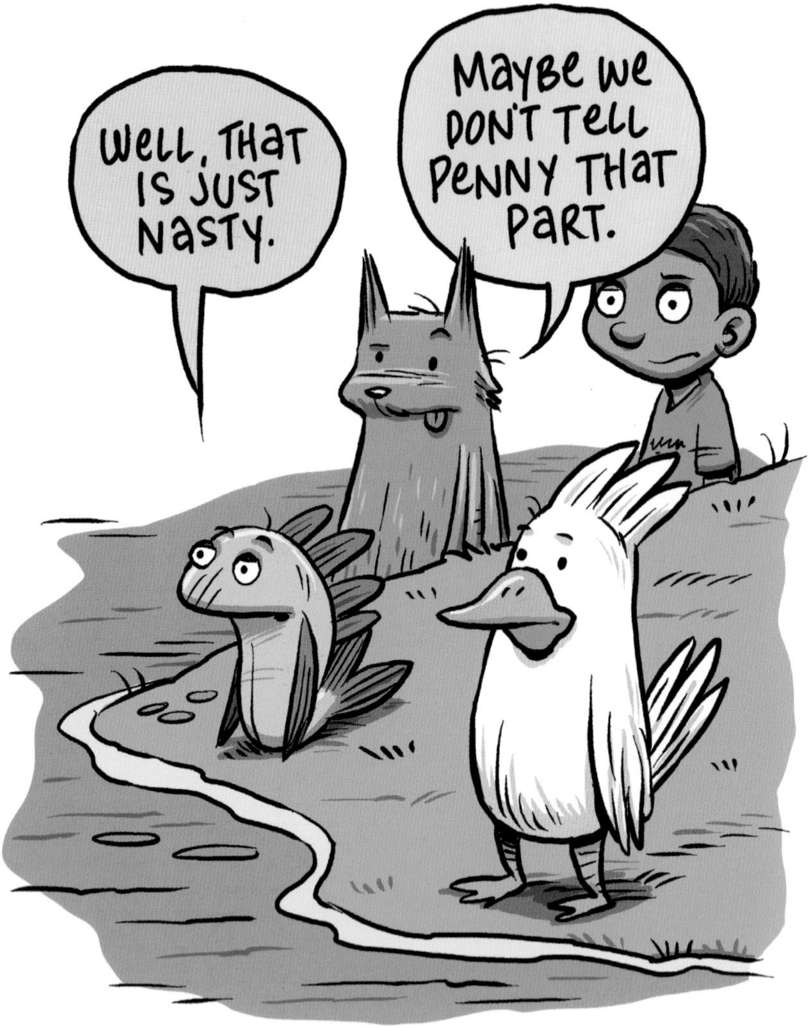
WELL, THAT IS JUST NASTY.
MAYBE WE DON'T TELL PENNY THAT PART.

CHAPTER FOURTEEN

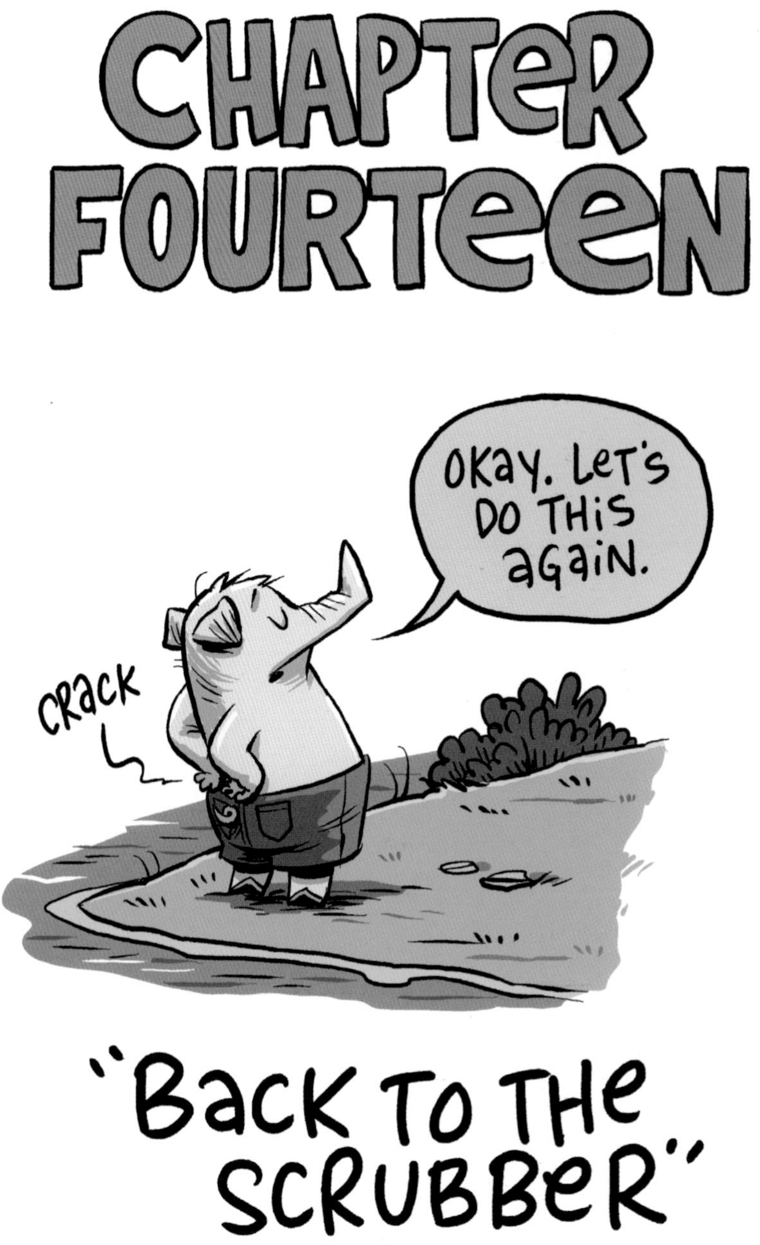
OKAY. LET'S DO THIS AGAIN.
CRACK

"BACK TO THE SCRUBBER"

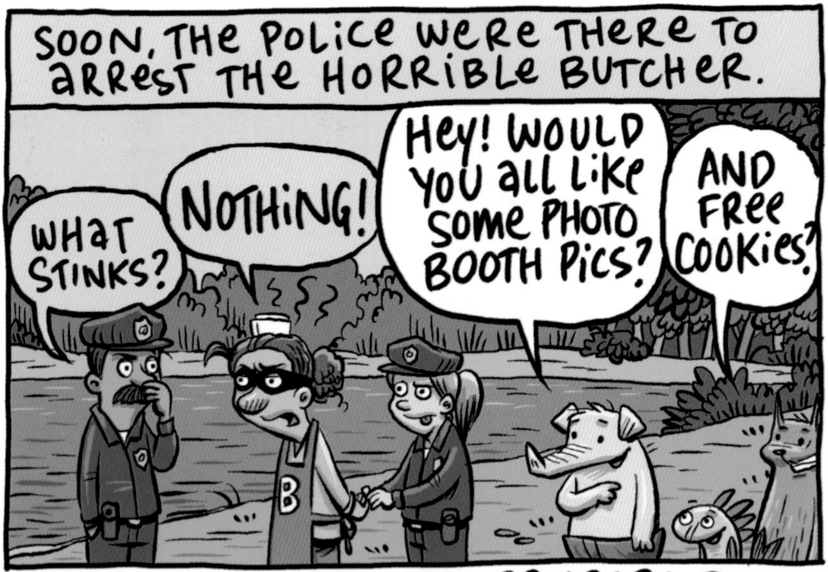
SOON, THE POLICE WERE THERE TO ARREST THE HORRIBLE BUTCHER.
WHAT STINKS?
NOTHING!
HEY! WOULD YOU ALL LIKE SOME PHOTO BOOTH PICS?
AND FREE COOKIES?

NEXT, THEY GOT THE CAMPERS BACK THROUGH THE PHOTO BOOTH.

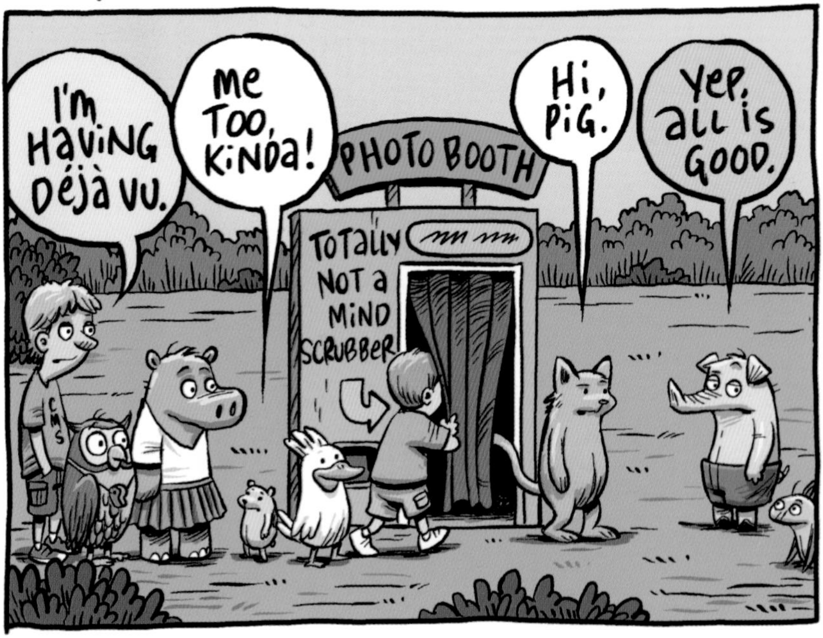
I'M HAVING DÉJÀ VU.
ME TOO, KINDA!
PHOTO BOOTH
TOTALLY NOT A MIND SCRUBBER
HI, PIG.
YEP. ALL IS GOOD.

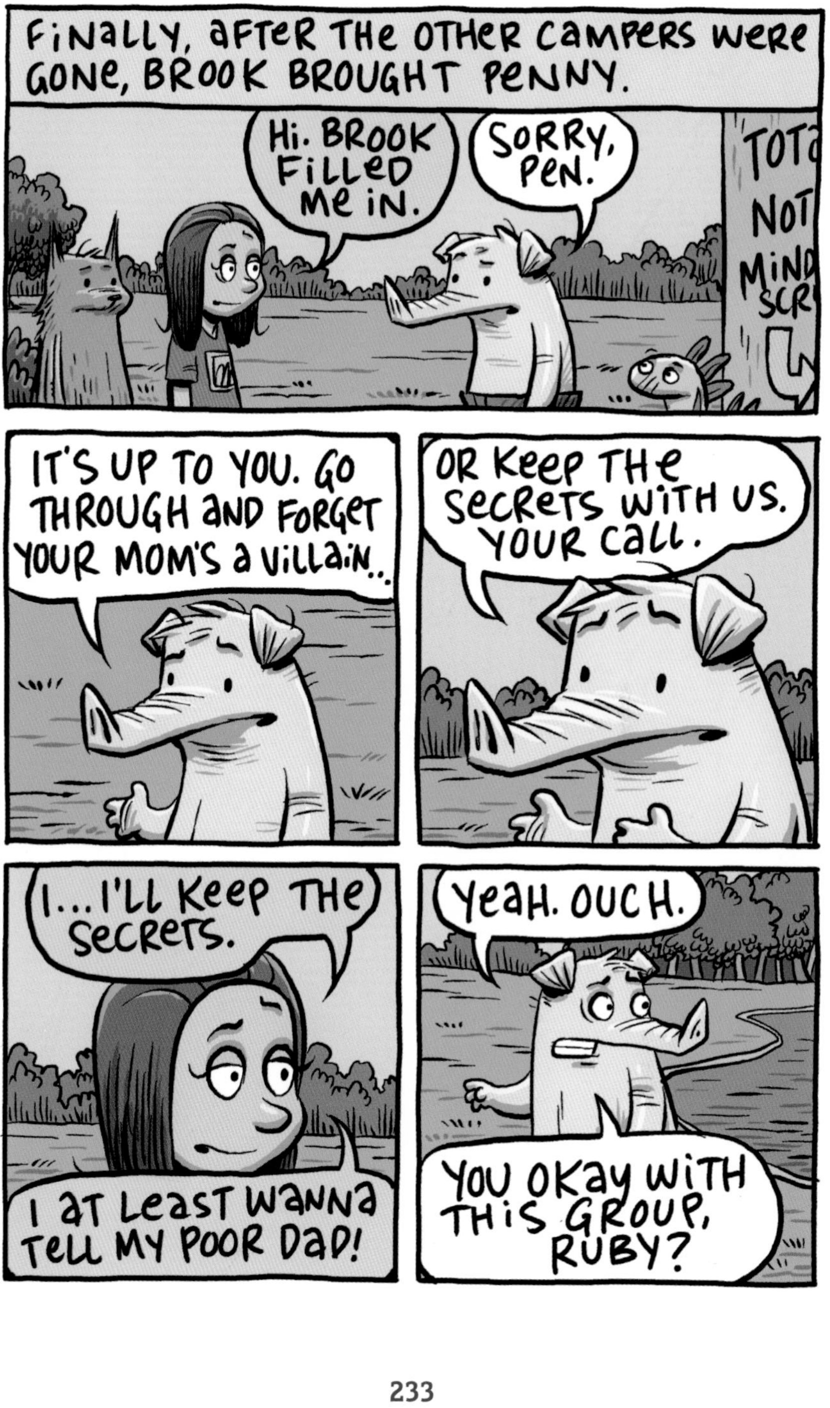
FINALLY, AFTER THE OTHER CAMPERS WERE GONE, BROOK BROUGHT PENNY.
HI. BROOK FILLED ME IN.
SORRY, PEN.
TOTA
NOT
MIND
SCR
IT'S UP TO YOU. GO THROUGH AND FORGET YOUR MOM'S A VILLAIN...
OR KEEP THE SECRETS WITH US. YOUR CALL.
I... I'LL KEEP THE SECRETS.
I AT LEAST WANNA TELL MY POOR DAD!
YEAH. OUCH.
YOU OKAY WITH THIS GROUP, RUBY?

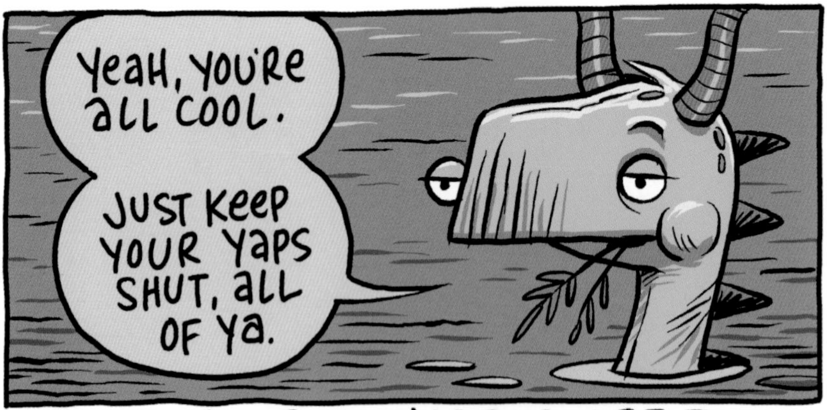
YEAH, YOU'RE ALL COOL.
JUST KEEP YOUR YAPS SHUT, ALL OF YA.

THEN GRUMBLES HEADED OFF TO HER WATERY MONSTER DIGS.

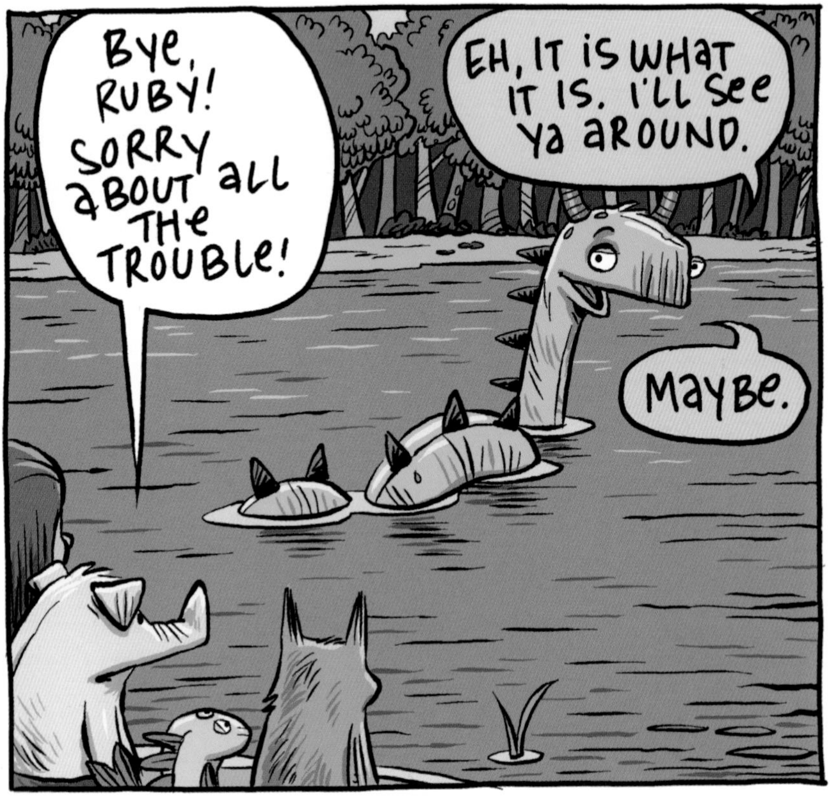
BYE, RUBY! SORRY ABOUT ALL THE TROUBLE!
EH, IT IS WHAT IT IS. I'LL SEE YA AROUND.
MAYBE.

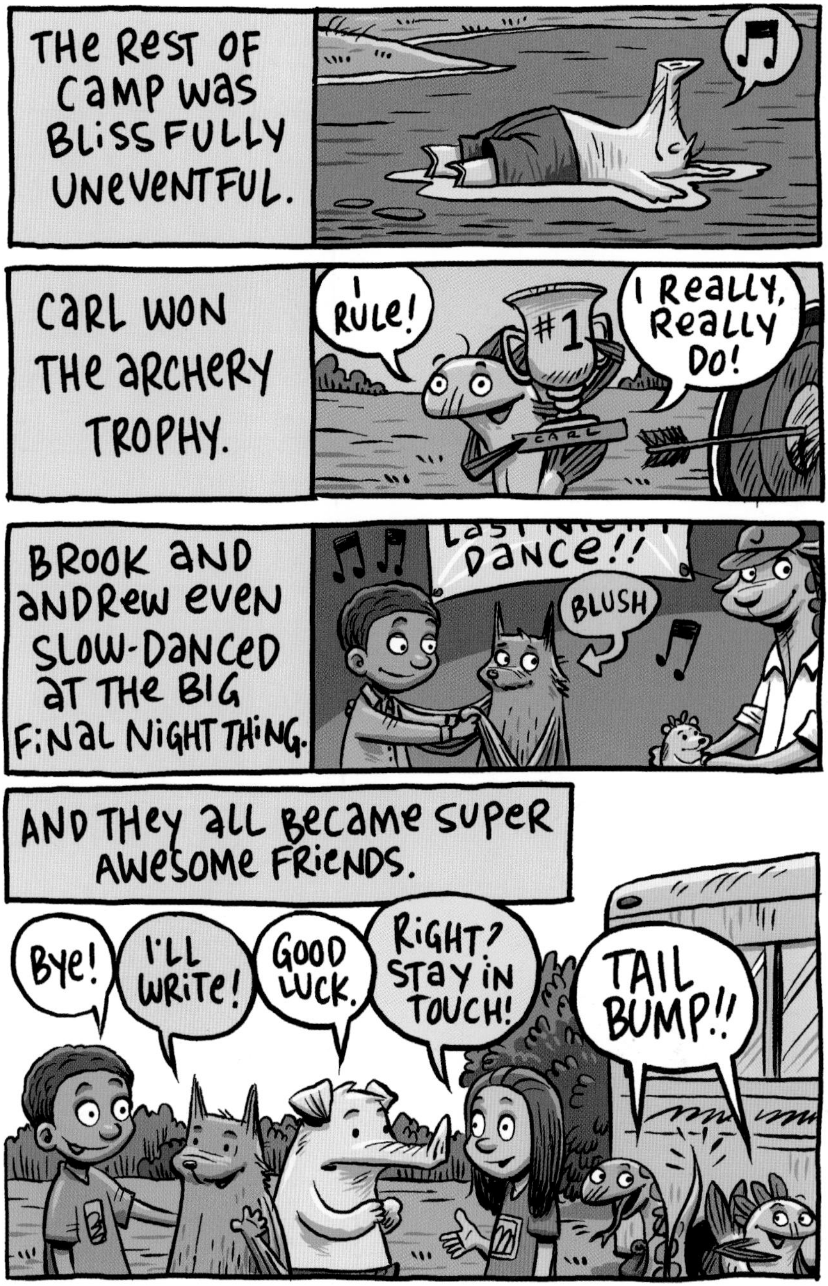
THE REST OF CAMP WAS BLISSFULLY UNEVENTFUL.
CARL WON THE ARCHERY TROPHY.
I RULE!
#1
CARL
I REALLY, REALLY DO!
BROOK AND ANDREW EVEN SLOW-DANCED AT THE BIG FINAL NIGHT THING.
DANCE!!
BLUSH
AND THEY ALL BECAME SUPER AWESOME FRIENDS.
BYE!
I'LL WRITE!
GOOD LUCK.
RIGHT? STAY IN TOUCH!
TAIL BUMP!!

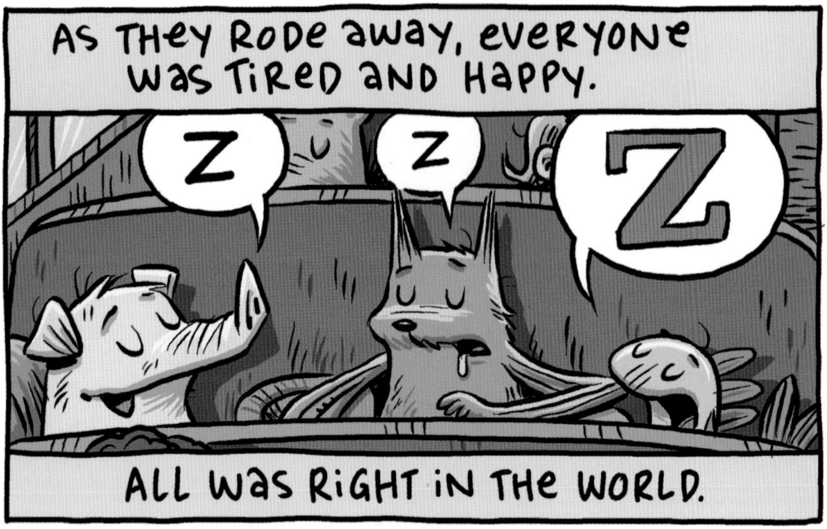
AS THEY RODE AWAY, EVERYONE WAS TIRED AND HAPPY.
Z
Z
Z
ALL WAS RIGHT IN THE WORLD.

WELL... ALMOST.

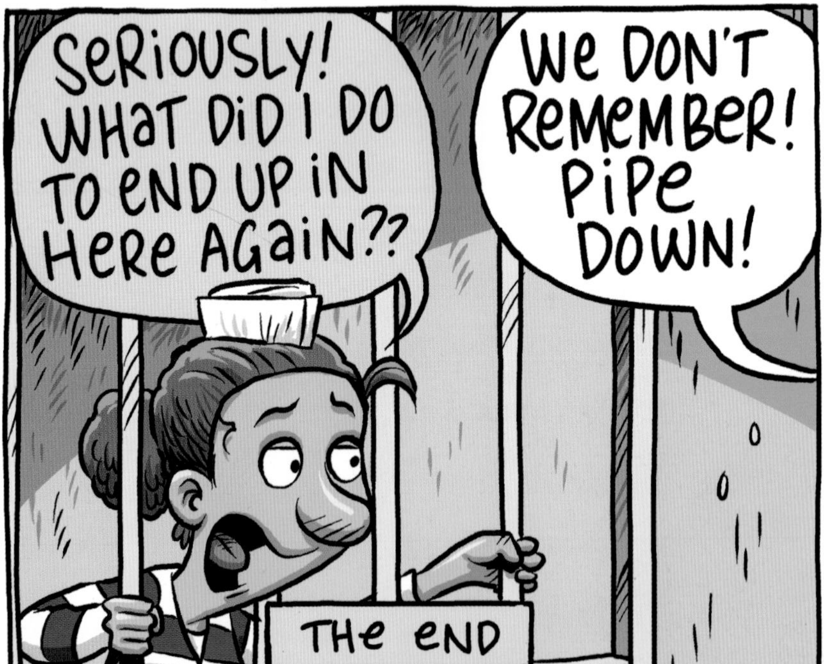
SERIOUSLY! WHAT DID I DO TO END UP IN HERE AGAIN??
WE DON'T REMEMBER! PIPE DOWN!
THE END

DON'T MISS ROB HARRELL'S **WINK**, WITH SPECIAL APPEARANCES FROM BATPIG!

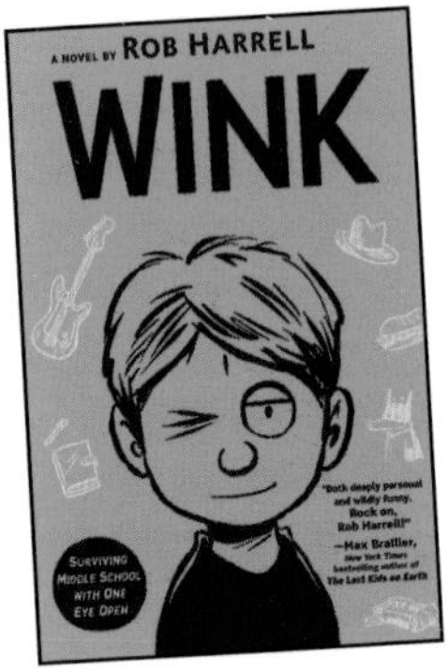
A NOVEL BY ROB HARRELL
WINK
SURVIVING MIDDLE SCHOOL WITH ONE EYE OPEN

TIME Best Book of the Year

Barnes & Noble Children's Book Award Shortlist

NYPL Best Book for Kids

NPR's Book Concierge Pick

Evanston Public Library Great Books for Kids

A Texas Lone Star Reading List Selection

An ALSC Notable Children's Book

"Harrell's genius is making all of it feel authentic for a seventh grader, a teenager who, like countless others, just wants to be normal . . . Bodies change, people change, life continues. It's a lesson a lot of us have been learning, and relearning, in recent days." —*New York Times Book Review*

★ "Filled with the same sardonic humor and celebration of atypical friendships as his Life of Zarf series, [*Wink*] draws from [Harrell's] personal experience to track the wild emotional roller coaster a seventh grader rides after being diagnosed with a rare tear duct cancer." —*Booklist*, starred review

★ "This page-turner is not to be missed."
—*School Library Connection*, starred review

★ "This lively novel showcases the author's understanding of middle school angst amid the protagonist's experience with a serious illness." —*Publishers Weekly*, starred review

ALSO BY

ROB HARRELL

Life of Zarf: The Trouble with Weasels

Life of Zarf: The Troll Who Cried Wolf

Life of Zarf: Troll Overboard

Monster on the Hill

LIFE OF ZARF
THE TROUBLE WITH WEASELS
ROB HARRELL

LIFE OF ZARF
THE TROLL WHO CRIED WOLF
ROB HARRELL

LIFE OF ZARF
TROLL OVERBOARD
ROB HARRELL

MONSTER ON THE HILL
RUMBLE
ROB HARRELL

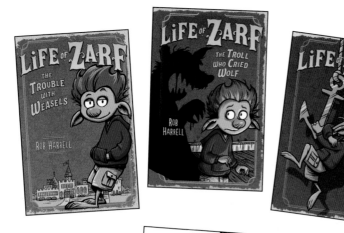

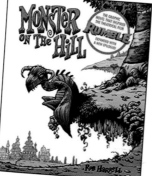

ROB HARRELL (www.robharrell.com) is the creator of the Batpig and Life of Zarf series, as well as *Wink* and *Monster on the Hill*. He also writes and draws the long-running daily comic strip *Adam@Home*, which appears in more than 140 papers worldwide. He lives with his wife and their dog in Indiana.